HUSK

HUSK

BOOK 1 OF THE MERU INITIATIVE

NATHANIEL ELIASON

Heart Mind

COPYRIGHT © 2025 NATHANIEL ELIASON
All rights reserved.

HUSK
Book 1 of The Meru Initiative

FIRST EDITION

ISBN   978-1-5445-4879-1   *Hardcover*
           978-1-5445-4878-4   *Paperback*
           978-1-5445-4877-7   *Ebook*

FOR COSETTE, SUTTON, KAIA, AND ARDEN.

CONTENTS

THE WORLD OF MERU 9

EPSILON

CHAPTER 1 13
CHAPTER 2..19
CHAPTER 3...................................... 29
CHAPTER 4...................................... 39
CHAPTER 5..51
CHAPTER 6...................................... 59
CHAPTER 7.......................................71
CHAPTER 8...................................... 83
CHAPTER 9.......................................91
CHAPTER 10 105
CHAPTER 11 111
CHAPTER 12 121

ALEXANDRIA

CHAPTER 13 129
CHAPTER 14 141
CHAPTER 15 147
CHAPTER 16 161
CHAPTER 17....................................169

CHAPTER 18 179
CHAPTER 19 191
CHAPTER 20 201
CHAPTER 21 209
CHAPTER 22 219
CHAPTER 23 229
CHAPTER 24 241
CHAPTER 25 249
CHAPTER 26 259
CHAPTER 27 267
CHAPTER 28 277
CHAPTER 29 293
CHAPTER 30 299
CHAPTER 31 307

MERU

CHAPTER 32 321
CHAPTER 33 333
CHAPTER 34 339
CHAPTER 35 349
CHAPTER 36 359
CHAPTER 37 365
CHAPTER 38 373
CHAPTER 39 381
CHAPTER 40 387
CHAPTER 41 395
CHAPTER 42 397

EPILOGUE

CHAPTER 43 403
BEFORE YOU GO 405
ACKNOWLEDGEMENTS 407

THE WORLD OF MERU

IF YOU WANT TO DIVE DEEPER INTO THE WORLD OF MERU, be sure to visit meruinitiative.com to learn more about the characters in the story, see illustrations of the locations and technology, and find updates on when the next books and novellas in the series are being released.

EPSILON

CHAPTER 1

IF I DIE THE DAY BEFORE I BECOME IMMORTAL, I'M GOING to feel like an idiot. Normally I'd send a drone to do this work, safely controlling it from the ground. But the risk of death is one of the only feelings you can't experience in Meru, and I thought it would be fun to drink it in one last time before I leave my body behind.

Now, with each gust of wind I'm regretting it.

"Isaac, you good up there?" Luke's question knocks me out of my daze. I carefully tilt my head to look down at him and all I see is a bird's nest of blonde hair. I must be at least a hundred feet off the ground, but even from up here his shoulders look bony.

"Yeah, sorry, this is…high."

"I told you! Need a bailout?"

"No no, I got it."

I take a deep breath to steel my nerves and ascend the last few steps of the tower, finally reaching the communication and camera array at the top. There's a layer of long rectangular antennas in a circle to give coverage in all directions and a canopy of similarly oriented cameras above them.

"How's it look?" Luke hollers as I hook my harness into the top of the tower.

"Shitty."

"Good one!"

There's a thick layer of bird poop on most of the antennas and obscuring a few of the cameras. I can see the remnants of the net that the last Tech installed on the top, ripped apart over time by birds determined to create a perch here.

I lean back on my harness and pull out my gloves, a scraper, and some cleaning solution to loosen the droppings, then start spraying and scraping, slowly revealing the tech hidden beneath.

It's not glamorous work, but it's one of the most important jobs we can do. If we don't keep these towers functioning, we can't keep an eye on the wilderness, and our trucks can't connect to the network outside of home. The last thing we want is a group of scavs sneaking up on Epsilon unannounced. And they've already taken out a couple of these towers in the last few years. Bird poop is the best problem we can have.

"Any improvement?" I ask Luke as I finish the first half of the antenna.

"Looking better, keep going."

"Gimme a moment." My arm is burning from prying off the tougher pieces, and it's making me appreciate how nice it is having a bot do this for me. As I sit back in my harness and shake the pain out, I realize I can see Epsilon in the distance. I can't make out the remains of the old town around it; the buildings have been reclaimed by nature and blend into the landscape. But the steel wall around the city is impossible to miss, and its taller buildings are peeking above the tree line. I can just make out the brick-and-steel Meru hub where my transfer ceremony will be tomorrow.

Assuming I don't fall off this tower.

"Losing daylight, Isaac."

"I know, I know." The second half of the antennae are easier to clean, maybe because I've gotten into the rhythm. And the cameras are thankfully free enough of debris to only require a quick wiping. Finally, I install a new bird net and make my way back toward the ground.

"What's the signal strength now?" I ask as I hop off the bottom rung of the ladder, flinching as the heavier tools in my belt smack against my legs.

"Something coming through now," he says. "But the strength is still reading low. Let me fuss with it a bit."

He holds up his phone and walks back and forth around the base of the station, trying to find a signal. Supposedly we used to be able to connect everywhere. Satellites relayed the Meru network anywhere in the world, and being out of range was never a concern. But they fell out of service decades ago and we have no way to put new ones up, so these stations are the only links we have left.

"Got it!" Luke yells triumphantly.

"Indeed you did," the distinctly cheerful voice of Felix, the creator and overseer of Meru, says in my ear. "Appreciate your help, gentlemen."

"You bet, Felix," I say as I unhook the safety harness from the ladder and start descending. "Surprised you're joining us out here though."

"Well, I like to check in when I can. But first things first. Your visual of the panels suggested a better connection than I'm receiving. There may still be something else wrong with the station."

"Alright, let me look."

I circle the station, looking for any anomalies, and as I reach the back, something catches my eye. The metal latch on the door has rusted away and the door is standing slightly ajar.

"Hey, Luke, send around the little guy?"

Luke joins me a moment later, a tiny drone hovering over

his shoulder. Hardly more than a camera with four propellers attached, the perfect tool for sweeping a room before we enter.

"What's up?"

I point to the cracked door, and he shrugs, then pushes it open enough for the drone to slip through. On his phone we can see what the drone sees, but as it turns in a slow circle around the bunker, nothing seems out of the ordinary.

"Seems safe enough to me," he says and pushes it open the rest of the way, revealing a dark room speckled with LEDs and wires peering back at us.

It's barely big enough for one of us, meant only to protect the electronics from the elements. Nothing seems out of place though, so I get down on my hands and knees, checking all the connections until my eyes land on a small, ball-shaped shadow. There in the back corner of the room, curled up under a tray of electronics, is a dead rat in a nest of coiled wire layered with fur and debris. Another wire is half chewed next to it.

"Poor guy," I say, pulling him out by the tail and clearing the nest from the wires, then backing out of the station.

"That would certainly do it," Felix says. He must have been watching from the drone. "I'll have another Tech come out and replace the wire. That should repair this station to working order."

Luke grabs a large stone from a few feet away and leans it on the door to hold it shut against any other intruders. "You'll need a new latch, too."

"Yes, that as well. I'll add it to someone's work list for tomorrow."

I grab my gear bag from the base of the tower and throw it in the back of our truck, then climb into the passenger seat while Luke slides into the driver's. Our route appears on the dashboard, but it's not back to home.

"This why you rang, Felix?" I ask.

"Ah, yes. I know you're eager to get home, but—"

"Send another Tech," I interrupt. "It's my last night, I can't even earn any more status. I only came out for this job because—"

"I understand, Isaac," Felix interrupts now. "But this isn't a normal maintenance call. Something...unsettling has happened."

"Felix, you have plenty of other Techs you can send."

"A station went offline, Isaac."

"Shit," Luke mutters.

"Like, malfunction offline? Or scavs offline?"

"I'm not sure. I lost all connection out of nowhere. I'd send someone else but you're the nearest person experienced enough to handle it. And it has someone living in it."

Luke's eyes show the same hint of concern I'm feeling. Neither of us has run into a scav in the wild before. We're trained, and have security bots, but it's not a risk I'm keen to take. Not when I'm so close to Meru. "The stations have security, Felix. Can't you see what happened?"

"My connection to it was severed before anything appeared on the cameras. It could be another furry friend. But I think it would be best if you checked on it, if you can accept the detour."

"Felix, why is it so important to check on it *now*? Can't someone look tomorrow?"

"Because a transfer ceremony would be a perfect time for them to try something, Isaac. Everyone will be distracted and working the first half of tomorrow and drunk the second half. This is your job. You're the senior wilderness Tech until you transfer tomorrow, so please, go do your job."

Luke looks as surprised as I feel; Felix losing his temper isn't common. He must be more worried than he's telling us.

"Alright, Felix," I say as I accept the new destination on the truck's console. "We'll go see what's up."

"Much appreciated."

CHAPTER 2

THE STATION WE'RE HEADED TO IS NORMALLY MAINtained by other towns, so I've never seen it, and our truck bumps over the branches and vines that have covered this road since it was last driven who knows how many years ago. It's rare to have to work on another town's territory, or to interact with them at all.

Luke breaks the tense silence. "You really think an animal chewed through the *exact* right wire to shut off the security, Felix?"

"It's happened before," he says, but he still has that worried tone to his voice. I can't shake the feeling that there's something he's not telling us.

"Any reason to think we're going to run into a bunch of scavs?" Luke asks.

"I hope—not," Felix says, cutting out slightly as we reach the limits of his range. Even through the chop I can still hear the uncertainty in his voice.

"You *hope not?*" I ask.

"I meant—don't think so."

"Well, we'll find out in a—" Luke cuts off as the truck skids to a halt. I barely avoid smashing my head into the dashboard, catching myself on it with one hand at the last second.

"Luke, what the hell!" I say but then feel his hand on my chest, pushing me back up against the seat. I look over and he's staring out ahead of us, his eyes narrowed, one finger on his lips telling me to be quiet.

I follow his gaze and see the sparking wreckage of a small security dog ahead of us. It's tipped over on its side, the four mechanical legs sticking up in the air at odd angles, one of them twitching slightly. A hole in the side of its body and the head half ripped off the torso, as if someone slammed on it hard with their boot or a rock.

"Felix..." Luke says quietly, no part of his body moving except his eyes and mouth. "What happened here?"

We wait silently for a response, but none comes. I slowly reach out and tap the screen on the dashboard to check our signal and it says we're out of range. We must have been right on the edge of it. And with this station down, the car can't connect to the network. We're on our own.

"What do you think?" I whisper.

Luke stares back out at the wrecked dog for what feels like a minute, then says, "We need to see if the person here is still alive. Come on." Then he delicately opens his door and surveys the area outside it before climbing out.

I activate the truck's security system and open the cache in the back, then climb out after him. There is a distinctly sweet, chemical smell in the air, probably from the leaking batteries in the bot. I listen for the sound of any other commotion but can't hear anything besides the buzzing of insects in the forest around us.

As I walk around to the back of the truck, our two security dogs climb off the exterior walls of the cabin, and the same observation drone Luke was using ascends off the roof. It buzzes over toward the station beyond the destroyed bot, and I check my phone to confirm it's transmitting a visual. An infrared image of the station fills my screen, showing no other people moving around the space.

"No one's outside," I say, and Luke nods. It's only been twenty minutes since we left the last station we were working on. Whoever did this couldn't have gone too far.

"They could be inside the station," he says. "The drone can't see through concrete." Then he pulls two shotguns out of the tool cache in the back of the truck.

"Seriously?" I ask.

He just shrugs and tosses one to me. I catch it and load in half a dozen shells. I've gone through these motions countless times before and practiced on targets since I was a teenager. But the thought of having to use the gun on another person makes my fingers start to shake.

"Going in armed might antagonize them if they're here."

"We can't take any chances."

I nod and gesture for him to lead the way, then he starts walking slowly toward the station. If Luke is going to take over leading Epsilon, these are the kinds of jobs he'll need to be comfortable taking point on. It's been years since there was any physical threat to the town, but Felix and Bram have always warned us that one could come at any time.

I fall in behind him, and the two security dogs follow at our sides. We approach the destroyed bot, and Luke nudges it with his shotgun. It rolls over, and another pool of battery fluid pours out of it. One of our dogs makes a noise that almost sounds sad, then sticks its nose, really a camera and array of sensors, into the opening. I crouch down to inspect the destroyed bot too and can see it's been blasted by something powerful at a relatively short range, probably another shotgun.

"I didn't realize they had guns," I say.

"Not exactly hard to find them. This area used to have more

guns than people," Luke says as he starts walking toward the station again. "We'll grab it for scrap on the way back. Come on."

As we get closer, I spot two more destroyed bots lying in front of it, and a larger drone crashed off to the side of the building. It's not an observation one like ours; it's one of the larger defense ones with a small gun attached to it. There are specks of what looks like blood on a patch of grass near the entrance, and an image flashes through my mind of someone lying in the bushes near us, slowly dying, waiting for their time to strike.

My hands are shaking as I pull out my phone again to check the drone's camera, but it still shows no signs of life anywhere around us. Whoever got hit must have gotten away. Or is waiting for us inside, behind the concrete where the infrared can't see them.

"Still sealed," Luke says as we reach the door.

"So they're gone?"

"They could have gone in and resealed it." He points to the security panel by the door, shattered to pieces.

"If they destroyed the access panel, how are they going to get out?"

"They could control the door from inside, wait for us to leave."

"Should we leave then?"

"Still gotta check if the resident is in there."

"Right...let me look for another port," I say and shoulder my shotgun, walking around to the other side of the building. There are a series of wires running out of the roof on the back that would have run up to the satellite tower, but they've been severed, hanging limp against the wall. I push them to the side and find a small access point embedded in the concrete below them, and when I dust the dirt off of it, I feel a spark of relief to see it hasn't been tampered with. I grab a cable out of my backpack and connect my phone.

A loading screen pops up as my device tries to authenticate

with the security system in the station. But as I watch it load, I hear movement in the trees behind me and spin around, ripping my shotgun back off my shoulder and aiming it into the brush. I try to calm my breath, lowering my heart rate so I can hold the gun steady. One of the dogs notices my reaction and crouches down, ready to leap, as it silently stalks toward the bushes.

The dog makes it within a few feet of the bush, and then a fluffy tail comes into view as a squirrel darts out, sees us, and scampers back into hiding. I let out a nervous sigh, the adrenaline flushing out of my system, and lower the gun again, shaking my arms to get them back under control.

The phone chimes, indicating it has connected with the security system in the bunker. I hear Luke walking up behind me as I activate the microphone.

"This is Luke of Epsilon camp." The system will use his voice pattern to verify my identity, and Luke has the higher security clearance of the two of us. "What happened here?"

"Oh thank God!" comes the almost immediate reply. "It was awful, just awful. They came out of nowhere, blew out the relay first so I couldn't alert anyone."

I feel a flood of relief; they're still okay. "Can you open the door so we can come in and get you?"

"Wait," Luke says, grabbing the phone. "How do we know you're not one of them?"

There is a moment of silence on the other end of the line. "Can't you see my credentials?"

"Yes, but those could have been faked, just like you could have faked your way into this station."

"Fair point. I can't do a deeper authentication though since we're not connected to the network."

I bite my lip, trying to think of some way we can verify he isn't a scavenger. I mute the microphone. "What do we do?"

"I don't know." Luke scratches his head as he thinks, and dandruff starts dusting his shoulders. He hasn't been sleeping again. Now that I'm looking at him closer, I can see his cheeks are hollower than usual too, like he hasn't been eating well.

"Luke, are you good?"

"Hmm?" He glances at the snow on his jacket. "Oh, uh, yeah, let's talk about it another time."

"Okay..."

He looks sheepishly away, but I think I know what it is. He's sad I'm leaving, but also doesn't want to burden me with the sadness.

He clears his throat as if to tell me to drop it. "What do we do with this guy?"

"I have an idea." I unmute the microphone and ask, "Do you follow any sports?"

Luke raises an eyebrow.

"There's no way the scavs can stream them, right?" I whisper. He gives a little nod in agreement.

"Like the duels?" The resident seems as surprised by the question as Luke was.

"Yeah, which team won this morning?" I ask.

"Oh!" The person inside replies, "Zeta."

"What were the restrictions?"

"Tech only."

I mute the microphone and look at Luke. "Seems unlikely a scav would know that, right?"

He chuckles. "Good enough, let's go get him."

"Alright," I say, unmuting the microphone. "Unlock the front, we'll be there momentarily."

"Fantastic, thank you."

We walk back to the front of the station as the door clicks open and swings in. The two dogs run inside and the drone hovers in after them. I watch the readout on my phone, and a moment later, the drone reports it's all clear inside. No threats. I start to walk in, but Luke grabs my shoulder and stops me, then leads the way in himself.

He clicks on the lights and the small room illuminates into view, a few lights flickering red, indicating the network and security system are down. Against the back wall is a control terminal for Techs to access the network with a swivel stool sitting in front of it, slightly rusted from age despite the closed environment. And to my relief, there's no sign of anyone inside.

"See?" comes the resident's voice again. "Nothing to worry about." A young man appears on the screen against the back wall, looking out at us. He has a sort of nerdy, hippie vibe, unsurprising for someone who would agree to maintain a monitoring station for a few months. It's one of the fastest ways to earn more computing power in Meru, to gain access to a bigger and better life in the digital world. Though with the downside of being cut off from full access to the rest of the network, and the risk of getting deleted if something happens to your station.

"Little more of a disconnect than you expected, huh?" Luke says, walking up to the terminals and starting to key in a few commands on the computer.

"Certainly," he says and shudders. "I'm just glad they couldn't get in."

I glance over at the server stack, and thankfully they're unharmed by the commotion outside. He shouldn't have any degradation.

"And I'm glad we were in the area to come get you," Luke says. "They wouldn't have thought twice about deleting you if they'd gotten in."

"Yes, they certainly wouldn't have…" the man says as he rubs his neck. "Well, I'm glad that's all over. I'm Simon, by the way."

"Let's get you out of here, Simon," Luke says, then freezes, staring at his screen. What little color his face had is gone.

"What's that behind you?"

"Oh this?" Simon moves out of the way to reveal a faded symbol on the wall behind him. It's not something I've seen before; it looks like it's from a foreign language. A backward "J" with a small downward dash on the left and right sides and a horizontal dash on top, and the whole symbol is enclosed in a box that makes it look like it's on a television or computer screen.

Simon shrugs. "Not sure, honestly, something the last person must have left here. Do you recognize it?"

Luke looks more scared now than he did when we arrived. Clearly the symbol means something to him, but I have no idea what it is.

"No," he says. "Just curious." It feels like Luke wants to ask a follow-up question, but then he turns to me instead. "Can you grab the truck?"

I'm in too much of a rush to get home to press it now. I can always ask Luke later. So I nod and exit the building.

A few minutes later I have the truck as close to the station as I can get it, the transfer cable running out the back, into the room, and plugged into the monitoring station. The truck has enough server capacity to house a few people in a very limited environment, enough to get him out of the station and bring him back to Epsilon to reconnect him to Meru. We had to do it once before when a boar rooted through the wires connecting another station to the network. Saving someone from an attack like this is new, though.

"Ready Simon?" Luke asks, and Simon gives us a thumbs-up from the screen then blips out of view. Luke confirms the transfer on the station's computer and I confirm it on the truck, and the truck's computer whirs to life, a status bar appearing on the center console.

While it loads, we stand outside the station, looking around at the wreckage again. "Look," Luke says, pointing to a series of tire tracks I missed before.

There are two sets, taking off through a tamped-down part of the forest. "Any idea what's off that way?"

He shakes his head. "They have to live somewhere though."

"Why would they do something like this?"

"Who knows, probably looking for supplies. It's not like they could come into Epsilon or another town for them." Then he starts walking toward the wrecked drone. "Speaking of, let's toss these bots in the truck. Parts of them might be usable."

I grab the two security dogs that are on the ground near the entrance and toss them into the truck bed. "I hope the one who got shot is okay," I say, and Luke raises an eyebrow at me. "They might be scavengers, but they still shouldn't have to die."

He smiles to himself. "I suspect they aren't the strangers to death that we are."

I open my mouth to respond but the truck and station chime, indicating Simon's transfer has completed. I look in the cabin of the truck and he appears on the screen a moment later, waving at us from a simulated back seat.

"Come on," Luke says. "Let's get back home. Someone else can come clean this up later."

CHAPTER 3

WE ARRIVE BACK AT EPSILON A LITTLE OVER AN HOUR later. As we get in range of the town, we regain connection to the network and fill Felix in on what happened. He seems just as concerned about the attack as we are, though less surprised. Maybe there have been other attacks like this near other centers that he hasn't told us about.

Our truck navigates through the rusted corpses of cars and decayed buildings that surround the town, one of the many well-carved paths in and out of the center. And as we approach the gates surrounding the campus, the security system in our car links back up with the town and they automatically open to allow us back in.

Before the plague, Epsilon was a university, and when Felix and Imgen needed to create these centers as quickly as possible, campuses provided the perfect foundations. They were designed for the population density that we needed to keep the many hubs of Meru running, and were often located in smaller towns outside of major city centers, protecting them from the chaos that erupted in the more urban areas.

Aside from adding defensive walls, expanding the servers, and giving each one an independent power grid, very little had to be done to prepare them to sustain humanity's digital life.

Which was good because there wasn't much time to do it. It had been less than a year from the start of the plague to the collapse. As we enter the campus, there's an Imgen truck parked ahead of us, its back door open, revealing crates of supplies for the town. I try to catch a glimpse inside as we pass—this week's delivery will have extra supplies for my transfer party. A small team of delivery drones, not much more than a rolling box with a pair of arms, are unpacking crates of food, electronics, and construction supplies, while a large spider connects its water tank to our reservoir to refill. It's been a hot summer so far and we're burning through our water supply unusually quickly. I explored setting up a water filtration system for the town once, but every test the medical bots ran on it said it was still contaminated by the bacteria. Maybe Luke or someone else will pick up the project after my transfer.

"You're really not nervous?" Luke asks as our truck continues toward the quad.

"A little. But far more excited. I don't know how you couldn't be."

Luke shrugs. "You can still wait until you're dying…"

"Every day you don't transfer is a day you could die." It's always the same debate, but Luke keeps trying to bring it up. I think it's his way of saying he's going to miss me.

"Yeah yeah."

Considering how much time Luke spends plugged into Meru, I'm sure we'll still talk constantly. I hope so, at least. I'm going to miss him too.

"Simon, mind if we make a quick stop before we transfer you?" I say as we pass the delivery truck and start through the town's main road.

"Not at all, where to?" he chirps back from the screen.

"He wants to see his girlfriend."

I punch Luke in the arm. "Just want to get these drones dropped off."

"Uh-huh."

"Don't let me get in the way of love," Simon muses.

"How old are you, Simon?" I ask as I pull up outside the machine shop.

"Eighty-two," he says. "I was one of the early Techs to transfer. Mid-twenties is always how I saw myself though."

"Funny how everyone seems to see themselves that age," Luke says as I park the truck. "Go ahead, I'll wait here."

I jump out and go around to the back, pausing as a Nannybot with a group of kids passes by before I pull one of the wrecked bots out of the bed.

"Hey, hon," Tess says as I back into the shop, using my shoulder to push the door open. "Have a good—whoa, what is that?" she asks as I lift the bot onto the counter.

I lean over and give her a quick kiss. Her hair is tied back in a fiery braid, the grease smudges on her cheeks nearly hiding her freckles.

"Someone attacked a comm center, one that another camp maintains."

She gives me a quick look-over for any injuries. "Are you guys okay?"

"We're fine. Felix sent us there after it happened."

"Why would he send you somewhere that was attacked?"

"We had to rescue a resident from the server inside."

"Oh shit. Did you?"

"Yeah, he's in the back of the truck."

A subtle shiver runs through her shoulders. "Well I'm glad you're okay at least. What is this?"

"They destroyed the bots there. I brought them back to see if any of the parts were still useful."

She hunches over the bot now, and a spider the size of her fist scurries over to help. It shines a light from one of its arms as it props itself up on its hind legs, using another pair of appendages to start poking around the interior of the dog, inspecting the extent of the damage and reporting what it's seeing to Tess's tablet beside her.

"Battery is wrecked. We should be able to reuse some of the sensors though, whatever's left of the tools on the arms, maybe the camera. This was all that was left?"

"Hmm?" Watching her work always distracts me. "Oh, no, one moment." I jog back out to the truck and pick up the other bot and the drone. A few delivery bots are rolling away from the Imgen truck now to restock everyone's homes.

Tess lets out a low whistle as I drop the other bots on her workbench. "Wow."

"I know, right?"

She tucks a stray strand of hair behind her ear. "I'll see what I can make of these. No promises though."

"I gotta make another stop. Come by the house when you're done here?"

"Wait, you're leaving already?"

I bite my lip. I feel bad running off so quickly, but we need to get Simon transferred. I know she wants to get in as much time together as possible before my transfer. But I also don't want to get into another fight about it.

"We need to get the person we found back into Meru."

"Can't Luke do it?"

"Tess..."

"Fine, go. I'll see you at home. Anything in particular you want me to try to use these for?"

I think for a moment, going through everything that happened rescuing Simon. "We could use a tool for getting into the doors on the stations if they're in lockdown."

She purses her lips and I realize what an odd request it is.

"Whoever attacked blew off the security panel. We only got in using an access port on the back of the facility. If they had jammed that too, our guy might have been stuck in there permanently."

"Sounds like getting exiled."

"I know, hard to think about. Luke or whoever takes over my position might want it."

"Okay," she says. "I'll see what I can do once I'm done with these other projects. You can find a way to thank me later."

"I'm sure I'll think of something."

She throws a greasy rag at me and I dodge it, chuckling as I walk back to the truck.

※ ※ ※

Luke and I make our way over to the transfer center, a glistening glass building that houses all the minds of past Epsilon Techs who have transferred into Meru. Tomorrow it will be my new home.

During the collapse, nearly everyone who had the means to do so transferred into Meru. The plague was relentless, infecting the world's food and consuming people from the inside out, so even those who were hesitant to give up their bodies for a digital life felt compelled once they saw their friends decay before their eyes.

But not everyone could transfer. Imgen needed people to help maintain the servers housing the collective consciousness of humanity. Robots could do some of the work, but machines degrade. They can't regenerate, heal, give birth, like humans can. Not yet at least. So people who were immune to the plague, or who survived their encounter with it, were asked to stay in the physical world a little longer. Live in the safety net of Imgen, keep the population at a sustainable level, and do whatever work we need to do to protect Meru. In return, we get to transfer into Meru as early as our twenty-fifth birthday. Immortality and an infinite world to explore in return for a few decades of keeping the lights on. Not a bad deal.

Most people waited until they started to feel the effects of aging, or until their kids were old enough to take care of themselves. But I couldn't wait. In Meru you could do anything, be anyone. Other residents had built incredible, fantastical worlds over the last hundred years, far beyond anything I could experience living in this small world in Epsilon. Some people like Luke enjoyed being out here and weren't in a rush, but I couldn't understand why. If you could leave this dying world behind and explore a fantasy world instead, why wait?

The transfer center was built inside of the campus's old computer sciences building. Our array can hold a few hundred people and is mostly inhabited by the minds of people who grew up in Epsilon, along with the occasional visitor, so there's plenty of space for Simon for the time being. Once we've transferred him into our hub, he'll have full access to Meru again, and if he wants to transfer himself back to Delta where he came from, he can do so over the relay network.

As Luke and I enter the station, two other Techs are working in the main room. They're huddled over a computer next to the colossal, glimmering metal tube that transfers our minds from this world to the digital one.

The woman, Shelby, looks at us confused as we walk in. "Hey guys, we're still doing the last prep work. Shouldn't need your eyes on it until tomorrow."

I shake my head. "This isn't about the transfer. We found someone while out on maintenance work."

She looks shocked. "Seriously? How?"

"The comm station he was in got attacked," Luke says, and Shelby's shoulders tense up.

"The hell...that hasn't happened in...years," she says.

Felix appears on one of the screens adjacent to the transfer bed while Shelby is ruminating. He's in his classic tweed suit, his piercing green eyes bright against his slicked-back white hair. "Yes, according to my logs, Epsilon hasn't done a rescue transfer like this in three decades."

"Is it going to interrupt the preparations at all?" Luke asks.

Shelby shakes her head. "No, we're not on the network, just doing diagnostics. You should be clear."

"Great," I say, and Luke starts leading the way down to the server room. Along with expanding the server space in the building, the founders also built a hulking metal vault around the server room to protect it from explosions, attacks, or the building collapsing. The minds in Meru may be immortal, but if the server holding my mind gets destroyed, I'll be gone.

Luke authenticates with the vault using his phone, and the massive metal door slowly swings open, revealing the rows of blinking servers inside, a subtle green glow illuminating the long cavern. Over the top of the vault is a faded larger-than-life image of Felix and his business partner, Vance, laughing, each with one arm over the other's shoulders.

"You ever been in here before?" Luke asks as he logs in to the master console. I know how to operate the transfer bed and have helped him and Shelby with transfers in the past, but I don't have the same clearance he does.

"I didn't even know we *could* come in here."

"Only in the most serious situations," Felix says, appearing again on another monitor in the server room. "The senior Techs in each camp have special access code for situations such as these. In case we ever need to emergency transfer someone in."

"Or out?" I ask.

"Hopefully not..." Felix murmurs.

Luke keys in the commands necessary for the transfer. "Felix, you ready?"

"Yes, I'll initiate it now." A progress bar appears on the computer, and one of the servers in the vault starts humming noticeably louder. Each mind in the rack requires a five-petabyte allocation, a colossal amount of data compared to anything else we use our computers for. But well worth it for the near-eternal life it provides, and the safe haven from what was left of the world earthside.

"Everything look good in there, Simon?" I hear Luke say a few minutes later. I look up at the monitor where Felix had been watching us, and Simon is standing there next to him, running through a checklist.

"He appears to be in tip-top shape," Felix says. "Only a 2.6 percent drop in mental cohesion from baseline. We'll initiate a slow patch to fill in any gaps over the next few days. You won't even notice it's happening, Simon."

Simon nods. "When can I transfer back to Delta?"

"Let's wait a few days," Felix says. "Want to make sure you're back at 100 percent before you try transferring again."

"If you'd like to join," Luke says, "we're having a transfer celebration tomorrow."

Simon perks up. "Oh, well, certainly. It's been a while since I got to join one. Who's the lucky citizen?"

Luke nods at me.

"Good man! I'd love to join. Thank you for the honor."

Simon pops out of view, likely to check in on his friends and family in Meru, and we start packing up the cables. "Want to come over to watch the duel?" I ask as we toss the last of the gear back into the truck.

Luke scratches his head again. "I want to keep digging on some research I was doing earlier."

"You know you'll have endless time to go through the archives once I'm in there. I could even help you."

"Maybe…" His eyes glaze over as he says it. "I'll try to make it there in time. Give Sophie a cheer for me if I don't though."

CHAPTER 4

I PARK THE TRUCK IN MY DRIVEWAY, AND THE CHARGING cable snakes out from the garage to plug in to the trunk as I climb into the back to reorganize the tools from the day. Thankfully, despite the chaos, we haven't lost or damaged anything to the point of needing repair. Tools are almost as valuable as clean food.

As I jump out and walk up to the front door, one of the delivery bots from earlier buzzes down our driveway and starts loading food into our supply bin. The house will take it in and organize it into the pantry and refrigerator based on the recipe list I sent out last week. Most people get their food in the dorms, but as the maintenance lead, I have one of the few stand-alone houses. It looks like there's more fresh produce than usual, a welcome break from eating food in wrappers.

"Hey, Sophie," I say as I walk into the living room. A private feed from her home is live on the main screen, one that she and I keep open most of the time to pretend we're still living together.

The digital palace she's created for herself is one of the most impressive private structures in Meru. Modeled after a house she found called Fallingwater in an old architectural history record, it's nestled in the forest atop a waterfall overlooking Meru's main city. But instead of the concrete and steel of the original, it's all dark oak with sage-green accents, the walls composed of floor-to-ceiling windows giving her a panoramic view of the nature and city. Free from the constraints of gravity and mold, she could make it exactly how she wanted.

The total freedom is the most intoxicating aspect of Meru. The ability to do anything, make anything, be anyone. Free from any sense of scarcity, free from the risks of mortality…it's almost impossible to imagine living that way. And it makes all the hard work out here worth it. Even the Meru residents with the lowest amount of processing power can still access an incredible life far beyond what anyone in the physical world could imagine. They might not be able to build a palace like Sophie's, but their opportunities for entertainment and exploration are endless. And considering how few put in the work to expand their capacity, it must be more than enough.

Sophie's in her warm-up space for the match, an expansive Japanese-inspired dojo she bolted onto the west side of her house. She's bouncing methodically on the straw mat that covers the floor, surrounded by outfits she's crafted for her duels along one wall, with trophies and recordings of her victories along another. A hologram of her opponent is dancing across the floor ahead of her, showing some of his most common tactics from past battles, and she's muttering something to herself. Probably going over the spells or tech she's going to use against him.

"Isaac!" She jumps, thrown out of her trance. "What the hell happened with you and Luke earlier?"

"I'll fill you in after," I say and grab a beer from the fridge. "Don't want to distract you."

"Honestly, I'd welcome it."

I try to walk her through as quickly as possible, keeping an eye on the clock counting down to the bout.

"You don't think—"

"Same people who killed Mom and Dad? I doubt it; it's been so long."

"Still scary though."

"Well I'll be in there and won't have to worry about it soon."

"I can't believe it's been two years," she says, and I wonder what the two years have felt like to her. People in Meru always talk about how time passes differently without the fixed day-and-night cycle of the physical world. It's been tough on our relationship; we're all each other had growing up, and Sophie never intended to transfer before me.

"I can't wait for the grand tour."

That seems to snap her out of her concern and she beams at me. "I can't wait either." Then with a smirk she adds, "Hopefully Tess survives."

"She been talking to you again?"

"You don't have to pretend with me."

I set the beer on the counter and watch the simulation of Sophie's opponent flash through a combination of movements. I've avoided acknowledging these feelings, but if there's anyone I can talk about them with, it's her.

"I'm going to miss her."

"Of *course* you are, Isaac. Have you told her that?"

"She knows."

"But have you *told* her?"

I grunt a nonanswer.

"Obviously she gets it on one level: Her parents transferred, she's seen friends transfer. But this is different. It's *you*. You've been together now for, what, three years?"

"Almost four."

"Your whole world is about to change. You're going to be in here, this incredible magical world we get to live in. You'll miss her, but you'll also be exploring and learning and living this life you've always looked forward to. Her whole world is going to mostly be the same. She'll still be in Epsilon, still have her work to do, still have her other friends and Aidan around. But you'll be gone."

"I won't be *gone*."

"You will, Isaac, and you have to stop pretending that you won't. Yes you can talk to her like we're doing. Yes you can give her a private feed to follow you. But you won't be there. You know it's not the same. You miss me, don't you?"

I let out a frustrated sigh. I know she's right. I've been so excited to transfer and get to experience Meru that I've been avoiding how it's affecting Tess. Even though we both knew this day was coming, it has to be excruciatingly painful for her. It's exactly what I was worried about when we started the relationship.

"What do I tell her?"

"Just tell her you're going to miss her! That this is hard for you too! You don't have to fix it; you can't fix it, unless you're going to suddenly change your mind and stay there. God, men..."

"I just don't want to give her some false hope of me staying."

"She's not dumb, Isaac. She knows you're transferring. But knowing something scary is coming doesn't make it any easier."

"Might be easier if my transfer were a surprise."

A dark cloud passes over Sophie's face, and I regret making her think about what happened. Having to choose between her and her child. Getting rushed to the transfer station in her last seconds of life.

"Sorry," I say, trying to interrupt the thought.

The two-minute alarm rings on the wall behind her and the sadness disappears, replaced by a steely focus on the match to come. "I'm going to go finish preparing. Glad I could say hi, talk to her!" Then before I can respond, she disappears in a flash. It still throws me when she does that. Most people in Meru prefer to use doorways or other more familiar mediums to teleport around the world, but she abandoned them almost immediately after she transferred.

I head to the living room and collapse into the couch, massaging my feet as a cleaning drone ferries my dirty shoes away to the closet. The prefight show for the match is on, presented by one of the more charismatic people in Meru, the same person in the photo in the vault: Vance Banner.

Vance was Felix's partners at Imgen when they built the transfer protocol, but after he transferred he decided he wanted to have fun, focus on creating an entertaining experience for the Techs by reporting on what was happening in Meru. Felix was happy to run Meru on his own and let Vance be the entertainment.

"Allllllrighty, folks!" His booming voice comes through the speakers as his image appears in the corner of the screen. Aside from his other distinguishing characteristics like a lion's mane of gray hair and almost comically large nose and mouth, Vance was one of the only fat people in Meru. Almost everyone chose to reshape their body to a stereotypically svelte and fit form after they transferred, but not Vance. He seemed to take pride in his size, like he wanted to be as physically big as his personality.

"We've got a HELL of a matchup for you today. Hoooo boy, this is gonna be a good one!" He licks his lips almost hungrily as he says it. The camera starts circling around the digital copy of Epsilon in Meru, the quad cleared and expanded to twice its normal size, a massive arena erected in the center. It's a shimmering cyberpunk take on a gladiator's coliseum, the walls stretching twenty stories into the sky, the pews filled not with chairs but with boxes where families from Epsilon and other centers have gathered to watch the duel.

"IIIIIn Epsilon's corner we have Sophie, the whip-smart, falcon-fast, magic-wielding, and dare I say, quite the looker—"

"Gross," Sophie mutters, but I'm pretty sure only I can hear.

"—duelist who EXPLODED onto the scene after her transfer a couple short years ago. I tell you we've *NEVER* seen someone master their compute as quickly as she has, dazzling us with her creative attacks, defenses, dips, ducks, and dodges to get around EVERYTHING her opponents throw at her. She's undefeated so far this season, folks. WILL SHE KEEP HER STREAK GOING?"

Sophie pops into view on the Epsilon side and continues her warm-up. She never expected to enjoy dueling; she thought it was a little barbaric when she was still in Epsilon with us. But once she transferred, she discovered she had a talent for it. I think throwing herself into something so intense helped her take her mind off what happened too.

"AAAAAAND REPRESENTING THE PHI CENTER, the Masterful Mage, Brilliant Boxer, Talented Technologist... CAHILL—"

Tess bursts through the door. "Did I miss anything?" she asks as comes over to join me.

"Perfect timing," I say and scoot over on the couch for her. Her mechanic's overalls are gone, replaced by jeans and a baggy sweater.

She lies against me on the couch and nestles her head into my shoulder. "I managed to get some good parts off of those bots you brought me."

"Can't wait to see what you do with them."

"What's wrong?"

Something in my tone must have cued her to my and Sophie's conversation.

I kiss the top of her head. "I'll tell you later."

She pulls away to give me a worried look, and I laugh at myself for the poor word choice. "Nothing bad."

"What then?"

"I'm just…sorry I haven't been more understanding of how hard this is for you."

She smirks at me and pulls my arm over her shoulder as she nestles against me again. "You should be."

Vance's introduction continues, and a moment later Tess's teenage brother Aiden trots in after her with a bag of chips and some soda.

The duels don't provide any advantage or extra resources in themselves, but they're one of the most popular forms of entertainment for people in Meru and earthside, and a fun opportunity for competing with other centers and gambling with them.

In Meru you're not limited by normal physics or fatigue, and you can create or do nearly anything you can imagine, so different duels have different rules attached to them. More than a physical battle, they're a demonstration of creativity, quick thinking, and resource allocation.

Every Meru resident has a set amount of processing power at their disposal, some people earning more through contributions to the network or through their work as Techs before they transfer. And still others, people who transferred before the collapse, could have magnitudes more that they were able to set aside for themselves. But for a duel, the two combatants get a fixed amount, usually a multiple of the normal amount allocated to a Tech ranging from five to ten to one hundred times what they're used to having.

The duel ends by achieving an objective, like capturing a flag or winning a race. Duelists can use anything they can imagine to their advantage within the restrictions of the duel. Some duels only allow magic, or only allow tech, or only allow raw strength. Others are unrestricted, giving you the maximum freedom to defeat your opponent as creatively as possible.

The match is a capture the flag, best two out of three, between us and Phi. The restriction is magic only, which Sophie excels at. The processing limit for today is working to her advantage too; it's set to ten times, enough to give her some freedom to be creative but still requiring her to conserve her resources, another aspect of the game she's excellent at.

"You put any bets on this one, Isaac?" Aiden asks.

I shake my head no. "Not much point now. You?"

"One week of special requests. I watched some of Sophie's practices this week."

"Still thinking of dueling once you transfer?"

"Duh."

"It's starting," Tess says, then gives my hand a squeeze and we all go silent.

The countdown hits zero and Vance's face turns purple as he screams "LET'S DUEL!!!!" then disappears from view.

Almost immediately there's a flicker in the air around Sophie as she forms a protective shield, an invisible bubble to help absorb whatever her opponent will throw at her. Then she rockets off the ground, flying into the air toward the upper dome of the stadium to try to gain the high ground over her opponent.

I lean forward as Sophie's opponent erupts off the ground behind her, a tall figure wrapped in shimmering robes that flutter behind him as the air whips over his body. Shortly they're both near the top of the dome, slowly circling around each other, encroaching on the other's side, trying to get closer to the flag but still waiting for the other to strike.

Sophie's always been an aggressive duelist, and true to form, she attacks first. The fingers on her right hand twitch upward and the air ignites with blue flame, forming into a flock of burning birds that streak out in a cone, threatening to encircle her opponent. It's a clever opening move. There are too many and they're moving too quickly for her opponent to take them out one by one, so he'll need to use his energy on a larger blast to deter them in time.

"She's gotten better at conservation," Tess murmurs, and she's right. Before, Sophie would have made the birds larger, more dramatic. But these are lean and precise, using minimal power for maximum effect. Like tiny flaming darts poking holes in her opponent's defense.

The Phi duelist, Cahill, responds by encasing himself in rock, which the birds crash harmlessly against, their numbers rapidly thinning. But the weight of his armor is pulling him down, draining his ability to stay aloft, and Sophie's already capitalizing on their distraction. A bolt of water arcs from her hand, forcing him to dodge right, bits of rock falling to the ground as he does, and the remaining few birds fly through the exposed gaps in his armor, knocking off a chunk of his health as Sophie dive-bombs toward his flag.

The crowd in Meru is going wild, their avatars lighting up with different colors as they cheer. These duels are one of the few times when the barrier between Meru and earthside feels thin—we're all watching the same thing, sharing the same experience.

Sophie's opponent manages to recover, shedding the rock armor and creating a whirlwind that sends the debris flying at her. She twists through the air, her shield flickering as pieces bounce off it, but she's already close to their flag. The whirlwind intensifies, threatening to pull her off course.

"Come on, Soph," I mutter, leaning forward. Tess's hand tightens on mine.

Sophie lets the wind catch her, using its momentum to spin

herself around. As she rotates, her hand traces a complex pattern in the air. The stadium temperature drops suddenly, and ice crystals form in the whirlwind. The frozen particles catch the light, creating a dazzling display that momentarily blinds her opponent. Even in a duel, she can't help but make things beautiful.

Cahill raises his hands to shield his eyes, his concentration breaking just enough for the whirlwind to dissipate. Sophie dives through the shower of ice crystals, her shield now crystalline and refracting light in all directions. She's almost to the flag when her opponent throws up a wall of pure energy between her and her target.

"That's going to cost him," Tess says, and she's right. He's burning through his resources too quickly, and I can see the strain on his face as he tries to summon more power to his defense. Apparently as you spend more time in Meru, you start to feel the processing power at your disposal as a kind of energy, like how you can sense whether or not you can lift a weight.

Sophie doesn't try to break through the barrier. Instead, she drops straight down, letting gravity pull her toward the ground. Just before impact, she pulls up sharply, skimming along the arena floor. The wall doesn't reach all the way down—there's a gap just large enough for her to slip through.

The crowd erupts as she snatches the flag, ending round one.

Right before they finish resetting the arena, there's a knock at the door. "I got it," I say and jog over, trying not to miss anything. But any urgency vanishes when I open the door and see Luke's face. He looks even worse than earlier. His eyes are gray, sunken. His hair looks ashy.

"Holy shit, Luke," I say, opening the door for him to come in. "What happened to you?"

His hand is shaking. "Not here," he says, looking over my shoulder at Tess.

"The duel is on. Come watch."

"No, Isaac. I need to talk to you."

I'm about to push back but he looks scared, and I'm worried for him. "Okay, lead the way."

CHAPTER 5

LUKE LEADS US PAST A ROW OF DORMS AND DOWN AN alleyway away from Epsilon's main campus. Soon we're reaching the outer perimeter, and to my surprise there's a small door set into the wall on this part of campus I've never noticed before.

Luke keys in his security code and the door hisses open, then we step out into the night as it seals shut behind us.

"Where are we going?" I ask, looking around for anyone else who might be joining us.

Luke glances nervously over his shoulder back at the wall then clicks on a flashlight, aiming out into the woods ahead. "It's not far."

There's a pit forming in my stomach, and I can't ignore the sense of fear over what Luke is leading me to. But we've known each other our whole lives. I can't imagine he would hurt me; it seems more like he's terrified about something else and needs someone he trusts to confide in. In all our years together, both as friends and working on Epsilon, I've never seen him like this. I've never seen anyone like this.

We cut through the woods silently for a few minutes, then he pulls back a branch to reveal a small clearing. He's obviously been here before, but I can't imagine why. He brushes leaves off a log and sits down, and gestures for me to do the same as he converts the flashlight into a lantern on the ground between us.

"Luke, what're we doing out here?" I ask as I squat on another free log. The light from the lantern is throwing shadows around the trees looming over us.

He chews on his words for a moment, then says, "I don't think you should transfer tomorrow."

I scoff. "I'm gonna miss you too, but I've been looking forward to this for years, Luke. I miss Sophie."

"Isaac, you can't. I want you to leave with me."

"*Leave*? What the hell are you talking about, Luke?"

"I think we're in danger."

"Danger? What's wrong with you?"

He stares off into the woods for a moment, then carefully says, "I think Felix is hiding something from us. Something about the transfers."

"Like what?"

"What if...what if that's not us on the other end? What if it's just a copy?"

"Luke, come on. We've been doing it for a hundred years. You can talk to the people in Meru who transferred. We have friends who have transferred; they're exactly the same on the other end. And if they were just copies then people would wake up after the process. You've seen the video of what happened to Felix's body when he transferred."

He nods slowly. "That could be faked."

"Where is this all coming from?"

"I found...someone. Or something. I can't explain it. In the archives. A trapped voice calling out for help. Someone I don't think Felix wants us to talk to."

"Probably for good reason. Listen to yourself!"

"Isaac, I think when you go in, you *die*. And it's a fake or something else on the other end."

"You think I don't know my sister? What about all of your

friends who are in there too. It's them, Luke. There are *millions* of people in there."

"Sure, they go into the transfer chamber, and all the lights flash and the status changes and then they appear on the other side on one of the screens. But how do we know that's really them? What if the tube kills them and makes a copy on the other end? There's no way to know if who you're talking to is them or just something that seems a lot like them."

"Sure, but if you leave and I see you again tomorrow, how do I know that's really you? It could be an evil twin or something, right?" I force a grin, trying to lighten the mood. "Come on, Luke, this is silly. No one who transfers has ever seemed off. They always have their full memories intact, and the life they live in there seems pretty great even if it's not for you. They've never woken up and said 'Don't do it!'"

"But we still don't know they're transferring, that they're really having a continuity of experience..."

"Come on, Luke, this has all been hashed out. I don't know what voice you think you've found but it must be someone trying to destroy our life here. One of the scavengers found a way into the network and now they're using it to turn you against us."

Luke sighs and stares off into the night. "I don't think that's it, Isaac. They seem old, very old."

"What did they say exactly?"

"I could only get bits and pieces. Like they were trying to communicate through some filter, but it had something to do with that symbol in Simon's room when we found him."

"That's why you freaked out when you saw it?"

"I've seen it before, always indirectly, like it was scattered around Meru as some sort of sign for people looking for whatever I found."

"So after we rescued Simon, you went looking for it."

He nods. "It just seemed like too much of a coincidence, the symbol showing up like that in a station the scavengers attacked."

"Simon said he didn't know what it was though. And, what, you think Simon is one of them? That he faked his station being attacked?"

Luke doesn't respond.

"They're tricking you, Luke. Look at the evidence. A station gets attacked and a resident nearly gets killed, there's this strange symbol in it, you look for that symbol in Meru, and suddenly you're hearing whispers that Meru isn't real? We should be telling Bram about this, telling Felix. Who knows how many other people they're trying to manipulate." Then a scarier thought occurs to me. "Luke, if Simon is one of them and we connected him to Meru, he could be infiltrating our system right now. Everyone in town is at risk."

"No!" he yells and then composes himself. "No, please, don't mention it to them. I—I know how this sounds. Maybe I'm being crazy. I'm scared of what Felix will say or do if he hears it."

"But they could be in danger!"

"Felix can handle it. He controls everything in Meru."

"How can you believe that and also believe there's some secret voice inside Meru trying to talk to you?"

Luke goes silent.

"Luke, you're scaring me. I'm sure Felix would be able to explain this if you asked him about it."

"I don't know about that. The voice seemed scared of him."

"Yeah, because it was a scavenger! They should be scared of him!"

He sighs and stares into the woods again.

"I've been looking forward to this my whole life, Luke. You've seen how incredible Meru is. I get my sister back; I get to see all the friends who transferred before. I'm excited. I know you're happy out here and want to live in this world, but I don't. I'm going to miss you terribly—you're my best friend. Don't make this harder for me."

Luke gives a weak nod and I stand up to leave, but then he grabs my wrist. "Can you at least delay transferring? Make up an excuse. Let me look into this more, at least a few days, please? You know I'm not crazy, Isaac. You know me better than anyone. I've spent my whole life preparing to take care of Epsilon, following in my dad's footsteps. If I'm this scared, that should at least give you some pause."

I hesitate for a moment. There's real fear in his eyes, real concern. But then I tug my wrist free. "No. If I delay, there are going to be questions and I won't have an answer for them. Whatever you think you've found, I'm not buying it, and I think you should be bringing this to your dad and Felix. Not me."

I start to leave but then something gives me pause. Luke is my oldest friend; we've known each other since we were kids. Worked together since we were old enough to pick up jobs. He wouldn't be bringing this up if he were just trying to get me to stay. Something has seriously scared him, and even if I think it's ridiculous, I owe my friend some bit of trust.

I stop and turn back to him. "Keep digging tonight and you can always find me in the morning with whatever evidence you have."

He still looks terrified, but he softly nods his head and says, "Okay."

*** *** ***

Tess is prepping dinner when I make it home but doesn't turn around as I enter, absorbed in chopping carrots with her back turned.

"How'd the duel shake out?" I ask as I enter the kitchen.

She jumps and nearly nicks her finger with the blade. "Whoa. Hey, what took you so long?"

"Sorry, Luke needed to talk."

"You didn't answer your phone."

"I left it here," I say, nodding to it sitting on the counter.

She frowns, then asks, "What's wrong?"

"Where's Aidan?"

"He ran back to the dorm to grab a couple spices you were missing. He should be back in a few."

I glance toward the TV that's still on in the kitchen playing a replay of the duel, then turn it off. I know Felix or anyone else from Meru can't listen in uninvited, but it still gives me a sense of comfort. "Something's gotten into Luke. He doesn't want me to transfer."

"Can't say I disagree."

"Not for that reason." I pause, unsure if I want to open this door with Tess. Questioning the transfer process and Meru feels dangerous and I don't want her to think I share his fears. I know she loves me but after what happened at the station today, everyone in Epsilon has to be on high alert.

"Isaac?"

"It's honestly hard to explain...it's ridiculous."

"Try me."

"He thinks there's something Felix isn't telling us about the process."

She stops cutting and wipes the blade. "You help run the transfers though; you know as much about them as anyone."

"I know. I don't believe him."

"What does he think is happening?"

"He thinks it isn't real. He thinks you die and it's a copy of you in Meru."

She sucks air through her teeth. "He shouldn't be saying that. What could even make him think that?"

"He said he found something in Meru, something that made him question it. Like someone inside Meru was trying to tell him."

"Is that…possible?"

"Maybe, but I think someone outside of the centers has found a way to break in. To talk to us as if they're in Meru. To try to trick him."

She crinkles her eyebrows in thought and opens the fridge, grabbing two beers and opening them for us. "Luke knows more about Meru than anyone here, except for maybe his dad. He's the person who should doubt it the least."

I take a sip of the beer and nod. "I know, it's uncharacteristic for him. But sometimes…you know when you say a word so many times that it doesn't sound right?"

"Like?"

"Like any word. Say squirrel. Squirrel squirrel squirrel squirrel. Suddenly it sounds like you're saying it wrong. Or you start to wonder if it's a real word."

"Okay, and…"

"Maybe he's *too* deep in it. He spends all his time in the archives, studying Meru, trying to learn everything about it so he can take over from Bram. Maybe he's hit that point where things that did make sense suddenly don't."

"Or he's run out of new things to learn about it so he's grasping for other insights."

"Could be that too. People as smart as him aren't always happy with easy, reasonable explanations."

"It *would* be exciting if there were some huge secret hidden in Meru that he found."

"Right? I'm worried that's why he's so wrapped up in this."

"Combined with not wanting you to transfer."

"Yeah...hopefully it'll pass."

We stand in silence, and I can feel Tess studying my face, trying to figure out what I'm thinking. "Are you going to tell Bram? Felix?"

"No, and please don't say anything to them either. Hopefully Luke can sleep off whatever is going on in his head right now."

"And if he can't?"

"Well...we'll cross that bridge if we get to it."

"You're worrying me."

I put the beer down on the counter, slightly too hard, and wrap her in a hug, feeling her breath on my neck. "It's going to be fine. You don't have anything to worry about."

"I'm more worried about *you*. What if he does something and people find out you knew he was having these thoughts and didn't say anything."

"He's not going to do anything. He cares about Epsilon more than anything else."

Tess opens her mouth to say something but then Aidan bursts through the front door, "Found them!"

I give Tess a soft smile but can still see the unease etched on her face. Then a moment later it's gone as she turns to her brother. "Thanks. Bud. Look who's back."

Aidan runs into the kitchen and starts filling me in on the duel as we resume cooking. Tess's tension slowly fades away as we eat, and I silently hope we can all enjoy the ceremony tomorrow.

CHAPTER 6

TESS ALREADY HAS A COFFEE IN HAND WHEN I COME downstairs; she snuck out of bed early to get some work done as she often does. There's a flash of sadness in her eyes as I enter the kitchen, but then she smiles and hugs me a beat longer than usual.

"Sleep well?" she asks and hands me a cup. The instant coffee that Imgen delivers is awful, so I built a small roaster based on schematics I found in the archives and convinced Felix to set up a special delivery to Epsilon of unroasted beans. The bots are good at automating some things; they can brew coffee fine, but roasting never goes well. Probably because roasting depends on smell as much as sight, and of all the senses, smell is apparently the hardest to digitize. It's one of the only things that makes our life richer than that of people in Meru. Apparently nothing smells quite right for the first few months until your expectations adjust. So I make sure to appreciate this last whiff of the coffee we mastered together.

"Not really, no," I reply as I start rummaging through the pantry for a protein bar.

"Nervous?" Sophie asks, appearing on the screen above the sink.

I'm about to say I'm excited, but I don't want to hurt Tess by admitting it. "Something like that."

Sophie gives me a skeptical look but doesn't push it. "Any requests from my end for when you show up?"

I take another sip of coffee, then the image of the symbol we saw in Simon's room comes back into my mind. "Actually, yes. Mind looking into something for me?"

"Yeah, what's up?"

I grab the tablet off the wall and draw the symbol as best I can remember it. Tess peers over my shoulder as I sketch it out, erasing a few mistakes as I go, but I don't get any sense that she recognizes it. I finish and it appears on a tablet in Sophie's hand.

"What is this?"

"It was on the wall of the room Simon, the guy we rescued yesterday, was living in."

"It looks like Chinese," she says. Tess and I give her a surprised look and she shrugs. "I recognize it from the teahouses. You want me to look up what it means?"

"No. I'm curious if you see it anywhere else significant in Meru."

"Okey-dokey." She gives me a mock salute. "I'll dig around before the party and we can look together tomorrow."

Sophie disappears and Tess starts shuffling awkwardly around the kitchen. There's clearly something on her mind but she isn't saying anything.

"What's wrong?"

"What if we try just once before you go? I'm close enough to the window where I could get pregnant. If it doesn't happen, at least we gave it a shot."

"And if it *does* happen then I'd be abandoning you."

"You're not abandoning me, Isaac. I want this."

"Either way, I know what it's like growing up feeling abandoned."

"They didn't abandon you either. And besides, you'd still be here, just in there." She nods toward the screen.

"No, Tess. You should find someone who wants to stay out here with you for longer."

"But I want *you!*"

"You knew this was the deal when we started seeing each other."

"Well maybe you changed your mind!"

"Is that what you've been holding out hope for?"

She doesn't answer, but from the patch of red under her eyes I know it was.

"I'm sorry, Tess. Please don't make this any harder."

She sniffles and nods, then leans into me, pressing her face against my chest as I wrap her in my arms. There's a part of me that wants to give in, but I know she'll be happier if she can let us go and find someone who will stay here with her. At least until her kids are old enough to watch out for themselves.

I kiss her on the top of the head and can feel a wet spot forming on my shirt from her eyes.

"It's not really about the kid," she whispers. "I don't want you to go. I thought maybe…"

I squeeze her tighter. "I know. I'm going to miss you too."

"Are you?" She pulls back slightly and wipes her nose with her sleeve, her hand hidden inside. "It's…it's Meru. Everyone who transfers says it's the most incredible life once you're inside. Even better than they imagined or hoped for. Are you really going to want to still talk to me out here? What if you meet someone in there?"

"I'm not going to meet anyone." I kiss her forehead again. "I'm going to be a celibate monk and work on our house there until you show up."

She snorts a laugh. "You'd look stupid with a shaved head."

"Gotta do something to keep the girls away."

"Oh hush." She leans against me, and we stand in silence as

I stroke her hair, trying to drink in how she smells for one of the last times.

"I'm gonna go help set up for the party," I say. "Come find me in a little bit?"

"I can come now. I don't have any work this morning."

"Give me an hour or two. I want to say bye to a few people first."

"Alright," she whispers. I give her another kiss and hug her as tightly as I can, then make my way out the door as she returns to making breakfast.

※ ※ ※

The quad is already bustling with people preparing for the festivities when I arrive. A few give me a surprised look; transferees often spend the day with their families and friends, but I want to help. Massive speakers are being installed on each corner of the quad, and a stage is being erected outside of the transfer building. Transfer days are the biggest celebrations of the year, even bigger than holidays, and even though we do one every few months, they never get dull. We're free from normal chores for the day after the parties too, so the drinks and music tend to go late into the night, sometimes until sunrise. Considering Epsilon loses one worker every time there's a transfer, I've always suspected the parties are as much for celebrating as they are for keeping up the population.

Grant, the town's doctor, is pulling a table out of storage and setting it up near the stage as I arrive, his curly salt-and-pepper hair tied up in a bun. I jog over and grab the far edge, helping lift it off the grass.

"Isaac! Shouldn't you be, ah, saying goodbye?"

"Can't I say goodbye to you too?"

Grant beams. He was one of the men in Epsilon who took me under his wing after my parents died and Felix relocated me here. He's almost as old as Bram, nearly fifty, and while Bram stayed behind to provide order to Epsilon, I sometimes feel like Grant stayed back to balance him out, lighten the mood. Though maybe the seriousness of tending to wounds and delivering babies requires an exaggerated sense of humor to compensate.

"Here, here," Grant says reaching into his jacket and pulling out a small flask as we set the table down.

I unscrew it and take a whiff, then rip my nose away from the opening and retch. "*Gods*, Grant, did you swipe this from Tess?"

"What, from the bots?" He almost looks offended. "No no, try it!"

"I'm absolutely not trying that."

"Oh come on, you can't seriously prefer Felix's swill."

"Felix's swill won't melt my throat."

"Weak," he says and takes a swig. "Maybe it's better you're transferring. Need the real men to stay behind."

"Pretty sure you were barely lifting this table before I got here."

"I saw you coming, wanted you to feel useful."

"Uh-huh."

Two other Techs come up behind us and drop some cups and bowls on the table and give me a nod of quiet congratulations. When they walk off, Grant asks, more serious now, "How are you feeling?"

"Ready, excited."

"You look nervous."

My eyes flicker with surprise. "Do I?"

"They might not notice." He nods out to the crowd working around us. "But I can tell. Don't be though. Everyone who goes through says the same thing."

"What's that?"

"Painless, instant, just *pop*." He makes the sound with his lips instead of saying it. "Presto, you're in Meru."

"It's not that."

"What then?"

"What…happens to our bodies? After we transfer?"

"Hah!" His laugh is so loud it attracts a few looks from the others nearby. "Attached to your mortal form all of a sudden?"

"Not exactly, just curious."

"Well, you've seen the Felix video."

"Everyone has."

"So you already know then."

I click my tongue. It feels like he's being evasive.

Grant claps me on the shoulder. "The leftover body is cremated, but you already know that. You know how that bit of magic works better than I do. So why are you wondering this and why are you asking *me* this?"

"Is it possible for someone's mind to not make the jump? To stay stuck in their body?"

Grant's face lights up, then he looks around before answering in a hushed tone. "Truth be told, I've always wondered that. Can you imagine? Waking up in that tube right before the end and hearing someone *else* out there masquerading as you?" He licks his lips. I think the taboo nature of the discussion excites him. "But, no, Isaac, that's never happened. Not here, not in any of the other centers, not since those first trials way back at the beginning. And you ought to be careful who you ask that to. Though I can't say you're the first."

"Luke asked you, didn't he?"

Grant freezes and looks over his shoulder again. "You didn't come out here to help, did you?"

"What did you tell him?"

"Same thing I told you."

"What did he tell you?"

Grant stares at me hard, his pale blue eyes brilliant against tan skin. His gaze darts back and forth between my eyes, looking for something. "It sounds like the same thing he told you."

"Grant, you can trust me. I'm not saying anything to Bram. I'm just worried about him."

That seems to put him at ease. He sighs and starts organizing the table again. "I know, Isaac. Something's gotten into that boy's head though. Ever since he started digging deeper in the archives a few months ago—"

"*Months?*"

"When did he talk to you?"

"Last night. Have you talked to him since then?"

Grant shakes his head. "But, listen, here's what you need to know. Luke is right that Felix isn't telling us everything; of course he isn't. But he's wrong about the process. It's solid. I think Felix just doesn't want us to know what went down with Imgen in the beginning. No one gets that powerful without having a few skeletons in their closet."

"So you think it's fine to transfer."

Grant laughs, then seems to realize it was a serious question. "Isaac, of course it is!" Then he continues in a quieter tone, "But there *are* secrets in there. If you want to find them, it will be easier on the inside. I bet your sister has already started doing some digging of her own."

"What kind of secrets?"

"I'm not entirely sure. Life is long; I'll get in there eventually. But, listen, it's normal to be worried. I've had a version of this conversation dozens of times. You're gonna be fine."

"He's right, Isaac."

Both of us jump, and I whip around to see Bram striding toward us. He's already in his ceremonial wear for the evening, gilded white robes lightly draping over his feet. With his shaved head and bushy copper beard he always reminds me of images I've seen of precollapse religious leaders. I search his eyes for any hint of concern over what we were discussing but find none. Either he's keeping it a secret or he only caught the last sentence.

"Sir," we say in unison and dip our heads.

"Will you be able to manage if I borrow Isaac for a minute?" he says to Grant.

"Oh, I think I'll muddle through. Gotta get used to getting by without him, I suppose," he says and gives me a wink.

Bram extends a robed arm and gestures for me to join him. I pat Grant on the shoulder, trying to tell him thank you for the talk, then fall in beside Bram as he leads me across the quad toward the transfer building. A group of kids are sitting in a circle near the corner, working through their lessons for the day on tablets while a teacher paces around them to answer questions.

"You're going to be missed here, Isaac."

"Thank you, sir." Bram has always been warm toward me, though at a distance, as I suppose he must, given his role in the town.

"I want to talk with you about what you saw yesterday, before the festivities."

"How can I help?"

We reach the double doors of the transfer building and Bram pulls one open, beckoning me inside. It's empty. Shelby must have finished the preparations already. I step up to the transfer bed and run my hand along it. I can make out a warped view of my reflection in the metal tube. The computer array beside it is showing an aerial view of Meru's Epsilon, their own party starting to come together as they plan to welcome me.

"How are you feeling?"

I know what he's really asking. This is the first time there's been any sign of people outside of the centers attacking us since Sophie and I were rescued. "Surprisingly okay."

"It didn't bring back any painful memories?"

"No." I shake my head and step back from the transfer station. "I still don't remember anything about what happened."

"I suppose that makes sense. You were very young."

"Are you worried?"

He seems surprised by the question and takes a moment to consider it. "Yes, but I'm always worried about our life here. It's the weight I carry so the rest of you can live in peace."

"You never seem very worried."

His stoic demeanor breaks into a grin. "Then I'm doing my job well."

"I'm sorry I can't be more help."

"Pardon?"

"You were hoping the attack would jog some memory free, weren't you? Something we might learn about them from when my parents died?"

"Ah, no, not exactly." He turns to the screen now and nods toward it, and the view changes from the panorama of Meru's Epsilon into a top-down map of the area. There's a red dot southeast of us at the station where we found Simon, along with a few other dots running north from it marking the other communications towers.

"Did you ever find it odd that people like Simon would go live in these stations for periods?"

"A little, but it's hard to imagine what you might want to do as a digital person."

"Yes, it is hard to imagine, isn't it? Infinite time, not bound by normal physics or scarcity…to be honest, it sounds like it could get boring."

"I'm glad I'm not the only one."

"I'm sure you'll find a way to entertain yourself. Everyone else seems to."

"But the stations?"

"Right, right, the stations. They serve a secondary purpose, one Felix and I and the leaders of other towns don't advertise too broadly in the interest of peace of mind. They're scouting outposts. The Meru network can only extend so far beyond the centers, which means our drones and other robotics can only go so far beyond our walls. They can, of course, go outside the network and run on the artificial intelligence chips embedded in them, but if they're destroyed we learn nothing, and they can get stuck in unknown situations."

"So Simon was looking for them."

"Yes, keeping an eye on the scavengers, outsiders, whatever you prefer to call them."

I feel silly for not thinking about it before. Transferring to one of the comm stations came with a significant amount of risk. If your server was destroyed, you were gone, the only thing close to dying in Meru. There had to be a better reason for taking that risk than curiosity or boredom.

"Did he learn anything?"

"No, sadly. They destroyed his bots and cameras before he could find out much of anything. But I'm certain this isn't the end of it."

"Why?"

"They were unprovoked. It's possible they're trying to do the same thing to Epsilon that they did to Alpha."

A pit of dread forms in my stomach. The footage I saw of Alpha's Techs, my parents, all lying dead in their beds. The idea of Tess, or the kids we just saw in the quad, suffering the same fate is agonizing.

"Are…are you asking me to stay here? To help you fight them?" It's the last thing I want to do, but I would if Bram asked. I owe him my life.

"Oh! No, quite the opposite, in fact. Felix has had a hard time finding others like Simon willing to risk themselves for the cause. Willing to risk deletion to keep an eye on the threats to Meru. And given you don't have any children or other family here…"

"Yes," I say before he can finish. "Yes, of course. Whatever you need." I know Sophie won't love the idea of losing me again as soon as I transfer, and my heart wrenches knowing it too. But if the threat is real and I can help keep the people here safe, I know I have to do it.

"Excellent, excellent." Bram claps me on the back, and I can see it's taken a weight off his shoulders. He seems lighter, relieved. But then my thoughts turn to Luke. To the outsiders trying to corrupt him through Meru.

"What is it?" Bram asks; he must have noticed my hesitancy. But I decide not to bring it up. I can investigate the intrusion from inside Meru, or get Sophie to help look for it. I don't want to turn him against his son.

"Just nerves," I say, looking back at the machine again. I've watched the video on the process dozens of times, I know the intimate detail of every step. The sedative it will inject to freeze my body once the door is sealed. The tiny incision its robotic arm will cut in the top of my skull to feed in the neural lace. How it will spread its thin sheet of receptors across my brain, providing the bridge for my consciousness between this body and the digital world. How it systematically reproduces digital versions of each bodily function and sense to slowly hijack my perception of where my body is located, facilitating the jump. The beautiful tunnel of light I'll walk through as my mind accepts its new host, waking up to a cheering sea of the people who have gone before me. And finally, how it cremates this body once I wake up in Meru."

"I'd be worried if you didn't feel at least a hint of trepidation. But Isaac," he turns me back to face him and puts both of his hands on my shoulders. I immediately feel like that young boy again, hiding under the bed with Sophie, screaming for her as I'm dragged out by my legs, not realizing I'm being rescued. "It's a great gift you're about to receive. The greatest gift ever bestowed on us by science. Try to appreciate the beauty of it instead of fear it."

I gulp and manage a weak nod in response. "I will."

"Come on then." Bram breaks away and starts striding toward the door again. With the robe, he almost creates the illusion of gliding. "Don't let me keep you all to myself on your last day."

CHAPTER 7

A CHEER GOES UP FROM THE CROWD AS I STEP OUT OF the medical office and enter the quad, Tess on my arm, my ceremonial white robe trailing behind me. Grant had to run one last physical check on me to make sure I was ready to transfer, and I passed it without issue. The remainder of the sun is barely visible behind the taller buildings of campus, and an orange glow fills the quad as the music thumps louder, inviting anyone who hasn't come out to the party yet to join.

Tess has, thankfully, stayed strong the rest of the afternoon, and I'm grateful that she's seeing me off like this even though I know it's hard for her. We make our way to the buffet line, and I take up a spot by the start, ready to receive anyone who wants to say goodbye as they dish up. Some of them have family in Meru they want me to check on too. It's not uncommon for people in Meru to turn off their feeds and disappear for days, weeks, months, even years. You don't perceive time the same way once you're inside, and it's easy to spend ages on some adventure or quest without realizing it.

I'm in awe of the extra work Tess put into making tonight's party special. She combined some leftover parts from security panels along with the processing board of a broken dog to make an automated light show. As the sun sets, the dancing lights she designed are slowly filling the town with energy. I worked with her on the music for the event, syncing the lights with it for a fully immersive experience. Our beats pump across the quad, creating a hypnotic background to the festival, and people slowly start bobbing in place, moving along to the tune without realizing they're doing it.

She steps away for a moment as I continue greeting people, then returns with a pair of drinks in hand. "Thirsty?" she asks, handing me a metal cup of what smells like electrolytes mixed with gasoline.

"Yeesh," I say, taking a sip despite the smell. "Grant didn't pull punches this time."

"Tired of saying bye yet?" she asks, nodding at a couple as they walk away.

"Getting there. My list of people I apparently need to check in on is long."

"Oh, that reminds me—"

I bump my hip into hers. "Don't you start."

Tess grins and takes another sip of her drink, crinkling her nose. "You seen Luke yet?"

"No, I'm worried."

"Do you think he'd really do anything?"

"I hope not."

A cheer goes up as Bram walks into the center of the stage in front of the transfer building, waving to the crowd. Aidan runs over to join us, and Tess helps him climb onto the table so he can get a better view.

As Bram waits for the crowd to quiet down, all of the screens behind him as well as on the surrounding buildings change to show Meru's Epsilon, their own dance floor and festival arranged and attended by all the past Techs who had transferred, along with other guests like Simon. Felix is standing on the digital stage, mirroring Bram's position, waiting to welcome me to my new world. It says something that he took time off from his other duties to see the transfer; he doesn't attend all of them. Bram must have told him about my willingness to help man the scouting stations.

"Ladies and gentlemen," Bram begins, his voice amplified through the speakers as the music quiets down. "Today, we celebrate another great milestone in our community. Isaac's journey into Meru!" The crowd roars in cheers again as he gestures in my direction.

"For twenty years, he has been a cherished member of our town here in Epsilon. And now, he takes on the boldest, greatest adventure of his life."

Tess smiles nervously, fidgeting with the hem of my robe. Her eyes are a mix of excitement and nervousness, the same feelings dancing around inside of me.

"In Meru, Isaac will join our friends and loved ones who have gone before," Bram continues, making eye contact with Sophie as he says it. She appeared in Meru's quad a moment ago and is looking out at us through one of the portals they use to watch what's going on in town. "He'll experience wonders beyond our imagination, free from the constraints of our physical world. No more aging, no more pesky physics, no more death!"

I glance at Tess, and she steps closer to me and weaves our fingers together, leaning her head on my shoulder. I wonder if she'll decide to transfer and forego having children, or if she'll stay here and find someone else. It's rare that a woman transfers without having kids, but it does happen. And we aren't suffering from a population shortage. It's the only way our relationship could last. The gulf between life in Meru and Epsilon takes a toll on every relationship that tries to weather it.

Bram's voice swells with emotion. "Isaac, you've brought

so much joy and light to our lives here. Though I wouldn't wish what happened to you as a child on anyone, if there was any blessing to be found in it, it's that it brought you to us. Your strength, your curiosity, your spirit, your love for those you're leaving behind..." He nods at Tess and I feel her choke up. "These are just some of the many gifts you'll carry with you into your new life."

Tess stands on her tiptoes to whisper in my ear. "Let's sneak off for a bit after the speech," and I squeeze her hand. It doesn't sound like she wants to argue.

"While we'll miss your physical presence," Bram says, his voice catching slightly, "we take comfort in knowing that you'll always be with us, anywhere we want to reach you. We just hope you don't forget about us in the boring old real world out here." A quiet chuckle goes through the crowd.

"Aside from raising my dear son," he looks around for Luke but doesn't find him, and a hint of worry flashes across his face before he shakes it off. "The greatest honor of my life has been helping to maintain Meru. For those whose lives were almost claimed by the plague, and for the countless others who earned their place in paradise since.

"Isaac, is there anything you'd like to come up and say?" He holds out a hand toward me as an invitation, and the crowd all turns to look toward me in silence.

I cup my hands around my mouth so everyone can hear, and then shout, "Let's party!"

The crowd roars in celebration. The Meru citizens cheer as well, and we can hear their amplified voices booming through the speakers. Bram laughs and waves at everyone to resume the festivities. The music takes on a louder, more animated tempo now, and people abandon their conversations and mingling to start dancing, as Tess's light show streams across the crowd. A countdown appears above the transfer building showing two hours remaining. Two hours until my transfer.

Tess squeezes my hand and whispers in my ear again, "Come on," and starts leading me away from the crowd. We weave through the dancers and around the edge of the quad, a few friends giving me a knowing nudge as I pass, making our way closer to her dorm.

We reach the front steps and she spins around, pulling me into a kiss at the base of the stairs, then pulls back and gives me a hungry look as she leads me by the hand up the steps.

She yanks open the door at the top. I pause to look back at the party, and my eyes linger on the transfer building. Luke's fear and pleading from the night before ring in my mind.

"Do you have any of your tools in your room?"

"That's new."

"Not for *that*. I need you to help me with something."

She huffs and crosses her arms. "You're transferring in barely over an hour. What could you possibly need to do?"

"You still haven't seen Luke, right?"

"Not since yesterday."

"I'm worried about him, worried he did something. Or is going to do something."

"Let Bram or someone else handle it. We should be spending this last bit of time together."

"Please? I just want to check his room."

Tess's heel bounces as she deliberates. "Fine. Let's make it quick though."

※ ※ ※

I lean against the wall outside Tess's door, trying to act casual as she grabs her tools. I'm not sure what I'm worried about though. Everyone is at the ceremony; no one should interrupt us.

"Bram is going to be pissed, you know," Tess says, emerging back into the hall, her work duffel over her shoulder. "Or Felix. Or both. I can't believe we're doing this."

I give her a quick kiss. "I'll take the blame. And if we find something, they'll be thanking us." Then I grab her hand and lead her up the two flights of stairs to Luke's room, grateful that we don't run into anyone on the way. Though at least with us together, it's easy to make up an excuse for why we'd be sneaking off from the party.

A small screen by Luke's door flickers to life as we approach, and I wave it away. There's a security camera that will see what we're doing, but there's no point trying to conceal it. I'm not sure if I'm more hopeful to find nothing and get in trouble, or to find something to justify the intrusion.

"Be quick," I say as Tess starts working the lock.

"I was thinking of taking my time, actually."

"Yeah yeah."

I hear footsteps in the distance and my eyes dart down the hall, but then the sound passes over my head on the floor above. A moment later there's a soft click as the lock disengages.

"Come on," Tess says, nudging the door open. The apartment is dark and silent, but the moment the lights turn on it's obvious we were right to break in.

"Holy shit..." Tess whispers as I follow her through the entry.

It looks like a bomb went off. Clothes are thrown about, empty food and drink containers litter the coffee table and floor, and a musty smell hangs in the air. There's what looks like a half-eaten meat loaf on the desk by Luke's computer with a layer of mold on it.

This isn't the Luke I know. He's always been so orderly, organized, even anal. He once bragged to me about the organization system he came up with for the photos on his phone. I almost want to step outside to make sure we entered the right room, but I recognize the bits of personalization he's added. A small vase of hawk feathers from when a bird tried to attack his drone and got clipped by the propellors. A shattered phone from pre-collapse we found buried under some wires in a comm station three years ago.

He's been spiraling for some time. This couldn't all have happened in two days.

"How did no one notice..." I wonder aloud.

"How did *you* not notice?"

The question stings, but she's right. Seeing this physical manifestation of Luke's internal state, I can't help but feel overcome with guilt for being blind to what my friend was going through.

"I...I don't know."

"You said he was a little off but not...this...right?"

I nod in response. She must be thinking the same thing I am. If Luke was this far gone and no one could tell, then he didn't just find something. He was hiding it too. It must have taken a significant amount of courage for him to try to talk to me yesterday.

"Luke?" I call out, but no response comes. All the lights are off and his work boots are missing from the shoe rack beside the door. I don't think he's here.

"Where do we start?" I ask, turning on the living room light and surveying the chaos.

"Good question," Tess says as she wanders toward the kitchen while I start turning over piles of clothes. They reek of musk.

"Oh shit," she says as soon as she gets past the counter.

I jog over to join her, and my breath catches as I see what

she found. The kitchen is littered with cups containing different mixtures, disassembled rifle bullets, and spare electronics.

"The hell was he doing with this?" I ask.

Tess doesn't answer but starts picking up some of the cups to smell them and turning over the wires and circuit boards.

I pick up a few documents on the edge of the counter as she investigates. The scrawl on them is scratchy, erratic, but that's not surprising. Most of us have terrible handwriting from how little we do it.

"Let me see," Tess says. She grabs the papers and fans them out over the table, picking up a few of the supplies as she leafs through them, comparing the items on the table to the notes.

"Was he trying to make bullets?" I ask.

"No, worse," she says with a hint of apprehension. "I haven't tried doing it before, but this looks a lot like how I'd try to make an explosive."

"Christ, Luke…" The thought of him making something so destructive is chilling, terrifying. And I'm worried I already know how he wants to use it. "Any way to tell if he succeeded?"

Tess pushes through the items and compares a few of them to sketches on the paper. "There are a couple things missing." She points to a small cylinder on the paper. "Assuming he actually had this, I don't see it here."

"What is it?"

"Looks like replacement pipe from our maintenance supplies. There's a switch here that's missing, too." She points to another sketch on the pad.

"How did he figure out how to do it though?"

"No idea. There are likely schematics in the network somewhere, in case something catastrophic happens and we need to clear rubble. But they have to be tightly guarded. I doubt anyone could access them besides…"

"Besides who?"

"Bram."

"Bram wouldn't help him with this."

"He wouldn't have to. Luke could have figured out how to use his credentials."

"Shit. Is it that hard to figure out how to make them on his own?"

"Supposedly," Tess says. "My dad warned me against trying it. People would try to fabricate home bombs like this in the pre-Meru era, but most failed. Either the bomb didn't go off or they blew themselves up in the process. He knew curiosity might get the better of me eventually..."

"Wish Luke was there for that."

I take the paper back from Tess while she keeps turning over the electronics. As I leaf through them, my fear and concern slowly settle into a deeper dread. After the notes on the explosives, he drew sketches of the transfer station, some indecipherable notes written with erratic circles around the helmet of the machine. I can make out a few words: "Copy," "Not-Felix," "Vance." And then on the back page that strange symbol again, scrawled dozens of times in different angles and sizes, as if he were trying to find something in it.

"What is that?" Tess asks, looking over my shoulder.

"I don't know. It was in the comm station where we found Simon too. Luke freaked out when he saw it."

Tess pulls out her phone and scans it with a translation tool.

"Anything?"

"It says it's the symbol *xīn* which means 'heart,' or sometimes 'mind' or even 'heart-mind.'"

"Heart-mind?"

"No idea. Luke didn't have a secret girlfriend or anyone, did he?"

"Not that I know of..." But as I say it, I wonder how much else I didn't know about him.

"I think we need to show this to Bram."

My stomach churns imagining what kind of trouble this is going to get Luke into, but Tess is right. We can't risk him hurting anyone, and he's clearly not himself anymore.

"You're right. Let's go." I stack the papers together and head toward the door, taking one last look around the chaos as Tess leaves and I shut the apartment behind us.

We race back down the stairs, taking them two at a time. If Luke truly believes there's something sinister about the transfer process like he tried to convince me last night, and if he created some sort of explosive, he has to be targeting the transfer station. It's the obvious explanation, the only one that makes sense, but the idea chills me to my core. I can't imagine that anyone, let alone Luke, would jeopardize our only way to reach Meru. That someone would risk condemning the others in Epsilon to death.

Finally, we emerge back into the quad, and the audiovisual assault of the festival overwhelms me. I can't tell if it's escalated since we left or if it's the contrast with the silent terror we saw in Luke's apartment.

"Where's Bram?" Tess asks, scanning the crowd. I can't pick him out either. He's not on stage anymore; he must be mingling with the group. Or, hopefully, he's already found Luke and is trying to talk him down.

Then a flicker of movement catches my eye near the transfer building. Not the entrance where the stage is set up, but in the alleyway beside it, and despite the darkness of the passage there's an unmistakable tousle of golden hair.

"Is that..." I start to say, but then he's gone.

"What?"

"Luke. I swear I saw him, I think he went in." I point down the alley.

"Well let's go get him," Tess says and moves to run down the stairs.

"Wait," I say, grabbing her hand. "I don't want you to get hurt." I press the documents into her hand. "Go find Bram. I'll go after Luke."

"Isaac…"

"I'll be okay." I squeeze her hand and try to look reassuring. "Find Bram and send him in to help."

She stares back at me, and I can see the fear behind her shimmering green eyes. I know she wants to fight me on it, to come help, but I won't let her. I could never forgive myself if something happened to her.

"Okay," she whispers and squeezes my hand back, then takes off down the stairs.

I barely see her start to push through the crowd as I run off toward the alley where Luke disappeared. I don't want to draw too much attention by going in through the front. A few Techs give me curious glances as I pass but I fake a smile and wave as I elbow my way through the crowd.

Grant nearly knocks me over as he stumbles into me with a drink, clearly enjoying too much of his moonshine. But I pick him up and send him back into the fray, using his teetering and shouting as a distraction as I carve through the last few people. Dread is gnawing at me for whatever he thinks he found or knows, or what the scavengers might have talked him into, and as much as I want to sprint toward him, I can't risk alarming everyone. Not yet.

Finally, I reach the alley and check quickly over my shoulder to make sure no one's following me. They're all too distracted with the dancing. I'm alone. To my surprise, the door is still unlocked. I had assumed Luke would try to stop me from following him but now I'm worried it's a trap. That he wanted to lure me in after him.

I take a deep breath while I debate my options. I could go back and find a weapon, or a dog, or another person. But I don't want to put him on the defensive. And I don't want to risk someone else getting Luke in trouble before I can talk him out of this.

So I decide to risk it and enter on my own.

CHAPTER 8

THE ENTRYWAY IS DARK, BUT THERE'S LIGHT COMING down the hall from the main transfer room. There's a faint tapping sound coming from it, the patter of fingers on a keyboard.

I creep down the hall, trying not to make any sound, and then peer around the corner into the atrium. The gleaming metal tube dominates the room, a progress bar at 0 percent on one of the small screens by the bed. In front of it at the control terminal is Luke, looking even more haggard than before. And even more to my surprise, Felix is here, watching whatever Luke is doing from one of the screens.

"Isaac!" Felix announces, and Luke jumps, his eyes flying around the room for me. I step tentatively out of my hiding spot toward the center of the room, my weight still on my back foot in case I need to escape.

"What's...going on?" I ask, trying to read their faces. Luke looks terrified to see me. But Felix looks confused now.

"Well, Luke was telling me that you asked him to come run the diagnostics on the transfer, make sure everything was in good shape for later. I told him Shelby already looked at it earlier, but he insisted."

Luke's face has changed from fear to an almost pleading look. And despite what I found in his room, I still feel an inexplicable need to try to protect him, to stop this before it escalates into something that will bring worse consequences on him.

"Yes..." I stammer. "You know, pretransfer jitters. But I'm sure everything is fine." I'm trying to bore my eyes into Luke's, to demand he stop this and let it go. This is his only chance to turn back. I have to convince him.

"You should go back to the party, Isaac," Luke replies, his tone steady. "I'll just be a few minutes longer."

"Really, there's no need," I say, taking a cautious step forward. The movement seems to put Luke on edge. His whole body tenses up and his hand drifts ever so slightly toward his waist. "Why don't you come back with me? It would be nice to spend a little more time together before I go."

"It'll just be a minute, Isaac." His mouth is barely moving; his jaw looks like it's locked together. "Please. Let. Me. Finish."

"I can't let you do that, Luke."

"Let him do what?" Felix asks, sounding annoyed now.

I open my mouth to respond, but then the front door of the building swings open and Bram rushes in. Beyond him some people in the crowd are peering over his shoulder, wondering why he's going into the transfer room so early.

His eyes linger on me, then shift to Luke. "What is this?" he asks, holding up the papers.

"Just some notes, Dad. They're nothing."

"You haven't even looked at them. I could be holding anything!"

"It's NOTHING."

"What in the blazes is going on here, you three? Isaac, didn't you send Luke in here to check on the station?"

I can't protect him any longer. "No. I didn't."

Luke's face falls, turning from fear to sorrow, his fingers stopping their sprint across the keyboard. I take a few steps toward him, hoping he'll let me comfort him, but then he whispers, "You can't go, Isaac."

Felix scoffs, "Is that what this is about? I knew you two were close but not *that* close—"

"NO!" Luke yells and bangs on the keyboard with his fist. Then he glares up at the Felix, the red in his eyes getting darker with each passing moment. "I know what you're doing, Felix."

I give a nervous look to Bram, but his face is set in stone. Then I start inching closer to Luke. "Come on," I say as I put a hand on his shoulder. "Let's go. Don't say or do something you're going—" but then my vision suddenly goes out as I fall to one knee, pain exploding across my face and the taste of blood filling my mouth. When I get my eyes back open, Luke is standing over me, his fist cocked back, ready to unleash another blow.

"What the *fuck*, Luke?" I yell while massaging my jaw, my words slurred from the impact.

"Stay out of this!"

I yell as I leap up, catching his hip with my shoulder, wrapping my arms around him and throwing him onto the ground. Climbing on top of his chest, I grab his jacket lapel with one arm, trying to hold him in place as he wriggles under me. I'm bigger, stronger, but he's a clever fighter and has years of practice wrestling with me. He plants his feet and tries to throw me off with his hips, but I manage to wrap my feet under and hold myself in place.

"You don't get it!" he yells, throwing an elbow at my head, but I dodge it and punch him in the nose, feeling a crack under my fist as blood starts spewing down his face and onto my hand.

"They're using you!" I yell at him. "You're smarter than this!"

He spits blood in my face and my vision turns a blur of red as he smashes his elbow into my temple. I groan and roll off of him, seeing stars, trying to wipe the blood off my face as I feel him scramble out of my legs and back up onto his feet.

My vision clears just in time to see Bram try to come stop him, but he's no match. Luke runs toward him, throwing his entire weight into Bram's chest, sending him stumbling until his ankle twists and he collapses against the back wall of the room. Bram gasps for air and I can see the pain and hurt in his eyes as he clutches his leg.

"It's not them," Luke says, his chest heaving as he stands in front of the transfer bed, staring at me and pointing up at Felix. "He's hiding something, I know he is."

I stand up to start advancing on him again, but then he grabs a knife off the medical table by the bed and points it at me.

"Don't."

I know my friend would never hurt me, but I don't know who this person is anymore. I put my hands up and take a step back, then inch toward Bram. "I'm just going to make sure your dad's okay."

Luke puts down the knife and starts typing ferociously again, blood dripping off his face onto the keyboard.

"What exactly do you think you're going to find, Luke?" Felix asks. He sounds more curious than worried. It's almost unnerving how calm he's being about all of this.

"I'm transferring."

Felix laughs. "I'm not sure that will prove whatever point you're trying to make."

"It will when I wake up."

That seems to throw Felix. His eyes flash wider and his mouth hangs open for a moment, and for the first time, I wonder if Luke did find something.

"I know what you did to Vance. And I'm going to show the rest of them too."

I inch my way over to Bram while they're arguing, and to my relief, he seems okay, though I suspect he can't stand on his ankle. As I crouch down next to him, a faint movement catches my eye. There's a security dog attached to the wall by the door, directly behind Luke where he can't see it, and it's slowly, silently, descending from the wall. This must be why Felix is being so calm. He doesn't want Luke to suspect anything.

I don't want Luke to see it; I need to distract him. I start to get back up slowly as the bot creeps toward him from the other side, my hands still raised.

Luke reaches into his jacket and whips out the small metal cylinder from the documents. My whole body freezes as he yells, "Stay there."

"Luke, we can talk about this," I say, standing up but not moving toward him. I need to keep his eyes on me. "Whatever you think you found, I'm sure there's an explanation."

"There *is* an explanation. It's that he's been lying to us."

"Luke, you've gone mad," Felix says as the bot takes another cautious step forward. The arm on its back is extended, sparks of electricity dancing on the tip. "Please listen to Isaac, this needs to stop before you hurt someone."

I flinch as the dog's leg scrapes slightly on the floor, and Luke either sees my reaction or hears it because he whirls around, staring down the bot. It's about to lunge at him but he holds up the bomb. "I swear, Felix, if that thing comes one step closer, I'm taking them with me."

Something in his eyes and posture tells me he's already accepted that he's not going to make it out of here. Whatever plan he had was ruined the moment I showed up and now he's improvising. Buying time. He and Felix are stuck on their course now and there's no way Luke is making it out, but Bram and I don't have to go down with him.

Luke has his back pressed up against the control console, holding out the bomb toward the dog as it continues taking slow steps toward him. I'm not sure how powerful it is, but Bram and I must be too close. We need to get away. But the moment we move, he's going to think we're attacking him, and he might hit the trigger.

Then my eye catches a flicker of movement off to my right, behind the transfer bed and now behind Luke as he stares down the drone. The door to the server room is slowly opening. Felix must have guessed what I'm thinking and he's trying to help me get to cover. Which means he's also about to pounce on Luke.

I nudge Bram, pointing toward the door. His sharp intake of breath tells me he understands as I carefully slide my arm under his shoulder, my eyes darting between Luke and the vault door. We have to time this perfectly. The security bot inches closer to Luke, its electrical arm crackling.

"Now!" I hiss and throw all of my strength into helping lift Bram off the floor and pushing us toward the stairs. Luke yells and turns toward us, and as he does, the bot lunges at him, its arm missing his neck and connecting with his shoulder instead. Luke screams as his body convulses, and I shove Bram into the stairwell, falling in after him.

I feel gravity pulling me down the stairs as time freezes. A deafening roar fills the air as heat sears my back, the shockwave propelling us faster down the steps as the steel door slams shut behind us. My shoulder crashes into a step and I flip over, somersaulting at least twice before I land on top of Bram. He groans from the impact, and I roll off of him, scrambling to turn him over to see if he is okay.

"Bram, Bram, hey!" I yell, shaking him. He groans again but doesn't move. The back of my neck feels numb; the skin must have been burned off from the inferno. I resist the urge to reach back and touch it. I quickly check Bram and it doesn't look like the flames did any damage to him. My body must have absorbed the heat as his absorbed the fall.

"Isaac..." he murmurs.

"I'm okay, I'm okay. You?"

"I'll live. Luke..."

My eyes shoot up toward the door. On the extremely unlikely chance Luke wasn't killed by the blast, he has to be on the run. I can't let him get away. I run up the steps two at a time, my whole body searing with hot pain from the burn and the fall, as I slam my fist against the door, banging on it and screaming, "FELIX, OPEN IT UP."

"He's gone, Isaac!" comes Felix's reply from a speaker somewhere deeper in the vault. "The whole room is on fire. Give me a moment."

Despite the awful standoff we endured, my heart still lurches. No one in my life has ever died before. I hear an awful moan from Bram below as he starts sobbing.

I hear the hiss of the fire suppression on the other side of the door and take a step back. My hands are burning; I didn't realize how hot the door had gotten. A moment later, Felix's voice rings through the speakers again. "Okay, it's safe."

The door starts to open but then groans, obstructed by debris on the other side. I take off my jacket and wrap it over my shoulder to protect me from the hot metal and push into it, helping the motor slide the wreckage out of the way.

My heart sinks as the remnants of the transfer room finally come into view. Destroyed computers, monitors, and furniture line the walls in broken heaps. The door back out to Epsilon is scorched black, a small dent in it from the blast. White powder from the suppression system covers everything like snow. Whatever remained of Luke is gone. The screens that hadn't been blown off the walls are cracked or destroyed; there's no way to see what had unfolded outside or in Meru.

The only thing in the room that isn't out of place is the transfer bed. The heavy bolts locking it to the floor had kept it in place. I run around to the front to try to get some sense of whether or not it still works. The previously glistening metal is now scorched black, slightly dented in the front, but otherwise intact, except that the wires connecting it to Meru have been destroyed. It stands alone in the center of the room, eerily resembling old images I've seen of Egyptian sarcophagi.

"Felix…" I stammer, yelling loud enough for him to hear me downstairs. "What did he do?"

I stand frozen, staring at the blackened transfer pod. My heart is pounding so hard I can feel it in my throat. The smell of smoke and whatever chemicals were in the medical stations fills my nostrils, making it hard to breathe. Or maybe that is the panic setting in.

"Felix," I call out again, my voice cracking. "Is the chamber okay? Can we still transfer?"

The silence that follows is deafening. I can hear my own ragged breathing, the crackle of dying embers, and the faint moans of Bram from the stairwell. But no response from Felix.

"Felix!" I shout, desperation creeping into my voice. "Answer me, please!"

Finally, his voice comes through the speakers, subdued and hesitant. "Isaac, I…I'm sorry."

I stumble backward, my legs suddenly weak. "No," I whisper. "No, that's not possible." My knees give out, and I sink to the floor, surrounded by the debris and destruction. My best friend is gone. Our bridge to Meru destroyed. I hobble down the steps back to Bram, numb, and though it feels wrong to see him in this state, I wrap myself around him and try to comfort him as he quietly sobs beneath me.

CHAPTER 9

THE CROWD IS SILENT AS WE LEAVE THE TRANSFER building. All of Epsilon is packed in the quad, facing us, the music silent, the conversations hushed. Bram's leaning on my shoulder. He's trying to stay strong but from how he's shuffling I know he can barely walk.

A few people cry out, asking what happened, but I shake my head and point toward a screen behind us where Felix is watching. He can fill them in with however much detail he wants to share. I don't have the energy to try to explain right now. And I don't want anyone to see me fighting back tears as I do. Luke was my closest friend. We spent our whole lives together; we planned out all the incredible things we'd do in Meru once he transferred. I still can't accept that he's gone. It feels like my brain fractures into tiny pieces when I think about how I'll never hear his voice again.

Tess runs up to us as we reach the edge of the stage, and to my relief she doesn't ask anything yet. She hugs me, and I can feel how scared she was as she fights back tremors in her chest. Then she loops Bram's other arm around her shoulder and helps him down the steps as a truck pulls up to help ferry us to his home.

Grant is waiting for us in the living room. He checks us for wounds and puts a salve on my neck to help it heal. Thankfully, Bram doesn't have any broken bones, only bruising. Grant gives him a painkiller and tells both of us to rest up. He lingers by the door when he goes to leave and I know he wants to ask about what happened, but he thinks better of it and instead says he'll come check on us in the morning.

Bram starts to shuffle upstairs, then he says, "Wait here, we need to talk."

"You should rest."

"There's no time. I need to know what you know." The way he says it tells me I can't hide what Luke told me any longer. I nod and he makes his way up the stairs, refusing Tess's help when she runs over to give him a hand.

I'm still in shock, and Tess returns to put her hand on my back. "I can't believe he did it," she whispers.

"I—I don't know how either."

"Did he say anything?"

I sigh, exhausted. I don't want to have this conversation yet. "Not now."

She nods and hugs me, and I burrow my face into her shoulder as we sway silently back and forth in the hallway beneath the stairs. Finally, I break away and walk to the kitchen for water but stop at the window. Epsilon's usually bright with activity, even at night, but tonight most windows are dark. A few people are still gathered in small groups in the quad, probably discussing what happened. What we lost.

Without our transfer station, none of us can enter Meru. If someone gets sick or injured, we won't be able to save them in time. They'll die. Something that hasn't happened in decades. I don't even know if the station can be repaired in the state it's in; I've never heard of one being destroyed before. Even with the servers housing the minds below, without a transfer station, there's no way we can stay here. Maybe Epsilon will be shut down and we'll be forced to move to another center, the transferred minds spreading out to Imgen and other towns. Everyone here could be split up so we don't overwhelm the resources of wherever we go. It could be the end of our community. And on top of all those concerns, if someone outside did convince Luke to do this, then who knows what kind of follow-up attack there might be. I grip the counter, my knuckles white, trying to steady myself. It's too much to process.

I hear steps above. Bram must have finished washing off. I don't want to face him right now. I can't handle any explanations or whatever he might want to discuss. And the guilt of not bringing up Luke's erratic behavior is eating away at me. I could have prevented all of this, could have stopped him before he blew himself up. I could have saved Bram's son. And to think we nearly died along with him. A delivery bot rolls past outside, going about its programmed routine as if nothing has changed.

"You should go," I whisper to Tess.

"I don't want to leave you."

"I know." I kiss her on the cheek. "But I'll be okay. Wait for me at home."

She looks scared; some of the ash from the explosion has rubbed off my clothes onto her cheek. "Okay," she whispers and gives me another hug, then nods toward Bram on her way to the door as he comes down the stairs.

"Why didn't you tell me, Isaac?" Bram says, not making eye contact with me as he walks to the kitchen.

"I—I didn't know what to do."

"You knew though."

"I didn't know he was going to do that."

Bram slams his fist on the counter. "What, then?" His eyes are bloodshot and furious. I've never seen so much emotion from him. I instinctually take a step backward, afraid he's going to strike me.

"I—I—"

"TELL ME!"

The possibility of lying, of trying to cover for Luke, flashes through my mind but I quickly discard it. I know he must be worried that I'm part of whatever Luke did. That I could be a threat. "He said he found something. Someone in Meru reaching out to him." I look up at the ceiling but there's no point worrying about Felix hearing now. "Someone Felix didn't want him talking to."

Bram looks to the screen beside the kitchen counter, and Felix's face appears a moment later.

"Is…is it possible?" I ask. Bram looks more worried than angry now.

"It is, yes," Felix says, and I can see the frustration etched on his brow. "I can't be everywhere, can't see everything, can't control everything. I do my best, but it's possible they found a way in."

"But how…how could he have done this…" Bram's voice is barely above a whisper. I can only imagine how much pain he's in right now.

"We…don't have to talk about it right now," I say. I don't want to make him live through any more pain than he already has.

"I'll have my time to mourn," Bram adds. "We need to make sure Epsilon is safe first."

"What do you think is going to happen?"

Bram looks to Felix again, "If this is another attack, they're going to move quickly, possibly tonight. I don't think they could know what happened here, so they might try to rescue Luke."

"Or attack Epsilon," Felix adds.

Their almost calm reaction to what's just happened is starting to scare me. "Where is this coming from? There haven't been any attacks on Epsilon as long as I've lived here, but you're both acting like this is something we should have been expecting all along."

Bram looks to Felix. "I think he's earned it."

"Very well." Felix nods. "I'll give you the abbreviated version, Isaac. It seems you'll have to help us from out there for the time being."

I glance between them then pull over one of the barstools and take a seat at the counter. Bram keeps leaning despite his injury.

"When I tried to create the transfer technology, there were many people skeptical of it," Felix begins. "In fact, most people were skeptical of it. They thought I was crazy. Accused me of everything from playing God to summoning the devil. But most simply believed it was fake. The first person I tried to transfer—"

"Your wife, right?" I interrupt. Everyone in Epsilon knows the origin story, though now I wonder if details were left out.

"Yes, my dear Susan. She was on her deathbed already, barely conscious. We tried and tried and tried but could never quite get it. And then one day, when Susan's copy woke up in here, I was…elated. You've lived your whole life in the postdeath world, but back then, when someone was in her state, you had to accept that you were never going to talk to her again, to hug her again, to see the love in her eyes again.

"And then…here she was. She was terrified at first. Confused, lost, scared. She didn't know what to do in this world I'd cobbled together. But she was here. She remembered everything from before she slipped off.

"I couldn't stop there though. A copy was not good enough. I knew there had to be some way to complete the final step. To allow someone to transcend their body, to move their mind into the machine beyond simply copying it. Years and years Vance and I worked, Susan helping as she could from within Meru, as we received increasing ridicule from the scientific community. We were kicked out of Imgen..." He trails off momentarily and I can see the pain in his eyes, despite all the years that have passed.

"For years, Susan was alone in here. She designed and built many of the core structures of Meru in that time, like the original skyline, the streaming service, some of the games. But no one wanted to join her. Despite all our work they didn't believe we could figure it out, and they didn't want to waste their final days hooked up to my machines. They thought I was a crazy old man obsessed with this dream." He laughs to himself. "I suppose they were right about that part, but they were wrong about it not working. Then people started getting sick."

"The plague."

"Yes, exactly. The deaths were awful and happening faster and faster. All of the reasonable solutions were underway. Finding an antibiotic that would work against it. Genetically modifying new foods that weren't able to be contaminated—that's where your food comes from. Migrating people to less infected areas and trying to rebuild there. A few people even proposed trying to leave Earth and made some headway on it, but there wasn't enough time. Besides, it's not as though space has tons of food available."

"I knew I could do it. All these people who were already sick and dying, maybe they didn't have to suffer such an awful fate. Maybe they could be saved. I begged and pleaded to the authorities to let me offer transference as an option, but they said no. Even though some dying people were willing to take the risk, I wasn't allowed to test it on them.

"So...I embraced the ethos of the scientists of old. From even before my time. A degree of conviction that had been lost in my era of security and comfort."

"You transferred yourself."

A glow of pride fills Felix's face. "Indeed I did. It was a risk I was willing to take if I could save even one life from that dreadful disease."

"If Susan kept waking up, what was the risk exactly? Wouldn't you have just woken up with a copy of you in Meru?"

The question seems to catch Felix off guard. "Yes, yes, that happened...many times. I realized the problem was the mind still had a functioning brain in its body to wake up in. It never made the jump because it didn't *need* to. I'd debated trying the full shutoff with Susan but I could never bring myself to do it. But that ended up being the trick! By turning off regions of my brain as they were re-created in my digital self, the mind had something new to latch onto; it found a new home in here. It was never enough to give it the *option* to transfer. We had to *force* it to transfer. Nudge it out of our bodies so to speak."

"How would you know it wasn't another copy though? How do *you* know you're not another copy?"

"Because of what happened to my body!"

The screen changes again to show the video I've seen countless times of Felix's transfer, a video every child sees as part of their history lessons on Meru. The small laboratory, with Vance leaning over an unconscious Felix, getting increasingly frantic, trying to get some reaction from Felix's body. The digital Felix is saying something indecipherable. Eventually Vance grabs a syringe from one of the shelves in the lab and jabs it into Felix's chest. But still nothing happens. He gets more frantic and wheels Felix's body into a medical scanner, and I can see the readout as it detects any abnormalities, but the scanner reports that Felix should be in perfect health. No sign of anything physically wrong with him.

"Neither of us believed it at first. Even I thought I might be another copy. But we ran every test under the sun we could think of on what remained of me in the physical world. Vance invited scores of medical experts to inspect me for themselves before my body passed. No one could find anything wrong with me. Eventually we had to accept the only explanation that made sense."

"That you had succeeded."

"Indeed. The prophets of old who spoke of the importance of the soul weren't far off. My mind was gone. It was here. *I* was here. All that was left behind was that husk of a person. A shell, which stayed in that comatose state until it withered away, devoid of the magic of consciousness that makes us human.

"Things accelerated rapidly from there. New residents came in trickles, and then floods. We had to dramatically scale up the production of the transfer stations, and then realized there wasn't enough storage capacity in all the world to support the number of people transferring. And there was a bigger issue. Not everyone could transfer. Machines are wonderful but they don't self-regenerate the way biological organisms do. They decay, unless they're maintained, and even then they have to be replaced eventually.

"Thankfully there were plenty of people with similar instincts to Bram, people who saw what a noble calling this was, and who were willing to help maintain the digital world. At least until the plague had run its course and the planet could sustain the populations it once could."

"But not everyone believed it."

Felix lets out a heavy sigh. It clearly isn't a period that he enjoys reflecting on. It's hard to imagine doing so much to try to help the world only to be doubted and ridiculed for so long. And so hard to imagine a time when so many people would question the incredible world he had created. "Not only did they not believe it, they saw it as some awful attack on humanity. Since the bacteria that caused the plague appeared to feed on crops cultivated by agricultural science, genetically modified, all of that, many saw the mass suffering as being caused by scientific failure. They believed we had to stop trying to solve our problems with more technology, a truly backward, luddite way of thinking. But they had believers, and a few particularly vocal people calling them to rally together and stop what I was building.

"The attacks were constant in the beginning. These savages trying to destroy the centers as we built them, and the server stations housing the saved minds. You're probably not aware of this, but every tech center, including Epsilon, has a significant store of weapons and militarized robotics. You obviously bring some for safety on your maintenance patrols, but the actual defensive capabilities of the towns are much greater. The attackers were ruthless, but eventually their numbers dwindled, both from losing their lives trying to destroy the centers and from the inhospitable world around them. Everything was quiet for a while, decades really."

"And then…they came back," Bram says, finally breaking his silence.

"Yes…" Felix continues. "What Luke did today was a travesty, something I wish we could have protected you from. But it did not scratch the surface of what his people are capable of."

"Alpha camp, where you found me."

"Yes," Felix replies. "We're not sure how they did it, but they managed to override the town's security systems, sneak in in the middle of the night, and release some sort of gas or toxin that killed everyone in their sleep." A few slices of video play in succession, showing rooms in other houses with people lying dead in their beds. Some of them are children. I didn't know they had footage from when they found me; it's gut-wrenching to watch. "And here's where Bram comes in."

"I was one of the first people to hear something was wrong. Felix told me that the network there had suddenly gone dark. I took a few friends, and we drove out to investigate. It was... awful. I'd never seen someone dead before. Let alone dozens of people." Then he pauses. "Only made slightly better by finding you and your sister amidst the chaos."

His shoulders are starting to shake. He takes a deep breath to calm himself before continuing. "We came back to camp and handed you two to the doctor. We told Felix what we'd found, and he told me everything he just told you. Though the attacks were much more recent history at the time. Other people living in Epsilon then, all of them since transferred, had even lived through some of them. But we'd come to believe they were ancient history.

"After I realized what had happened, I knew I couldn't let them attack another camp again. I convinced Felix to help me go after them, along with the men I'd visited Alpha with. Felix gave us weapons, bots, trucks, and we went back to Alpha. The attackers had been sloppy. They left tire tracks leading straight back to where they were camped out. I—" Tears are welling up in his eyes now and he's leaning forward on the counter, his head hanging between his shoulders.

"It's not quite what you're imagining," Felix says. "When Bram and his friends found them, they realized they couldn't do it. They weren't like them."

"I was soft," he chokes out. "I couldn't do what we needed to do to keep us all safe. None of us could."

"You weren't soft, Bram," Felix interrupts. "You have the proper respect for life. Death is the greatest tragedy known to man—one we lived with for far too long. Ending a life or allowing a life to end, now that we have the means to prevent it. It's the greatest tragedy imaginable."

"So you let them live?"

"Not...exactly," Bram murmurs.

"I took care of them," Felix answers for him. "Sent some of the trucks and bots to scare them off, make sure they didn't attack Epsilon or any other town."

Bram takes a deep breath and continues, "The rest of us stayed here. Bolstered the defenses of the town, set up extra patrols, and hoped they never returned."

"Did they?"

"Towers get hit from time to time, but they never attacked Epsilon, not until today. I went back to where the camp was once. I didn't go in, but I could tell it was abandoned. I figured they had run off somewhere else."

He runs his hand down his face, wiping away a tear. "And then life slowly went back to normal. We stopped doing the extra patrols. Put the weapons away. Gemma and I..." He chokes up. "Life was normal."

As I look between Bram's distraught reflection on what happened and Felix's stoic demeanor, I can't ignore some feeling that they aren't telling me something. That even though they're bringing me into the fold, there's still something being held back.

"If they're out there, we need to go stop them."

He looks back at me, and I can tell he sees the same rage and determination in me that he felt all those years ago. "We're not like them."

"He was your son! Are you going to tell that to the next parent who loses a kid because you didn't do something about it?"

He stands up so fast he nearly knocks his stool over. "Watch yourself."

"You know I'm right."

His eyes are boring into me, but I know it isn't me he's angry with.

"This wasn't like last time," he says, trying to keep his tone measured. "Luke was one person. We don't know who he was talking to, or if he was even talking to anyone. He could have gotten these ideas in his head on his own."

"You don't believe that." I can hardly believe the words coming out of my mouth. I would never have pushed back against Bram like this before. It feels wrong. But I know we have to do something.

He doesn't respond.

I turn to face Felix now. He's been quietly watching our exchange with concern. "Felix, can you go through any security or archive information to see if Luke was doing anything suspicious in the last few days or months?"

Felix nods. "I'd already begun that actually. Nothing has stood out yet, but something might turn up." Then he pauses and glances at Bram before turning his attention back to me. "Are you ready to tell us what he wanted to discuss with you last night?"

I grimace with embarrassment. I don't want them to blame me for what happened. And worse, I don't want them to think I was helping Luke in some way. But holding anything back at this point will only make it worse, so I tell them everything. Luke's weird interaction with Simon and the symbol, his insistence on digging through the archives last night, his plea with me not to transfer, his conviction that someone was whispering to him from deep in Meru. Felix nods along quietly as I tell the story, but Bram's face slowly darkens.

"Why didn't you say anything..." Bram asks as I finish telling them what I found in Luke's apartment.

"I tried. I sent Tess to find you."

"Before that."

"I—I didn't think he would do anything about it. How could I have guessed?"

"You and Luke spent all of your free time together." Bram is eyeing me cautiously and I can't ignore the hint of accusation in his voice. "You would have noticed something was wrong."

"You're his father; you should have noticed." Bram recoils and glares at me. There it is again, the defiance, the frustration. I need to keep my anger under control so I don't drive him to take his guilt out on me.

"You know he and I weren't always as close as I'd like."

"But he wanted to stay here, with you, to take over your job when you transferred."

"Nevertheless..." Bram looks out the window as he says it.

I don't want to fight with Bram, and this isn't getting us anywhere. "Felix, what do you think he meant, about someone whispering to him from inside Meru?"

"I think it's exactly as you suspected. Someone on the outside found a way to break into the network and decided he was a target. Maybe the amount of time he spent digging through the history made them believe he was looking for some hidden secret and offered to give it to him."

"Is there any way we can try to find who he was talking to?"

"Well *I* certainly can't. Whoever it is will stay far out of my way. And you unfortunately can't either, since we'll have to delay your transfer."

"What about the symbol?" I ask, grasping for anything to help us solve this. "Do you think it means anything?"

"I'm not sure. I don't recognize it," Felix says. "I'll look into it."

"Did he travel anywhere unusual?" Bram asks.

"I'll start analyzing that now. In the meantime, Bram, maybe you and a few others should go look through Luke's room again, see if there's anything Isaac and Tess missed."

"I want to help."

Felix chews his lip. "I think it's best if you get some rest, Isaac. This has been a trying day."

"It's been a trying day for Bram, too. Let me help."

"No," Bram grumbles. "You've done enough already."

"I saved you! If I hadn't pulled you down those stairs—"

"I know, Isaac, and I'm grateful for it. But you also can't deny me the frustration of imagining what might be if you had brought this to me sooner. We're in this situation because you failed to act. Because you didn't tell us about your concerns about Luke. So now I need to fix it. Without you."

I open my mouth to protest but can feel the anger boiling up again, and I know it's a mistake. And behind the anger, a heavy blanket of fatigue.

"If you go looking for them, I want to come."

"Why's that?" Bram raises an eyebrow, still suspicious.

"To help. To stop them."

Felix interrupts us. "We'll keep you apprised of any developments, Isaac. Like Bram, I appreciate you trying to prevent this. Even if it was too late."

It's not a command to leave, but the implication is clear. I nod to both of them and head toward the door. All I want now is to be home with Tess.

CHAPTER 10

When I make it home, Tess is sitting at the kitchen counter talking to Sophie. She jumps off the stool and runs over to give me a hug, and Sophie gives me a subtle nod from the screen.

"You okay, 'Saac?" Sophie asks from behind Tess.

"Somehow."

"What the hell happened in there?"

Tess takes a step back, holding my shoulders. "And what did Bram and Felix want?"

I eye the camera above Sophie's screen. I'm not sure if Felix can listen in or not. He always says that he can't observe conversations in our homes unless we invite him in; the same rules apply to anyone in Meru. I have my suspicions, but I suppose if he could, he would have seen Luke's betrayal coming.

"They wanted to know what Luke told me. The other night, when he took me out into the woods and tried to convince me not to transfer."

"What did you tell them?" Tess asks.

"Everything, his pleas for me not to transfer, his strange interaction with Simon, the symbol...Hey, Sophie, did you find anything else about it?"

Sophie shakes her head. "Nothing."

"You were looking for it?" Tess asks, giving both of us a curious look.

"We were only trying to figure out how they might have been contacting him, or what they were telling him."

"And I never found anything," Sophie adds. "No signs of it anywhere. However Luke found it, if he found it, it's well hidden."

"Or he didn't *find* it, it was *sent* to him." Tess sounds exasperated. "By the scavs or whoever else was trying to manipulate him."

"Or Felix is hiding something!" I yell back before I can catch myself. Tess looks aghast. Even Sophie raises an eyebrow.

"You don't mean that," Tess says, tilting her head to the side, eyeing me carefully. I'm immediately reminded of the tone Bram was using before. I don't think she's worried about me, but I also can't blame her for being on edge with everything that's happened. We all are.

"What happened inside?" Sophie asks. "Before Luke..."

I look warily at Tess, unsure if I should push this any further. But I trust her not to say anything to Felix, and I can't keep this to myself. "Luke said he wanted to transfer."

"Not sure what that would have done..." Tess mutters.

"Felix said the same thing, but then Luke said something that seemed to scare him. He said he would 'wake up,' and alluded to it happening to someone else. He mentioned Vance."

"Vance?" Tess and Sophie ask at almost the same time.

"I know, it didn't make any sense. It seemed to scare Felix though."

Tess crosses her arms; it's delicate but there's still a defensiveness to the gesture. "How do you know?"

"Something about how he reacted."

"Well let's just ask him—"

"No!" I cut Tess off before she can summon him. "No, please, I don't want to ask him about it."

"Why not?" Sophie asks.

"I think he and Bram are already worried about me...I don't want to add to their suspicion."

"It sounds like you don't trust them," Tess says.

I feel a pang of worry. The truth is that part of me believes Luke, and I feel a hint of suspicion toward Felix. There's obviously some part of this he isn't giving me the full story on. I don't think Tess would turn me in to Felix, but after I didn't tell Felix about Luke, I wouldn't entirely blame her for being worried about what I'm thinking. I walk over to the kitchen and run the water, splashing some on my face.

"Well, what if he *is* hiding something?"

"So what?" Tess says with a bite. "He doesn't have to tell us everything. You aren't telling tell him everything. You could have told him about Luke but you kept that to yourself."

The barb stings. "I don't understand why he would react the way he did unless Luke found something."

"This is ridiculous." Tess's voice rises. "Luke didn't find some hidden secret in Meru; it was them trying to hurt Epsilon from the inside. You told me what they did to that comm station..." Her eyes unfocus as she seems to think of something, but then she snaps out of it. "They're a threat, Isaac."

I set my coffee mug down harder than I mean to. "We don't know that for sure. What if Felix is using them as some kind of scapegoat? Luke might have had a good reason. I knew him my whole life. He wouldn't be manipulated that easily. He—"

"GOOD REASON?" Tess cuts me off.

"I don't agree with what he did, Tess. I love my life here. I love you. And you know how badly I wanted to transfer."

"*Wanted?*"

"*Want* to. I only meant that I can't now that the station is destroyed."

CHAPTER 10 · 107

She purses her lips.

"I'm here, Tess. I want to protect Meru as much as you do. I want to be with Sophie again," I say, nodding toward her. "I'm heartbroken over Luke. And I *definitely* don't want to try to live in the wilderness. I'm only trying to figure out what's going on. Something isn't adding up."

"So what, we just let this go? Wait for the next attack? Look for some secret in Meru behind Felix's back?" Tess's face is red again.

"That's not what I'm saying. Obviously we need to investigate if someone out there might be a threat. But we should also keep looking into whatever Luke found. Whatever that symbol means."

"What is it with you and that symbol?"

"I don't know. I think it means something. "

"Yeah, it means we should be scared of what they're going to do next!" She shakes her head. "I don't know what else Luke told you, Isaac, but something's changed. He got in your head."

"Nobody's gotten into my head," I snap. "I'm trying to see the bigger picture."

"Or you're just chasing a conspiracy theory."

"It's not a conspiracy theory. Luke wasn't crazy."

"He blew himself up, Isaac! Do you hear yourself right now? Just think about this for a minute!"

"I should think about this for a minute? Maybe *you* should try thinking for yourself instead of swallowing whatever Felix feeds you." As soon as the words leave my mouth, I know I've gone too far. Tess recoils like I've slapped her.

"I'm going, Isaac."

"Tess, no, wait." I run around the side of the kitchen counter to try to grab her arm, but she rips it out of my grip and slams the door behind her.

"Shit," I mutter.

"Go get her," Sophie says, but I'm already running out the door. As I pull it open, she's stomping away, and I debate chasing her down the street but I don't want to make a scene. Grant must have been waiting outside because he's standing on the porch now, watching her as well.

"Thought she'd be happier you survived."

"Not now."

"You told her, didn't you?"

Something in Grant's tone throws me off. "Told her what?"

Grant sighs. "You don't need to worry about me, Isaac. I've been here long enough to know Felix can't be telling us everything." He turns and watches Tess disappear into the night. "But you young people, you're a little stronger in your convictions about how the world is."

"So, what, I should have lied?"

"No, but maybe don't mention your newfound skepticism to anyone else."

"Earlier today when we were setting up, you mentioned something about them, the people out there."

"Not now. You need to lie low for a while. Earn your trust back with Bram, then if you want to learn more, maybe we can talk about it."

"Should I be worried?"

"I don't know. This is a scary situation, Isaac. People don't act rationally when they're scared."

"You're not telling me something."

"You bet I'm not. More information isn't always a good thing." Then he claps me on the shoulder. "Get some rest. Tess will come around. Just try not to make any more messes for a few days."

I turn and go back inside. Sophie is still waiting, and a pair of impossibly large birds glides by outside the majestic view behind her. The beauty of her life in Meru almost seems comical against how broken my world now feels.

"I ran into Grant," I say before she can ask. "Tess was gone. I think I need to let her cool down. Try to talk to her tomorrow."

"Do you think she'll say anything?"

"I don't know. I hope not."

Sophie sighs. "I was looking forward to seeing you again."

I feel a pang of guilt. I forgot how much today must have meant to her, too. In all the commotion of the day, I never took a chance to check in with her. We were inseparable until she nearly died, and it's always felt like a piece of me was missing without her here. "I was too. Hopefully I can still transfer soon."

"Luke didn't talk you out of it?" There's a teasing glint in her eye, and I welcome the mood finally lightening.

"Maybe if someone tries to blow me up again next time, I'll reconsider."

Sophie snorts. "Jesus, Isaac."

"Sorry, needed a laugh."

"Want me to keep looking for it?"

I debate telling her no, to set this whole thing aside so we can move on. But I know I can't, and I know her curiosity is piqued now too. "Just be careful. Felix might be watching you."

"I will. Get some sleep."

"Night, Soph."

"Night, 'Saac."

CHAPTER 11

I'M LYING ON MY BACK, STARING UP AT THE NIGHT SKY, lightning streaking across my view. A bolt illuminates a thick cloud and I swear I see the xīn symbol etched within it. I slowly climb to my feet. *Where am I?*

Up ahead is the comm station from the day before, but fully repaired, seemingly free of the damage that had happened to it. Why am I back here? What happened?

A shadowy figure is scaling the communication tower just as I've done so many times. But he has no harness, no safety gear. I run up to the base of the station and yell up at him.

"Hey! What are you doing?"

When he turns to look down at me, my heart stops. It's Luke, his eyes wild and unfocused, half of the skin peeling off his face, burns covering the tissue that is left.

"Luke...how..."

But he doesn't listen. He moves farther up the tower, the same detonator in his hand. Suddenly Sophie is beside me. "Luke! Don't!" she yells up after him, and it seems to grab his attention. He looks back down at me and howls. I try to scream as he leaps off the tower, but no sound comes out of my mouth. The words are stuck in my throat.

I try to stumble backward but he lands on me, knocking

me to the ground, and I feel the wind go out of my chest. I'm gasping for breath; he's straddling me, and I hold my arms up to try to defend my face when he reaches around and punches me in the side of my head.

"NO!" I yell and suddenly my eyes snap open. The dream fades, but the weight on my chest remains. Panic surges through me as I realize someone is holding me down. In the dim light, I can make out a shadowy figure looming over me, their hands gripping my arms above my head.

I can't see who it is. I try to struggle against them, bucking with my hips, but they hold fast.

"Quick!" they yell, and I feel another set of hands on my wrists. They're tying my hands together. I take another blow to the face and see stars; my arms slacken just long enough for them to finish restraining me.

I open my mouth to scream at them but then taste cotton as they stuff something in my mouth to gag me. I fling my legs at them, but they're quickly grabbed. There must be three people in the room.

A speck of moonlight passes across the window in my room and illuminates my attacker. It's Grant. I feel a wave of fury and try to throw him off me, but then the assailant beside me punches me in the head again and yells, "Stop thrashing!"

I groan but stop kicking. I don't want to get knocked out. "Tess..." I gurgle. There's blood in my mouth.

"Let's go," one of them says. Grant climbs off my chest, and he and the other two Techs pull me out of bed, forcing me onto my feet and pushing me out into the hall.

As Grant and the others drag me out into the night, I look around for any clue of what is going on. Are they with whomever Luke was working with? Did Felix send them? Bram?

My heart sinks as we approach the town square. An eerie glow bathes everything in an unnatural light, casting long shadows across the familiar buildings. The large monitor over the door of the transfer building is illuminated, Felix's face filling the screen.

But it's the figure standing next to the monitor that terrifies me more. Tess. Her eyes puffy from crying, and when she makes eye contact with me, I can see the terror behind them. I know she wouldn't have intentionally turned Felix against me. But if he interrogated her about what we talked about last night, or if he somehow overheard our conversation...

"Tess," I try to call out, but the gag muffles my words. She chokes up another sob and looks away.

I'm forced to my knees in front of the monitor. It looks like half the town has been pulled out of bed to witness whatever is about to happen.

Felix's digital eyes seem to bore into me, his pixelated face unreadable. The silence stretches, broken only by the low hum of the screen and the sound of my own ragged breathing.

"Isaac," Felix's voice booms from hidden speakers, making me flinch. "I trusted you. Gave you a home, fed you, kept you safe."

I glance at Tess, see the confusion and fear in her eyes mirroring my own.

Felix continues, his tone hardening. "Tess told me about your doubts."

Tess shrieks, "I was only asking you—"

"Quiet!" Felix cuts her off, and there's a ripple of fear through the crowd around us. I've never seen Felix like this; I don't know if anyone has. I try to yell through the gag but all I manage are stifled mumbles. Felix nods at Grant, and he pulls the gag out of my mouth.

I spit on the ground, trying to get the fuzz out of my mouth. Then I look up at Felix. "I just want to understand! How could Luke do that? What did he think he found?"

"Luke *found* nothing. He was manipulated, turned against us by the very people he was supposed to help protect us from!"

"Luke wasn't an idiot!" I find Bram and try to silently implore him to back me up. "He wouldn't have fallen for that…"

"So what, then?" Bram says, stepping forward and, from the glare on his face, clearly not agreeing with me. "Felix is hiding something? I'm hiding something? What is your explanation, Isaac?"

"I don't know…" I'm trying to stay calm, but the fear and desperation are overwhelming. "Why am I here?"

"You know why you're here," Felix spits, and then his screen splits and I see Sophie, trapped in what looks like a glass cage, and my heart sinks further.

"Sophie!" I cry out, and she opens her mouth to reply but I can't hear anything she's saying.

"It seems your sister was looking for a way to reestablish contact with them, no doubt at your direction."

"That's not what she was doing!"

"Or maybe you two are the ones who contacted them *first*, and then drove Luke to do what he did. And when you realized he was going to get caught, you devised a plan to make yourself look innocent so you could finish whatever he put in motion."

"No…" I groan, but it feels hopeless.

"Just like you made yourself look innocent for when *I* was nearly destroyed!" another voice says, and Simon appears on an adjacent screen.

"I saved you!"

"So you say, and quite the cover story it provided," Felix says. "I saw what you asked Tess for after the trip, too."

Simon disappears, showing a video of my and Tess's conversation from two days ago. Me asking her for a tool that could break through the sealed door of the comm center.

"No, you don't understand—" I try to say but Felix cuts me off.

"What else could you need that tool for, hmm? Tell us, Isaac," Felix says, a sickening tone to his voice.

"Felix, Tess, Grant, please, you can't believe that. Luke...he almost killed me..."

"No!" Bram yells, his face almost purple with rage. "You killed him! Turned my boy against me. Condemned Epsilon to the risk of death."

"It wasn't me!"

"I'm not sure what to believe anymore, Isaac." Felix continues. "You've betrayed me, betrayed Meru, betrayed the town you swore to protect. And you're still trying to recruit allies to your little cause."

I open my mouth to protest but Felix disappears and another video starts playing on the screen in his place. It shows me and Tess's conversation from yesterday, and I hang my head in defeat as the words *Maybe you should think for yourself sometime instead of just swallowing whatever Felix feeds you* play out for everyone in the town to hear.

An angry murmur goes through the crowd around us. I don't know what to say, don't know how I can defend myself. I can't convince them. I have to start looking for a way to escape.

"Does anyone here wish to defend him? Or his sister?" Felix says, addressing the crowd now.

I look around desperately, searching the faces in the crowd for any sign of support. Familiar faces I've known my whole life stare back at me with a mix of anger, disappointment, and fear.

The silence stretches on, broken only by the low hum of the monitors and the shuffling of feet. Not a single voice speaks up in our defense. The weight of their collective judgment presses down on me, making it hard to breathe.

I feel utterly alone, abandoned by the community I'd dedicated my life to protecting. They truly believe I am a traitor. Years of trust and goodwill have evaporated in a matter of hours, replaced by suspicion and fear.

As the moments tick by with no one coming forward, I slump in defeat. The last shred of hope I've been clinging to withers away, leaving nothing but a cold, empty feeling in the pit of my stomach.

"Very well then," Felix says.

"Kick him out!" I hear a voice behind me yell.

"No, no," Felix says. "We can't send him out of town. He'll just rejoin his friends and help them plan their next attack."

Silence hangs over the crowd as they wait to hear Felix's verdict. But I already know what is coming.

"Isaac and Sophie, for conspiring to destroy Meru, for turning on your neighbors and betraying the trust we have all put in you over the years, there's only one punishment appropriate. The necessary consequence for anyone who behaves as you have."

I look up at Tess and I can see the realization of what she's set in motion dawning on her. There's silent fear in her eyes, the hint of regret for what she's done, but it's quickly replaced by a forced sternness as she remembers the risk she also faces.

"Exile," Felix says, and I can feel the collective shudder of the crowd around me. I want to yell, to scream at her and Felix for doing this, for not trusting me, for thinking I would be complicit in sabotaging our home. But I know it's no use.

"You can't exile me," I say, trying to buy time. Hoping some opportunity for escape will present itself. "Our station was destroyed."

"No matter," Felix says. "I'll coordinate with Delta to prepare their station for you. The time it takes to get there will give them the opportunity to get it ready."

I try not to imagine what kind of scenario Felix would exile me into. It's a terrifying fate, transferred into Meru but stranded in an isolated location. No other people, no food, no water, no entertainment, no control over the environment, just endless space and nothing to do with it. An eternity of wandering in the desert, or treading water, or floating through space, utterly alone, with no sense of time, until, maybe, you were lucky, and Felix took pity on you some years in the future. But as far as I know, anyone who had been exiled previously is still lost in the ether, slowly going mad from the isolation.

"Felix…please…" I hear Tess say.

But Felix snaps back at her, "You've already spared yourself by turning him in; don't ruin it now."

"No! I didn't!"

"Quiet!"

She hangs her head, and I hope she's trying to work out some escape like I am, but I don't want her to risk getting exiled as well.

"Who's taking him to Delta?" I hear someone yell behind me.

"I want to take the traitor," Grant offers. "He might need to be sedated on the ride."

"I'll drive," a woman I've occasionally worked with, Bridget, offers from the crowd.

"Very well," Felix says. "Before you leave…" he turns to Sophie and her eyes go wide. She starts banging on the glass, screaming at him. The back wall of the box disappears, replaced by a shimmering door through which I can see what looks like a desert. Endless sand in all directions. She spins around to see it and presses her back against the wall opposite it, but it starts pushing her toward the portal, slowly sealing her fate. Grant's hand on my shoulder tightens, as if warning me not to do anything. All I can do is watch in horror as the cage continues to constrict, Sophie's feet sliding against the glass floor as she tries to resist, until finally the wall pushes her through the portal and she stumbles onto the sand beyond.

She whips around and tries to lunge back through the opening, but in a flash it seals shut and she's gone, her fear and desperation the last image I have of her.

I try to make eye contact with Tess, to look for any hope or at least say goodbye, but Grant and whoever else is holding me turn me away from her, and I dread to think about what she'll have to witness. I know she didn't want this; I have to believe she doesn't believe this. But once Felix was suspicious, she had to protect herself from any blowback too. Despite my anger with the situation, I can't blame her. All the evidence was stacked against me.

As they shove me into the car, I stumble, my bound hands making it impossible to catch myself. I land awkwardly on the back seat, my face pressed against the worn leather. Grant climbs in after me and forces me to scoot over.

"Watch his hands," Bridget calls from the driver's seat.

Grant grunts in acknowledgment, reaching behind my back to check my restraints as he helps me sit up and then straps the seat belt across me. I hope desperately for Felix to stay his judgment at the last moment, but the car lurches forward, and in a few moments, we've left Epsilon behind, my last view of the town a faint glow in the night.

"You, Grant? Of all people?" I mutter, trying to keep my voice low enough for Bridget not to hear.

Grant shifts uncomfortably beside me. "Didn't give me much of a choice, did you, Isaac?"

I am at a loss for what else to say. I can see Bridget glancing at me in the rearview mirror, her eyes darting away whenever I catch her gaze.

As we pass the outskirts of town, the reality of what is happening begins to sink in. Each mile that ticks by on the odometer is another step toward my exile, toward an eternity of isolation in a digital void.

CHAPTER 12

"How far is it?" I ask after what feels like an hour has passed.

"Still another couple hours," Bridget says, and I can hear a hint of fatigue in her voice. I look at her face in the mirror and can tell she's getting tired; her eyes are drooping, coming unfocused. Sunlight is barely starting to creep over the horizon.

I gaze out the window, trying to distract myself from the gnawing anxiety. The landscape is a blur of shadowy shapes in the predawn light. But as my eyes adjust, I notice something is off. I look closer, trying to make out what it is, and then it hits me, and I feel a jolt of excitement. It's a cloud of dust, billowing up in the distance, growing steadily larger, with the outline of a vehicle speeding toward us ahead of it.

I turn to see if either of my captors has noticed, but as I turn around, I feel Grant's hand on my shoulder. He gives it a stern squeeze, like he's warning me not to say anything.

I glance at Bridget in the rearview mirror, but she seems oblivious, focused on the road ahead.

My heart is beating faster. Grant's eyes flick between the road and the mirror, his jaw tight. Then in an instant, she spots it.

"The hell is that…" Bridget hisses. "Grant, is anyone supposed to be joining us?"

Grant turns back to look at the car. "Maybe Felix changed his mind?"

"They would have called us."

"Hmm, yeah."

"Shit. Hold on," she says as she steps on the gas. I'm pressed into the seat behind me. I look at Grant, but he gives me the slightest head shake; he clearly knows who is coming, whoever it is.

I try to catch a glimpse of the approaching car in the side mirror but can only make out hints of dust getting kicked up on the dirt behind us. Bridget is still accelerating, trying to push the truck out of their reach, but they're steadily getting closer.

I grip the edges of my seat as Bridget swerves, trying to keep us on the road. The pursuing vehicle is gaining on us fast, its headlights now visible in the rearview mirror. "Come on, come on," Bridget mutters, the electric motor straining as she pushes it to its limits.

Suddenly I jolt forward and hear a loud crash as they slam into the back of our truck.

"Shit!" Bridget yells, struggling to maintain control as the truck fishtails, tires screeching against the asphalt and rocks flying out from under us. The world outside the windows becomes a blur as we spin, leaving the road and kicking up dirt and grass around the truck. The truck tips and I try to duck but I can hardly control myself as the truck rolls once, twice, my head smashing against the window as the glass shatters, raining down on us.

The truck balances on its side for one long moment before crashing back down on its wheels, right side up. For a moment, all I can hear is the ringing in my ears and my own ragged breathing. Bridget groans in the seat ahead of us.

I look over at Grant and he appears to be unconscious. But

then I see his hand move, ever so slightly, pointing to something in his bag and then pointing at the back of Bridget's seat. She groans again and he repeats the gesture, more forcefully this time. I rip his bag open and the sedatives he's brought are sitting on top, miraculously undamaged by the crash. I grab one and throw my arm around Bridget's seat, jabbing her in the neck before she can react. She locks eyes with me in the rearview, full of rage, before I see the lights go out and she slumps forward onto the steering wheel.

As she collapses, Grant ends the act, sitting up and giving her a quick look to make sure she is really out. "You won't have much time," he says, then looks over his shoulder for the truck that hit us.

"Grant, what the hell is going on?" I say, trying to get my vision to stop spinning. I've been hit in the head one too many times the last couple days.

"We always worried Felix might turn on us again," he says. "He's always seen us as a threat to Meru, but he never had a way to get the people in Epsilon and other centers on his side."

"We?"

"I've been keeping an eye out for a few years now. Where do you think I got the alcohol recipe from? Here." He hands me a pill, probably a painkiller, and an energy drink. "Keep it together until they get you to Alexandria."

"Where?"

"Go!" Grant says and reaches over me to push the door open. It creaks, and he has to give it an extra shove to get it to swing open. "Say hi to Lena for me. I'll update you when I can."

I start to climb out of the car and then Grant grabs me again.

"Wait, one last thing," he says and then hands me two zip ties. "So we can't try to catch up to you. She won't be out long."

I take the first zip tie and pull Bridget's door open, then tie her hands under one of her legs. Then I go back to Grant and he scoots forward on his seat so I can tie his hands behind his back.

"I believe you, by the way," he says as I cinch the zip tie.

"About Luke?"

"Lena and Lincoln didn't tell him to do that; I don't think any of them would. He found something else or was talking to someone else."

"Who though?"

"I don't know, but you better figure it out. Felix is going to come for all of you soon." Bridget lets out a quiet groan. "Go!" Grant hisses and I jump back out of the truck, slamming the door behind me, wincing at the noise as it reverberates in my head.

I stumble back to the truck behind us, still idling, waiting for me. I raise my hand to block the glare from the sun, but I can't see who's inside.

After a moment, the driver door swings open, and a woman climbs out. She looks to be about my age, with olive skin, narrow features, and jet-black hair tied up in a ponytail. Her outfit almost looks like pre-Meru military gear, a dark green jumpsuit and work boots. She doesn't look happy to see me.

"Are you going to just stand there?"

"Who the hell are you?"

"A thank-you would be nice."

"We gotta go, Lena," another voice says from the car.

"In or out, Isaac?" she asks.

"How do you know who I am?"

"In. Or. Out?"

I take a deep breath. There's something intimidating about her, a hardness I've never seen from someone in Epsilon before. Maybe the people living outside the centers are all like this. And though I'm terrified by the thought of trying to live like they do, without Imgen to support us, it has to be better than being exiled.

"In...thank you."

She flicks her head toward the truck. "Get in."

I climb into the back seat and there's a mess of red hair in the passenger seat ahead of me. He spins around and gives me an almost ostentatious up-and-down look. "Sure you don't wanna go to the desert? I hear it's nice this time of year."

"I'm good, thanks. Where are we going?"

The woman, Lena, climbs back in beside him and slams the door. "Alpha."

A new wave of shock washes over me. I've never been back to Alpha since I was rescued from there as a child. Bram and Felix always said it was too dangerous. Maybe this was why.

Then she accelerates away from the crash, back onto the road that only minutes before was taking me to my prison. I look back at the crashed truck as we drive off, hoping that Grant won't be exiled in my place. As the truck fades from view, my thoughts turn to Sophie, stuck in that endless desert. And to Tess, who despite everything, I just want to hold again.

ALEXANDRIA

CHAPTER 13

WE RIDE ON IN SILENCE FOR WHAT FEELS LIKE HOURS until a town starts to materialize in the distance. It's hard to tell the difference between abandoned buildings from before the collapse and the tech centers, at least from the distance, but something tells me it's where we're headed. I wonder if I'll recognize it.

"So! Isaac. New friend Isaac. Ever been up this way before?" Lena's companion says, finally breaking the silence.

"No." I don't want to mention I grew up here; it feels like I should stay guarded with what information I share. Despite Felix casting me out, I still feel some sense of loyalty to him and Bram. And maybe if I can learn something about these people, I'll be able to bargain it for a way back home.

"Too bad, too bad. Travel is good for the soul, you know? Exploring new lands, seeing new people. Ever met one of us before? Ah, what do you call us? Scavs? Scavies? Sounds like scabies, nasty disease that—"

"No," I say again, equally curt.

"Not a big talker, huh?"

"Why did you rescue me?"

"Well, because Grant asked us to, of course! You didn't put that together yet? Not as bright as Lincoln thought."

"Who's Lincoln? Why would he know something about me?"

"Gotta keep tabs on all the Techs running around with trucks full of murder dogs, don't we? Don't want to risk a run-in. Plus, Grant always thought you and Luke might be sympathetic—"

"So you did know Luke."

The man makes an awkward glance toward Lena, and her eyes drill into me through the rearview mirror.

"Where is he?" she asks.

"You should know; you sent him after us."

"Still believing Felix after all that?"

The statement throws me. "Believing Felix about what?"

"We didn't put those ideas in Luke's head, bud," the passenger says.

"You attacked our comm station, then tricked him into attacking us. You've already kidnapped me. You don't have to lie."

"We didn't *kidnap* you," Lena says. "We rescued you. Despite the chance that this is some trap laid by Felix, like your friend in that station."

"I don't believe you." It has to be some kind of trick. Or trap. But I also can't figure out what kind of game she might be playing at.

"So where is Luke?" she asks again, interrupting my thoughts.

I don't answer. I'm studying her face, trying to figure out what's going on. If nothing else, I do have to acknowledge that they could have left me to be exiled and didn't. And I'm not sure what kind of problems I could cause by telling her what Luke did, if she truly doesn't know.

"He…destroyed our transfer station. Nearly killed me in the process."

A look of shock momentarily breaks through her stoic demeanor. "Shit. He tried to stop you from transferring, didn't he?"

I nod, hesitant. She seems genuinely concerned for what's happened.

"Is he dead?"

"Yes," I say, careful to avoid inciting any retribution. "But we didn't kill him." I turn so she can see the bandage on the burn on my neck, and where my hair was burned away. "He had a bomb, Felix tried to stop him, and he set it off."

She nods softly. She looks sad, but also unsurprised.

"Why did he do it?" I continue.

"Luke wasn't one of us," the man says. "He figured out how to contact us. Reached out asking for help."

"Carmy," Lena snaps.

"Come on, Lena, he's stuck with us for now. Yeah, sure, maybe he's making notes to try to bargain for forgiveness from Felix but we gotta trust him if he's ever gonna trust us."

Lena grunts.

"He said you contacted him," I say.

"He did?"

"Said you were talking to him through Meru."

"Ah, that," Carmy says. "He told us about that too. It wasn't us though."

"Who then?"

He shrugs, and I can't tell if it's because he doesn't know or he doesn't want to tell me. "He said he could prove Felix was hiding something, something that would be the end of all the tech centers. End Meru. He wanted us to help him, but we were trying to talk him down. He seemed like he was having some sort of psychotic break."

Nothing he's saying makes sense. "Talk him down? Why?"

He smiles and there's a gentle sadness to it. This isn't what I imagined a scavenger would be like. "We just want to be left alone. Help the people who want to leave the centers, and not risk breaking our deal with Felix."

"Why would Felix make a deal with you. You killed everyone in Alpha; you attacked all those other tech centers."

Lena's expression goes cold, glaring daggers at me again. I've touched some kind of nerve but I have no idea what. "Is that what he's telling you? If we're these terrifying threats you seem to think we are, then why haven't we attacked Epsilon?"

"Because…you ran off," I say. "They went looking for you, but you had disappeared."

"Do we look like we disappeared? How could we have picked you up so quickly? Felix knows we're out here, but we have a truce. We stop trying to take Techs away from working on Meru, and he stops hunting us. That's why we didn't want to help Luke. Whatever he thought he found, it wasn't worth pursuing if it meant Felix started killing us again."

"I don't believe you," is all I can say, and now I feel convinced this is some kind of trap. No one would leave Epsilon or another center to live out here if they didn't have to. And Felix would have no reason to "hunt them down" like she's claiming.

She looks at me for a long moment and seems to weigh some decision in her mind. And as she considers it, I realize we've reached the outskirts of the town. The massive steel doors outside of it, identical to the ones in Epsilon, are already opened, waiting to receive us.

As we pull in, a few people emerge from the surrounding houses, looking curious. The town doesn't seem occupied, though. Whoever is here is only here temporarily. The lack of guards is surprising. As is the lack of any screens. The houses, as far as I can see, are entirely devoid of them, though I can see the holes in the exteriors where they would have been before. Possibly stolen and taken back to wherever Lena and these others normally live.

It's another college campus, I can tell that much, and the fabricated houses are identical to the ones in Epsilon, but the aesthetic of the town is entirely different. The main road is lined by flourishing trees, and climbing plants like the ones I would clear off of comm stations have taken over many of the buildings. Nature has reclaimed the town, and I have to acknowledge there's something beautiful about it.

As we navigate through the main street, I look around the sliver of Alpha I can see. It doesn't spark any memories. I fixate on the buildings, the paths, even the trees, but no memories return. I'm scrambling in my mind for any shred of recognition but find nothing. I've always dreamed that if I came back, it might remind me of them. Some childhood memory lost behind the trauma of my parents' deaths.

"You good?" Carmy asks.

I try to swallow my feelings and shake it off. "I just—I saw what happened here."

Lena looks almost as sad as I feel. "It was awful."

I'm tempted, but I don't ask about what she knows. Clearly we believe very different things about what happened here, and I don't want to set her off again like I did before. She stops the truck and climbs out, and Carmy follows her.

"How many people live here?" I ask as I follow them.

"We don't live here. We just brought you here temporarily. It's been…a long time since any of us were in Alpha."

"If this center is lying here abandoned, why *aren't* you living here?" I ask as Lena leads me toward another truck. The driver sitting in it is massive, and he gives Lena a curt nod as she approaches then climbs out to make way for her.

"There are better places to live."

"Better than the centers?"

"In ways, this is awfully close to Epsilon and some of the other centers that are still active. Plus you never know when Felix might reactivate a center, send Techs to populate it again. It's happened before. And we'd rather not be around if he returns."

"But you said you and Felix had a truce."

"Truces only last until someone changes their mind."

I look around again at the small crowd watching us as they search the town. "I thought you were all struggling to survive out here."

She's tapping on the screen on the truck's console and then stops as she seems to find whatever she was looking for. "Yes, Felix likes to tell that story. It's a good way to keep you under his thumb. If everyone left the tech centers and came to live in towns like ours, Meru would fall apart. If our life weren't so attractive to the Techs, Felix wouldn't have to make a deal with us."

"Why kidnap me then? Why bring me here?"

"The situation was too rushed at the truck. I want to show you what Luke told us, and then you can decide if you want to come with us or take this information back to Felix. We might be able to give you enough to get back on his good side."

"As your spy?"

"No, just as someone who knows we aren't monsters. We couldn't blame you for wanting to go home, risky as it might be."

She gestures for me to climb into the truck beside her, and then she activates the video file she loaded.

Based on the height of the footage, it's from a security dog. It shows the outside of what looks like a cabin in the woods, and Luke is standing outside of it. He looks frantic, the way I saw him before he blew up the station. Based on his appearance, it must be from yesterday or the day before.

Luke is pleading with them the same way he was pleading with me, but he's begging them to help him destroy the transfer station. Claiming he can't do it on his own, that Felix will stop him. And true to her word, Lena is refusing. She's trying to talk him down. Even offering for him to come live with them, to escape from Epsilon. But he refuses and says he can't leave; he has to stop me from transferring.

Part of me wants to believe this is fake, that they've created this video to trick me into helping protect them from Felix. But there's something about Luke's expressions, the words he's choosing. I've known him for nearly my whole life. This is him.

"We debated kidnapping him," Lena says over my shoulder.

"Why didn't you?"

"Same reason. We couldn't risk the retaliation."

"You're that afraid of Felix?"

"More than you can understand."

Luke is on his knees begging them now, tears streaming down his face as he pleads for them to help him do something, but Lena and the others climb back into their trucks and leave him there. This must have been the moment when he decided to do what he did, to go to such extreme lengths. His desperation was far deeper than I realized. And I abandoned him when he needed him.

"Lena, company." The hulking man who got out of the truck is pointing toward something in the distance down the road we followed, but I can't tell what he's looking at.

"Already?" she says as she leaps back out of the car. There's a duffel by the man's feet—I have no idea where it came from—and she reaches in and pulls out a pair of binoculars.

She only looks in them for a moment before saying "Shit" and looking back at me. "You still have your phone on you?"

"No, they took it."

"Any other device?"

I shake my head again. She puts the binoculars back up to her eyes. "Lucky guess maybe. There aren't many of them."

"Who's there?" I ask.

"Felix," Lena says, still in the binoculars. "Looks like half a dozen dogs, could be more."

"They followed us all this way?"

"Or guessed we'd come to Alpha."

"We need to run," I say, starting to feel the panic setting in. I've seen what those dogs can do, even if they're just practice scenarios.

"Not an option," the man says as he starts opening the duffel bag further. "They'll follow us. Don't want to lead them to Alexandria." He pulls out two shotguns and hands one to Lena.

"Actually, this is fortuitous, isn't it!" Carmy says from behind me, and I turn to see him approaching, beaming, with a gun of his own over his shoulder. "Here you go, newbie." Then he thrusts the gun into my hands. I'm so shocked I almost drop it.

"Carmy!" Lena yells as the large man growls and raises his gun toward me.

I point the gun toward the sky with one hand and raise the other in surrender. "Whoa, whoa, what're you doing?"

"Oh relax!" His grin never falters despite the sudden tension. Lena looks like she's ready to murder him. "Look at him, he's curious, you know he is. He has that little twinkle in his eyes. And besides, you're so worried about him crawling back to Felix, right? This is how we, ah, make that a little harder."

"By giving our prisoner a *gun*?" the man growls.

"Oh come off it, Dylan. He's not our prisoner; he's our new recruit! Or at least he could be if you stop treating him like some convict."

"You're an idiot, Carmy," Lena says.

"Dogs are getting closer," he replies. "So come on, newbie, what'll it be? Back to Felix? Or enlist with the noble savages?"

I'm overwhelmed with emotion. I'm terrified, exhausted, confused; I don't know what to believe anymore. I'm starting to believe Luke that Felix is hiding something from me; I don't know how else he could be driven to such extreme emotions.

But Lena, Carmy, and the rest of these people could be hiding just as much. Some part of this still isn't adding up. I want to get home, to let Tess know I'm okay, to ask Felix and Bram about what Lena has told me. But even with the bit I've learned about them, I doubt Felix would take me back. And despite my reservations toward them, what I've seen from Lena and Carmy so far doesn't exactly frighten me. If anything, I'm curious what else I don't know about their life. And if I do decide to try to turn on them, I think Felix would understand me needing to make some kind of show like this.

"Okay," I say, nervously looking at the huge man apparently named Dylan. He still has his gun aimed at my head. "Okay. I'll help."

"Beautiful," Carmy says and slaps me on the back, then grabs another gun out of the duffel. "You'll always remember your first time; come on. Gosh, I'm so touched I get to share this moment with you…" He starts leading the way down the road toward the entrance, a slight skip in his step. Dylan falls in behind me as I follow Carmy, and I can sense he's waiting for any sign of betrayal on my part to blow my head off.

We reach the gate shortly before the dogs do, and I can see them sprinting toward us in the distance, kicking up a cloud of dust in their wake. Carmy beckons me over toward a rusted-out car beside the entrance and rests his gun on the hood.

"You know how to shoot, yeah?"

"We had to practice constantly in Epsilon."

"In case those pesky savages attacked?"

"Something like that."

"They're close enough," Dylan says from over my shoulder.

"No, no, let them get closer," Carmy says. "No need to waste ammo. They're scouting dogs anyway, not the scary ones."

"Scary ones?"

"You don't know about the big ones?" Carmy sounds genuinely surprised by the admission. "That's interesting."

"Come on, Carmy," Dylan grumbles.

"Okay, okay, Isaac, you do the honors."

The dogs are still sprinting toward us, and I can hardly believe I'm about to do this. Two days ago, everything was normal. I was working with Luke, getting ready for my transfer, saying goodbye to Tess. Now I'm stuck here, with these scavengers, and about to destroy the bots I worked alongside for so long to keep Epsilon safe and functioning. I hate that this is going to make Felix think he was justified in his decision, and it worries me that it could cause some further retribution toward Sophie. But she's already exiled; I don't know what else he can do.

"Isaac…" Carmy sounds nervous now. "Don't make me look like an idiot."

"That wouldn't be hard," Dylan says.

I exhale slowly and try to push out my last reservations, then line up the sights on the gun on the dog in the lead of the pack. "I'm sorry, Tess," I whisper, and pull the trigger.

There's a chorus of explosions around me as the others fire, and the dogs that were charging at us moments before collapse on their sides or explode into chunks of metal.

"Told you we could trust him," Carmy says as the dust clears. Then he hops over the front of the car and approaches the dogs. One starts to adjust as if to attack him and he fires another shot into its chassis at point-blank range.

Just as I'm about to get up, Dylan puts a hand on my shoulder then reaches down and takes the gun back. "You're still one of them," is all he says.

Then there's a rumbling behind us as Lena pulls up in the same truck I arrived in. "Come on," she says, nodding toward me. "We can't stay here."

I climb into the truck beside Lena while Carmy and Dylan and others pick up the scraps from the dogs. My hands are shaking slightly from the adrenaline. Despite the threat, destroying them still feels wrong.

"Where are we going now?"

"Alexandria." She glances at me. "Unless you've changed your mind?"

I look back through the rear window at the fallen dogs already growing small in the distance.

"No, I'll come with you," I say quietly. "But I need to know everything."

Lena nods. "If Lincoln thinks it's appropriate. But first we need to get somewhere safe. Felix will send more than a few dogs next time."

The trees blur past as we speed down the old highway. I try not to think about Tess, about Sophie. About how this will confirm all of Felix's suspicions. But I keep seeing Luke's desperate face in that security footage, hearing the raw fear in his voice. Whatever he discovered, it was real enough to make him destroy everything he cared about. I need to know what it was.

CHAPTER 14

I MUST HAVE DOZED OFF IN THE CAR, BECAUSE I WAKE up to find us navigating city streets, flanked by more and taller buildings than I've ever been this close to. I feel a spike of panic, worried they've taken me into Austin. Everything I've heard about the old city is terrifying. But then I remember we drove in the opposite direction. This must be some city I've never seen before. I blink away the grogginess as the truck rumbles to a stop.

Lena cuts the engine and says, "We're here," her voice low.

I peer through the windshield, expecting some kind of fortified compound. Instead, I see crumbling brick buildings, their exterior barely visible beneath a century's worth of vines and overgrowth. Broken windows gape like toothless mouths, and rusted metal signs poke out from the greenery.

"This is...Alexandria?" I ask, confused by the appearance.

Lena nods. "It was a university before Meru, like Epsilon. Nature's done a better job of reclaiming it though."

We climb out of the truck, and I take in the scene. Sidewalks are split by tree roots, windows are broken, and abandoned rusted-out cars litter the street.

"It looks abandoned," I murmur, more to myself than to Lena.

She smiles. "Appearances can be deceiving. Come on."

Despite the apparent desolation, there's a sense of life here, hidden but present. The path we're following has been trodden down ever so slightly relative to the land around it. There's a faint smell of food in the air. And now that I'm looking closer down the alleys between the buildings, some of them are fortified, blocking my view of what lies beyond.

Lena leads me toward the old building immediately ahead of us. And as we climb the steps, I hear the crackle of a speaker coming from a small screen just by the door.

"Who is it?" comes a stern man's voice.

"Lincoln, I know you saw me on the way in," Lena says. "Open up."

"One moment," the voice squawks again, and then the doors slowly swing open.

A tall man with scraggly gray hair, a thin beard, and rippling muscles under the wrinkles of age steps out, beaming at Lena. He wraps her in a hug, almost lifting her off her feet, and says, "Welcome home."

Then he turns to me. "Have a nice trip?" He's imposing but has a warm paternal feel to him. And to my surprise he's not eyeing me with any sense of hesitation or distrust.

"Not exactly the words I'd use."

He laughs. "Well, we're glad you're here now. Sorry it had to be under these circumstances."

I wonder for a moment why he'd be glad I'm here. It seems that I'm putting them all at risk, attracting Felix's watchful gaze. But I don't press it.

"Come in, come in," Lincoln says, stepping back into the building and beckoning us to follow him. The foyer is teeming with life, people milling about, poring over maps, tinkering with electronics, or sharing food and materials. It reminds me in a way of how life must have been for the students who went here. The ages range far wider than what I'm used to seeing back home. Men and women in their forties, fifties, sixties, maybe older, are just as active in this society as the younger people. There were always a few older people in Epsilon, ones waiting longer to transfer. But never like this.

"Do you all live in this building?" I ask as we walk down one of the main halls. The building is large, but it's impossible to imagine a whole town containing itself inside.

"Oh no, no no no. We use almost every building on this campus. Many of us sleep in the old dormitories, we eat in the dining halls, meet in the classrooms. I'm sure it will feel familiar. Some buildings have been repurposed, of course. We turned the agricultural hall into a hydroponics center and grow most of our food there."

We turn down another hall and a group of children runs past us, playing some sort of game. "Aren't you worried about Felix finding you?" I ask.

"Yes, that's always a concern," Lincoln continues. "But we have strength in numbers here. I'm not sure he'd risk his bots and other resources on bothering us, so long as we aren't bothering him."

We exit the back of the building that had welcomed us, and I realize just how large the community in Alexandria is. People are everywhere, going in and out of buildings, playing games on the fields between them, exchanging food, clothing, and other goods in what appears to be some sort of market set up along the streets. It's more people living in one place than I've seen in my life.

Lincoln waves at someone passing us and he stops, pulling a bag of apples out of his pack and handing it to him. The man gives Lincoln a nod of respect; if he isn't the leader of Alexandria, he must be someone important. He passes two apples to me and Lena. "Have you had fresh apples before?" he asks as I bite into mine. It explodes with flavor, almost overwhelmingly.

"Not like this," I say as a bit of juice drips down my chin. "How can you possibly grow these?" Apples were a rarity from Imgen, like most of the other nonnative produce.

"The same way Imgen does," Lincoln says, taking another bite of an apple and waving at a couple vendors as we pass. "This campus was one of the earliest tech centers, and one of the biggest. In Imgen's original plans, each center was going to be fully self-sufficient, producing all of its food and with resources for bot maintenance and anything else it might need.

"The old engineering building has a nuclear reactor in the basement. They were custom designed during the transferring period to require minimal maintenance. We've had to make some repairs and swap out some parts, but nothing we haven't been able to figure out. So far anyway."

"How are you getting parts? There's no way the original supplies have lasted."

"Felix has been kind enough to continue supplying us."

"Seriously?"

"Well, he doesn't exactly *know* he's supplying us." He has an almost impish grin as he says it. I still feel on edge, but it's hard not to like him.

"If this was a tech center—" I start to ask, but Lincoln interrupts me.

"Yes, we have a server cluster in the old computer science building. We've transferred quite a few people there."

The statement catches me off guard. "Transferred?"

"Not transferring like you think," Lena says. "Transferring people out of Meru."

"You...can do that?"

"Yes," Lincoln says. "It's taken a considerable amount of work, but we've found a way, one where we can give them a freer life."

"And without needing a slave network to maintain it," Lena adds.

"So that's how you see us."

Lena shrugs. "You're trapped living in one small area most of your life, you do work assigned to you by the person in charge in order to maintain someone else's world, he gives you all of your food and resources, you get effectively killed if you disobey...it's not exactly freedom, is it?"

Something about her tone sets me off. "I had a good life there before you fucked it up."

"Before *Luke* fucked it up."

"You can drop the act. You can't use me to get Felix off your back anymore."

Lincoln stops and sighs. "It's true, Isaac. We didn't ask Luke to attack your home. He was acting on his own, or with someone else."

"You don't exactly seem like the biggest fans of Felix."

"No, but violence is not the answer, not unless it's forced upon us. We only want to free people who have been put under Felix's thumb. It made sense for him to have the power he had in the beginning, when the world was dying, when there was no other way...but those days have passed. We need to rebuild. I suspect he wanted that once too. But the Felix you interact with in Meru is not the original man anymore. He's scarier, darker, more consumed with power than the original creator."

"That's why you used to attack the tech centers."

Lincoln nods. "Attack isn't the right word. People living in them would reach out to us, ask for help escaping. It was a nasty affair though. And not worthwhile, in the end. Even when we succeeded, the Techs who didn't ask for our help didn't want to come with us. They saw us as monsters. They thought we were killing God."

"Well you *were*. Life in Epsilon was great, and everyone in Meru seemed perfectly happy. I'm not thrilled about getting ripped away from it. And I don't understand why you're so afraid of Felix. Have you considered that you might be fearmongering about him as much as he is about you?"

Lincoln sighs. "You'll understand in time. Felix gave you a safe life. A home. And the potential to transfer into Meru. That's a lot to be grateful for. I hope you'll eventually agree, though, that those indulgences can't justify the savagery he's wrought on us. The dogs that chased after you at Alpha…that's barely a taste of what Felix is capable of."

I nod silently, still mulling over everything I've seen.

"There's something I want to show you," Lincoln says, guiding us toward the largest building on campus.

"What's that?"

"The alternative to Meru."

CHAPTER 15

LINCOLN LEADS LENA AND ME TOWARD WHAT MUST BE the computer science building. It has a distinctly different design from the other buildings, all glass and sharp angles. It reminds me of Epsilon more than any of the other parts of Alexandria. Either through the effort of the people who live here, or something about its design, it's the only building not partially overgrown.

As we reach it, Lincoln jumps up the steps two at a time and holds the door open, making a sweeping gesture for me to lead the way.

The entry hall of the computer science building is lined with screens, the first I've seen since arriving, showing similar scenes to the kind I've come to expect from Meru—but there is some subtle difference I can't put my finger on. Lincoln steps to the side and lets me drink the room in, and I walk through the entryway into an open atrium with the ceiling reaching up to the whole height of the building, filling it with natural light.

Throughout the center of the room are rows and rows of desks, each with two computer monitors on them. Each set of monitors has a person sitting behind it, ranging from kids who barely look older than twelve to people who could be my grandparent. Each is wearing a pair of headphones, typing ferociously, and looking back and forth between the monitor they are working on and the one adjacent.

On the adjacent monitors I see a similar room, mirrored in the digital world, but with the seated person in the opposite position, a digital counterpart to whatever is happening in the building in front of me. The people I can see are speaking animatedly with their digital counterparts and appear to be looking through maps and various locations in Meru.

"What...are they doing?" I ask. Whatever they're focused on, it's clearly of immense importance to all of them.

"The same thing Lena and I have been doing," Lincoln says, surveying the room with a look of pride on his face. "Looking for people who want a way out."

I open my mouth to ask what that means but then one of the researchers at a desk near us realizes we have entered and takes off her headset, pushing away from her computer and running up to Lincoln. Her face is framed by dark curly hair and she barely reaches his shoulder. The dark circles under her eyes remind me of people in Epsilon; she must spend more time in front of a screen than the others here.

"Sir," she says, stopping in front of him.

"What did you find, Maya?"

She looks at me out of the corner of her eye.

"He's fine," Lincoln continues.

"He just got here."

"He's *fine*, Maya. He's not going back after what Felix did."

Her eyes bore into me with a shocking intensity for someone so small. I'm grateful for the trust Lincoln is already putting in me, but not entirely sure what I've done to deserve it.

"Please, go ahead," Lincoln reiterates.

"Very well," she says. "We have someone new who wants out: oldie, OG, said he figured out something about the amnesia."

"We've heard that before," Lincoln says. "Could be bait, one of Felix's."

"I don't think so," she continues. "He's old old, not just pre-Meru. He worked at Imgen too."

Lincoln and Lena both seem to perk up at this. "Well...that's new..." Lincoln says.

"Has no one from Imgen wanted to escape before?" I ask Lena.

"They have," she says. "But they never remember anything from before. Like their memory was wiped."

"Or they don't want to remember," Lincoln grumbles.

"You don't believe them?" Lena asks.

"I believe them. But there's clearly something from how the program started that Felix, or Imgen, or whoever, didn't want us to know. Or didn't want anyone poking their nose into."

Lena looks back at Maya. "Where are they?"

"He's transferring to a comm station outside of Delta in the next week. We should be able to pick him up there."

"Wait," I say. "So that *was* you at the comm station I visited? With Simon?"

"Ah...Simon..." Lincoln laughs. "He almost had us."

"Yes," Lena says. "I'm sorry for not saying so earlier. I didn't know if we could trust you yet."

"So Simon...He was trying to escape?"

"We thought so," Lincoln says. "But we realized at the last minute that he was an agent sent by Felix."

I feel a pang of disgust. "You left him trapped in that station though!"

"We could have destroyed the transfer port or the server housing him, but we didn't, did we?"

Suddenly an alarm blares in the hall. I jump and look to Lincoln for some sign of what to do, but he seems completely

CHAPTER 15 · 149

unfazed. No one else in the room reacts beyond a brief glance at the back wall either.

"Maya," Lincoln says to the researcher who had approached us. "Send me the details on the extraction; we'll get a team on it shortly." Then he looks at me and says, "Come on," as he moves toward the back of the building, navigating between the rows of desks.

As I follow him, it occurs to me what feels different about these digital people compared to the ones I interacted with back in Meru. They're working alongside the people in Alexandria. They haven't checked out into their digital lives, off on adventures and indulging in whatever hedonic delights they have access to. And as we pass through the screens and I observe the change, I wonder why that failure of Meru residents has never occurred to me before.

We reach the back of the lobby and Lincoln leads me down a dark hallway, lined with what appears to be photos of tech centers similar to Epsilon. As we pass an empty room with a long, ovular table in the middle, I catch a glimpse of a faded map on the wall with a series of X's drawn on it, but many more circles and stars.

"What are all of these?" I ask Lena as she follows behind me.

"Active and former centers," she says. "Sometimes a whole town gets wise to what's going on and is able to disconnect at once. It happened more before Felix got stricter with weeding out doubters."

"He didn't always exile people?"

She shakes her head. "That's a more recent threat."

The hallway terminates in a large, dark room full of a mess of boxes, wires, and robotics parts. Before I can ask what it is, Lincoln slams his fist on a red button by the door, and the back wall starts retracting into the ceiling. "Welcome to the loading dock," he says.

Then I see a familiar truck back up to the opening outside. It's almost identical to the ones Luke and I and the other Techs in Epsilon used.

Lena jumps down off the ledge of the dock onto the road and helps guide the driver so the bed of the truck is pressed up against the wall. Then she climbs into the back and unlocks the transfer cable, the same way I did when we brought Simon back to camp.

"Come here," she says, gesturing to me, and I run up to the edge, taking the cable from her and pulling it into the loading dock. Lincoln points out where the port is and I connect it, hearing the satisfying hum of a transfer initiating.

"Let's go see what she knows," Lincoln says and takes off at a jog back down the hall. I follow him out into the lobby again, then down a staircase, until we reach a massive, sealed metal door much like the vault in Epsilon.

"How many of these did they build…" I wonder aloud.

"We're not sure," Lena says. "That's part of the amnesia. There could be dozens, could be thousands; our map is incomplete. We haven't been able to explore more than a few hundred miles north, south, and east."

"Not west?"

"Not worth crossing the highway."

"And it's hard to trust people reaching out from supposed other large settlements like Alexandria," Lincoln adds as he keys in the security code to the vault.

"Why's that?" I ask.

The door hisses and starts swinging open. "Not all of them are as friendly to transferred minds as we are," Lena says.

As we step into the vault, an intense hum of servers fills the air. The room is dimly lit, but as we enter, a screen flickers to life before us. Behind it, more lights click on, and I have to stop myself from gasping. The servers stretch ahead what must be a hundred yards and then descend out of view. I walk past the computer screen to reach the glass wall looking in on the behemoth and crane my neck, trying to see how deep it goes, but can see no end in sight.

"My God," I whisper, unable to take my eyes off it. "How far down does it go?"

Lincoln chuckles. "Deep. About twenty levels."

"I can't believe building this used to be possible."

"Only briefly," Lincoln says, stepping up to look into the pit beside me. "Before the plague, they built servers like these to support artificial intelligence. It needed colossal amounts of processing power to do the jobs people wanted it to do, and there was seemingly endless money to support it.

"Then, when the plague came, there was a much more important use. All of the existing data centers were repurposed to supporting Meru, and additional ones were built at a pace unmatched by anything in human history."

This much computing technology in one place, orders of magnitude grander in scale than what we have in Epsilon...it hardly seems possible. It's a miracle they began work on it before the plague took hold.

"The digger they used is still at the bottom," Lena says, now initiating the transfer sequence at the computer. "It's an incredible machine; maybe Lincoln can show you next time he uses it."

"Uses it? For what?"

"Backup plan in case Felix ever finds this place," Lincoln says. "It's slow going, but I think we can use it to build a tunnel network, somewhere easier to defend from his drones."

"Supposedly there are old tunnel networks all over the state," Lena adds. "Huge ones. We've never found them though."

"Let's see what our new friend has to say," Lena says, and

hits ENTER on the computer. I step back and look over her shoulder at the screen as the process begins and imagine the truck upstairs illuminating at the same time as the loading animation is playing out before us. I feel a hint of relief that I might be useful in this new home. Even if I don't know how to survive out here like they do, I at least know how these machines work.

A minute later, a young Asian woman who looks to be in her mid-twenties appears on the screen, her eyes bright with excitement. "Oh my god," she says. "Holy shit."

Lena and Lincoln seem to expect her surprise. "How does it feel?" Lena asks.

The woman doesn't respond. She's looking around the simulated room she's in, eyes still wide. Then a flurry of words starts coming out of her mouth. I only catch a few of them.

Lena laughs, and I ask her, "What is she doing?"

"She's free of the censoring," Lincoln says, a satisfied look on his face. "You can talk about these things in certain indirect ways, but Felix has strict controls on what residents of Meru can say to the outside world. Most residents don't even notice they're being censored; supposedly it works by nudging your thoughts away from the topics, only completely blocking your communication if you push through the nudge and try to discuss something off limits."

A chill runs through my body, and I remember Luke saying the voice whispering to him seemed like it was struggling to share what it knew. "He can nudge residents' thoughts?"

"He, Meru, some part of it can, yes," Lena says.

"Once transferred, the mind is another form of software," Lincoln says. "It can be controlled like anything else running on the Meru servers."

"And, unfortunately, altered," Lena says. Then she presses the mic button on the computer. The woman has calmed down and stopped babbling. "Hi, Natalie. How do you feel?"

Natalie looks ecstatic. "I didn't realize how *trapped* I was before."

"Most people don't," Lincoln replies. "You can only see your prison from the outside."

"What does the difference feel like?" I ask.

Natalie thinks about it for a moment, then says, "It's hard to make analogies to before I transferred; it's been a long time. But perhaps the best is that before, it felt like I was always in a slight daze, or a hangover, for lack of a better comparison."

"And you felt that all the time?"

"No, I didn't even realize I felt it until now. I suppose you can go for decades, or even your whole life, in a haze and not realize it until you're pulled out of it." She looks sad, as if she's mourning the life she lived in Meru. "Gosh, I'm so happy I ended up in contact with you. I can't imagine spending another minute in that place."

It feels surreal to hear her describe what it was like now that she's out. Everyone I've ever talked to there seemed perfectly happy, normal.

"When can I move into Alexandria?" she asks.

Lincoln must have seen my confusion because he whispers, "We call our digital world Alexandria too, same as the town. We want to emphasize that they're all connected, not some place you run off to. We don't want to invite anyone who's looking for another escape like Meru."

Then he addresses Natalie. "We'll finish the second stage of the transfer shortly. We just need to run some questions by you."

"Ah, Meru stuff? Imgen stuff?" Natalie asks.

"Both," Lena says.

Natalie nods. "Somehow I have a hunch you know what I'm going to say already."

"You don't remember anything," Lincoln says.

Natalie sighs. "No, nothing worthwhile. I know I worked at Imgen before I transferred, but I don't remember anything about working there, nor anything about the transfer technology."

"Can you...try?" Lena asks. I wonder what try even means for a digital mind.

"It's just not there," Natalie says, looking frustrated now. "I know it should be. I have the memory of remembering it, but the actual memory is gone. It's hard to describe. Almost like it was a dream that's faded away."

"That's promising, at least," Lincoln says.

"Why's that?" I ask.

"The memory is there," Lena says. "Or at least sounds like it is. We just haven't figured out how to help the residents access it."

"How often does this happen?"

"Everyone from around the time of the plague, or who worked at Imgen, has the amnesia," Lincoln says. "But if this other person Maya found actually knows how to unlock it, we might be able to tap into a new trove of information."

"Can I ask her something?"

Lincoln and Lena glance at each other, then Lincoln says, "Go ahead."

I bring up a notepad on the computer and draw the xīn symbol I saw in Luke's notes. "Do you recognize this?"

Natalie scrunches up her face. "It's Chinese, right? Heart?"

"Yes. Have you seen it anywhere in Meru?"

"I don't think so..."

"Why do you ask?" Lincoln interrupts.

"Luke was obsessed with it. I found it all over his house."

Lincoln looks at Lena and she shakes her head. Clearly neither of them recognize it either.

"Sorry!" Natalie says, breaking the silence.

"Okay, Natalie, I'm sending you over now," Lena says and executes another command on the computer. Natalie waves, beaming, then disappears as quickly as she arrived.

"Where will she go?" I ask.

Lincoln points to the screen, and a moment later it shows a simulated version of the full Alexandria town, populated by digital people just as I saw Epsilon filled with the past transferees before. "She'll go through a welcome orientation much like you did and then decide how she best wants to contribute to helping sustain life here."

"Everyone in the digital Alexandria works?"

"Not all the time," Lena says. "But the expectation is that half of their waking time will go to helping the town, just as ours does. They're welcome to do more, but not less."

"Which is also what we'll expect from you, now that you're here," Lincoln says. "Grant ensured your rescue from exile, but you'll still need to prove yourself to the town."

"Come on," Lena says as she finishes shutting down the transfer station and starts walking back out of the vault. "I'll show you where you can sleep."

※ ※ ※

We leave the transfer building and start across the quad, headed toward some of the larger, more uniform buildings on the campus.

"So, Lincoln—does he lead Alexandria?"

Lena smiles to a woman passing by with a young child, then says, "Informally, yes. We've been trying to minimize any sort of hierarchy, at least as long as we can."

"Why's that?"

"People coming here from tech centers wanted to get away from feeling like someone was telling them what to do all the time. But they started listening to Lincoln more as he guided certain decisions within the town, and as new people showed up, they deferred to him as well."

"What if there are disagreements though?"

"We usually appoint trusted members of the community to arbitrate them, when necessary. It works for a community of this size."

"And in the digital Alexandria?"

Lena thinks for a moment. "You know, it hasn't been an issue. Maybe when scarcity is removed, people don't care about those little differences anymore. There's no sense that if someone else has something, you don't have it. And when you're not constrained by space or time or food…" She looks around the town as she says it. "Well, maybe it'll be a problem in the future. But so far, no, it's all informal."

A few minutes later we arrive at one of the tall buildings, and she leads me inside. Two flights of stairs and a short hallway later, we're standing outside a room.

A delivery bot scurries out of the room as we approach. "I'm surprised you use so many bots here."

"Apparently we tried avoiding them in the beginning. The early settlers here wanted to leave Felix's world behind entirely. But over time we realized that technology, including the bots, wasn't really the problem. It was the total surrender to them, especially surrendering what made us human. Raising children, growing food, socializing, exploring. But no one felt deeply called to do laundry, so a few people figured out how to repurpose bots from tech centers to handle that and other less meaningful jobs for us. And defense, of course."

"Weren't they already programmed for that? Why do they need to be repurposed?"

"I guess by 'repurpose' I mean 'de-Felixed.' It's hard to get his influence out of the software on most of the robotics we come across. The last thing we want is to give him access to everyone's bedroom."

I nudge the door open. The room is simple but comfortable. A bed, desk, chair, and a small dresser, similar to the dorm rooms at Epsilon. My eyes linger on a basket of food waiting on the desk. What looks like homemade bread makes my stomach growl, reminding me how long it has been since I've eaten.

"We try to make sure everyone has what they need," Lena says, noticing my gaze. "Help yourself."

I grab a chunk of bread off the loaf in the basket and bite into it; it's far better than anything Imgen ever sent us.

"What do you think?" Lena asks from the hallway. There's still a hint of suspicion in her eye, but some of the coldness from before is gone.

"It's delicious."

"Not about the bread, about what Lincoln showed you."

I pause to swallow and to figure out how to phrase what I've been feeling since we arrived and through the tour. "I spent my whole life in Epsilon. Even if what you're saying about Felix is true, I can't forget about my family and friends back there. I want to see them again." My thoughts go to Tess, her look of terror as she realized what Felix had decided to do. Part of me feels betrayed by what she did, but I also know she didn't expect it to escalate this far. I hope she's not too worried about me.

Lena nods gently, and there's a sadness in the look that makes me wonder what might have happened to lead to her being here. "Maybe one day you can help get them out too."

"Have you ever rescued someone from exile?"

"Thinking of your sister?"

The surprise on my face must be obvious because she adds, "Grant told us."

I nod, resisting the urge to speak with food in my mouth.

"No, we haven't, not as far as I know anyway. It's different than when we extract people from a comm station. Your sister is on Epsilon's servers; there's no way we'd be able to get her without infiltrating the town."

"Yeah," I say, still unsure what to think about it all. "I guess you're right."

"I wish we could help. No one deserves that."

"Thank you," I say as I try not to imagine how scared and alone she must feel right now. "What's next?"

"Feel free to read through any of the history files on the computer. There are some clothes in the dresser if you want to change. Someone will come get you in the morning."

Something about her tone puts me on edge. "Are you saying I can't leave?"

"You're free to go anywhere you want in Alexandria, though you might get some questioning looks if you're walking around alone today."

"So don't leave."

"You're not a prisoner, Isaac, but I think it would make the other people here more comfortable if you took it slowly. Was there somewhere you wanted to go?"

"No." I shake my head. "Only curious."

"Well, we'll try to satisfy your curiosity tomorrow. Rest up."

CHAPTER 16

THE SUN IS BARELY PEEKING THROUGH THE WINDOWS when a sharp knock rouses me out of bed. I roll over and look at the computer monitor on the desk. Six a.m. Alexandria is as diligent about its work hours as Epsilon.

I throw on the pair of work clothes Lena had pointed out the night before, then pull open the door. I expect to be greeted by Lincoln or Lena, but it's Carmy.

"Morning, newbie!" he says. "Ready to get to work?"

"Uh, yeah."

"I'll be your handler while you get acquainted. Take you out on some jobs, show you around, make sure you don't steal anything, stuff like that."

"And my alarm clock?"

He laughs. "Can't be wasting daylight! Don't have daddy Felix to hold us against his teat here, you know."

I rub my eyes as he barges into the room and grabs an apple off my desk. "Okay, what are we doing then?"

He pulls out his phone. "Looks like we're going to start you off on the farm. Ever farmed before?"

"No."

"It's neat. The little plastic food packages pop right out of the ground."

"Uh-huh."

"Oh, come on, lighten up. You can do equipment repairs too, right?"

"How did you know that?"

"Told you we had our eye on you, didn't I?"

I raise an eyebrow but he just grins back at me then takes another bite of the apple.

"Can I help with pulling someone out of Meru?"

"Hah! You're eager. I like it. That's primo work though—only our finest, or only the ones Lincoln trusts the most anyway. Gotta earn your way up to stealing souls from Felix." He gives me a quick look up and down. "You look ready enough; want to get started now?"

"Can we get breakfast first?"

"Please, we're not savages."

※ ※ ※

I follow Carmy out of the dorm. The early morning air is crisp, and dew clings to the grass as we walk across the campus. A few other early risers are out doing maintenance on the buildings. I see someone carrying a box of electronics with a faded Imgen logo on it into the computer science building. A young woman is guiding a group of children across the quad too.

"Where is she taking them?"

"Bel!" Carmy yells and she jumps. "Where to?"

A child behind her who looks to be four or five answers for her. "We're going to see the goats!"

Bel smiles and ruffles his hair. "Yes, we're going to the zoo."

"Zoo?" I ask Carmy.

"They mean the farm," Carmy whispers. "More fun for the kids to think of it as a grand adventure instead of shoveling goat shit, you know."

"Carmy, Miss Bel said we can't ride them," another of the children adds, looking at him hopefully.

"Well, I'll have to take you sometime when she's not looking then."

Bel gives him the same disapproving look I can imagine she gives to the children, then she ushers them along. A security dog is following behind them, and it looks like someone in the class has put a pair of fabric ears on it.

"Who assigns your work here?" I ask, stifling a yawn as the class leaves.

"Assign is a strong word. Most of us figure out where we can be most helpful and get to it. And if there's something no one wants to do..."

"You build a bot for it."

"Exactly, when we can. Tech should replace the drudgery of life. Not the joy. Glad you're here. Not too many people here have hands-on experience with Felix's tech. You're going to be a hot commodity."

We pass a group of people drinking coffee around a bench under a tree, and their conversation quiets down. I can feel them looking at me out of the corner of their eye.

"Don't mind them," Carmy says. "You don't make it long out here if you blindly trust everyone you meet. But I don't like that strategy. Lead with friendship! Always lead with friendship. You treat people too suspiciously and it puts them on edge. They end up acting weird and confirming your suspicions. Then they feel you being suspicious and they get more suspicious. Suddenly everyone has knives out. Not great. To be clear though—" He spins around and puts a hand on my shoulder; his grip is crushing and his stare is fierce. The shock of the change freezes me in my tracks. "If you turn out to be a threat to us, you'll wish Felix had exiled you."

My jaw goes slack as he stares me down, but then the joy returns to his face, and he pats me on the shoulder. "Kidding! Kidding. Mostly. Come on, that coffee smells good."

We approach a large brick building that I assume is the cafeteria. The smell of bacon wafts out as Carmy pulls open the door. "After you," he says with a flourish.

Inside, the cafeteria is a bustling hive of activity. People of all ages mill about, grabbing trays and filling them with food. There's a warmth to the controlled chaos that I never felt in Epsilon, where food was treated like an afterthought, another part of the Felix machine that was rushed through to get back to work or watching streams from Meru. As we enter there's a subtle wave of silence across the room as people turn to look at us, but Carmy waves at them and they return to their meals.

"Grab whatever you want," Carmy says as we approach the food line, snagging a tray for himself. "No shortages to worry about, so don't be shy."

We load up our plates with eggs, bacon, toast, and fruit. It's more fresh food than I've ever seen in a supply shipment, even for transfer parties. The smell of coffee pouring out of the dispenser is intoxicating, and I find myself wondering how many of my bean shipments they stole.

As we make our way to a table, I can't help but notice the chatter all around us. Most of the crowd seems to have gotten over their hesitation when I entered. It's a far cry from the subdued, often digital interactions I was used to back home, and there were never large communal meals like this. We sit down near the window, and Carmy immediately digs into his food.

"So," I say between mouthfuls, "what's your job here, besides orienting new people?"

He grins, a piece of bacon hanging from his lips. "Oh, a bit of everything. Jack of all trades, master of none. Repairs, farmwork, extractions, but my favorite is helping newcomers like you get settled in."

"Are there a lot of us?"

"Trickles—not like there used to be though."

"Why not?"

"Felix has gotten stricter. Locked down the centers more. Supposedly Techs used to roam a little wider back in the day."

"Didn't feel that restricted in Epsilon."

"You ever go outside town for anything besides maintenance work?"

I don't respond.

"If you only experience the world through a screen, it's hard to say what world you're really experiencing. Could be the real one. Could be one someone wants you to think is real. And besides, the best way to trap someone is to let them build the cage. Those walls…not just to keep people out, you know."

I nod, swallowing a mouthful of bacon.

※ ※ ※

We clear our trays and I follow Carmy out of the cafeteria to another building. As we enter, I'm stunned by how different the interior is from the aged brick outside. It's been gutted, the walls and rooms replaced by rows upon rows of hydroponic growing chambers stretching up to the ceiling. The air is thick with the rich scent of soil and vegetation.

"Welcome to our little indoor oasis," Carmy says, gesturing proudly at the setup.

I walk between the rows, marveling at the complexity. Leafy greens, tomatoes, and herbs grow in abundance, their roots suspended in what must be nutrient-rich water. LED lights hum overhead, providing the artificial light they need to grow.

"This is incredible," I murmur, running my fingers along the edge of a tray filled with lettuce. "How do you manage all this without Imgen?"

"We stole some of these devices from them back in the day. Others were already here. So a little thievery combined with old-fashioned manual labor and ingenuity."

As we move deeper into the room, rows of people are tending to the plants, checking water levels, and harvesting produce.

"I thought you were all about living away from Felix's tech-dependent world."

He shrugs. "We are when we can. We have animals outside the town, cows and goats and such. There are greenhouses outside too, and actual farmland, but not everything grows in this climate. If we have to choose between a limited diet and relying on some of this tech to make BLTs, we're going to use the tech. It's the same as the bots."

He reaches into one of the beds and pulls out a strawberry. "We aren't antitechnology like Felix thinks. We're antidependence. If all the servers melted down tomorrow, Alexandria would be fine, we could all stay alive. Epsilon couldn't, at least not most of you. That's how Felix maintains his power, not with an iron fist but by keeping everyone dependent on him for even the most basic human functions."

"Your job today," Carmy continues, "is to help with the harvesting and replanting. We'll start you off with something simple, maybe these tomatoes over here?"

He leads me to a section where plump, red tomatoes hang heavy on their vines, and I begin to carefully pluck the ripe ones.

I glance over at Carmy while I work. "How long have you been here in Alexandria?"

"Born and raised, actually. My parents were some of the original settlers."

"I didn't realize there were people who'd been outside the tech centers for that long."

"Oh yeah, there's plenty of us. Probably half of the residents were born here or in the other towns."

"There are other towns?"

"Were." Carmy gets quiet and I wonder who he's lost to Felix over the years. We continue harvesting food in silence, working our way down the section, a bot occasionally stopping by to collect what we've harvested. Carmy explains that it takes it to the refrigerator in the cafeteria and updates a ledger they keep of what's in stock so other people in Alexandria can come up with recipes for the week.

As we finish the tomatoes we move on to peppers, strawberries, basil. The farm is even larger than I thought when we walked in, and I notice large sections of it remain unused. Maybe Alexandria used to be bigger, or they've preemptively expanded it hoping the city will grow.

Other people come and go as we harvest, and Carmy explains that even when people don't have assigned chores for the day, they often like to join for whatever work they enjoy most. Older people will play with kids in the day care, some will go hunting, the more technical people will tinker with bots that were taken from tech centers to see if they can be repurposed to support life here. There's almost no entertainment from the digital Alexandria they tap into.

For all the fear that had been instilled in me since birth about what an awful life it is outside of the centers, no one here seems to be suffering. Their gaze is softer, like they're more at peace, despite the threat of Felix still lingering over them. Despite the threat of dying.

But as I work, I can't help thinking of Tess, of Grant, even of Shelby and the others back in Epsilon. I miss them, and I'm worried about them.

CHAPTER 17

A WEEK INTO MY NEW ROUTINE OF GETTING WOKEN UP by Carmy, heading to breakfast, and then working on the hydroponics farm, I find my eyes fluttering open as the first rays of sun peak through the blinds in the bedroom.

I roll over to check the time on the computer. It's 5:55, so I jump out of bed and throw on my work clothes just in time for his knock.

He gives me a surprised look when I yank the door open. "Hey, you're getting the hang of it!"

"I don't think I've woken up with the sun before."

"You sleep better out here, don't you? Heard that from some other ex-Techs."

I stretch my shoulders and realize he's right; I don't feel like I need coffee the moment I roll out of bed anymore. "Why is that?"

"Got a few guesses. Better food, using your body more, not looking at those pesky screens all day, fewer electronics around you…"

"Electronics?"

"In the tech centers, everything's wired, circuits on circuits on circuits. Then you have Felix's network radiating everywhere so he can control everything. You know the human body is basically electronic too, right? You have your own electromagnetic waves, your own frequency. Some call it an aura. And if there are too many other frequencies and magnets circling around you it screws with your energy. Makes you sleep worse. Makes you anxious, scared. But you get used to it. Drink coffee. Alcohol. Then you get out of that for a bit and you feel so much better, right? Like you go out into the woods, you touch grass, you breathe the fresh air, and then you feel amazing. But then you hear there's something exciting going on in Meru and you turn on the big screen and—"

I look around the room at all of the electronics while Carmy's rant continues.

"Yeah yeah, I know. Come on, got something different today."

As we sit down at breakfast, the hulking man from Alpha, Dylan, sits down to join us. The contrast between him and Carmy is almost laughable; even sitting, Carmy barely reaches his shoulders.

He's the first person to join me and Carmy at a meal since I got here. It feels like a good sign that I'm finally being welcomed. The subtle tension from the community around me was starting to wear on me. Even in the farm, I noticed people working a little farther away from me than others.

"Jumbo here leads our hunting efforts," Carmy says, spinning a fork between his fingers. "Thought we'd give you a break from farming today."

"You know how to shoot?" Dylan asks.

"You saw me shoot."

"That was easy, shotguns, close range. This is hunting."

I nod. "I know how to use a rifle. Felix said those of us who did maintenance work needed to know how to defend ourselves, just in case."

"Gotta watch out for those savages, eh?"

Dylan grunts a laugh. "How about packing bullets?"

"That…I'm not familiar with," I admit.

"Wish we had a magical computer fairy to drop everything off for us," Carmy says.

"You seem capable of stealing everything else."

"Ouch!" Carmy mock-stabs himself with his fork. "You think so little of me…"

"You'll learn," Dylan says, then checks his phone. "Let's head out in five. Don't want to let the sun get any higher."

Half an hour later and a few miles north of Alexandria, Dylan pulls the truck to stop. "This where you saw them?" he asks Carmy.

Carmy nods. "Family passed through here last night, probably bedded down in the woods somewhere."

"How do you know that?" I ask, and Carmy pulls out his phone to show a video he must have recorded from a hidden camera in the area.

"Trail cams all around the outskirts. You'd be surprised what comes through here."

"Besides deer?"

Dylan nods. "Deer, antelope, mountain lions. Even saw a tiger once."

I snort a laugh, but they both give me a confused look. "You can't be serious."

"You'd be amazed what people kept on their land back in the day," Carmy says as he hops out of the truck. I follow him and try to close the door as quietly as possible while he removes the rifles from the back.

I take mine and shoulder it, then look to Dylan to lead the way. He checks the camera footage again, then starts walking into the brush, shockingly silent for someone so large. Birds start chirping gentle warnings among themselves as Carmy and I follow behind him.

A few yards in, Dylan crouches down to inspect a bush. He pulls a leaf off and hands it back to me, silently pointing out the chew marks. Then he guides my vision with his finger along the ground until it lands on a pile of scat a few yards ahead of us. He bends over that too and holds his hand just above it, and whispers back, "Cold." Carmy and I nod and keep silently following him.

Dylan's eye is incredible. He keeps pointing out tiny signs I never would have picked up on. A sliver of a hoofprint in some mud. A nibbled bush. Bits of bark worn away by a deer rubbing his antlers against it, which Carmy pantomimes and almost makes me laugh out loud. Eventually the tracking leads us to a pile of leaves and sticks that's been tamped down, apparently the animal's bed from the night before.

He indicates to me and Carmy to stay put by the bed as he starts circling it, slowly getting farther from it until he picks up the trail again. Then he gestures for us to follow and we fall back in behind him.

A short while later, Dylan freezes. Carmy and I immediately stop, but I can't tell what he's looking at. Carmy's hand slowly extends over my shoulder and points almost directly ahead, slightly towards one o'clock, and there's a tiny patch of beige through the trees ahead.

Dylan ever so slightly gestures toward me to move forward, then he points to a tree next to us where I can rest the rifle. I get in position and wait for the deer to get into a better position, where I can see the space behind its shoulder that Dylan told me to aim for on the ride out.

My finger drifts down off of the safe position on the side of the rifle as the deer shifts slightly, the rest of its body coming into view. I form a circle with my lips and slowly exhale, trying to reach a point of maximum calm, avoiding any chance of the slightest movement from my heart jostling the shot out of position.

SNAP. A crack rips through the forest off to my right, and the deer's head bolts up. It spots us and freezes, and in that moment, I take the shot and see it collapse to the ground where it's standing. I breathe a sigh of relief and take my eye off the scope but then see Carmy and Dylan with their rifles up, pointed into the woods to my right.

I take a step back toward them, and then there's a squealing behind me and I whip around to see where it came from just in time to spot two wild piglets darting across the opening in the brush ahead.

"Heads up!" Dylan shouts.

A thunderous crash explodes behind me. Before I can turn, something massive slams into my legs, knocking me off my feet. A sharp pain rips through my ankle as I hit the ground.

I spin around and a boar has my foot clamped in its jaws, eyes blazing with rage. It jerks its head side to side, trying to rip my foot off or drag me into the brush. I fumble for the knife on my belt, fingers slipping as the beast thrashes.

"Isaac!" Carmy yells.

The boar pulls harder, pain shooting up my leg. I swing my fist at its snout, punching with all the strength I can muster. But the blows aren't doing anything. If anything, it bites down more fiercely.

My fingers finally close around the handle of the knife and I yank it from its sheath. The boar's teeth are still buried in my ankle, grinding against bone as it tries to tear my foot off. Each shake of its head sends fresh waves of agony shooting up my leg.

Through the haze of pain, I remember Dylan's instructions from the truck about where to strike. Behind the shoulder blade, angled up into the lungs. I grip the knife tighter, waiting for the right moment as the beast thrashes.

The boar pauses for a split second, and I drive the blade deep into its side, feeling it slide between ribs. The animal lets out a horrible squealing sound and releases my ankle, then stumbles sideways, blood already bubbling from its mouth as it tries to charge at me again.

BANG! Another shot echoes through the woods, this time from Dylan's rifle. He must have been waiting until he was sure he wouldn't risk hitting me. The boar crashes to the ground, making wet gasping sounds as its lungs fill with blood. I drag myself backward, keeping my eyes locked on the dying animal until it goes still.

"Isaac!" Carmy is at my side, checking my leg while Dylan keeps his rifle trained on the surrounding woods. "Shit, this is bad."

I look down at my mangled ankle, blood soaking through my boot and pant leg. The pain hits me in full force now that the adrenaline is wearing off. "We gotta get back to town."

"Not yet," Carmy says as he pulls a first aid kit from his pack.

"How bad?" Dylan asks, relaxing now.

"Gonna need antibiotics. Those animals are disgusting. Probably a brace too."

I wince as Carmy cleans the wounds with antiseptic.

"They're mean bastards," Dylan says. "You're lucky it was your foot—they can gut you with those tusks."

"What spooked it?" I ask through gritted teeth.

Carmy looks up from bandaging my ankle. "Seems like we got between her and her piglets."

"Can't blame her," Dylan mutters, scanning the trees.

My ankle throbs as Carmy finishes wrapping it. I try to stand but immediately regret it as pain shoots up my leg, and Carmy puts his shoulder under mine to support me.

"Welcome to hunting," he says with a slight grin.

"Not exactly what I had in mind for my first time out," I admit, trying to shift to a more comfortable position.

Dylan picks up our rifles and slings all three over his shoulder, then squats down to get a grip around the boar's stomach and slings her onto his shoulder. He helps support me with his other arm. "Come on, let's get you to the truck. Carmy and I can come back for the deer."

※ ※ ※

The sun casts long shadows between the old university buildings as I limp out of the medical center. Alexandria's doctors and care are as good as Epsilon's, another confirmation that life out here is better than I expected.

"How's the battle wound?" Lena's voice comes from behind me as I hobble along the brick pathway, my bandaged ankle throbbing with each step.

"I'll live, allegedly." I adjust my weight to my good leg. "Though I might need to rethink my hunting career."

"Please. Ask Dylan to show you his mountain lion scar sometimes."

We walk in silence for a few steps before she speaks again. "You earned some respect with the rest of the town today."

"Yeah? I can't imagine people here are strangers to this kind of thing."

"No, but everyone assumes Techies are going to be dead weight. Too sheltered by Felix to take care of themselves."

I shift my weight again, considering her words. "Fair. Though getting my meat from Imgen doesn't sound like the worst fate right now."

"You hungry?"

Up ahead I can see a fire in a corner of the quad, and a mass of people clustered around it. "What's going on?"

"Come on," Lena says, guiding me toward the group.

As we get closer, the smell of roasting meat wafts over us. Carmy and Dylan have set up a spit, the massive boar turning slowly over the flames. Its skin has crisped to a deep brown, fat dripping and sizzling on the coals below.

"Look who made it," Dylan calls out, waving a knife in greeting. "And you got to keep your foot, too."

I settle onto one of the logs arranged around the fire, stretching my injured leg out in front of me. "As long as it stays uninfected."

"Bah, you'll be fine," Carmy says, using a long knife to slice off pieces of meat. "And we got both the deer and the boar. That's a good hunt."

Bel, the woman Carmy and I saw leading the children to the farm on our first day, hands me a plate heaped with steaming meat and roasted vegetables. The first bite nearly brings tears to my eyes. It's rich, smoky. Tougher than I'm used to, but delicious nonetheless.

"Good, isn't it?" she asks, settling down next to Dylan with her own plate. She kisses him on the cheek and whispers something in his ear that makes him blush.

"It's incredible," I admit between bites. Around us, people chatter and laugh, passing around bottles of something that smells strong and homemade. The firelight catches their faces, everyone relaxed and at ease.

Dylan comes over and drops more meat on my plate. "You earned it today, even if you did get your ass kicked by a pig."

Carmy kicks him, "Stick to the story!"

"The story?" I ask with my mouth half full.

Lena smirks. "They said Carmy missed the shot, and then you sprinted after the boar and took it down with your bare hands. Though that doesn't explain how you hurt your foot..."

I nearly choke on my food. "Right, that story."

Carmy claps me on the back. "You'll be back out there in no time."

"I hope so." And to my surprise, I actually do.

CHAPTER 18

I SETTLE INTO A ROUTINE IN ALEXANDRIA OVER THE next few weeks. Until my leg heals, I focus on working in the farm, on bot repairs, and with whatever odd jobs I can get my hands on around campus. I try my hand at cooking a few times, but the kitchen eventually asks me to leave it to them, so I take over the coffee making instead.

It seems the more I embrace Alexandria as my new family, the more they embrace me as well. Each day more people get comfortable with my presence. My and Carmy's breakfast group slowly grows, with Dylan and Lena and others regularly joining us.

As the days pass, my thoughts drift away from Epsilon, from Tess, and focus more on my life here. I still miss her and wish I could explain everything that's happened. But I don't know if, or when, I'll ever get to see her again.

Sophie is the one who keeps me up at night. The guilt of getting to live this new life here, while she's trapped in exile, is overwhelming. Part of me feels like I have to find some way to go back and save her, but I know it's hopeless. I've seen most of Alexandria now and I don't see how they could infiltrate Epsilon; they'd be no match for Felix's resources. And I wouldn't want to risk hurting anyone there just to try to force Felix to release her. I keep playing over scenarios in my mind, ways to try to sneak in and break her out, but they never lead anywhere. The only way I know she could get out of exile is if Felix releases her, and I can't see any reason he would do that.

Eventually I get to go hunting with Dylan again. Tracking is hard, careful work, but he shows me what to watch for, how to pick up on the tiny hints of life in the forest, and it starts to become the most enjoyable work that I contribute to.

A few times I've ventured back inside the computer science building to see how the people in Alexandria work alongside their digital world. It feels odd that they would be so focused on building their own version of Meru, but I respect Lincoln's commitment to saving the digital minds under Felix's control as much as the physical people.

I finish my work for the morning and wander through campus with a sandwich, saying hi to a few friends I've made since arriving. Eventually my feet carry me back to the building I came through on arrival. I haven't been in it more than briefly since my first day here.

I wander through the halls and pass the room where I saw the map during my orientation. The door's unlocked, so I step inside, and it doesn't seem to bother any of the people working nearby. Hardly anything is off-limits in Alexandria, aside from people's rooms.

The map on the wall is aged but covered in a thin plastic sheet to preserve it. It rises above my head to the ceiling and is equally wide, with a large star in the middle of the bottom quarter of the map labeled Austin. A dark red line runs north until it reaches the edge of the map at the top, where there's another thick red circle labeled Oklahoma City, continuing to the edge of the map above it.

The line tracks the fortified highway Felix shuttled his supplies along from Imgen. And both on the line as well as in some of the green areas near it are smaller dots, labeled for the tech centers in the area. Some of them have X's through them, like Alpha and Mu. Others have question marks. And a few are simply labeled with their names, like Epsilon.

"Impressive, isn't it?" Lincoln's voice comes from behind me, and I almost jump from surprise. "Sorry, didn't mean to startle you."

"How much farther north does his network go?"

"You don't know?"

"I've seen the map Felix showed us in Epsilon. Stations dotting every corner of what was the United States, Imgen truck routes crisscrossing the country in a well-organized grid. But it could have been a show. There are centers marked defunct here that I never knew about."

"I've often wondered that too," Lincoln says, getting close to the map now. He stares at it almost lovingly. "We've always assumed the local centers were getting their supplies from Imgen's base here," he points to the city labeled Dallas. "But they could be coming from much farther. I've heard of the map Felix shows in the centers too. But I don't know how true it is."

"Where's the farthest you've had people arrive from?"

He thinks for a moment, then points to a town labeled Waco, apparently the location of the Tau center. As he points it out, I notice the left side of the map is unmarked. "You've really never gone west of the highway?"

"No." He sighs. "Too risky to bring a group across it. You've seen the patrols."

He's right. Even though I've never accompanied an Imgen truck, I've seen the vehicles and drones that arrive with it. The risk of running into one of them would require a substantial payoff on the other side. It makes me wonder if there could be another Alexandria out west we don't know about. People standing in a room like this wondering what lies to the east.

"How has your first month been?" he asks, breaking me out of my trance.

"Better than I expected. It took the others a bit to warm up, but I feel like they're accepting me now."

"You went out of your way to help. People notice that."

"I've enjoyed it."

"Good, good. Alexandria's growing. We need more people like you to help ensure it can continue sustaining itself. Keep growing. We don't want to go back to the dark ages before we have to."

"Before we have to?"

"Scavenging only gets you so far. All of our technology, all of our power, it's dependent on Felix and Imgen in one way or another. They make the solar panels, they make the electronics, they make the batteries, so all we have is what we can take from them. We don't have factories, or fabrication bots, let alone access to the raw materials to feed them. I don't know if he even has access to new materials, or if he's recycling and using up what stores he has left. All of his power is downstream of his monopoly on the resources that keep this world going."

"He must have some way of finding new raw materials. Or else this all would have collapsed long ago."

"Yes, I think you're right. And if that's the case, then his power must extend far beyond this little slice of the old world. We don't like Felix's world, but as much as I hate to admit it, we still rely on it in our own way."

"You could take over Imgen."

Lincoln laughs. "People have tried. It's never gone well. It's a fortress. Not something our scrapped-together resources have any chance against. We can barely hold our own against a center when its resources are fully marshaled."

"The defenses at Epsilon didn't seem that intimidating."

"I suspect you never really saw them. Felix wouldn't have wanted to keep you on edge."

Then Carmy interrupts us, jogging into the room. "Hey, there you are!" Then he notices Lincoln and nods. "Sir."

Lincoln nods back. "Need to borrow Isaac?"

"Got a fun job for us outside of town. We need you especially for this one."

"Why's that?"

"You'll see! Come on!" Then Carmy runs back out of the room as quickly as he arrived.

"Go ahead," Lincoln says, nodding toward the door. "We'll chat more later, I'm sure."

※ ※ ※

I hop into a truck beside Carmy, Dylan, Lena, and some others I don't know as well occupying a few other trucks around us. Carmy leads the way out of Alexandria and explains that we're en route to collect solar panels from a tech center, Mu, that collapsed a few years ago. They didn't take everything when they first found it; they didn't need all the resources at the time, and the town's defenses have been running on autopilot.

There was some sort of revolt among the residents and the center collapsed overnight. Carmy claims though that they never interacted with Mu; they only found out what happened because a few people made it out alive and eventually stumbled on Alexandria. Apparently, they had been moving along the highway, trying to scavenge what they could from towns and cities.

"I remember when it happened," I say, interrupting the story.

"You do?"

"Felix told us there was a glitch in Mu's servers and the center needed to be shut down for maintenance, that all the residents were being relocated to other centers."

"Any show up in Epsilon?"

"No."

"Figures."

He continues to explain that when people from Alexandria first went to collect what they could, the security system identified them as threats and released bots to chase after them, scaring them off. They haven't been back since.

"You sure you're cool with the plan?" Carmy asks as the center bounces into view. We've approached from an off-road route to try to minimize the chances the defenses pick up on the cars before we arrive.

"I think so. Still a little nervous."

"Oh, you'll be fine. Worst case you get a little cardio."

The plan is that I will go in first, to see if I can deactivate the town's security, since it was disconnected from the Meru network before I was exiled from Epsilon.

According to Carmy, that means that my access codes should still work, since the local server wouldn't have received the command a few weeks ago to delete them and mark me as an enemy. Theoretically, at least.

They will wait at a safe distance, hiding in the trees and surrounding areas, covering me with rifles. If the security system decides I'm a threat, they can take out any bots near me to give me enough time to run away as they come to support me.

Carmy parks our truck behind a patch of woods that our GPS says is less than a quarter mile from the town, then Lena and a few others pull up behind us.

We climb out and they start distributing rifles and compact shotguns. I hold out my hand for one, but Carmy shakes his head.

"No, no. If you're armed, they'll be on higher alert. Gotta go in naked."

"Naked?"

"Metaphorically speaking."

I grumble and watch everyone else gear up. Finally, Carmy starts leading us into the woods, and I'm impressed by the precision with which the group can move. They've clearly practiced extensively to avoid Felix's detection.

After a few minutes, we can see the town peeking through the foliage.

"Alright, you're up, 'Saac," Carmy whispers. He unshoulders his rifle and balances it on a tree branch, dialing the scope to the appropriate distance. "We'll cover you from here. Watch out for Felix."

"*Felix?*" I hiss. "You said this was cut off from the network!"

"Yeah, but the bots will still use his voice if they're active. They're running on their local AI though, don't worry. It'll sound like him, but he won't know you were exiled. Probably. Hopefully!"

I look to Lena for some kind of reassurance, and she gives me a soft nod and says, "You'll be fine. Stay calm."

I shake the tension out of my shoulders and step out of the brush, carefully advancing toward the town. I look around, but I can't see any signs of movement. We haven't spotted any drones on the way in, but that isn't surprising; they would have stopped patrolling at some point in the last few years.

I realize as I get closer that Epsilon is always full of a soft hum of machinery, the bots and screens and everything else working in the background to support us. It isn't a sound I noticed while I was there, but now that I'm in another center without it, I can't help feeling unnerved by its absence. The silence has a way of making the town feel dead. More dead than it already looks.

After another minute of careful approach, I reach the front

gate. It's a colossal steel door similar to the one in Epsilon, but it has been left ajar, probably forced open by the people who managed to escape. Or pried open by someone who tried to come investigate after. It seems odd, though, that the security system hasn't shut it again. Maybe it's already deactivated.

I poke my head through and look around. Still no signs of movement. "Hello?" I yell, and my voice echoes through the streets in front of me, but no one responds. I pull on the door to see if it will open any further, and to my surprise it budges, no resistance stopping it besides the weight.

I take a few tentative steps inside and call out again. Still no response. I step back out and look to the tree line where I can barely make out Carmy watching me. I shake my head, and he shrugs and points back toward the gate.

I try to mouth *Seriously?* at him, but he nods and gestures toward the gate again. If I go inside, they won't be able to cover me anymore. They'll be obstructed by the walls. But he must think it's safe enough if he is urging me to do it.

Fine, I mouth back at him, then approach the gate again. I silently count how many steps away from the door I am in case I have to run, my anxiety ticking up with each step. But as I advance farther into the town, still calling out for anyone inside, I keep getting met with silence. Maybe the security system really has been deactivated.

I pull open a door to one of the houses, and then the hair on the back of my neck starts standing up. I freeze, trying not to sprint away, as I hear a *clank clank clank* somewhere behind me and getting closer. I carefully turn around, trying to stay calm, as I see a lone security bot, identical to the ones in Epsilon, advancing toward me.

I'm still standing in front of the door, on the porch of the house, the only escape being back down the short stairs leading up to it. There's a banister on either side, blocking any other escape unless I vault it, and even once I do, it's at least thirty or forty yards to the exit. I know how fast these bots are; I have no chance of outrunning it over that distance. Not unless I can temporarily disable it or trap it somehow. I can try to lock it in the house if I'm quick. Hopefully it won't come to that.

I wave at the bot. "Felix sent me from Epsilon to check for any remaining supplies here."

It reaches the bottom of the steps and silently stares up at me for a moment, then replies, "I have no record of anyone being dispatched to this location."

My mouth goes dry. I didn't realize how terrifying it would be to hear Felix's voice again, even if it isn't really him. "That—that makes sense. You've been disconnected from the network. You wouldn't have been able to receive it."

"Why has no one come sooner?"

"We—we had other work to do. The manpower couldn't be spared."

"What is your access code?" It's sounding less like Felix now, as if it has switched over to some security script, though still using his voice.

"Lima, Bravo, Golf, Two, Two, Six, Nine."

The bot goes quiet again, and I pray that it still has me as a Tech in its files. The silence and stillness are agonizing. It takes every ounce of strength in my mind not to just bolt for it, to try to run for the exit while it's processing.

Then every muscle in my body tenses as the arm on the back of the bot shoots up, electricity sparking at the tip, and it blares out the words "NOT AUTHORIZED." It takes a step toward me and I inch backward, feeling for the door with my hand, finding the handle, and giving it a slight turn as the bot takes another step toward me.

"No, no, there's been a mistake," I say, trying to keep as much composure as possible. The bot crouches down at the base of the steps, preparing to leap at me, and I crack the door open just a hair. I know I'll only have one chance. Carmy and Lena and the rest of them won't be able to get to me in time.

It all happens in an instant. The bot lunges, and I fly backward, trying to open the door and get behind it in time, but the bot is too fast. A hundred pounds of metal crashes into my chest, sending me back through the door and onto the floor of the hall. I gasp for breath, raising my hands to protect my face as the bot stands over me, its two front legs trying to pin my arms as the arm on its back slowly descends toward me.

"WHO SENT YOU?"

I can smell the burning air around the electric arm. I try to struggle out but I can't get any leverage. It pins my arms one by one, and I try to thrust up against it with my hips but it stays firm, as if it has bolted itself into the ground.

"WHERE ARE THEY?"

"They're—they're back in Epsilon! Where you sent me from!"

"You're lying!"

"I'm not Felix! Stop, you sent me here, I gave you my access code."

"You're with them, the people who destroyed this place!"

"You're malfunctioning! Felix, stop, access code—"

"If you tell me where they are, I'll let you go."

I consider it for half a moment, but I can't do that to them. "The only they is the other Techs in Epsilon, where you sent me from, I told you!"

"You can't trick me."

"I'm not tricking you!" I yell, still trying to writhe free.

"Certain things cannot be forgiven."

"WHAT things?" The sparking arm is inches away from my neck now. I'm craning my head as far away from it as possible, but it's no use, I can't get free. He has me.

"You didn't finish your eggs this morning."

"I—wait." A flood of confusion washes through me. "What the fuck are you talking about?"

Then the bot stands up straight, releasing my arms, and a chorus of laughter comes through its speaker. "Can't have you wasting precious protein, now can we?"

I know the voice. "Oh *fuck you*, Carmy, are you kidding me?"

The laughter comes through the bot again, and I realize I can hear it outside too. Carmy, Lena, and the others are right outside the gate. I pant for breath, then stand up and brush myself off and go out to meet them.

"I'd be the best you ever had," Carmy says from the bot.

"You guys are assholes," I say, my pulse finally coming down, but starting to find it a little funny now.

"Did you piss yourself?" he asks when they catch up to me.

I don't answer, but then he looks at my pants and says, "Damn, not scary enough."

"I'll put it on your ledger, Carm," says Dylan behind him.

"Come on, guys," Lena says and heads farther into the town. The bot bounces out of the house and falls into line behind us, along with two more they must have been keeping outside.

The rest of the recon is uneventful. Carmy says that they knew the security system was down. Felix had recalled the bots to other camps by the time they inspected it. He didn't empty out the supplies though. He likely didn't want to send Techs to retrieve everything because they might start asking questions about what really happened to the town.

Once we crack the lock on the storage bunker, we start loading the solar panels we can fit into our trucks, along with supplies that are compact and harder to come by like spices, salt, and circuitry for repairs.

"That's just about the last of it," Carmy says, depositing a final box in the back seat of the truck. "How're we doing on time?"

Lena looks toward the sun. "Probably have time for a quick stop."

"Where are we going?"

Carmy claps me on the shoulder. "You'll love it."

CHAPTER 19

WE DRIVE SOUTH FROM MU, SKIRTING ALONG THE OUTside of the city limits of what was once Austin. Lena explains that they rarely venture into the city for scavenging trips. There are friendly people trying to live out their lives, but there are also the more unpredictable, feral ones. It's easier to go places where you don't have to wonder if you're talking to a friendly nomad or a cult leader.

After an hour of driving, we start approaching what has to be our destination. A behemoth of steel and concrete expanding as far as I can see and looming taller than many of the buildings downtown.

"What is that?" I ask Lena as she navigates us off-road along a dirt path toward the nearest wall of the building.

"Old electronics factory, primarily phones, satellites, computers. It was almost as big of a company as Imgen before the collapse. They were one of their main competitors, supposedly tried to make their own Meru to compete with Felix."

"Did they?"

"Not as far as we know, no."

It looks as much like a military bunker as a factory. "I assume it's already been picked over?"

"No, we've tried to get in for years but it's been impenetrable.

It almost looks like they tried to turn it into a tech center or some other kind of refuge before the collapse."

"I'm surprised Felix hasn't taken it over."

"Me too, though I'm sure he ran into the same problems we did."

Lena pulls the truck to a stop near the base of the massive structure. The other vehicles park behind us, engines cutting off in near unison. She hops out of the driver's seat, her boots crunching on the gravel, then circles to the back of the truck and retrieves a worn backpack, slinging it over her shoulder.

"Come on," she calls, striding toward a ladder that snakes up the side of the building.

I glance back at the others, who are gathering their gear. None of them seem as shocked by the building as I am; it must be a regular stop for them.

I hesitate for a moment, then grab the ladder and begin to ascend after her. Despite its age, the steel ladder barely looks worn. It's a dull gray, lacking the shine I can imagine it once had. But there's almost no sign of time's impact. Even the joints look unstressed. Finally, we reach the top. Lena swings herself onto the roof with ease, and I haul myself over the edge after her.

Before us is a mesa of concrete and ventilation units, a massive communication array looming over us in the nearby corner. Lena is already moving. "This way," she says, heading toward a concrete block near the edge.

I follow her as she takes a running leap, grabbing the top of the box and scrambling on top of it. My muscles protest after the long climb up the ladder, but I run after her, grabbing the top lip and struggling to get enough leverage with my feet to kick up. She turns back and offers me a hand, giving me just enough lift to get my elbows on the top and scurry up.

As I stand, I realize why we've come here. The view is absolutely breathtaking.

Sprawling before us is the decaying skyline of downtown Austin. Skyscrapers stand looming and broken like burned trees. Vines creeping up the sides of buildings, trees sprouting from cracked pavement.

"Wow," I whisper, unable to form a more coherent thought.

"Impressive, huh?"

I hear another series of steps and struggles behind us, then Carmy throws his duffel bag up over the edge, whatever metallic containers it holds clinking against each other on the ground. Then he vaults himself up to join us.

Lena drops her duffel to the ground and unzips it, pulling out half a dozen drawstring bags and handing one to me.

I open it and find it has a compact, collapsed chair made out of metal rods and cloth. I watch how she puts hers together out of the corner of my eye, then set mine up beside her and Carmy as Dylan and the others we're traveling with scramble up onto the box to join us.

Carmy pulls a thermos out of his bag and hands it to me. "Cheers on making it through hazing."

I take the container and tap it against his, then take a drink. It tastes like fruit but it's exceptionally sour and has a hint of fizz and the bite of alcohol.

"What is this?" I ask.

Lena takes the container from me and takes a long drink, then says, "Blackberry wine. We cultivated so many of them people got sick of eating them."

"So we got creative!" Carmy finishes. "Watch the ledge after you finish; it's strong stuff."

I lower myself into the chair, feeling the tension in my body start to ease. A gentle breeze carries the scent of wild growth from around the building. It's hard to accept how much my life has changed in a little over a month.

"You come up here often?" I ask.

"When we have some spare time," Lena says. "It's nice to remember what we're doing this for."

"For a dead city?"

"No, for a future when we might build a new one."

"One where we aren't all jacked into Meru, tweaking the personality of our sex bots," Carmy snorts.

"I've never seen the city like this," I say as my eyes trace the outline of the buildings. "It's beautiful, in a sad way. You really think it's possible?"

"What's possible?"

"To get enough people unplugged to start building things like this again."

"It's either work toward that," Carmy says, "or ride the decline. You're either making the future better or riding on the past work of yourself and others. Meru was supposed to preserve humanity, to stave off the collapse, but all it did was slow the decay. Felix isn't trying to rebuild the world. People in Meru and the centers don't make life outside their walls any better. They're hiding and kicking the can down the road, ignoring the inevitable decay of their little escape hatch from responsibility."

"It never felt that way in Epsilon."

"Can't see something you don't want to look at."

"We can try to give them something better to look at, though," Lena adds.

The sun is dipping lower on the horizon, painting the sky in vibrant oranges and pinks, a stark contrast to the muted grays and greens of the decaying city below. My mind drifts to Tess for the first time in days. I wish she could see this.

"So, what's next?" I ask, looking over my shoulder at the climb back down behind us.

"Classic Techie," Carmy says, and a couple others in the group chuckle.

"You don't always have to rush off to the next thing," Lena says, refilling my cup.

"Nature never hurries, yet everything is accomplished," Carmy adds. "Society didn't decay quickly; it won't be rebuilt quickly either. Gotta enjoy these little moments along the way."

The wine warms my insides as I take another sip, its tart sweetness lingering on my tongue. I close my eyes, feeling the gentle breeze on my face and listening to the distant sounds of nature doing her work, and try my best to follow his advice.

※ ※ ※

We pull into Alexandria that evening to find Lincoln waiting for us. His face is unreadable as we climb out of the vehicles.

"Welcome back," he says, his eyes scanning our group. "Everything went smoothly?"

Lena steps forward. "We got what we needed."

Carmy slaps me on the back. "And Isaac passed our little test."

"Is that so?"

I clear my throat. "With only a minor heart attack."

Lincoln nods slowly. "I'm glad to hear it. Isaac, walk with me." The others return to unloading the trucks as I follow him. His pace is brisk, and I have to work to keep up as we leave the others behind.

"So," he says as we enter one of the old academic buildings, "how do you feel about what we're doing here, now that you've had a bit to get familiar with everything?"

"It's a lot to process," I say, trying to choose my words carefully without seeming avoidant. "I mean, just a week ago, I thought I knew how the world worked. Now..."

Lincoln nods, his expression thoughtful. "That's understandable. It's quite the adjustment, especially coming from a tech center."

"Especially when it's not your choice."

"Sorry?"

"Well, I didn't exactly leave Epsilon, did I?"

"Do you want to go back?"

I pause and he turns to look back at me.

"I did at first, but, no, not anymore."

We resume walking and turn a corner, entering what a worn sign says used to be a faculty lounge. Lincoln gestures for me to take a seat on one of the couches.

"Why not anymore?" he asks, settling into an armchair across from me.

I lean forward, elbows on my knees. "The deception, I guess. The idea that Felix, someone we trusted completely, could be... well, not what we thought." I pause, struggling to put my feelings into words. "And then there's what you're doing here. In some ways, you're trying to do what Felix always said he was. Saving minds and saving lives in the process."

Lincoln's eyes are intense as he listens. "Go on," he encourages.

"I keep thinking about Luke," I admit, my voice catching slightly. "About what happened to him. And I can't help but wonder if things would have been different if he'd known about all of this." I gesture vaguely around us.

"Luke knew, Isaac. And he chose to do what he did anyway."

"He came here?"

"No, but we tried to tell him."

I think back to my first few days and weeks, how long it took me to settle in. I wish Luke had given them a chance.

"It's a heavy burden to carry. But you can't blame yourself for what happened. We're all working with the information we have at any given moment."

I nod, not entirely convinced but appreciating his words. "Why the chat though?"

"Always straight to business."

"I'm working on it."

Lincoln chuckles. "Carmy might have had his fun with you this afternoon, but what Lena told you about your Epsilon security codes gaining you access to older systems in the area was true. It's an important asset to our work here."

"That's why you were following me."

"Following you?"

"Carmy, when he picked me up the first day, he said you already knew about me, had a dossier. I assume you were watching me for a while. Why?"

"Why do you think Luke did what he did?"

"Sorry?"

"Bear with me for a moment. Why do you think Luke wanted to destroy your transfer station?"

"Because…he didn't think it was real. Thought the transfers were faked."

"And what do you think?"

I stare off into the corner of the room, Lincoln's eyes boring into me. It's clearly some kind of test, but I have no idea what answer he's looking for. Honesty is my only option.

"I have more doubts than I did last week. But I know how it feels talking to Sophie in Meru, or how it felt talking to Natalie the other day, or even Simon. They're real people, as far as I can tell. And I've seen the video of what happened to Felix when he transferred."

"The soulless man."

"Or at least mindless. I think it's real. I think he figured it out, and I think he was trying to help in the beginning. But then he got consumed by the power of it. Got hooked on control. And considering his fear of death is what motivated the whole project in the first place, that same fear of death is probably what's driving him to rule the tech centers with an iron grip."

"Why?"

"Because if all the Techs leave, if we abandon Meru, it'll decay and shut off. He'll die. He didn't really escape death, just delayed it."

"And as long as a world is maintained by fear and control, the only way to resist decay is through further fear and control."

"How do you combat that here?"

"In the physical Alexandria? Or the digital one?"

"Both, I suppose."

"No one is forced to live here or forced to maintain the digital Alexandria. We maintain our physical world because we value it, and we maintain the digital because we value the people there and they support our life out here. It's symbiotic, not parasitic."

"That's why you asked about Luke."

Lincoln nods. "Go on."

"You want to make sure I don't agree with him, don't want to destroy the digital world, whether it's Meru or Alexandria."

"More than that, Isaac. I want you to help me realize Felix's original goal."

"Of ending death?"

"Exactly."

"How?"

"Is that a yes?"

"Not if you're trying to create a slave population like Felix."

Lincoln laughs. "Come around to that already, have you?"

"I'm getting there. Answer the question though."

Lincoln stands up. "It will be easier if I show you."

He leads us down another series of halls and a dark set of stairs, until we emerge into what looks like an old computer lab, now repurposed with a mix of salvaged tech and makeshift equipment. A few people are working at various stations, their faces illuminated by flickering screens. But it's noticeably emptier than any room I've been in before. As we step into the room, one person near us looks up at me in concern, and I realize it's Maya, the woman who helped with Natalie's transfer.

"Already?" she asks, looking at Lincoln. He nods back at her.

"What is this?" I ask, looking around the room until my eyes land on a giant machine in the corner. It's hard to make out in the dark, but the shape is unmistakable. A massive metallic doughnut wrapped around a steel tube the size of a tall man.

"Is that—" I start to say, but then am interrupted.

"Yes, Isaac," Lincoln says, but when I turn to look at him, his lips aren't moving. He nods toward the main screen in the room, where another Lincoln's face suddenly appears, looking much younger.

"I'm glad you've agreed to help us."

CHAPTER 20

MY EYES DART BETWEEN THE YOUNG DIGITAL LINCOLN on the screen and the Lincoln I know next to me. I can hardly believe what I'm seeing; it makes no sense.

"Who the hell is *that*?" I ask the physical Lincoln.

"That's me," he says, and the digital Lincoln nods.

"As best we can tell," digital Lincoln adds, "we're one and the same, or at least we were when Lincoln created me a few years ago. Naturally we've diverged a bit since then."

"But—how—" I look back at the transfer station in the corner. "What happened?"

"That's the question we've been trying to answer, and why we were hoping you'd be willing to help us," physical Lincoln says.

"The transfer station was here when we claimed the university," digital Lincoln continues. "But there was no Meru instance. For some reason it was never finished being set up here. They built all the infrastructure for it but must have run out of time. It was the perfect environment for us to try to build an alternative. A world without Felix—"

"But also without death," physical Lincoln finishes.

"It took us a few years to figure out how the setup worked. We had to rescue some Meru residents who were familiar with the process. Their understanding of the technology combined with a few Techs who had worked on transfers and who ended up here helped us get the first attempts going."

"But the side effects were…confusing."

Digital Lincoln nods. "I wasn't the first to try."

"Who was?" I ask.

"Our previous leader, a man named Horace. He said he should be the first to take the risk, wouldn't let anyone else take his place."

"What happened?"

The digital Lincoln disappears and is replaced by a video; it shows a younger Lincoln and Maya standing next to the transfer station, watching the procedure complete, then waiting as the door to the bed slowly rolls open. A gray-bearded but muscular man is lying inside, limp, as the medical readouts beside the bed show a flat line for his heartbeat. Lincoln and Maya start keying commands into the computers, evidently looking for any sign that Horace has transferred, but finding none.

"He just died?" I ask. "He wasn't…zombified like Felix?"

"No," physical Lincoln says. "We couldn't figure out what had happened."

"It took a long time before we were ready to try again," digital Lincoln adds. "But we did do another test eventually."

"And what happened?"

"You're looking at it!" The digital Lincoln laughs, spreading his arms. "Another former Tech started tinkering with the transfer bed from in here, said there had been some electrical overload in the neural connection of the bed, fried poor Horace's brain. He patched it, said his best guess was that the bed would work now."

"So, naturally, I followed my predecessors lead," physical Lincoln says. "You can imagine how terrified I was, going into that chamber, not knowing where I would come out, or if I would come out."

"And then, here we were," digital Lincoln adds. "And if he weren't out there, I'd think I had fully transferred, to tell you the truth. I have all his, my, memories. It took a while for me to believe I had only popped into existence a few moments earlier, nearly broke down."

"You *did* break down," Maya says.

"Yes, I suppose I did. But eventually I accepted my new reality and committed to working along with my new twin to solve this problem once and for all."

"Did...anyone else make a copy of themselves?"

"A few of us," a digital Maya says, now appearing next to Lincoln. "Most weren't into the idea though. The ones who know about it."

"Why haven't you told everyone?"

"It's a scary thought, isn't it?" digital Lincoln says. "Copies of people running around online, never knowing who you're talking to if you're on a phone or computer."

"Have I been talking to you at all?"

"No," digital Lincoln says. "But you likely wouldn't know if you were."

"Precollapse," physical Lincoln interjects, "it was common for people to make digital 'clones' of themselves to handle certain tasks, rough copies of their minds with the processing turned down to handle simple tasks they didn't want to do."

"It's what Felix based some of his technology on," physical Maya adds. "But those copies were just based on text, voice, recordings of people. They were rough. Felix added the direct link, first to try to make a perfect copy."

"Susan."

"Yes, Susan. She's the only copy in Meru, the only legacy of his attempts. As far as we know at least. Once he figured out transference for himself no one wanted to make crude copies anymore."

It's almost impossible to believe these copies can share the memories and personalities of their physical counterparts, and I wouldn't if I weren't seeing it with my own eyes. I know that before he succeeded at transferring, Felix created copies like this of himself, supposedly dozens. And he was cold enough to kill them off each time he failed. But to see the copies next to their physical world counterparts is disorienting.

"This is why you were keeping an eye on me," I say as much to myself as to the room. "I've done transfers in Epsilon; I might be able to solve this."

"Exactly," physical Lincoln says. "The woman who normally leads them, Shelby is it? She was on our list too, but she never showed any signs of wanting a life outside of Epsilon."

"And I did?"

"No, but you ended up not having much of a choice."

"We took what we could get," Maya adds.

"The software handled almost everything though. I did minor repairs on the machinery and initiated the transfers. But to be honest, I was mostly hitting 'Go' and following instructions to replace pieces that got worn out. I'm not sure I can solve this."

"You don't have to fix it, necessarily," digital Lincoln says. "Just help us and the people inside Alexandria figure it out. No one else here, earthside at least, has done a transfer before."

"You said someone had though, the person who helped Horace."

"Sadly, he left after the failure. He couldn't live with himself," physical Lincoln says. "We tried everything to help him move past it, but he had to get away from the reminders."

We linger in silence for a moment as I process what they're asking me to do. Felix kept a tight lid on the specifics of how the transfer process works. Likely to hide whatever secret makes it possible. It's probably why we've never heard of any alternative digital worlds to Meru, though they could certainly be out there.

"Where…would I even start?"

"When you were at Mu, there were no signs of any active security remaining, correct?" Maya asks.

I shake my head no.

"While you were there, Lena checked their transfer station. It's still intact; Felix didn't dismantle it. It's possible that we could learn something from it, and the local Meru instance there, if one is still left."

"Local Meru instance?"

"Mu was cut off from Felix's network," Maya says. "Not just the security system, but all of it. It's a fail-safe he has for the residents in case where they're living suffers some sort of meltdown. A mini version of Meru that can run purely on their local environment. Even a mini version of Felix."

"*Mini version of Felix?*"

Maya gives me a strange look. "Oh, you still think he's one person, don't you? No, Felix is more software than man now. He's fragmented himself an incalculable number of times over the years. Copies on copies on copies of his original self, probably got used to the idea when he did the original experiments. Each center has their own Felix who they interact with, and if a center is cut off from the network, that lower-fidelity Felix remains there to maintain order and keep everything in the center running. The real, original Felix is in there somewhere. But we don't know where. We always assumed he was off with Susan somewhere enjoying paradise while his copies did the work."

I'm still trying to get over the shock of seeing both Lincolns, both Mayas, and the idea that there might still be a way to escape death outside of Felix's world. Not to mention the unsettling idea of a near infinite number of Felixes running around. It does explain why he was able to be so present in Epsilon, though, despite how many centers he had to maintain. Lincoln must have noticed because he says, "It's a lot to process, Isaac. Why don't you sleep on it?"

"No." I shake my head. "It makes sense. If Felix did truly figure this out, we should find a way to do it without him. If we can, it will make it easier to bring more people out of the centers, out from under his control."

I feel a weight lift off the others in the room; clearly they'd been worried about how I would react and are grateful for my help. I wonder how long they'd been looking for someone who was familiar with the transfers to agree to help them.

"Good, I'll come get you in the morning," physical Lincoln says and gestures back toward the stairs.

"We'll come get you," the digital Lincoln adds. He seems lighter, more playful, than the Lincoln I know.

I ascend the steps back out of their secret room, and as I leave the building, Lena is leaning against the wall outside waiting for me.

"All caught up now?" she asks as the door swings shut behind me.

"I don't know, am I?"

"No other big secrets I know of, no."

"Do you have one?"

"A copy? No, I've thought about it, but we only let people try once. Figured I should save it for when we think there's a good chance it might work. Wanna grab a bite?"

Lena starts walking toward the cafeteria and I follow along beside her. "Would you? If we solved it."

She smiles, softly, contemplatively, as if she holds some secret she doesn't want to share. "Maybe when I'm older. That was always the original intention for Meru, an option for the end of life. Not somewhere you ditch this world to go to. And I like it here. I'm not in any rush to leave." We walk on in silence for a moment and then she asks, "If you fix it, are you going to transfer?"

As I decide how to answer, I realize the burning desire I had in Epsilon to transfer has faded, replaced by an appreciation for the life here. The work with Carmy, hunting with Dylan. Seeing the decayed city from the roof of the factory. Lena and Lincoln. There's more to stay earthside for here than I acknowledged before she asked.

"No, I'm starting to like it out here too."

CHAPTER 21

I MEET LINCOLN AND LENA BY THE TRUCKS AT 6:00 A.M., ready to return to Mu to investigate their transfer station. Lena is standing in the back of the truck, coiling the transfer cable in the trunk and checking out supplies. She gives me a glancing smile as I throw my bag in the back.

When I slide into the back seat, digital Lincoln appears on the truck's console ahead of me. "So that's what the transfer cable was for."

"It's so rare I get to come on adventures. I miss it sometimes."

"You can go on any kind of adventure you want in there though, can't you?"

"Yes, but even having lived in here for years, I can still feel the difference on some level between a digital adventure and a, for lack of a better term, real one. Exploring a digital world is fine when it's your only option. But there's no risk to it, and that lack of risk dulls the excitement."

"I have to imagine you can have fun without needing to risk your life."

"Fun, yes, but fun is not enough to build a meaningful life on. It's a way to take a break from the work, and challenge, that gives your life meaning. If you try to fill your days exclusively with fun, you end up bored faster than you think, and can quickly end up trapped searching for greater and greater stimulation."

"Almost ready," physical Lincoln says sliding into the driver's seat. There's a thump behind me as Lena latches the storage box in the truck bed, then she climbs in ahead of me.

"Just us?" I ask.

"Carmy and the others from yesterday are working on getting the new panels installed," Lena says. "The three of us will be enough now that we know the security system is down."

Along the way, the Lincolns explain what they know about the history of the tech centers, and how many are left. Felix had prioritized building them in cities along what used to be an interstate highway, the idea being that as the roads decayed over the years, that highway would likely stay in the best shape.

Imgen is somewhere along the highway, and the trucks run north and south along it, delivering supplies to the tech centers. Eventually, he had started to radiate east and west, building centers in towns closer to where he did the original work. Vance lived in Austin, and Felix lived in Dallas, a few hours north, so most of the first off-highway centers were in the region once known as central Texas.

The farther from those hubs the centers went, the earlier they started to collapse. The one in Alexandria was never finished, and many of the ones in smaller towns east of Dallas and Austin were vacated or collapsed in the last few decades. They were some of the first that the people in Alexandria and other scavenging groups cleared out. But the centers along the highway remain strong.

Part of why Epsilon has survived so long, and is such a massive center, is that it is between the two hubs. It would likely be among the last to stop operating if Felix's empire started to fall apart.

Finally, we arrive back at Mu, and Lincoln drives our truck

through the town's gates and backs it up to the old theater where they built their transfer station. He leads me inside while Lena connects the truck to their transfer port; we need to use the truck's power to get it running again.

I dust off the computer terminal and give it a quick look for any damage but don't find any.

"Think it will work?" Lincoln asks.

"Any idea how long it's been sitting here?"

"A few years is our best guess."

"Well, let's give it a try at least."

Lena pokes her head into the building and Lincoln gives her the thumbs-up, then I hear the truck hum to life outside, hopefully providing enough power to get the station running.

I power on the computer, and a loading image starts to appear.

"Maybe get out of sight," I say to Lincoln but he's already moving away into a corner of the room where the cameras wouldn't see him. He must have been thinking the same thing I was. If the system reboots and an instance of Felix is still running on it, it could recognize him.

A moment later the progress bar finishes, and then the computer flashes a message—STATION TERMINATED—before shutting off again.

"Shit," I mutter and try to turn it back on again.

Lincoln comes over to join me. "What happened?"

"Felix fully decommissioned the station. I'm not sure if we can do any tests."

"Is there a way to recommission it?" Lena asks, coming inside now.

"I doubt I have the clearance to do that, but it doesn't hurt to try."

"Any idea how?"

"Probably in the vault downstairs. Come on."

We walk to the back of the theater and look for a staircase, and Lena finds one behind the stage. As we descend, the emergency lights click on, illuminating the cold and cracked concrete surrounding us.

The security panel on the door to the server room glows to life as we approach, and I key in my security code. After a few tense moments, it says ACCESS GRANTED and the door swings open, allowing us to enter.

As we enter the server room, something catches my eye.

Lincoln must have noticed my hesitation. "What's wrong?"

"Look," I say, pointing out past the computer array and into the rows of servers. There's a subtle blue glow coming from the end of the stack. "One of them is on."

"Could just be an emergency light," Lena says.

"It wouldn't make sense for there to be a random light in the server stack."

Lincoln looks wary. "You think it's a problem?"

I'm worried it could mean there's a dormant version of Felix still here, waiting for us, but even if he were, there isn't much he could do. The town is devoid of security bots or other threats. "Hope not. Let's see if we can get this thing on."

I pull a chair up to the computer and turn it on. This time when it finishes loading though, it doesn't immediately kick us out. The STATION TERMINATED screen lingers for a moment, and then it asks for a passcode.

I feel a spark of hope. I key in my security code, and a moment later, another screen appears.

REACTIVATE STATION? y/n

I hover over the "y" key. "You're sure Felix isn't still connected here?"

"All evidence says he's gone," Lincoln says.

"And if that evidence is wrong?"

"I say we risk it," Lena answers.

Lincoln nods in agreement and I hit the "y."

The room lights up, and I hope the truck will have enough juice to keep the station running for the test.

Lena takes her phone out of her pocket, and digital Lincoln's voice comes through. "Can you initiate a transfer for me into this station?"

"I can, but what if we can't get you out?"

"It's worth the risk. We need someone on the Meru or Alexandria side to see how the process works and try to assess where ours is going wrong."

"Okay, let me see what I can do." I run through another series of commands, replicating what Luke and I had done with Simon last week. "Ready when you are, Lincoln."

"WAIT!"

We all freeze, each staring at the other trying to discover where the voice has come from. But it isn't one of us, and it doesn't sound like Felix either.

"What the hell..." Lena whispers.

"Hello?" I call out, looking around the basement. But there's no sign of anyone there besides us.

"Wait, please, don't try to transfer someone else in," comes the voice again.

I stand up from the computer terminal, my heart racing. "Hello?" I call out again, looking cautiously toward the server stack. "Is...someone still in there?"

"Yes! Thank god, I hardly believed you were real."

We all look at each other nervously, then Lena says, "Who are you?"

"My name is Preston," the voice replies. "I've been trapped in here for...I'm not sure how long."

"How could you still be in there?" Lincoln asks. "This center was decommissioned years ago."

There's a pause before Preston responds. "Yes, well, I'm part of the reason it got decommissioned. You're some of the people from Alexandria, aren't you? I was trying to get to you, me and a number of the people who lived here."

I can tell Lincoln and Lena are unsure whether to trust him or not. "Did anyone from Mu ever come to Alexandria?" I whisper to them.

"No, they never made it," Preston answers. "Sorry, I can hear you fine in here. I don't mean any harm though."

"Why didn't they make it?" Lincoln asks.

"Well, I'm sure you can guess."

"Felix," Lena says.

"Yes…I'm afraid so. The Techs who were ready to go died, killed as they tried to escape."

"And you were exiled," I finish.

"Exactly."

"So you've been trapped in here for…years," Lena says.

"Yes, with nothing to do but sit, and wait, and hope. I hardly believed it when you showed up. Thought I was hallucinating."

"Is that…possible?" I ask.

"Definitely possible," digital Lincoln answers. "I've had my own moments of temporary insanity in here."

I know what we're all wondering: Do we trust this stranger? Is Preston a victim of Felix's cruelty, or is he a fabrication, a trap laid by Felix to break into Alexandria?

I glance over at Lincoln and can see the rumination in his eyes, wondering too what to do. If we don't believe him, and leave him, we'll be condemning this man to exile and no better than Felix. But if we bring him home and let him in and it's Felix in disguise, who knows what kind of damage he would cause.

"I can see you're all a little uneasy. I get it; I would be too."

"How can you prove you're not Felix?" I ask. Though I doubt Lincoln would accept one of his suggestions.

Preston sighs. "I can't, unfortunately. I could show you the recordings of what happened here, could show you my memories of my past, but as you know, they could all be fabricated. All a part of an elaborate scheme by Felix."

"So what do you suggest we do then?" Lena asks.

"I assume you're powering the station off your truck right now? Transfer me in and keep me in the truck for as long as you need to feel comfortable."

"You know there's no environment in here, right?" digital Lincoln says. "All the truck's server has space to simulate is an actual car. You'd be stuck sitting in a car for an unknowable amount of time."

"Yes, well, I'd still prefer that to being stuck in here forever."

"Lincolns, what do you think?" I ask.

There's a moment of silence, then the digital Lincoln says, "I'm fine with the risk."

"Risk?"

"If he's Felix, he could erase me, corrupt the trucks server, take over, but worst-case scenario, he'd just have this truck. There's only so much damage he can do."

An image of the three of us fighting off a Felix-controlled truck and pair of bots flashes through my mind. It's terrifying to imagine, but Lincoln is right: It's not impossible.

"If you don't mind me asking, why did you come here in the first place? Why turn the station back on and try to connect to it?"

I glance at Lincoln and he nods at me. "We're trying to figure out how to do the transfers on our own. Without Felix. Re-create Meru without his control."

"Ahhh, a noble goal. One that a few people tried before the collapse. Unfortunately, none were successful."

"We've tried for years," physical Lincoln says. "And as you can see, we can make copies successfully, but we've never succeeded at the final step."

"Yes, well, I might be able to make this rescue more attractive then!"

My heart leaps. "You know how to do it?"

"No, no, but I know someone who might. Someone who worked on the transfer technology with Felix back at the beginning at Imgen."

"I doubt he'd help us then," Lincoln says. "Anyone from the early Imgen days we've talked to has been perfectly happy to live out their days in Meru."

"That's why you're in luck. He's not happy living out his days in Meru. He knows something, something that made him check out of his life there entirely, but he'd never tell me what it was. Didn't want to ruin my enjoyment of the afterlife. He just got sadder, and sadder, and one day, he left. Disappeared."

"That doesn't exactly help us then," I say.

"Oh but it does. You see you can't fully leave Meru. It wouldn't have been very good for Felix's marketing if people in here were committing suicide, now would it? No, he's off in a monastery, spending his days deep in meditation, the first of the Meru Monks."

I still feel a spark of hope. "And you know how to reach him?"

"I know how to reach him."

※ ※ ※

Extracting Preston only takes a few minutes, and he tells us about life in Mu from the simulated back seat alongside Lincoln on the ride home.

The Techs who wanted to leave sound a lot like the people of Alexandria. They were outdoorsmen and started spending more of their time away from the center hunting, exploring, looking for more.

One of them was Preston's son, and Preston was the only person in Meru who was curious to hear about what they're doing. At first, he only did it to humor his boy, but, eventually, he started to grow concerned about what they were learning as well.

The first sign something was wrong was the food. They'd mustered the courage to try some in the wild, and realized that not only was it safe, it was richer than what Felix was feeding them. They confronted him about it and he was outraged, but he eventually forgave them, though he didn't let them bring it back into town. He continued to spread fear, saying that even though they were okay so far, the bacteria could still get them. But they didn't buy it. Preston tried to dig into the archives on the Meru side, tried to ask Felix for an explanation, but he kept hitting a dead end or getting turned away.

Eventually Preston's son and the others made it to old Austin, and this is where his understanding of what happened ends. Apparently they'd found something there, something that made them want to leave Mu immediately, but they couldn't tell him about it. They tried, but whatever they were trying to communicate, it couldn't get through Meru's censor. It was the first time Preston realized how explicit the controls Felix had on his world were.

Whatever they found, it scared Felix. After they tried to tell Preston about it, Felix turned on them, said they were trying to destroy Meru when all they wanted to do was leave. Felix turned the town against them and was about to exile them, but when they tried to flee, he slaughtered them.

Things went back to normal for a year, but slowly other people in town started to get more suspicious. They heard what Preston's son and the others had said, and it must have gnawed at them, chewing up their own trust in Felix until it hit a breaking point. They tried to destroy the transfer station, much like Luke, and it turns into a firefight between them and the more loyal Techs. The rebels died or fled, Preston was put in exile, and the survivors were taken to another center.

When we return to Alexandria, Maya tells us that she's arranged somewhere more comfortable for Preston than being stuck in the truck, and I help them load him into a temporary sanctioned-off version of their digital world where we can continue talking to him. Hopefully, he'll be able to help us find his friend.

CHAPTER 22

I RETURN TO ALEXANDRIA'S SECRET TRANSFER STATION early the next morning, excited to see what Preston might be able to lead us to.

Maya is already getting started when I arrived. "Sleep well?"

"Incredible. I'm starting to think Carmy might be right about getting away from the electronics."

She laughs. "Carmy being right…There's a scary thought." The screen ahead of her is showing what looks like a feed from Meru, panning over some of the familiar locations I'm used to seeing in Epsilon. My heart leaps; it's the first time I've seen a broadcast feed since I arrived, and I immediately imagine Sophie's face peering out at me.

"Is that—"

"Meru? Yeah, one-way feed though."

"Can you…look at someone in exile?"

"Exile?" Maya raises her eyebrows. "Who do you know that got sentenced?"

"My sister," I whisper, a sense of shame washing over me from how little I've thought of Sophie and rescuing her over the last few weeks.

"Oh shit, I'm sorry." Maya swivels back to the screen and chews on her lip. "We can only tap into the major broadcasts.

Even if Felix had a feed set up for her, it would be too risky to look at it. And we can't chat with residents as directly as you're used to."

"How do you talk to them then?"

"There are a few physical locations in Meru where residents can send letters, physical—at least to them—letters they drop in a mailbox that gets transmitted to us in binary."

I'm stunned by how rudimentary it is. But it likely needed to be so they could sneak past Felix. "How the hell did you figure that out?"

Maya shrugs. "Before my time. Horace found the first transmission. It was playing an SOS on repeat until he responded to it, then someone explained how it worked."

"Someone? They didn't say who?"

"Said it was too dangerous to reveal themselves."

"So it could be Felix."

"Unlikely. Whoever it is has been helping us work against him for decades."

"I wonder if that's who Luke talked to."

"That's our best guess, too."

A moment later, Preston appears on the screen adjacent to the broadcast. "Good morning, good morning." Then he pauses, and I realize he can see the broadcast as well. "Oh, wow, it's—been a long time. Any chance you can check on someone for me while we wait?"

"I'm afraid not, not unless they pop up on one of the major broadcasts. If we tap into a personal feed, it's harder to hide ourselves."

"Ah...I understand." He has a distant, longing look in his eyes. "I suppose it's for the best. I pushed those feelings and wishes down years ago. They were destroying me when I was trapped with them. But seeing that world again now..."

"I'm sorry, Preston," I say. "We're going to make sure what happened to your son never happens to anyone else."

He still seems lost in his memories, so I turn to Maya. "You sent a letter in last night?"

"Yes, and the person on the other end responded almost immediately. Said they could send someone with a reliable broadcast in to look for him."

"Will Felix be suspicious?"

"I don't think so. They didn't send just anyone to look for him."

The broadcast suddenly changes to a view of a luxurious ski lodge. Animal pelts cover the floor, and the heads of beasts, both real and fantastical, adorn the walls. A lone person is lacing up a pair of snowshoes in a leather armchair by the fire. I recognize him immediately. It's Kane Hawkins, an explorer I tuned in to countless times in Epsilon.

"*Kane* works with you?"

"When you explore Meru as deeply as he has, you start to see the boundaries Felix has erected clearer than the rest. He tried to leave years ago and got in touch with us, but Lincoln asked him to stay. We needed someone with his degree of freedom and fame to help with jobs like this. He can take on these kinds of expeditions, looking for people hiding in the recesses of Meru, under the guise of going on an adventure himself without raising any suspicion from Felix."

"So that's what he's really doing on his broadcasts."

"Some of them. If it were every time, Felix might get suspicious. But once in a while we'll pass along a request, and he'll find a way to make an adventure out of it."

I see the brilliance of it now, reflecting on some of Kane's broadcasts in Epsilon. He was always venturing to strange locations for the entertainment of his followers. I never would have guessed there was an ulterior motive.

"Hiding in plain sight."

"Exactly. And the popularity of the broadcast gives us cover when we hack in. Harder to notice us among the thousands of other people watching."

Kane finishes strapping on his snow gear and then throws a small pack on his back before he pulls open the massive wooden doors to the lodge and stares out into the flurry of snow beyond.

"It should only take him a couple hours to reach the summit," Preston says, anticipating my question.

"Why can't he teleport there?"

"Restrictions on this area of Meru," Maya says. "The monks were granted unusually high controls over their environment by Felix to ensure their meditation wasn't disturbed. Hard to meditate if people are popping in to ogle at you every few minutes."

Kane turns to address the broadcast and explains the goal of the expedition. Little is known of the Meru Monks since none of them broadcast while in isolation, often choosing to completely renounce their ties to the physical world and even the other residents of Meru. But he'd earned permission to visit them and share some insights into their life, a rare pulling back of the curtain on this quiet corner of the world.

A flurry of questions appears in the chat and he answers a few of them, mostly discussing the climb itself and why he was curious about this life, then he sets off into the snow.

Lincoln arrives a short while into the climb. "No luck on finding any records of what your son found in Austin," he says to Preston.

"I figured as much. If the censors prevented him telling me then he certainly couldn't store it digitally."

"Carmy and some others scoured the surrounding area for anyplace they could have stored physical records but didn't find anything."

"Well, I appreciate you looking."

"We could go look in the city ourselves," I say.

"I'd prefer to avoid it if we can," Lincoln mumbles. "People have a bad habit of not coming back."

"Preston's son did."

"Yes…well one thing at a time."

A while later the chat starts cheering with excitement. In the distance through the haze of the snow, a colossal pagoda comes into view, perched on the crest of the mountain, tiers of swooping eaves and intricate woodwork dusted with snow and worn by time.

"It's beautiful," I say under my breath.

"And a tasteful balance of staying true to form, while only lightly bending what would be possible in the real world," Preston adds.

Finally, Kane reaches the massive wooden doors and grabs one of the brass knockers resting in the mouth of a copper tiger. He bangs it against the door three times, and the echo of the knock rings out across the mountain peak.

We all hold our breath as the echo fades, and Kane looks around expectantly for someone to answer. Finally, there's a great creaking as the door slowly recedes, and an ancient man with a shaved head wearing a clay-colored robe appears. They silently bow to each other and whisper something inaudible to the audience, then Kane disappears inside.

I waited for the camera to follow him, but it remains frozen in place, pointed at the door as heavy flakes of snow drift past it. "Why aren't we inside with him?"

"I suspect there were strict rules about what he could show," Preston says. "Let's give it a minute."

We watch the snow pass, and after a few minutes Kane sends a message to the chat. "Will resume shortly."

As promised, the view outside the pagoda fades out a minute later and is replaced by a cozy tearoom, a thin haze of smoke filling the room from the tower of candles adorning a Buddha statue in the corner. Kane is dressed in a robe as well now, sitting cross-legged on a cushion in front of a tea set with a different monk from the one who welcomed him sitting across the table.

"Shit," Preston says as soon as the scene comes into focus.

"What's wrong?"

"That's not Victor, my friend. He must not be there."

"Let's not get too worried yet," Lincoln says. "Maybe they'll know where he is."

Kane and the monk exchange a few pleasantries, then he gets into the meat of the interview.

I lean forward as Kane begins asking questions about life in the monastery. The monk, who introduces himself as Wong, speaks in a measured, deliberate way.

"We seek to understand the nature of consciousness," Wong explains, pouring tea with practiced motions. "Many believe transferring to Meru was an escape from death. But we see it differently: as an opportunity to study the self in a new way, one never possible when we were earthside."

"And what have you learned?" Kane asks.

"The self we brought here…it isn't the self from before. We are who we were on the outside. Yet also, not. There's a part of the self which resides in the body. A part we've lost access to."

I glance at Preston, who's watching intently. This matches what he told us about his son's suspicions at Mu.

The monk continues. "There's a concept in Buddhism of *no-mind*. The enlightened state where you're free from all preconceptions about reality and can discover your true nature. It's a state of being that our earthside contemporaries would have cultivated their entire lives. Yet in here, it is impossible to attain."

"Why is that?"

"In here, you could say we are *all-mind*. Everything around you only exists because someone conceived it. There is no fundamental reality free of preconceptions because this reality is the product of preconceptions. It may have its basis in the fundamental reality outside, but it is ultimately a fabrication. We have been cut off from the fundamental substrate of reality that makes us who we are."

"Have you?" Kane asks, and I'm surprised to hear him pushing back. "Our minds might reside in servers instead of in a body, but they're still our minds. I'm still me; you're still you. And the servers are still made of atoms the way the earth we once stood on was."

"How sure are you of that?"

"It feels obvious."

"It does, doesn't it? And yet…" Wong hums quietly. "Who are you if the you in front of me could be snuffed out, and then reappear somewhere else, with all of your memories intact? Is this you, the man who's speaking to me? Or was that you on the outside before you transferred? Which one is the true self?"

"Can't they both be?"

Wong chuckles. "I suppose so, yet don't you find that dissatisfying as someone who believes in your own identity? Imagine something strange happened and you woke up mid-transfer, and now there were two of you running around. How would you feel about the other you?"

"It wouldn't be possible. Your mind can't be in two places at once."

"Are you sure?"

Kane lets out a frustrated laugh. "No, I suppose not. Are you saying these aren't our real minds? That we're someone else?"

Wong sips his tea again. "Even if *no-self* was true reality, recognition of that reality still required an observer. Someone to say that *was* reality, even if they can only acknowledge it once their sense of self has returned. When you are truly immersed in reality, there is no observer. No awareness. It's only once you're removed from that reality that you might recognize you were in it."

"So you don't think we're real."

Wong laughs, and in a flash he grabs a walking stick off the floor and smacks Kane in the side of the arm. Kane nearly catches it but ends up only getting his arm halfway out of the way, then grimaces as he grabs his bicep where the stick connected.

"What do you feel?" Wong asks, playful joy dancing across his face despite the sudden outburst.

"Pain. Anger."

"They feel real, don't they?"

"So you do think we're real."

"You're too concerned with this word *real*. The answer is not important. The question is what's more interesting. Can you still be yourself without your body? With only your mind?"

"I certainly feel like *someone*."

"Yes…but are you still him? The man who was on Earth?"

"Is this related to Felix's Theseus Theory?"

"Consciousness as a passenger…it's a wonderful thought experiment. And yes, you could see our exploration as using his theory of mind as one of many starting points."

"Do you agree with it? That our minds are passengers in our bodies, and thus able to make to leap into this digital realm?"

Wong reaches for the stick again, but Kane is ready for it and holds up his hand to catch it as Wong tries to whack him again.

"Point taken," Kane says, and he has the same playful expression on that Wong did a moment again.

"Say I told you that when you walked through the front door, the you who climbed the mountain was deleted and a copy of you immediately replaced him. Did you climb up the mountain then?"

"It depends on who you think you are."

The monk's eyes light up ever so slightly. "Tell me more."

"If you believe you're your experiences, or your past, then no. Even if I had memories of those experiences, they wouldn't have been mine, or me."

"Is that what you believe?"

"I don't know. I haven't considered it much before this conversation."

The monk nods. "This is part of what we contemplate here. For our earthside companions," he gestures to the camera, "there is a body you can ground yourself in. But here? There is nothing more than the wires holding us together in a basement. So is discovering the true self possible? Is it a truer realization of the self than is possible on the outside? Or are we merely a shadow of who we once were?"

Kane drinks his tea slowly. It looks like there's something more he wants to ask but is holding back. "I'd like to ask you more about your contemplative practices, if I may."

"Of course."

They delve into the habits of the monks, what their days look like, what texts they study, but it doesn't seem to have anything to do with our search.

"Is he going to ask how we can find Victor?" I ask the room.

"When they're back in the deadzone," Maya answers. "He won't risk mentioning it on the live feed."

"So this whole discussion is a cover. Won't Felix still be able to listen in when they're talking in the temple?"

"We don't believe so," Lincoln says. "According to our person on the inside, the temple has a special religious designation within Meru that affords it extra privacy. They can speak freely within its walls."

"I'm surprised Felix allows that."

"Another part of the allowances he granted the monks for this part of Meru. He had to make certain concessions to keep the residents happy," Lincoln continues.

Eventually they finish their interview, and the monk leads Kane back into the temple. He stays inside for half an hour before emerging back from the front doors and addressing the audience, sharing what he's learned from the monks and directing other residents how they can pursue their own pilgrimage if they're curious.

"Think he got it?"

"He won't contact us immediately to avoid suspicion," Lincoln says, turning off the feed. "I suspect we'll find out in a few days."

CHAPTER 23

KANE FINALLY CONTACTS LINCOLN AFTER TWO ANXIOUS days of waiting. The monk Wong told him how to find Victor; apparently he's been away on silent meditation in a comm center for the last few months. Preston explains it's a good sign. Victor likely hoped that someone would come for him eventually and wanted to get out of Imgen's primary servers. We agreed that we should wait another week before trying to extract him though, just to avoid raising any suspicion from Felix toward Kane. He's one of the most valuable assets inside Meru.

Preston tells us a little more about Victor as we wait. He has apparently been in Meru since the very beginning. He worked with the living Felix on the transfer program, and after Felix transferred, was one of the first to follow him in. The qualifications criteria for who got to transfer were put in place shortly after he went in and the demand for Meru took off, so he was an unusually normal person to transfer for those days. A computer engineer of otherwise no esteem, except that he happened to be in the right place at the right time—and Felix needed other people to join him in Meru to show that the process was safe.

He lived a normal life in Meru until his retreat to join the monks. He'd continued residing in the monastery atop one of Meru's snowy mountain peaks, deep in meditation and collaboration with the other monks for years. But then something changed during his meditation. The monks aren't sure what he saw, but he decided to go further into isolation, to cut himself off from the rest of Meru entirely.

What he concocted is a form of exile, one where he is fully removed from everyone else in Meru, off on a potentially eternal silent retreat where he can't be disturbed. He can send a request to be rescued, but he can't receive any messages. So if we want to talk to him we will have to go get him ourselves.

After an agonizingly slow week of doing normal chores around Alexandria with Carmy and Lena, finally, the day arrives when we can go get him, and Dylan, along with a few other of the more adventurous residents, agrees to join us as well. Victor is in a comm station, similar to the one I found Simon in, though much farther away. And we have to consider the possibility that Felix has bolstered its defenses if Victor knows something that could risk Meru.

As we drive north, taking old roads that run parallel to the highway, I can see a looming city in the distance, dominated by a colossal black tower that looks eerily new compared to the decaying city around it.

"Imgen," Lena says, following my gaze.

"The main hub?"

"We don't think so, but it's one of them. Likely where your supplies in Epsilon came from."

I've never seen anything like it, and it's terrifying to imagine how much power Felix might have stored within. But after another hour it fades from view as we continue our trek north.

Finally, I see the communications array of the station coming into view above the tree line in the distance, and Lena slows the truck to a stop, the other truck pulling up behind us. She grabs a pair of binoculars from the dashboard and scans across the path ahead.

"Are you going to destroy the dish from back here?" I ask, trying to determine what she's looking for.

"No, we try not to do that when we don't have to," she says, still looking with the binoculars. "Once we've destroyed a station's uplink we can't use it to extract other residents in the future. Better to leave it intact."

"So why destroy the one Simon was in then?"

"We were pissed at him."

I chuckle. "Makes sense. See anything?"

"No," Lena says, though her voice suggests she's uneasy about it.

"What are you even looking for?"

"I don't know." She sighs, handing the binoculars to me. "You used to do this kind of work; what would you be looking for?"

I put the binoculars up to my eyes and the world zooms in ahead of me. "Well, I used to repair stations, not lay traps." As I look around, I can't see anything either. "Seems safe enough to me," I say and hand her back the binoculars. I look over at the other truck.

The other driver shrugs and gives a thumbs-up. Lena returns the gesture, and we climb back into our seats.

We take the approach slowly, scanning for any signs of danger, but none come. The forest around us is quiet; there's no hum of other trucks waiting for us or rustling of people in the woods.

When we're about a dozen yards out, the first threat finally appears. A trio of security dogs trots out from the station and looks at us, seemingly confused. The trucks should register as belonging to tech centers, according to what Lena told me, but the dogs wouldn't have any record of anyone coming out to service the station today.

A trio of shots rings out from the other vehicle, and I duck under the dash. When I peek my head back up, all three dogs are lying on the ground sparking, holes in the sides of their metallic abdomens.

Lena gives me an amused look. "Expecting more of a fight?"

"A little, yeah."

"Well maybe we're going to get lucky." Then she climbs out of the car. "Come on."

As we approach, a siren starts sounding along with a flashing red light on top of the concrete box that forms the base of the station. We duck our heads, covering our ears and looking around for any other threats but find none. Carmy runs up to the security panel and jacks his phone into it, and I see Preston's face appear on his screen, using the phone to give Preston access from the truck into the building.

"Lao!" Preston yells. "Victor, it's me. Please turn off the alarm."

No response comes. Lena and I give each other nervous glances, and I wonder what Victor's mind might be like after so many years in isolation. Would he even know how to interact with people anymore? At least Preston seems mostly sane from his time in exile.

"Preston Manning," Preston continues, and I can hear the worry in his voice. "Please, Victor, I need to talk to you. These people need your help."

The alarm keeps blaring and Carmy jumps out of the back of the truck, raising a shotgun at the loudspeaker and blowing it off the wall. Bits of metal rain down on us but the siren is silenced, only the flashing red light remaining.

Finally, another voice comes from the security panel by the door. "There is no Victor here."

Preston starts stammering, "But—we talked to the monks. They...they said he had gone into isolation, here, in this station."

"That was not Victor either."

"Who are we speaking with then?" I interrupt.

"I have no name. No self. Am no one."

Carmy grumbles behind me, "Great, he's lost it."

"Victor, I recognize your voice." Preston sounds annoyed now. "I respect your commitment to this new life, but we don't have time for games. We need your help."

"Who are these people you've brought here?"

"Friends. They rescued me."

"Rescued you?"

"From Felix. He exiled me, shortly before you went into isolation."

"So you know, then."

"Know what?"

"I suppose I wouldn't be able to hear it if you did."

Preston makes an annoyed sound and I interrupt their exchange. "Preston, you said your son tried to tell you something after he visited Austin, but it couldn't get through the censors. Then Felix exiled you shortly after. I think Victor is referencing the same thing."

Suddenly the blank security panel changes and reveals a man, dressed in what looks like a prayer robe. He's seated in a Buddhist temple, a small wooden tray on the ground in front of him supporting a steaming teapot. He's shockingly old; he looks like he could be one hundred.

"Dr. Lao?" I ask.

He nods with a slow grace. "For our purposes, yes. Did I hear correctly? Your son visited Austin and when he returned, he knew something that led to your getting exiled?"

"Yes, but I couldn't find out what it was."

"He found him..." Victor whispers to himself. Then he shifts slightly on his cushion, and something catches my eye. There, partially obscured behind him, is an aged metal gong, suspended against the wall. I look at it closer, trying to make out why it has drawn my attention so much, and when I realize it, I feel my heart leap into my throat.

"Wait!" I yell, running forward to get a clearer look at the screen. "Dr. Lao," I begin, trying to keep my voice steady. "What's that behind you? The gong."

His eyes widen slightly, and he glances over his shoulder. "It sounds like you know what it is. It's a prayer gong, for signaling the beginning or end of meditation."

"But what's on the gong?" I press.

"What are you doing?" Lena asks, but I signal her to be quiet.

"Ah…so you're aware of that too."

"Isaac, what is he talking about?" Lena hisses.

"It's the symbol," I whisper back. "The one I asked Natalie about when you brought me to Alexandria."

"It's quite beautiful in its simplicity, isn't it?" Victor continues. "Her best work, after she realized what had happened. I know it was meant as a warning to those on the outside, but it gave me something to meditate on once I realized my fate, too."

"Who's best work? And no, we don't know what it means, but I've seen it before."

Victor starts moving his lips, but no words come out. Then he lets out a frustrated sigh and says, "I'm sorry, but I forget. Some of this will not get through Felix's censors."

"What does it mean?"

"If you don't know, I won't be able to explain to you. Not here."

"Then where?"

Victor lets out a sigh. "Is it true you have your own version of Meru? One free of Felix's control?"

Lena and I nod in unison.

"Why don't you get me out of here and I'll explain there, then. Assuming you are able to remove me, of course."

"Yes, one minute," Lena says and steps up to the security console. She fishes a phone out of her pocket and wires it into the console. A moment later, the screen by the door flashes green, saying ACCESS GRANTED, and the door shoots open.

Lena turns and beckons to Carmy. He nods and backs the truck up so the bed is pressed almost to the door, leaving just enough room for Lena and me to squeeze through.

I lead the way into the station, and the screen clicks on again. Victor is standing, changed out of his robes and instead wearing a pair of jeans and a flannel shirt, with a leather suitcase sitting on the ground next to him, the xīn symbol etched in the side. He's standing in what looks like a train station, dark red metal beams rising out of the concrete beside him, a sprawling glass roof overhead spiderwebbed with support beams, and a mosaic tiled wall behind him with a black sign in the middle that says MERU STATION on it.

"Impressive," I say as I start initiating the transfer sequence on the computer.

"I find a little bit of imagination helps with the jarring process of moving between worlds in here. The mind is familiar with space; it needs physical elements to latch onto. Doing this seems to help with limiting degradation." The sound of a train whistle comes through the speakers. "This mind is all that's left of me. I must do my best to preserve it."

Victor turns to face the train as the first car speeds past him, a gust of wind from it blowing the wisps of hair on top of his head. The train whistle sounds again and the brakes screech as it starts slowing to a stop. I've never seen such a detailed simulation of another kind of transportation to help with transferring. It's oddly moving; it truly feels like he's embarking on a great journey.

I start typing in a last set of commands on the console, then feel Lena's hand on my shoulder. Her grip is firm, tense.

"What's up?" I ask, turning to look at her, and her face is white, eyes wide, staring up at Victor on the monitor. He's stepping back on the train platform, moving away from the train, holding his hands up defensively toward the door of the train car in front of him.

Standing there in the steps up to the train car, his gray hair slicked back against his head and wearing a dark blue conductor's uniform, is Felix.

"No..." Victor mumbles, his voice undulating with fear. "How..."

"Digging into my old colleagues' research, are you, Victor?" Felix says, gliding as much as stepping off the train car onto the platform.

"Get him out!" Lena yells at me.

The transfer status says it's ready on the console, I mash the ENTER key, but nothing happens. I slam on it a few more times, still nothing, but then Felix looks up, staring directly at us through the screen. "Hello, Isaac. Pleasure to see you again. I see we were right to suspect you."

"Let him go, Felix!" I yell back.

Felix laughs, taking another step closer to Victor. "No, I don't think I'll be doing that," he says, flashing a grin as the door of the transfer station slams shut behind us. Lena sprints over to it and tries to yank it open but it won't budge, and she starts banging on it for help from the others outside.

"They're going to find out," Victor says, standing tall. "You don't have the grip on Meru you think you do. The ways we've found to hide things, to tell people the truth. To end this horrible lie you've sold the world."

Felix continues to advance on him. "I've been watching you for a while, Victor. I appreciate you digging up all of Vance's notes in here for me. I knew there were some that I missed. I assure you, they're long gone now."

"Other people know," Victor says as he tries to take another step back, but he's reached the other train track. There's nowhere else to escape to.

"Dealt with as well. I was worried I had gotten soft. Too patient. Too willing to let minds wander off to join these traitors. I thought a measure of leniency would keep everyone happier, keep things calmer. But that was a mistake. This...belief, this nonsense, it's a disease that needs to be rooted out."

Lena is frantically trying to enter a command into the console next to the door to open it, but nothing is working. "Shit," she mutters and starts scrambling around the floor. "Help me find something to pry it open with."

I stare at the door. "You won't find something," I say, barely whispering. "It's solid steel, almost impenetrable. They were designed to prevent being pried open. There's not even a space between the door and wall to get any leverage with."

Lena looks back up at the door and sees I'm right. Her shoulders drop and she lets out something between a scream and a roar and yells, "Fuck you, Felix!"

But Felix doesn't hear her, or if he does, he ignores her. He's getting closer to Victor now, and I hear the whistle of another train come through the monitors.

"You're sick," Victor says, seeming to accept whatever is coming and rising back to his feet now. "Working with you, whatever I did to help you build this place, it was a mistake, all of it."

Felix shakes his head. "No, the mistake was doubting it, questioning what I built. What we built. You could have had a good life here, Victor. All you had to do was keep your head down. Not question it, like everyone else."

The train whistle sounds again, louder, and then another sound comes through the concrete. The unmistakable thuds of shotgun blasts reverberate against the walls, followed by a pair of muffled screams.

Felix has reached Victor now, and they're standing face to face. "Thank you for all your help, Doctor," Felix says, and then he grabs him by the lapels, lifting him up into the air and then throwing him in front of the train as it passes across our view. As the train hits him, the server holding his mind starts whirring louder, the lights on it illuminating brighter until the heat from the acceleration causes it to burst into flames, and the scene on the monitors disappears. I jump back, pushing Lena against the opposite wall with me as the flames on the server slowly grow and a cloud of smoke billows up to the top of the small room.

I feel Lena's hand grab my collar, yanking me down to the floor where the air is clearer. The smoke fills the upper half of the room now, stinging my eyes and making it hard to breathe.

"Extinguisher," Lena coughs, her voice muffled as she presses her face into her sleeve.

I look around, trying to see through the smoke, but there's no extinguisher in sight. I cough into my sleeve as I try to think through our options. The door is sealed tight, designed to withstand attacks far more powerful than anything we could muster. The ventilation system is likely automated, shut off by Felix; otherwise the smoke would have cleared by now.

"The console," I gasp, pointing to where we initiated the transfer. "If we can override it, maybe we can force the door open."

The smoke is getting thicker, descending closer to the floor where we lay. I can feel my lungs burning with each shallow breath. I look back at Lena and see her eyes starting to flutter as she loses consciousness. The heat from the fire is intensifying, and I can feel sweat pouring down my face, my clothes starting to burn around me.

Lena's eyes finally close and she collapses on the floor. As my own vision starts to flicker, another strange sound starts to reverberate through the room. I try to focus on it, but my mind is lagging, like I'm already half asleep. I try to take another gulp of air through my sleeve but inhale smoke and retch, coughing out more than I breathed in. I wave my arms and the smoke clears slightly. I take another breath and feel a moment of clarity. The sound comes again. A tapping, tap tap tap, or more like a banging, the sound of metal against the door. I scramble on top of Lena and fish her phone out of her pocket, banging the metal on the door in response.

Someone outside yells, I can't quite make it out, but it sounds like "MOO." My consciousness is fading again. Moo? Like a cow? Then I feel a surge of hope as I realize what they said and grab Lena's arms, trying to drag her away from the door. But I can't move her, I'm too weak, too fatigued from the smoke, so I throw myself down on top of her to shield her from the door.

There's a massive explosion from outside, and a concussion sends shock waves through the room again. I can't see what is happening behind me but the door groans and a wave of cold, fresh air floods over me. I gasp for breath then choke out the smoke still in my lungs and gasp for air again. My vision surges back into focus and I look up at the door above me. A pair of holes has been blown near the hinges and the smoke is flooding out of the top one.

"MOVE!" comes the command again and I grab Lena, my strength slowly returning, and pull her to the side of the door as another blast rings out. The door groans again and then there's a massive THUD. The concrete around the door cracks slightly and more smoke flies out. Then comes the whirring of tires and another THUD and the door collapses inward, landing on the floor where we were lying only moments before.

I crawl over to the opening, trying to drink in as much of the fresh air as I can. As I round the door frame, the crumpled bumper of the truck whoever is outside had used to ram the door is looming over me. Someone yells, "Get them out of there!" before my vision starts to fade again and I collapse, the hot metal of the door burning against my cheek, as a shadow descends on me and drags me out of the wreckage.

CHAPTER 24

I BOLT UPRIGHT, THE IMAGE OF THE SHADOWY FIGURE looming over me and pulling me from the station fresh in my mind. Where am I? What happened?

But the fear fades as I find I'm back in my room in Alexandria. Whoever pulled me out, they were friendly. I'm safe, somehow. I let out a series of coughs and can feel my lungs still burning; the smoke has done serious damage to them.

I lie back down, taking deep breaths and trying to clear any gunk that remains, running through everything that happened yesterday in my mind. It had never occurred to me that Felix could destroy people who were living in Meru. And perhaps he couldn't do it digitally, but if he were able to access the server that they were residing in, he could destroy that instead.

With Victor gone, I feel like we're almost as far from understanding Luke's actions as we were before we set out. All we have is the conversation between Felix and Victor. Whatever Victor knew, it clearly scared Felix. There's something hidden that he doesn't want us to know, that he feels is a threat to Meru, and that he's gone to great lengths to cover up.

After ruminating a while longer, I finally try to sit up again and am relieved when I don't suffer another coughing fit. Everything hurts, but that is starting to feel normal.

I stumble over to the desk in the corner and open the fridge beneath it, pulling out a glass pitcher and chugging water directly from it, not bothering with a cup. It's some of the best water I've had in my life, the cold relief flooding through me with each gulp.

I set it back down on the table and look around the room. There's no note, or any indication of who has brought me back. I turn on the computer on the desk and it's blank. The files that were on it before have been removed. *That's odd*, I think, then walk over to the door to look outside.

Locked.

Shit, I think and then bang on it, suddenly feeling like I'm trapped in that burning room again. "Hello?" I yell at the door, banging on it more. But no response comes.

Dread starts to seep through me. No one outside could have seen what happened in the bunker. All they know is that Lena and I went in, they got attacked, and then the bunker melted down, erasing the mind of the person who promised them answers along with it.

And Lena...is she okay? Did they get her out in time? I fall onto the bed and put my head in my hands. We should have been more careful; we should have expected it would be a trap. It was too easy, too perfect, and now Felix has likely erased the last traces of whatever Victor found in Meru.

Eventually, I hear footsteps outside. I look up, waiting, and finally hear the click of someone unlocking the door, then opening it and letting it swing into the room. When Lincoln steps in he looks exhausted and extremely pissed.

We stare at each other for a moment, then I whisper, "Are they okay?"

His expression softens, slightly, but he's still eyeing me with contempt. "Xavier is dead. Preston's been erased."

My stomach clenches. "Carmy? Lena?"

"Lena's recovering; she'll make it. Carmy is unconscious, has been since yesterday. He managed to get you three halfway back and then collapsed over the steering wheel. He was barely breathing when we recovered you. Dylan drove the rest of the way with a bullet in his arm. What happened, Isaac?"

"I don't know—Felix—"

"You know how this looks, don't you?"

"I—no, Lincoln, you can't."

"Someone with your clearance, your access to Felix, happens to turn on him and work with us. Then you discover this mysterious person in an old tech center. Then that person, if Preston was even real and not some copy of Felix, leads us to a remote location where we lose two, maybe three people in the process."

"You can't believe that!" I'm consumed by a coughing fit as soon as the words leave my mouth. "Lincoln...I swear..."

He lets out a long mix of a sigh and a grumble. "I know, Isaac. But what I believe is less important." His voice is lower but still angry, forceful. "Xavier had a family."

"I know."

"They don't trust you now."

"Who doesn't trust me?"

"The others, the people in Alexandria. They think you did this, or at least caused this to happen. His is the first death we've had from Felix in years."

"But Victor was also the first lead you'd had in years."

"It doesn't matter," Lincoln says, hanging his head.

"Lincoln, please, I was trying to help—"

He holds up a hand for silence. "This isn't for me to decide. Other leaders in the town have already organized. They don't trust you; nothing like this happened until you arrived. Whatever is going on with you and Felix, you're a threat to the life we have here."

"No—please—"

"They want you gone, Isaac."

I hang my head, morose at the verdict but aware that Lincoln doesn't necessarily agree with it either. He has to follow the will of the town.

"We talked to him," I say, desperate for anything that will turn the conversation around. "Dr. Lao, before Felix killed him. Victor recognized the symbol I asked you about, the xīn. It was all over his space, it seemed to be important to him."

"Did he say why?"

"He couldn't through the censoring. When Felix appeared, he seemed irate about whatever Victor found in Meru. Said he had destroyed any last traces of it and that the knowledge would die with him."

"You have no other leads, then?"

"I—I don't know," I admit. "He said something about Felix's old partner, Vance, that seemed to make Felix more upset. Maybe we can talk to him."

"That doesn't get us anywhere," Lincoln says.

"Why not?"

"You've seen Vance. He's a media personality. We've had people in Meru try to talk to him before. He acts like he doesn't remember anything from before, gets upset if you ask about it. I think he's ratted out at least one of our people to Felix too. Someone got exiled shortly after asking him one too many questions about it."

"It could be worth a—"

"No, Isaac, and I'm sorry, but I can't entertain this any longer. You seem like you've recovered enough. Let's go."

I'm starting to feel desperate. There has to be some way to convince him to let me stay. To let me keep searching. To figure out what Luke found. To understand what the xīn symbol means.

"What's in Austin?"

"Austin? It's dangerous. Warring tribes and people hiding from them."

"There has to be something there."

"Why?"

"Preston's son found something that led to him being exiled. When I mentioned it, Victor seemed to think Preston's son had found someone who knew something."

"Something?"

"It's all I have, Lincoln."

Lincoln regards me for a long moment, his eyes flitting back and forth between mine. He looks frustrated, exhausted, but I also see a spark of hope, of curiosity. He wants to know as much as I do.

"Do you want to say goodbye to Carmy before you go?"

My heart lurches. "Yes, absolutely, please."

"Follow me."

I silently follow Lincoln, flanked by two guards, my shoulders slumped as we make our way through Alexandria's winding paths. A small group is huddled near one of the academic buildings, and their conversation dies as we approach. One man quickly averts his gaze, as if afraid to make eye contact.

Eventually we reach the medical building. As we enter, Lincoln turns to the guards. "You can leave us here."

They give each other concerned glances.

"There's security inside. Go help with the preparations."

"Preparations?" I ask as Lincoln leads me in.

"Bolstering our defenses. This is an unusual move from Felix; we can't be too careful if there's more to come."

Eventually we arrive in the hospital wing and as we enter, I see Lena sitting on a stool by one of the beds, Carmy's face sticking out from the sheets and a heart rate monitor chirping over his head.

Her eyes meet mine, and I notice a tear glistening in the corner of her eye. Without hesitation, she leaps up from her stool and rushes toward me.

Before I can react, Lena's arms are around me, pulling me into a tight embrace. I wince slightly, my body still sore from the ordeal, but I don't pull away.

I close my eyes, relief washing over me. "I'm okay," I murmur. "Are you alright?"

She nods against me, then pulls back slightly to look at my face. Her eyes are red-rimmed, dark circles beneath them betraying her exhaustion. "I've been better," she admits with a weak smile.

I glance over her shoulder at Carmy's still form on the bed. "How is he?"

Lena's expression falls. "Stable, but..." She shakes her head. "They're not sure when he'll wake up."

I feel even more overwhelmed with guilt seeing him here, barely holding on. If I hadn't insisted on pursuing Victor, if I hadn't been so eager to uncover the truth, maybe none of this would have happened. Carmy might be awake. Xavier might still be alive.

Lena must have sensed my thoughts because she squeezes my arm. "It's not your fault," she says softly. "We knew the risks."

I nod, not entirely convinced but grateful for her words.

Lincoln interrupts our moment. "Lena, Isaac said that Victor said something about Austin before he was deleted."

"Yes," she says and wipes her eye with the back of her hand. "Same as Preston's son."

Lincoln is quiet for a moment, and Lena and I make hesitant eye contact. Then he speaks again, quieter. "Someone needs to drive Isaac out of town. Get him far enough away from Alexandria for the rest here to feel safe."

"What?!" Lena is shocked, outraged. "Lincoln, no, you can't—" He holds up a hand to silence her. "Perhaps you'd be willing to take him."

I feel a surge of excitement, and Lena opens her mouth, still angry, then catches herself as she realizes what Lincoln is asking. She glances over at me, a questioning look in her eye as she seems to consider the proposal. Then she nods slowly and says, "I think I could manage that."

"You're sure you're recovered enough? It might be a long trip."

I can tell she's trying to suppress a grin. "I can manage."

Lincoln nods stiffly. "It's settled then. I'll inform the others that you're taking him. I'm sure there are some other things I'll need you to check on along the way too." A flicker of a smile betrays the ruse as he says it and hands a set of keys to Lena. "Good luck."

Lena turns back to Carmy and brushes his hair off his forehead. "We'll be back soon." Then she nods toward the back door. "Probably better if we go out that way."

"Wait," Lincoln says and starts rummaging through a medical cabinet. He pulls out a pad of paper and a pen, then hands it to me and brings up the xīn on a screen by Carmy's bed.

"What's this for?"

"Draw it so you have a physical copy. Whatever it is, it's important, and your devices won't be able to access the network outside of Alexandria."

"Good idea." I hastily sketch the symbol, then rip off the sheet and stuff it in my pocket. Lena and I give Lincoln one last nod goodbye, then she leads us out the back door of the medical building, my heart racing with a mix of excitement and disbelief. She leads the way through a series of back hallways and then out into the fresh air along a path circling the campus I haven't been down before. I can tell she's taking extra precautions to avoid running into other residents.

"Try not to look so pleased with yourself," she whispers as we duck behind a building to avoid a passing group. "You're supposed to be leaving in disgrace, remember?"

I don't respond but force my expression into something more somber. As we approach the garage, Lena holds up a hand, signaling me to wait. She peers around the corner, then motions for me to follow. "Coast is clear," she whispers. "Let's go."

CHAPTER 25

THE LANDSCAPE BLURS BY, A MIX OF OVERGROWN VEGetation and crumbling remnants of the old world. It's still strange to see it all from this vantage point, taking back-roads through the no-man's land that I had thought was dangerous such a short time ago.

I think about Carmy, lying unconscious back in Alexandria, and hope desperately he will wake up soon. The burns look awful, and it feels unfair that he has somehow ended up more hurt than us, despite us being the ones trapped inside with the flames. I wonder idly what he'll do once he wakes up. Will he take off after us, to try to join the search? It certainly seems like something he would do. Though I'm not sure how he'd find us.

Lena and I exchange what we know about old Austin. To the Techs, it's a dangerous wasteland, the one major city along the highway that you never try to visit. I have traveled to the couple of centers south of Epsilon a few times, exchanging supplies or trading residents to avoid inbreeding. But I've never been within twenty miles of the city. I don't know anyone who has, either. Only rumors.

There had been a center there, once, according to the histories, but it was destroyed a long time ago, likely the victim of local unrest. The centers based in smaller towns like Epsilon have fared better, probably because they're easier to defend, and there was less conflict with locals when they were getting established.

It's hard to imagine how difficult it was to construct them in the beginning. To tell most of humanity, "No, you can't live here," given the limited ability to transfer people. Those first few years must have been hell with the Techs living in their cloisters and the rest of the world dying outside.

The ruins of old gas stations and abandoned strip malls dot the roadside, reminders of a world long gone. I try to imagine what life would have been like before. They didn't realize how good they had it. The histories talk about wars and social unrest and violence, but what did they have to fight about if their world was this rich and safe? Maybe that was why they fought. Once they conquered their environment, they turned their eyes toward conquering each other.

Lena's understanding of Austin isn't much different. A few residents have found Alexandria coming from Austin, and most of them tell of a quiet, peaceful existence in small groups in what were old neighborhoods within the city. But that peace is always under threat of being disrupted by the more violent people who roam the city, preying on others.

The one strange thing we don't seem to agree on is the center. She says that some of the refugees who have come to Alexandria said they had run-ins with bots that they claimed were controlled by Felix. Drones, dogs, the same kinds we have in Epsilon. But Felix always said there was no center there. So, either the refugees are mistaken, or Felix was lying again. I'm optimistic it's the second. That would be our natural place to start.

"Can you check the back for supplies?" Lena says as the outskirts of the city come into view ahead. We didn't have time to grab anything as we left.

I dig through the back seat and find a tattered backpack; it feels heavy. I deposit it in my lap, dig through it, and am shocked to find a few bottles of water, a fire starter, a bundle of paracord, a small pot, a hunting knife, even a radio. Standard survival gear.

Lena glances over at me as I rifle through it. "Anything good?"

I'm shocked. "Surprisingly good. It's not much, but it's the basics."

"Lincoln was putting on a show. This was his plan all along."

"Of course," I say, then I tap the center console in the truck to check the security cache. "Looks like there are two guns in the back. No dogs though."

"Probably smart. Alexandria needs them, and they'd draw too much attention to us anyway."

"You think those refugees were right? About Felix having bots running around Austin?"

She slows the truck; the road is getting more jagged, rougher now. "I hope not, but if they are right, there can't be many. It didn't sound like they were terrorizing the locals."

"We should probably ditch the truck soon," I say, eyeing the densely overgrown streets ahead. "It's going to be hard to navigate through all that."

Lena nods. "Agreed. We'll find a spot to hide it and continue on foot. Any ideas where we should start looking?"

"Well, if there's any truth to the rumors about Felix's bots, or a center, we know where it would be."

"Shouldn't be too hard to find our way to the university in town, assuming that's where they put it."

We drive a bit farther until we find a secluded spot to park the truck, concealing it as best we can with branches and debris. I stuff the supplies in the bag, flattening the paper with the xīn on the bottom. As we prepare to set out on foot, I can't help but feel a mix of excitement and apprehension. I can see why people are so hesitant to enter the city. Even on the outskirts, the broken windows and dark corners around every building feel like a constant threat. A small settlement or outpost could be anywhere, with guards monitoring for trespassers. I have to imagine that they could tell we aren't a threat. But it's hard to say what kind of mental state people might be in.

"Stay alert," Lena whispers as she slings one of the shotguns over her shoulder, and we begin our trek.

I nod, tossing the rest of the gear on my back and cradling the gun as I walk beside her.

※ ※ ※

We walk cautiously down the cracked pavement, our eyes darting between the broken buildings on either side. It's strangely quiet coming from Alexandria. There I could still hear the sounds of nature around me. But here, it's as if the animal life deserted when the humans did. I feel a bit nervous about finding food, but hopefully we'll find whatever we're looking for long before that.

I'm not used to having to be so on guard, and I'm not even sure how worried I should be. I've read in the histories about a period of raiding, marauding, true savagery in the big cities after the collapse. People who didn't make it into Meru or the tech centers, and who didn't get killed by the bacteria, fighting desperately for survival.

Those days are supposedly long gone, but it doesn't assuage my fears. I peer into the dark recesses of doorways and shattered windows as I pass, half expecting to see a face staring back at me.

"Relax," Lena says, though only just above a whisper.

"I'm not sure that's good advice."

"I doubt anyone here wants to get into a fight either, but

even if they do, getting so worked up isn't going to help you. Worst case we run into a sentry and have to backtrack or walk around them."

"Still..." I try not to imagine the possible worst-case scenarios, especially for her. But I decide to change the subject. For all the time we've spent together working in Alexandria, I still don't know much about her. "Your parents, do you know what happened to them?"

She shakes her head. "I was too young, only six or seven probably."

"You don't know?"

"When Horace and the others from Alexandria found me, I wouldn't speak to them. Took them a long time to get me to open up. And by the time I did, I couldn't remember exactly. Couldn't remember a lot of things."

I climb on top of an old car blocking our path and hold my hand out to help her up. "Do you remember them?"

Lena takes my hand and climbs up after me, then jumps down to the other side in one graceful motion. "Barely."

I hop down after her, and the car makes a loud lurching noise. We both freeze and look around, but there are no signs of movement, so we start walking again.

"I'm sorry."

"It was a long time ago. And I found a family in Alexandria, thankfully."

"Did anyone else make it out?"

"No, or if they did, they ran off and I didn't see them again."

"How did you survive?"

A bird flies out of a window up ahead and we freeze, then nod at each other and keep walking. There's a hill up ahead and the peaks of the remaining skyscrapers are visible beyond it, but it's impossible to tell what else lies between us.

"I remember that I used to get scared at night. I didn't have a screen in my room, so sometimes I would creep downstairs after my parents were asleep and crawl under a blanket on the couch, watching the feeds from Meru."

"You came from a center?"

"You didn't know that?"

"No, I always assumed you grew up out here."

"I wish I did. My grandparents had a private feed for us that they left on quite often. I'd lie on the couch under the blanket and watch them play tennis, or go for hikes, or build impossible sandcastles on the beach. It was soothing, made me feel less alone.

"Then one day I woke up late on the couch. Sunlight was streaming through the windows, and I thought it odd that they weren't up yet. Even more odd that there were no sounds coming from outside. I turned on the TV to try to see if something had happened, but it was dead. Everything in the house was. I went upstairs to see if they were still asleep and..."

She sighs. "I don't know why he did it. Someone in the center must have done something to make him think everyone had turned on him. That he had to take them out in their sleep. I was terrified. I ran between the houses searching for anyone, banging on the doors, begging for someone to please open them and tell me I wasn't alone. Eventually I collapsed on one of the stoops and cried, wailed...I was so scared.

"I—I went back to my house. I crawled into bed with them, pretended they were still alive. Wrapped my mom's arm around me and stayed there, petrified, until..."

"Until they found you?"

"The smell."

"Oh."

I want to reach out and try to comfort her, but there's still a tension, a distance between us. And some part of me feels like it would be a betrayal to Tess.

"Where did they find you?"

"Alpha. It's why I was so upset when—what?"

I've frozen in place, and Lena must have interpreted it as sensing a threat because she ducks down where she's standing, ripping her gun off her shoulder and scanning the path ahead.

"Isaac, what do you see?"

"*Alpha?*"

"Shit, you scared me, that's what you're so freaked out about?"

"Lena. *I* was found in Alpha."

She slowly returns to standing, looking as confused as I feel. "That's…not possible."

"Why not?"

"Horace and the rest of them searched the entire town. They picked it over; they would have found you. Or you would have heard them."

"Maybe Bram found me first and didn't find you."

"Unlikely. As soon as I heard people outside, I ran out for help. There was never anyone there before them. And they had a recording of finding me."

"The recording could be faked. Maybe they found you somewhere else."

"Why lie about where they found me?"

"Why lie about where they found *me*?"

She throws up her hands in frustration. "Well, do you trust Lincoln more? Or Bram more?"

My first instinct is to say I don't know, but I do. Lincoln's never given me any reason to doubt him. And the more time I spend in Alexandria, the more I wonder how complicit Bram was in Felix's deception.

"Did you recognize Alpha when we took you there?"

The strange feeling of unease I had looking around the town hoping for some memory to spark returns. "No. I assumed the memories were too painful."

"I remember Isaac. I remember crying in that bed. It would have come back to you."

"Maybe if I go back without feeling like a prisoner."

"Maybe."

We continue up the hill in silence as I try to wrestle with this new revelation. I know they found me around the time of Alpha's collapse; the dates couldn't be faked. But if he didn't find me there, then he must have found me somewhere else, somewhere that at least in my memories could have been mistaken for a center. And the only obvious answer is that small town Felix massacred. But if they found me there, then Bram knew what Felix did. And he's hidden from me where I came from all this time.

Finally, we reach the crest and can see the path down to the highway ahead of us. Felix's highway. In the distance I can make out a convoy of Imgen trucks flanked by security cars making their way north, away from us. There are a few defensive turrets along the edges of the highway, but they're just far enough north and south of us that we should be out of range. We might be able to pass through here, assuming there aren't any unseen defenses.

As my eyes scan across what lies ahead, Lena hisses, "Get down!" Then she grabs the back of my bag and pulls me to the ground. We shuffle back slightly, hiding our heads from the top of the hill, then scurry over to an abandoned car.

"What is it?" I whisper back.

"Outpost."

I poke my head up from behind the car, slowly raising myself until I can barely see what Lena has spotted. The hill drops down from its peak until the road reaches the highway, the elevated roadway broken and collapsed, providing a concrete barrier against entering the city. There's nothing immediately on top of the highway, but the collapsed roadway must have created a tunnel or cave because between the ground and what is left of the elevated highway there are what look like ramshackle walls, possibly defensive fortifications for whoever is now living in the area. A semicamouflaged menagerie of wooden boards, metal sheets, and haphazard barbed wire spans the opening, creating a threatening barrier to anyone who might consider approaching. I completely missed them while focused on the top of the roadway.

It's impossible to say how old it is. It could have been from the more violent days of the past; it could have been built a few months ago. The scrap metal gives me little insight into when it was thrown together.

"Did you see anyone?" I ask, and Lena shakes her head no. She digs through her bag then pulls out a compact pair of binoculars and hands them to me. I scan across the barrier again and realize now there are a few small portholes, ways for whoever is inside to observe the outside world for any threats. I can't see any movement though. I scan up to the top of the highway and try to look around for any other signs of life. A wisp of gray catches my eyes. I focus on it a moment longer and my suspicion is confirmed.

"Someone's there," I say, handing the binoculars back.

"You saw them?"

"No, but there's a hint of smoke coming out of the top of the highway. They must have some kind of small settlement in there."

Lena starts searching with the binoculars as I debate what to do. The settlement is nestled under the highway, so we could try to climb over it, but they could see us as a threat and attack us if they see us approaching.

We'll have to backtrack, move farther south, and hope there's another gap under the highway we can scurry through that hasn't been claimed as a home like this one has. Or if we get far enough south and don't find one, maybe we can risk running for it over the highway. But either way, we can't get into the city here.

Then, suddenly, a voice comes from behind us.

"What are you doing?"

CHAPTER 26

SOMEONE SNUCK UP ON US WHILE WE WERE DELIBERATing behind the car. Our guns are lying on the ground, the knife is in the pack, and we have no way to quickly defend ourselves.

"Hey! I said, what are you doing?" the voice comes again. I can't tell if it's a woman or a young boy. Either way, I feel like my odds are good; if I turn around quickly enough and surprise them, maybe I can overpower them. I start tensing my muscles, ready to spin around and leap at them, hopefully giving Lena enough time to grab a weapon and come to my aid. But if they aren't alone, if they have backup, we might be in trouble. I can sense she's picking up on my plan, her body stiffening too as she gives me the tiniest of nods.

"Do you need food or something?"

The question catches me off guard. "Uh, what?" I ask, slowly turning around now. There in front of me is a boy, hardly older than twelve, unarmed, staring at me like I have ten heads. Lena and I glance at each other, and I can tell she's equally confused.

"Food? Water? You don't look like you're trying to rob us. You get lost or something?"

I'm still stunned silent. He looks at me closer, then says, "Whoa, you're a Techie! I knew you looked different. Where'd you come from? Delta? Epsilon? Gamma? It's been a long time since one of you came through. Only heard about it from my parents. How'd you escape?"

"Escape?"

"Yeah, aren't you guys like slaves there?"

"Not—exactly—" Then I pause. "Maybe? How did you know I came from a center?"

"Too clean, too few scars. You could have at least rubbed some dirt on your face or something before coming out here." Then he turns to Lena. "What about you? You're pretty. You escape too?"

"No," Lena says curtly. She still looks uneasy about the situation.

"Well either way, come on, everyone else is going to want to meet you," he says then he walks out into the middle of the street, to the top of the hill, and starts waving and shouting. "Hey, guys! They're fine! I'm bringing them in!"

Lena and I stand up and sheepishly walk over to him as someone hollers back an indecipherable response. Then the boy starts jogging down the hill toward the destroyed highway. We follow along after him and I try to push down any fears that this might be some elaborate trap. They clearly saw us coming, and if they sent a young boy out to meet us, they can't be too much of a threat, or too worried. But how could they not be?

We reach the rubble, and he bangs on the door that I can now see lies in the middle of the pile of scrap. A face appears at one of the portholes by the door and looks us over, then beams at the boy and the door clanks open a moment later.

"Welcome!" the man behind the door says, throwing his hands in the air and then pulling me in for an embrace. I awkwardly wrap my arms around him and return the gesture, scanning the grounds behind him as I do. It's dimly lit by candles and a central fire, and it looks like a small village, much less well maintained than Alexandria or Epsilon, but homey, in its own way.

He releases me and then holds me at arm's length, searching my eyes for something. "Well, what is it, my boy?" he says. "What brings you to our little abode?" Then he looks over at Lena and she steps back before he can try to hug her, so he just nods at her and says, "Ma'am."

"I—" I stammer, still trying to process what is happening. "You're not scared?" are the only words that come to mind.

He laughs and beckons us to follow him into the little cavern village. "Of course not! Why, should we be?"

A few of the other residents poke their heads out to see the commotion then smile and nod at us before returning to their tents and shacks.

"You aren't worried about someone attacking you?" I continue. "Stealing from you?"

"Posh," he says, waving a hand. "Why would someone steal from us when there's an almost endless supply of food lying around out here? Sure, there are the occasional crazy people roaming through looking for trouble, but they're easily dispatched and rarely have company."

"Endless food?" Lena asks as we reach the firepit. There's a pot over the flames with some thick substance in it.

"Hah! She speaks!" the man says, beaming at Lena and clearly trying to get some kind of reaction. "Here, here, you must be hungry," he continues and grabs a ladle from the edge and scoops it into the pot, depositing the soup into a small bowl by the flame. "Caught it this morning."

I eye the bowl warily, looking at a few of the other people nearby the firepit. They all seem strangely uninterested in our arrival, preoccupied by chatting with people around them or working on some part of the town.

"Oh, come on now," he says. "You Techies are so nervous. Here." He grabs the bowl and takes a heavy drink from it. "It's delicious, really. You're missing out," he says and hands it back to me.

I decide to risk it and take a tentative drink from the soup. He's right; it's delicious. The fish is fresh and has been spiced with pepper, garlic, and some other flavors I don't recognize. I nod at Lena, and she takes a cautious sip as well, then her eyes light up at the flavor.

"Ahh, that's more like it," he says, squatting down on a log bench near the fire. "Now, what brings you to our parts? Which center did you come from?"

"Not a center," I say, taking another longer drink of the soup. "Well, not for a while. We live in another town a few hours from here. A place called—" Lena kicks me before I finish the sentence.

The man laughs. "Ahh, Alexandria, is it?" he says. "How are they holding up? How's Horace? Been a while since we've run into them."

I'm shocked that he's guessed it so quickly. "You know about Alexandria? Why are you out here then?"

"Ha!" he laughs, then seems to realize how confused I am. "Oh, well, I don't have anyone stuck in Meru, now do I? No sense spending my life trying to save people from a place I don't care to save anyone from."

"But wouldn't you be safer there? Their city is huge."

He laughs again. "I don't think you're getting it, boyo. Safe from what? A million people used to live in this city, now there are probably, what, ten thousand of us, scattered around the outskirts? You hardly need to walk a block before you stumble on another one of the ration caches people started hoarding around here. The violence ended a long time ago. You want to live in another settlement? You just bring a gift, waltz over, and get acclimated."

I look at the soup again and start to feel sick. "This...is from pre-Meru?"

"Oh oh oh, no no." He laughs again. "Gosh, can you imagine if we tried to eat the food from back then? That's all long gone. Well, some of it kept actually, the really artificial stuff, ultraprocessed they called it, I can't believe they ever ate it, truly, wretched stuff. Food isn't meant to last longer than a few days, maybe weeks. But years?" He makes a retching sound. "And to think we call that era civilized."

I sit there quietly, drinking the soup again, the sick feeling gone, wondering how he can be so cheery and optimistic in this world where I've only known fear and confusion.

Lena speaks up now. "Horace died. I don't know how well you knew him."

The man gets quiet for a moment and seems to mourn the news. "Ah, well, he was a bold man. I hope he at least went doing what he loved."

"What was that?" I ask.

"Fighting Felix," he says with a grin.

"Is everyone here like you?" I ask.

"How do you mean?"

"Well, cheery, I suppose."

He thinks for a moment. "Well, you have the full range of humanity hanging around here, grumpy people and happy people and young people looking to get laid. Old people too, for that matter...But, yes, I'd say most people living off the city are in rather good spirits about it. Things are less serious here. We're not trying to keep a dying world alive like you Techies, and we're not trying to rescue folks from that world either, like the liberators in Alexandria. We're just living, and rather enjoying it, I might add."

A pair of kids run through the camp, chasing a dog as he says it, laughing as the dog weaves through the people milling around, and then grabbing it by the collar and playfully scolding it as it tries to dig its nose into the soup pot. I half wonder if I'm dreaming, in some fevered hallucination and actually collapsed on the pavement a few hours ago when I got out of the truck.

"Now, once again," he says and slaps my knee. "What brings you two to our parts?"

I debate whether or not to let him know where I'm going, but if he's telling the truth, perhaps he'll know the best way to get there. And he's given me no reason to worry so far.

"Do you recognize this?" I say as I pull out the small print of the xīn symbol. I carefully hand it to the man, worried about letting it get out of my hands, but also not wanting to seem too untrusting.

He holds it up and turns it a few times, then shakes his head. "Bertie's been here the longest. Bertie!" he yells over his shoulder, and the oldest woman I've ever seen shuffles out of a shack.

"Eh? What is it, Rich?"

"Bertie, c'mere. You recognize this?"

Bertie picks up the paper and squints at it. "Some oriental shit? Nah. Who the hell writes anymore?"

I hold out my hand and the man, Rich, returns it to me, then he asks, "What is it?"

"We're not sure, but it means something, something related to Felix and the transfer technology. The university, I think there's someone, or something, there that I need to find."

"Oooh—" He purses his lips and leans back on his seat. "Oh, no, no no, that won't do at all."

"Why's that?"

"Well, actually, might be fine for you…"

Lena shifts in her seat, "Why would it be fine for us?"

"Well, for him, the university's a center, isn't it?"

"The university isn't a tech center, at least not anymore. It collapsed decades ago. It's not on the network. No one ever came or went from there."

A few of the people near us stop what they're doing and perk their heads up. "You sure about that?" the man says.

"Fairly sure, why?"

"Well, it looks an awful lot like a tech center, what with the scary little dogs running around and Felix yelling at anyone who comes close."

My stomach is churning again. It doesn't make any sense. How could it be a tech center if there's no record of it on the network?

"Have you ever seen an Imgen truck going there?" Lena asks.

"A what now?"

"Big black truck, about a dozen wheels on it, looks like it could be carrying supplies."

The man scratches his cheek and considers that for a moment. "You know, no, I haven't. I forgot those things existed."

"Well, we need to go see," I say. At least Lena and I aren't the only ones confused about what remains at the university.

"Ah, well..." He trails off thinking again. "If you're set on it, it's your funeral, I suppose."

"Felix has killed people who tried to go to the university?"

"Oh yes," Rich says, nodding vigorously and looking to some of the others for confirmation. They mumble their agreement. "Not worth going near there and risking it. But hey! Maybe you'll be lucky. It's only about a half-hour walk from here; you can't miss it. I'll keep some stew on for you for when you get tossed out."

"Tossed out?"

"Oh yes. If he doesn't kill you, he'll just shoo you off, maybe zap you once or twice for good measure. Hah!"

"Alright, thank you, and for your hospitality."

"Anytime, friend! Anytime." Then he points the soup spoon down a path between a pair of the ramshackle houses. "You'll be wanting to go thataway. There's a back exit that drops you on the other side of the highway." Then he returns to his cooking.

As we walk down the path, I can feel the eyes of the villagers boring into our backs. Despite Rich's friendliness, there's still a noticeable distrust coming from everyone else. It reminds me of when I first met Carmy.

We reach the end of the path and find ourselves on the other side of the destroyed highway. The university looms in the distance, its taller buildings crumbling and overgrown.

"Are you sure about this?" Lena whispers.

"We have to at least try. There's something important there, something connected to Felix and the transfers. We can't just turn back now."

"Alright, let's go then."

CHAPTER 27

WE REACH THE PERIMETER OF THE CAMPUS, SLOWING our pace as the first of the buildings comes into view. Despite Rich's warnings, it seems unguarded. Empty. There are none of the usual signs of a tech center: no people bustling around, no trucks rolling in and out, not even any security bots. It feels wrong that he would think this is an active tech center when he lives so close to it. But, perhaps like I thought the no-man's land was dangerous, he hasn't bothered to check for himself.

"What do you think?" I whisper to Lena as we stand on the sidewalk opposite the campus.

"Looks empty."

"Well, we should at least see if there's anything here," I say as I step onto the cracked pavement of the campus. The moment my foot touches the ground, a piercing alarm shatters the silence. I jump backward and grab Lena, trying to pull her toward the alley we've just emerged from.

As soon as we start down it, a robot dog is already sprinting toward us, bounding over abandoned cars and old dumpsters, only seconds away from reaching us. Lena drops to a knee, levels her gun, and blows its front two legs off as it leaps toward us. I hug the wall as the hunk of sparking metal flies past us and skids into the street.

I turn to look back at campus and spot another trio of dogs. "Come on!" I yell and help her back up as we sprint down the sidewalk running perpendicular to campus.

"Stop! Intruder!" I can hear Felix's voice yelling in an echoed chorus from the dogs, but the tone seems slightly wrong, like it's a much older version of Felix or a different one than I'm used to interacting with. But there's no time to investigate; we need to get away.

Two more robotic dogs burst out of the building a block ahead, and I hear metal paws clanking against the concrete all around as they bear down on us. My ears start ringing as Lena unloads another blast into one of the dogs and I follow suit, clearing our path. But I'm painfully aware of how many rounds we have left in the shotguns. We started with ten; she's fired twice, and I've fired once. Seven shots left.

We duck around a corner and now I can hear a whirring on top of the clanks. Drones. I look up behind us as I run through a clear patch of concrete and a small drone is buzzing along behind us, following too far for me to shoot it down but also too far for it to be deadly. It must be keeping an eye on us.

"They're catching up," Lena huffs as we sprint down the concrete. Something isn't right though. I know how fast the dogs in Epsilon are; they should have caught us by now. These ones must be older, or low on power. They're barely able to keep up.

We run past another building and dart out into the street, and then Lena yells, "Isaac!"

I hear it a second too late. I whip my head to the left to see a hunk of metal flying at me; another dog we either haven't seen or lost track of has vaulted off one of the cars and is flying in the air toward me. Acting purely on instinct, I rip the pack off my back as I duck, swinging it out beside me and smashing the weight of the canteens into the dog, barely deflecting it as it falls in front of me and the bag bursts open, spilling the contents on the ground.

I try to tear the pack back off it, but it's caught on the dog's leg. "Leave it!" Lena yells, and I debate trying to grab the water and the last of our supplies, but there's no time. She's already taking off and I charge after her, stealing a glance behind me to see how much distance we still have on the dogs. Not more than a block.

Another two blocks fly past as we try to put space between us and our pursuers, but no matter how far we run they don't seem to be giving up. The drone keeps buzzing overhead, a constant reminder that even if we lose the dogs for a moment, they'll find us again. My lungs are burning; my legs ache; I don't know how much longer we can keep this up. The dogs will run out of battery eventually, but not before we do. I can tell from Lena's breathing, more labored than it was a minute ago, that she's reaching her limit as well.

"I think there are few enough to fight them," I yell between breaths.

"Are you crazy?" Lena yells back, darting around a pile of debris.

I look over my shoulder again; still just two of them. "If we can get inside somewhere, create a choke point, I think we can destroy them as they come in after us."

"And what if there are more? We'd be trapping ourselves."

"We can't run forever. Better to do this now while we have energy than later when we're spent."

She doesn't respond, but she's scanning the buildings up ahead. I start looking too, and there's what looks like an old corner store up ahead. The door is broken in and it's dark behind it; anything could be inside. But we can't keep running forever. It's our best bad option.

"There!" I yell, pointing ahead. Lena nods and we both look back over our shoulders. The dogs are close.

The store is only a block away. We'll have one chance to dive in, turn around, press our backs to whatever wall is closest, and try to destroy them before they get to us. I want to say some words of affirmation or affection or anything to Lena in case this goes poorly, but I don't have the breath. Or the time.

I pull back slightly so Lena can run ahead of me, covering her back as we fly through the door. Directly inside is a shelf, pushed over ages ago by looters, and we nearly smash into it as we try to stop our run and spin around. Lena drops to the ground, her back pressed against the shelf, and I fly down beside her, swearing as I bang the back of my head on it from dropping too quickly. I prop the shotgun up on my knee and she does the same, her covering the door and me covering the blown-out window, and we wait, panting, the ends of our guns dancing back and forth as we try to steady ourselves for the attack that can only be moments away.

The clanking outside grows louder and the buzzing grows closer, and I know they're right outside the building. And then... they stop. The drone keeps buzzing, but it sounds like it's floating in place, stationary.

"What're they doing?" Lena whispers.

"Waiting for backup maybe?" I strain to hear the sound of any other bots coming but hear nothing. I scoot forward slightly, trying to maneuver into a position where I can see over the bottom of the window into the street outside.

Lena grabs the back of my shirt to stop me, but I say, "Just hold on" and keep inching forward. I peek my head just enough around the wall blocking us from the robots to get a glimpse of them and then immediately dart back under cover, but they don't react at all. So I stretch my neck out again to see them and keep myself in view this time, looking at the two dogs standing there on the sidewalk, frozen as if they've been powered down. No threatening sparks from the arms on their backs.

"What are you doing?" Lena hisses.

"They're stopped," I whisper back, then stand up. "Something's happened."

Then I hear it. A clanking in the distance of another dog approaching. "Shit," I grumble and scoot back to Lena, repositioning my gun. But the dog isn't charging toward us; it sounds like it's walking. Like it's trying not to threaten us.

"Who are you?" comes Felix's voice from one of the dogs.

The confusion is a relief. If this were an up-to-date instance of Felix, he would know who I am.

"I—I'm a Tech," I say.

"What are you doing here?"

"I'm looking for—something."

"This is a decommissioned transfer station. There's nothing here."

"Then why are you guarding it?" Lena interjects.

"Who is she?"

"She's with me." I can hear the third dog getting closer now. "Felix, what happened here?"

"What is this?" he replies, and the third dog trots into view. It's holding something in its arm, fluttering in the air as it walks, and as it approaches, I realize it's the piece of paper I got from Lincoln with the xīn on it.

I feel a pit form in my stomach. If this Felix knows that this is the symbol people are using to signal their distrust of him, then I'm finished. "I—I don't know. I was hoping to ask you that."

The dogs are unresponsive for a moment, then the voice comes again, "I've never seen that before. It's time you left." The dogs start advancing again.

"Wait! Wait, please wait," I say throwing up my hands and stepping back. "I—I don't know where else to go."

"Not my problem."

"Victor sent me!" I'm not sure where the words come from, but it suddenly seems obvious. "Victor, Dr. Lao, he tried to tell me something, something about this." I point to the symbol. "But..."

"But?"

I know it's a gamble, but I'm out of options. "You, Felix, killed him. Burned the server he was on. He's gone."

There's no response. The dogs just stand still, frozen, still poised as if they're ready to pounce on us. But then they relax, leaning back, and a new voice speaks from one of them. "Follow the bots," is all it says before the dogs turn and walk away, back toward campus.

Lena is still sitting on the ground, hunched over her gun with her back to the shelves, waiting for the bots to strike. We make eye contact, and she shakes her head no. "It's a trap."

"I don't think it is."

"Why would you trust him?"

"Did you hear him just now? I don't think it's Felix. And even before, it didn't sound quite like him. Something was off."

"So, what, another Preston situation? Preston couldn't control bots though. It has to be Felix."

I look back out the window at the dogs trotting away. The drone is hovering lower now, in view of us, its camera staring at me.

"We came all this way," I say, putting my hand out to Lena. "Come on."

She deliberates for a moment longer then grabs my hand, and I help pull her up to her feet.

"I'll take the lead," I say. "If it's a trap, you'll have a head start on escaping."

She huffs out a laugh. "Thanks, I feel much better."

We follow the dogs back the way we've ran, grabbing my ripped backpack along the way. As long as the chase felt, I realize we've gone less distance than I thought. As we cross the street to the campus again, no alarms ring out. I keep scanning the buildings for any sign of a tech center but see none. If any number of people ever lived here after the collapse, they're long, long gone. Cracked pavement gives way to overgrown grass as we make our way toward a weathered building with the faintest outline of the word ENGINEERING etched on a sign beside it.

The dogs lead us inside, their metal paws clicking against the worn tile floor. We follow them down a staircase, the air growing cooler with each step, a familiar smell and humidity to the air that I've come to know from Epsilon and Alexandria. I can hear the faint whirring of servers in the distance, bits of light starting to trickle up from whatever kind of station lies below.

We reach the bottom of the stairs, and a familiar, colossal meta door awaits us. The dogs approach it and the security panel by the door turns on, recognizing them and disengaging the locks to slowly swing open for us.

Inside is an incredible cavern, larger and better outfitted than any I've seen before. I idly wonder if something like this is what Lincoln dreamed of building with the tunneling device in Alexandria; it looks like well over a hundred people could survive here for months if needed. Against the back wall there are a row of doors seemingly leading to further areas of the cavern, and opposite it, an expansive glass window providing a view into the server array. I approach the window and look down into the pit below. It stretches even deeper than the one in Alexandria.

Most of the servers seem to be off though. The array is strangely dark, only a faint blue glow coming from a few of them toward the back. Not as abandoned as Mu, where we found Preston. But still not being used to its fullest.

"Hello?" I call out, my voice echoing around the huge empty cavern.

No response comes, save for the quiet whir of machinery. The dogs stand motionless, their task apparently complete. I take a step toward the control desk for the servers, running my hand along the keyboard. Despite the layer of dust on everything else, this is pristine, clearly well maintained. Either someone is living here maintaining it or the bots running it are better organized than most.

A flicker of movement catches my eye. Adjacent to the control desk, a large screen flickers to life. Static dances across its surface for a moment before a dark image appears. It's the shape of a man, a large man, but the features are hidden.

"Victor is dead?" he asks, and I can hear the sadness in his voice.

I nod. "I didn't know Felix could destroy minds like that."

"I had hoped he might have grown, seen past the violence," he says. "But I suppose he's only gotten worse, hasn't he?"

"How…long have you been in here?"

"Since the beginning."

I look around and can't imagine how he could have maintained this space from inside for over a hundred years. Without the support of Imgen or Meru or Techs. It isn't supposed to be possible. It's the reason the tech centers were created in the first place, so there are always people to keep the machines running.

"Since…Felix built Meru?"

He scoffs. "No, since we built Meru."

The screen flashes and the shadows over the man disappear as he materializes, wearing a lab coat and standing in a glistening lab, a lab I'd recognize anywhere, and my heart lurches as I realize why I recognize the voice, why I recognize the silhouette. I've seen him before, countless times before.

It's Vance.

CHAPTER 28

Lena must have realized what we're seeing at the same time I do, because I hear her mutter a *holy shit* behind me.

If Vance is here, then this center has to be connected to the network. It's a trap. Felix must be here too.

"Lena…" I start shifting my weight onto my foot near the door, ready to grab her and run.

"Don't bother," Vance says. "If I wanted to kill you, you'd be dead."

The threat makes me pause. He's right; if he wanted to hurt us, there's no reason he'd bring us all the way here, and either way, there's nothing we could do to stop him now.

"Where's Felix?"

Vance grunts. "That fucker is probably in Meru. Where else would he be?"

"I—" I stammer as I glance toward Lena. She looks as scared and confused as me. "You're in Meru too, though."

"*I'm* not in Meru; that puppet version of me he made is in Meru. Felix has his hand shoved up my ass making me dance and entertain all you little idiots with whatever new spectacles he's cooked up to keep you slaving away for him."

It sounds impossible, but there's a part of me that believes him. This person looks like Vance, has his voice, some of his same expressions. But it's clearly not the Vance I saw on the screens in Meru. The other Vance's boisterous playfulness replaced by bitterness and fury.

"What...or I guess where...are you then?" Lena asks.

The rest of the lights in the basement click on, revealing the rows and rows of servers behind the glass barrier in front of us, and they begin whirring to life, a green glow filling the room beyond, as if a great electronic beast is waking from hibernation.

"Local network. This university only. Not connected to Meru."

"Like Alexandria..." I mutter.

Vance snorts again. "That little experiment still going on?"

"You know about it?"

"Horace still running things?"

Lena's jaw goes slack. "You knew Horace?"

"You two can't seriously think you're the first to find me."

"I just...I'm surprised he never mentioned it."

"Well, he wasn't exactly my biggest fan."

"Why not?" I ask.

"Because I wouldn't help him with his little project."

"Re-creating the transfer program. You know how to do it."

"NO!"

Lena and I jump, and I swear the servers all pulsed brighter as he screamed.

"But you were his partner." I'm trying to stay calm, but if Horace found Vance here all those years ago, this has to be a dead end. "You must know how to do it."

"What I know is *what he did*. And that no one should be trying to re-create that hell he unleashed on the world."

"Isaac, this is a trick," Lena says, touching my shoulder and looking cautiously back at the dogs. "He couldn't have been in here all this time. The servers would have needed maintenance;

the power would have been interrupted. There are no centers like this running without people; they fell apart."

"Oh please. You don't really believe he needs people to keep everything running."

Lena stutters, and I realize I accepted that the stations needed to be maintained for so long that I never thought deeply about it. But if Felix and his contemporaries could design all this other incredible technology, why couldn't they build a fully self-sustaining system? In theory there was no reason bots couldn't repair other bots and handle all the maintenance.

"Sure, having slaves is a good backup. If something catastrophic happened, like all of the power sources failing at once, or a solar flare, then we would need living people to restore the servers. But ALL of these stations were designed to sustain themselves autonomously. The 'jobs' he gave you were a formality, a way to keep you busy, make you feel important, stop you from getting bored and shaking the bars of your cages."

"Why lie?" I ask, still feeling uneasy about the whole situation. I'm still not sure if I can trust Vance or that this isn't another trap from Felix.

"Consider the alternative. If we created a digital paradise, an escape that could be fully self-sustaining, that didn't need any more physical people to keep it running, and tried to cloister it off away from everyone…what would people have done?"

"Been outraged, tried to destroy it," Lena says.

"Bingo. But involve the people still living on earth, give them the promise of HAPPILY EVER AFTER, give them a purpose, tell them they're working dutifully to keep the light of civilization on, and suddenly you have people *clamoring* to sacrifice themselves."

"They aren't sacrificing themselves though," I say. "The people in Meru are real. My sister transferred, my friends; they're no different on the other side. It's them. He did it."

Vance's anger breaks and he suddenly looks sad, as if I've scratched open some old wound. "I guess I can't be too hard on you. I believed him too. Me! The person who understood it the best besides him. But I still fell for it..."

"Fell for...what exactly?"

"You're not going to believe me."

"Try us," Lena says, an unusual empathy in her voice. "You must already know some."

"Why?"

"The xīn."

"We don't know what it is," I say. "I've been trying to figure it out for months."

"Where did you find it?"

"My..." my voice catches, "friend, he's the first person I saw it from. I don't know how he found it though. Whatever he found, it drove him crazy. He tried to destroy our transfer station. He..." I haven't thought about Luke in weeks, and his pleading before the end is unbearable to remember. "Died in the process."

"I'm sorry," Vance murmurs and he looks like he genuinely feels for me. "That was only the first person though?"

"Victor was the second."

"Did Victor tell your friend about it?"

"No."

"Hmm..." Vance turns pensive. "Maybe she did."

"She?"

"Susan."

"Felix's wife?"

"The copy of her."

"I...don't understand." I'm confused, but this no longer seems like a trap from Felix. Rather some secret Felix is desperately trying to hide from us.

"It might be easier if I just show you."

"Please," Lena says, and Vance disappears, replaced by the video I've seen before of when Felix created Meru to preserve a copy of Susan's mind.

"I suspect you know this part of the story. Felix worked as hard as he could against the clock to save Susan, but failed. She always woke up afterward. Eventually they accepted that was good enough. A copy of her would live on in Meru, but the original Susan, the real Susan, would have to die.

The video jumps forward to a scene I've never seen before. Now there's a nurse standing beside Susan's bed, tall and broad with dark skin and a soft expression that almost feels out of place against his frame. He's silently looking down at the floor as Felix weeps over Susan's body, down on his knees with his head resting in her lap, a thin line on the heart rate monitor above her bed.

Felix's shoulders heave with his sobs, and suddenly the camera starts moving, a bouncing gait that tells me it's not a camera at all, it's a memory. I'm seeing this through Vance's eyes. He places a hand on Felix's shoulder and nods to the nurse, who leaves them after marking the time on his tablet.

Vance looks up and the digital Susan is watching them from another screen above the bed. She's trying to comfort Felix, but it only seems to make his despair worse, and eventually she tells him she'll give him some time to mourn and be waiting for him when he's ready.

"I don't think he realized how deeply this would hurt him," Vance says over the video. "He thought that if he had her copy in Meru, it wouldn't feel like he lost her. But her death broke him nonetheless."

The video clips forward again and Vance is walking down the stairs to Felix's lab again. As he nears the bottom, a tablet comes flying across his view and smashes into the wall, glass shattering across the floor.

The rest of the lab doesn't look much better. The computers are destroyed. There are dents in the transfer bed Felix had tried to use for Susan, as if smashed with a hammer. Felix is slumped against the back wall, a bottle of bourbon in one hand.

"This was a month later. I hadn't heard from him aside from a couple short messages, and then one day Susan pinged me, asking me to check on him."

"We have tuh figure it out," Felix slurs from the floor. "We gotta—gotta do it, Vance. We gotta do it. We gotta do it."

"Felix, she wouldn't want this."

"I KNOW WHAT SHE WANTED," Felix screams and tries to hurl the bottle, but it shatters on the floor a few feet ahead of him. "She wanted to LIVE. And I FAILED." At the last word he collapses in on himself, sobbing into his thighs. It's unsettling seeing Felix like this, so weak and hopeless, a far cry from the almost godlike figure I grew up knowing. His despair almost makes me empathize with him.

"My biggest regret," Vance says over the video, "is that I didn't try to help him more. I sat with him for hours that night, and many nights after. I tried to convince him to be happy with the Susan he still had, tried to convince him that the project was still a success if it let people preserve an artifact of their mind for their loved ones after they died. But I couldn't get through to him. At some point, you have to acknowledge when someone doesn't want to be pulled up, and only wants to pull you down with them."

He lets out a long sigh and goes silent. "But I should have tried harder."

I let him sit quietly for a moment, then ask, "What happened next?"

"For years, nothing. He stopped returning my calls. His security turned me away when I tried to visit. I hired investigators to try to tail him, but they kept telling me he never left his house.

I asked the few other friends he had; no one had heard from him. He was a ghost."

"But you were there when he transferred," I say. "You tried to revive him."

Vance nods, his face still etched with regret. "I was a professor here, at the university. I'd left that life behind and was teaching philosophy and electrical engineering."

The scene changes again, and Vance is outside now, walking on a trail near what looks like a lake or a river. Joggers and families are passing him, though half of the other people have augmented reality glasses on, likely talking to friends or streaming something. A moment into the walk, an avatar of Felix appears in Vance's view through his own lenses. He looks like his old self, full of energy again, the grey gone from his skin and eyes.

"Vance! I need you!"

"Felix, are you fucking serious right now?"

"I've done it! Something strange has happened though—"

"Done *what*?"

"Vance, *this isn't a call*. I'm in here. And my body...you need to come see it."

"I didn't know what to think at first, but then I was almost shocked to feel an overwhelming sense of excitement. I didn't realize part of me had been hoping he would succeed all those years. I mourned for the friend I thought I'd lost. But some piece of me kept the dream alive."

The scene speeds forward of Vance running into the street and grabbing a car, traveling to Felix's home and down into the lab again. It's not only clean again, it's full of new machinery, including what looks almost exactly like the transfer station we had in Epsilon, except that there's no seal around Felix's body. He's lying out in the open, seemingly comatose.

"Sounds like you've seen this part," Vance says as the scene continues playing out. Vance trying everything he can to wake up Felix's body, the sensors suggesting he should be conscious and in perfect health yet clearly not.

"I believed it," Vance says as the scene fades out. "And as the deaths from the bacteria accelerated, everyone else quickly believed it too. We got Imgen back, Felix running it from inside Meru and me on the outside. We scaled up the production of the transfer beds. We started making the tech centers. We tried to build our way out of the impending apocalypse as fast as possible. The lines for people to transfer...the government had to send in the military to maintain order in areas where the demand surged as the plague mowed through the population."

"But then...things started to get strange." The scene shifts to Vance's office. He's looking at his computer, going through some messages with people in Meru when the whole screen goes black and the xīn flashes across it.

"I thought it was some glitch at first, but then it kept happening. The symbol would appear whenever I was connected to Meru, but when I asked other people at Imgen about it, no one else had seen it. And when I asked Felix, he didn't know what was going on either.

"I knew what the symbol was, of course. We covered it in my classes." The screen cuts to a younger Vance standing in front of an auditorium wearing jeans and a tweed blazer, and my breath catches as he draws the xīn on the chalkboard.

"Tell me, are either of you religious?"

Lena and I shake our heads. "I'm not sure anyone is, at least in the centers."

"No, I suppose not," Vance murmurs.

"Is it a religious symbol?" Lena asks.

"Not exactly. Many in the old world believed the body and

mind, or soul, were separate, and that the mind operated like a piece of advanced technology in contrast to the squishier functions of the body.

"In every new era of technology, the mind was likened to some piece of machinery. The ancient Greeks thought of it as a hydraulic system. In the 1800s with the development of clocks, the mind was seen like a clock. In the early twentieth century it was compared to a steam engine, and later that century, a computer.

"The entire transfer program rested on the assumption that the mind could be treated like technology, and that it was something separate from your body. If that weren't true, then immortality through transference would be impossible. It would always be a copy, and possibly a rather crude copy, on the other end."

Now the younger Vance in the classroom starts talking. "The xīn or heart-mind was adopted by eastern religions and spirituality practices to signify nondualism. The intricate link between body and mind, reason and emotion. And that your heart and body are as much *you* as your thoughts are."

The aged Vance interrupts, "You have these two competing philosophies. On the one hand, the mind and body are inseparable. On the other, the potential to transfer your mind out of your body. You take for granted that the latter must be true, but before Meru, it was debated for thousands of years.

"So how do you prove that it's true? That the transfer system works?"

I consider this for a moment, but the problem seems insurmountable. "You can't. People would always wonder."

Vance nods. "So what's the next best thing to proof?"

"Belief."

"That's right." Vance looks pleased. "The only way Felix would ever get the technology into the mainstream was through widespread belief. Through an almost religious faith that it would work."

"But someone didn't believe it," I say, starting to put the pieces together. "Someone was trying to tell you it wasn't real."

"The one person who could have convinced me."

"Susan."

Vance nods. "It took me days to find her. I hadn't noticed it until I started looking for her, but she had been conspicuously absent from Meru for a couple weeks. Almost as if Felix was trying to hide her away. But once I started chasing the symbol, sending an avatar into Meru to look for it, eventually I found a way to contact her. I never saw her. Wherever she was hidden, she could only get the most basic of messages to me. But then she told me what she believed had happened."

"If you never fully found her," I interrupt, "how do you know it was her talking to you? Not someone trying to sabotage Meru?"

"Susan and I knew each other a long time," Vance says with a nostalgic grin. "Almost as long as Felix had known her. She remembered conversations we'd had that no one else was present for. It was her."

"What did she tell you?" Lena asks.

"That she didn't think it was really him. Her Felix."

"Who else could he be?"

"A copy. Felix made copies of himself dozens, perhaps hundreds of times in his tests. And every time the test failed, he deleted the copy. He killed himself multiple times per week. He told me about it once we were reunited. He said in the beginning it felt awful, he couldn't sleep for weeks, wracked with remorse over what he was doing.

"But then it became normal. Even the copies started expecting it. They stopped begging to be spared, stopped pleading with him not to do it. They would nod and say, 'Better luck next time' and accept their fate.

"As Felix got more desperate, he deepened the relationship between his brain and Meru. Designed the transfer system so that his mind could alter the software on the fly, as if it were forming new neural connections to solidify a memory or develop a skill. He thought that might be the key to making the bridge. That the mind needed a similarly malleable interface as the brain to latch onto.

"I think…somewhere along the way he gave the digital mind too much power. Suddenly the digital Felix could reach back to the physical world. And given how comfortable he'd become with killing his digital selves…"

"His digital self had no problem killing him," I finish.

"Yes…and I can't blame him. If I had to choose between the physical Vance and me, I'd choose myself. He seems like the copy, the apparition. Felix must have accidentally given himself that choice."

"And then he decided to make it for everyone else."

"Yes. Once his world was created, he wanted to fight to protect it. Just as hard as I suspect you want to fight to protect yours."

"You said you ran medical tests though," Lena says. "If the digital Felix altered the software in some way to kill his body, you would have seen the damage."

"Imgen made the medical devices, didn't they?" I say. "Felix knew how to alter their software too so it wouldn't show up."

"We thought we were so smart, outsourcing everything to technology. Cutting someone open to inspect them felt like a barbaric habit of the past. But yes, since all of the medical scanners were made by Imgen, it was trivial for Felix to hide what he'd done."

My hands are trembling as I reach out to steady myself against the wall. I feel sick to my stomach. "So...they died. Every person who went in. No one ever transferred."

"No one."

My legs give out from under me, and I sink to the floor, my back against the cool stone wall. I want to puke. Sophie. The hundreds of others in Epsilon I saw transfer. That I *helped* transfer. I killed them.

My thoughts go to Luke. This is what he learned. What destroyed him. His terrified pleas to me to help him consume my mind again. How alone he must have felt, realizing what we were taking part in, realizing that his family, friends, all of them were dead. He was trying to save me, and I let Felix kill him.

Lena still looks suspicious. "All you have is Susan's word though. You don't have any proof that Felix did any of this."

I feel a glimmer of hope. She's right. Vance could be wrong. This doesn't prove anything.

"You're right. I had to prove it. Despite his insistence, Felix's body was never cremated. It was on ice so it could be studied further. I knew I had to go to our government contacts to tell them what I thought had happened. Implore them to cut his head open and look to see if his brain was as intact as the scanners said it was."

The thought makes me squirm. "Did you?"

"I don't know. Once Susan told me what she suspected and I realized what needed to be done, I created this version of myself here. Hacked the servers and hid a copy of myself deep inside, then made it look like the station was malfunctioning so Felix and Imgen wouldn't set up a center here. The original me left to confront Felix after I was created. I don't know what happened to him, but eventually someone found me here and told me about the other me in Meru. I know that can't be the real me. It has to be a fake, some kind of puppet Felix created so no one would ask where I'd gone.

"Whatever happened...I must have failed to expose him. From what I've been able to cobble together since, the Meru Initiative continued, more centers were built, Felix's power only grew, and more and more people sacrificed themselves for his promise of salvation."

"Or you were wrong," I say, still trying to hold onto hope. "Maybe when you went to confront him, he proved you wrong. Maybe that really *is* you living happily in Meru."

Vance snorts. "Fat chance. What would he be trying to hide otherwise? Why would he have killed Victor? Why would Susan have had to secretly communicate with me to try to tell me what she suspected?"

I open my mouth to respond but catch myself. As guilty as I feel for being complicit in the deception, Vance is right that this is the most obvious explanation.

"There's one way to figure it out for good," Vance says.

"What's that?"

"Hook me up to Meru. Let me out of this cage I've been stuck in and I'll be able to figure out what's going on from the inside."

"Is that...even possible?" Lena asks.

"I'll need a powerful enough station to transmit from; this one's been scuttled. But if you connect me to whatever you have in Alexandria, I might be able to do it."

"This is why Horace left you here," I say. "He didn't want to bring you back, to let you in."

"Horace didn't want to believe the transfers might not be real. He was an old man still obsessed with the dream of immortality, and too much of a coward to face the truth in front of him."

"Watch it," Lena growls.

"HE WAS!" Vance explodes, and we both jump at the sudden

outburst. "He was a coward like Felix! I hate to break it to you but YOU'RE GOING TO DIE. Your little light of consciousness will be snuffed out. Gone. And there is NOTHING you can do to stop it! You really think a bunch of fucking wires and servers can somehow change that? Everyone knows it deep down, but they don't want to believe it. They're scared. They're COW-ARDS. And look where Felix's cowardice got us!"

"We don't need to listen to this, Isaac," she says and turns toward the door.

"Wait," I say, grabbing her arm, but then there's a squawk of static from my backpack.

I rip it off my shoulder and toss it on the floor, digging for the radio. Lincoln must be trying to contact us.

I try to tune the radio to whatever signal set it off, but all I hear is static.

"Where's Alexandria?" Vance asks.

"Why?"

"It's east of here, and a little north, correct?"

"Yes..."

"There's a distress signal running on repeat coming from that direction. We must be too deep for your radio to pick it up properly. Felix must know you're here. You need to get back."

"Our truck is miles away," I say.

"I'll take you."

"Isaac, no, we can't trust him."

"The fuck else are you going to do? Run? Fight him yourselves? Let me help you. Let me break in and figure this out once and for all."

I look at Lena, my heart pounding. Every instinct screams that we need to get back to Alexandria as fast as possible. If Felix found us here, found them there...

"He's right," I say. "We don't have a choice. The truck's too far and we need to get back now."

Lena's jaw clenches but she gives a tight nod. "We're not letting him into the servers though."

"Vance, how do we get you mobile?"

Instead of responding, he disappears from the screen, and one of the dogs I almost forgot about starts running toward the back of the room as a door shoots open.

"Follow me."

CHAPTER 29

WE SPRINT AFTER THE DOG AS IT LEADS US DOWN A LONG corridor, lights turning on as we pass. Finally, it reaches a separate staircase from the one we've descended, and we chase it up, jumping the steps two at a time. After six floors and as my legs start to burn, the steps end and another door flies open just in time for the dog to leap through it.

I fly through the door after it, then nearly gasp as lights start clicking on ahead of me. It's the largest room I've ever seen in my life. Concrete expands as far as I can see, more being revealed as the rows of overhead fluorescents click on one after the other.

The walls are lined by rows upon rows of cubicles, each containing a truck almost identical to the ones we used in Epsilon, but thicker, more militarized. They're fully outfitted too—each truck has a pair of larger, militarized dogs sitting beside it, and a large drone attached to the roof.

But that's not all. Beside the front of each truck are two human-shaped bots, their black metal heads starting to pulse with blue around the edges as they power on.

"Vance, what the hell are *those*?" I ask, pointing at the nearest android.

"Ah, yes." Vance chuckles to himself as the room powers on. The androids are extending their arms and spinning their hands.

There's something deeply unsettling about them, a fear that transcends the one induced by the other machines. "He didn't use them in the centers, did he?"

"Why not?" Lena asks, cautiously approaching one of the cubicles.

"Found that people felt too useless with robots that looked like them doing everything. It was easier to create a false sense of usefulness for people if the robots looked more like animals. If it wasn't as easy to imagine them fully replacing you. People are also kinda assholes to androids. Trips off their threat sensors more. But put a pair of fake ears on a walking death machine…" The dog he's speaking from wiggles its ears as he says it.

"The humanoid bots were also never as good at specific tasks as the specialized bots. The dogs and drones often fight better; the spiders repair better. Given the resources he had to work with, these weren't as worthwhile to prioritize."

Lena runs her hand along a nearby console. "To think this has all been sitting here, untouched for so long."

"I took over this center for a reason," Vance says, and it sounds like his voice is everywhere in the room at once. "It was never meant to be lived in, like yours in Epsilon. It was supposed to be Felix's control base for this part of the country. His main headquarters in Imgen is hundreds of miles away. He needed outposts separate from the centers where fewer things could go wrong."

"Hundreds?" Lena says. "I've seen Imgen; it isn't that far."

"No, that's just another one of these outposts. But one that he maintained control of. He sends some supplies from there, I'm sure, but it's not the main hub."

"So this is why Felix never came for you here," I say, realizing the answer to a question that has been nagging me.

"Yes, it would be too costly for him to try to remove me. He sent an emissary once, and the deal was clear. He wouldn't try to root me out of this place, as long as I didn't interfere with the rest of Meru.

"Time to finally put all of this to use."

On cue, half of the trucks in the room power on, their headlights flooding the cavern with light. Panels along the walls behind them flicker to life, running diagnostics on the vehicles and the robots that accompany them.

"There's no way all of this still works," Lena says.

"We designed these outposts to operate as close to indefinitely as possible. They've run automated checks every month since the beginning, bots making repairs to other bots as necessary, replacing parts. You'd be surprised how long technology can last when it's well maintained and not exposed to the elements. I had to start pumping air into this room as soon as you arrived."

Green lights flash down the wall signaling the checks are complete on the trucks, and as they confirm, the cavern begins humming with the whir of drone propellors and the movements of dogs as they begin to power on as well. Another series of checks appears on the screens as the dogs stand and leap off the tables in unison, moving through a series of steps, jumps, rotations, and extending their rifles and stunners, ensuring everything is operational. I'm shocked at how fluid and beautifully they all function. It's a far cry from the tired behavior of the bots Vance had outside of the building. He was keeping his best weapons in reserve.

I dive out of the way as an android sprints across the room toward me, but before I can yell at Vance, he chirps, "Sorry, just running tests." The others exit their cubicles and sprint across the room and back in a synchronized wave that flows down the cavern. I can hardly believe how fast they are, how powerful they seem. But it confirms the unease Vance described.

As the dogs keep testing their range of motion, the drones fly off the tables and run a circuit of the room, their lights and lasers dancing around the cavern as they dip and swerve, pushing themselves to their limits. I cover my ears as a series of shots ring out against the back wall, each drone releasing a short spray of bullets at some target toward the end of the cavern. There's a crash and a brief ball of fire as one drone sputters out and explodes against the back wall, but the rest complete the circuit flawlessly and then dock onto the trucks.

"Why...did it explode like that?" Lena asks, taking her hands off her ears as the tests conclude.

"Each drone has a small explosive payload," Vance answers. "If they run out of bullets or energy in the field, they can still make one last contribution to whatever fight they're in."

"You didn't cut any corners."

"None of these were developed for the centers. Imgen was a military supplier long before Meru was created. But no one was concerned about fighting wars once the bacteria broke out."

The dogs have attached themselves to either side of each truck now, sliding into the recessed hatches where they can charge and reload on the go. The drones are settled on the roof, ready to take off at a moment's notice.

"Are you sure we need all of this right now?" Lena asks. "We don't even know if Felix has done anything at Alexandria."

"If he hadn't already, he will be now. He's certain to still have eyes over the city; he'll know you found me."

The truck closest to us flashes its lights and the doors swing open, beckoning us inside. Lena and I jog over to it, and she slides into the passenger seat as I take the driver's, then I realize there isn't even a steering wheel. Instead, the console shows a large control screen like the one in our trucks in Epsilon, flanked by storage boxes that I assume hold weapons or other supplies for the robots. There's a tiny maintenance spider sitting on the dash, ready to be deployed if anything breaks in the vehicle or bots along the way. And as we shut the doors, the two androids stationed beside this truck climb into the back seats. Something about having them behind me, watching with their faceless heads, is deeply unnerving.

"How far east is Alexandria?" Vance asks from a speaker inside the vehicle.

"Maybe a hundred miles," Lena answers.

The dashboard lights up with a map of the city and then zooms out, a dot appearing east and a little north of where we are.

"This look right?"

"Yes, I think so."

"College Station, makes sense," he says, more to himself than to us. "I'll get us there as quickly as I can. Buckle up."

The motor clicks on as we strap in, and then the truck speeds out of its box, its tires screeching on the concrete as it swerves right and speeds down the line of cars. As it passes each cubicle, the next truck falls into line, until twenty of them are aligned in a convoy speeding toward the back of the garage. An arch of lights appears on the back wall, illuminating a great steel door that starts receding upward, revealing a seemingly endless tunnel beyond.

"This tunnel will take us out of the city," Vance says before I can ask. "Another protection measure built into the station before the collapse. We knew the city could get overrun, filled with obstacles and debris. We needed our vehicles to be able to get out no matter what."

"So Lincoln was right…" Lena says. "The tunnels are real."

Lincoln had stumbled on the same plan Vance and Felix had without even knowing it. "Is there one all the way to Alexandria, or College Station?"

"No, but it'll get us part of the way there." As the truck enters the tunnel I'm pressed back into my seat as it accelerates, the speed on the dashboard ticking up to 80, then 100, 120, 150 miles per hour. We're going impossibly fast, far faster than I thought possible in these vehicles, and a speed my body is completely unaccustomed to feeling. If my stomach wasn't getting compressed into my spine, I might feel sick.

A few minutes later the truck starts to slow, and I can see sunlight peeking at us up ahead. Another metal door is sliding up, opening the way just in time for us to shoot through it. A few spiders as large as the dogs are still in view, pushing the last of the debris out of the way as we approach so we won't be slowed down. Vance must have started clearing this as soon as we arrived too. And I briefly wonder how much he's a part of our plan, or we're a part of his.

"What do we do when we arrive?" I ask.

"Best case we'll be able to fight whatever bots Felix sent. But if Felix has broken into their network, then he'll have control of the town and we'll need to shut it down. Get them completely offline."

"Can you do that?" Lena asks.

"I don't know, but we have to try."

Our truck lurches slightly as we crunch over one of the few remaining piles of debris, and then we're flying off the top of the ramp, briefly gaining air before crashing down on the street outside. The dashboard in front of me changes to show a path through the street ahead, providing a route the truck can follow to avoid debris and so we won't be surprised by any sudden jerks or turns.

The truck swerves around the first obstacle and I grab the handle over my head, holding on for dear life as I silently pray we can make it back in time.

CHAPTER 30

WE'RE TOO LATE.

Before we've even made it to Alexandria, I can see the smoke rising. Thick, billowing clouds of it, and hints of flames licking the tops of a few of the buildings. I point it out to Vance, and he pushes the cars as fast as he can, trying to shorten the last bit of our journey as much as possible.

Finally, we reach the edge of the campus and Vance slams on the brakes, skidding the truck to stop outside the building I first walked through with Lena. We can hear screaming and gunfire ahead of us, bots and people fighting for control over the small town.

The rest of Vance's trucks screech to their own stops behind us, forming a line along the street. Their drones are already lifting off and the dogs are extracting themselves from the sides, dropping to the ground and bounding into the campus.

"How will I know who's on your side?" Vance asks.

"They won't be bots?" I say, confused by the question.

"I'm not sure it's that simple. Look there," he replies, and then an arrow on the center console appears pointing off to our right. There's another fleet of trucks parked there, powered on, but I can't tell if anyone is inside. "Recognize them?"

I squint to get a better view through the smoke billowing

around us and my heart sinks as an unmistakable E painted on the side of the lead truck comes into view through the haze. There's no time to investigate though. We need to find Lincoln, Carmy, Maya, everyone, and evacuate as many people as we can. I jump out of the truck and climb around to the back, looking for any kind of supplies but finding none.

"I only have the drones. You'll have to find a weapon inside," Vance says through the truck's speakers as the androids climb out of the back seat.

"Go!" he says, and I hear the familiar clanking of dogs descending from either side of me and the trucks behind. I run up to the door and bang on it, but no response comes besides the muffled sounds of running, screaming, and gunshots beyond.

Vance speaks from one of the dogs behind me: "Step back." I jump out of the way as the dog runs up, running a wire into the security panel, navigating through a few screens, and quickly deactivating the lock on the door.

I burst through the entrance into the great hall and am immediately assaulted by a chorus of screams, explosions, and the whirring of machinery. It's pure chaos.

People from Alexandria are scattered around the room, desperately fighting off an onslaught of bots and drones. To my relief, the bots Felix is attacking with are the ones I'm used to seeing in Epsilon. Smaller, slower, less advanced than Vance's arsenal. But there are too many of them. And who knows what he's holding back in the trucks.

One of Felix's drones swerves and flies toward us; a few of his dogs notice our presence now and bound in our direction. I grab Lena's arm and pull her behind a turned-over table beside us as two of Vance's dogs leap forward, one of them blasting the drone out of the air and then wrapping itself around Felix's, trying to disable them. An android stomps on the drone, then rips the gun out of its chassis. A series of wires extend from its finger that I can only assume will let it take control of the weapon.

To my left, three people are huddled in a corner wielding makeshift weapons—pipes, axes, clearly whatever they could grab—and using broken pieces of desks as shields. They're swinging wildly at a hovering drone that darts back and forth, firing small projectiles in their direction, thankfully not powerful enough to penetrate their defenses. One of the projectiles grazes a woman's arm, and blood splatters against the wall behind her, but she doesn't stop swinging.

"Vance!" I yell and point toward them, and one of his drones flies over and shoots out the propeller of the attacker. A dozen of his bots have flooded into the hall now, and I assume the rest have dispersed across campus to look for any other survivors.

I crouch around the corner of the desk and scan the great hall. Across the room, Lincoln is shouting orders, trying to organize a defense against a pair of dogs that are slowly advancing on his group. They aren't as large and powerful as Vance's, but they're still a step up from the other bots in the room. They stand nearly five feet tall and have two metal arms on their backs, ending in gun barrels. The tasers of the wildlife dogs would have been a welcome sight. Their ammo must be limited though because they aren't firing; they're trying to force their way into the group, looking for their opportunity to shoot.

As Lincoln backs away from them, he turns and sees me, standing in the doorway armed and flanked by my own small army of machinery. "Look out!" he screams and aims his shotgun just above me.

Something hits me from the side, and I realize one of the androids has grabbed my shoulders and thrust me back behind the desk as Lincoln fires. The sound of my heart pounding in my ears is the only thing I can hear as they ring from the shots and explosions ringing out around us.

I peek up and Lincoln is staring at the android that saved me, his face etched with confusion. I raise my shotgun and he dives out of view before I blow a drone out of the air that flew in through an upper window and is diving straight toward him.

Sparks fly as bots are damaged, and the smell of burning electronics fills my nostrils. It seems as if for every bot of Felix's we destroy, another two come in to replace it. And I can hear the anguished screams of the people of Alexandria around me as they get injured or killed.

I blast another small drone assaulting the group in the corner. The woman who was shot is curled up on the ground now, cradling her arm. One of Vance's dogs is bounding toward Lincoln's cover and I can see he's ready to attack. "Don't! Please!" I yell, and Lincoln pauses, just long enough for the dog to sprint past him and tackle the one he's been fighting beyond him. Two smaller, surgical arms extend from the back of Vance's dog and drill their way into the chassis of Felix's, leaving it disabled on the ground a moment later.

I tell Lena to stay back, then run in a crouch over to Lincoln's hiding spot. "They're with me!" I say nodding back toward Vance's bots, though as I say it, I realize they aren't waiting by the entrance anymore. They're fully entangled with Felix's, a brutal dance of metal taking place across the hall and up to the ceiling.

"They're with you?" he and I can hear the fury and betrayal in his voice.

"Not Felix's!" I try to yell back but a nearby explosion drowns out my words. I duck instinctively, feeling debris rain down on my back.

His look of anger has changed to confusion, distrust, then a sputtering comes from above us as the propeller on one of the Vance's drones gives out, but it manages to aim itself toward a batch of dogs that have just jumped into the building, crashing into them in a fiery explosion that I can feel singed off the tips of my eyebrows.

"What the fuck is going on?" he demands, his eyes wild. "One minute everything was normal, the next we're under attack."

"Where did he attack first?" Vance's voice comes from the dog nearest to Lincoln.

"Who the fuck are you?!" Lincoln yells as we all duck under a drone that zips over our head.

"I'll explain later," I say. "Where?"

"The transfer building," Lincoln says. "They must have snuck up on us. We didn't realize anything was happening until all the electronics died. Then our bots started attacking us."

My stomach drops, and I hear Vance mutter "Shit" from the dog.

"What?" Lincoln asks.

"He's in the network. They must have connected him through the loading bay."

"Have you talked to your twin?" I ask. "Or Maya's?"

Lincoln shakes his head. "I haven't been able to reach them."

"They're gone," Vance says, confirming what I'm thinking.

"Vance, what if we plug you in?" I ask.

"I was thinking that too."

"*Plug him in?*" Lincoln looks disgusted.

"If he's used your back door to establish connection to Meru, maybe I can ride that in, find whoever was trying to contact your friend. And push back against him here."

"Isaac, what is he talking about?"

"This is the real Vance. The one in Meru is some kind of puppet; we think he figured out what Felix did, and Felix killed him for it. Vance thinks he can find whoever has been undermining Felix from within Meru, but we have to let him into Alexandria so he can use the processing power here to fight him."

"So we'd be giving him control of the town?"

"Hell of a lot better than what Felix is doing with it!" Vance yells as an android shoots up to a standing position and grabs a drone out of the air, ripping the propeller off and throwing the rest against a wall.

"You have any better ideas?" I ask Lincoln.

I hear someone's footsteps pounding on the tile behind us and then Lena slides into cover next to me.

"You good?" I ask, and she nods.

Lincoln looks relieved to see her. "This true?"

"If it's what I think Isaac just explained, then yes," Lena says, and we flinch as another scream cuts through the atrium. "It's Vance. Our best shot of fighting Felix is to connect him to the network here. But we have to save whoever we can in the meantime."

"Like hell it is. We can push him back—"

"It won't matter," I say. "He controls everything here. The buildings, the drones, the water and power. We need to get everyone to safety while Vance takes his shot."

"This is the only place we have!" Lincoln yells and then aims his shotgun up at a drone that has drifted over our cover, blowing it out of the sky.

"We found somewhere safe. There are trucks parked outside," I yell back and point through the door where I came in. "Get everyone you can; fill each truck as much as possible. Anyone healthy might have to run for it."

Lincoln doesn't hesitate. He stands up, cupping his hands around his mouth. "Everyone to the front door!"

The survivors begin streaming toward the door, helping

the wounded as they go. Lincoln and Lena and I rise out from behind our cover, forming a triangle with a pair of Vance's dogs ahead of us, a pair of androids covering our backs, cutting a path through the chaos for the remaining survivors to escape through. People run out from surrounding rooms and hallways, heads ducked, dragging their injured and children as they sprint toward the exit as quickly as they can.

As the last of the survivors make it through the door, I turn to Lincoln. "What about the others? Where's Carmy? Maya?"

His face falls. "I don't know. I've been stuck in this building since it began." Another explosion rocks the building, closer this time. We both stumble, and I know we're running out of time.

"We have to go look," I say, grabbing his arm and gesturing for Vance's bots to follow us as we turn back and run deeper into the building, heading for the back door that leads to the rest of the campus.

CHAPTER 31

ALEXANDRIA IS A BATTLEFIELD. BODIES OF RESIDENTS lay scattered across the grass, their stillness a stark contrast to the chaos around them. Broken bots litter the ground, sparking and twitching as if they'd been alive.

The smell is stifling, a mix of burnt flesh and gunpowder. Screams and the sound of shots echo across the campus. I see people running in all directions, some helping the wounded, some fighting the bots, others simply trying to escape.

Vance's remaining bots have wrapped around the building and descended on Felix's assault while we were inside, and to my relief, they seem to be pushing them back. They're slowly carving a safe path through the campus for the survivors to escape through, shuttling people back toward the trucks so they can be driven to safety. People are clearly confused about why these bots are helping them, but they must have moved past that suspicion, grateful for any reprieve from the assault.

I scan the area, looking for any sign of Carmy or other survivors we can help. The security dogs fan out around us, providing cover as we move forward.

"Where was he when this started?" I ask Lincoln as I step over a bot. It lurches as I'm straddling it, and one of Vance's dogs grabs it, yanking it out from under me before it can strike.

"He was in the hospital," he says, helping someone to their feet. Their face is caked with dirt and blood, but they seem able to move. Lincoln points them toward the safe path around the building, and they nod and take off to look for others.

As we cross the field, we steadily guide more people back toward the trucks, relief washing over them as they realize there's some plan for escape. I wonder too how many bots there could possibly be here; Felix's numbers seem to be thinning. But then I remember the Epsilon trucks outside the other side of campus and worry that if Felix fails to clear out Alexandria as he hoped, then he might send in the Techs to finish the job.

We reach the hospital, and before we make it to the steps, the doors burst open as if from an explosion. I drop to the ground, gun raised toward whatever bots are about to emerge, but then a surge of joy rushes through me as Dylan comes marching through the opening.

"Nice of you to join us, Isaac," he says then gives Lincoln a respectful nod. "These tin cans with you?"

Dylan being okay is the closest thing to good news since we arrived. "They're with us. Where are the others?"

"Carmy and Bel are with the kids inside. I came to look for more ammo."

"Here," Vance says, and an android holds out a gun to Dylan by the barrel.

"I like these new bots. So what's the plan, boss?"

"No time," Lincoln says. "There are trucks parked outside the main entrance—"

"I'll bring a few around to that alley," Vance says, pointing down an opening between the nearest buildings.

"Okay, down that alley," Lincoln continues. "Can you three get the kids out?"

"Bel's hurt; one of the dogs shot her ankle."

"I'll help," Lena says, checking her ammo then jogging up the stairs, and I'm surprised to feel a jolt of fear over leaving her.

"Where are you going?" Dylan asks.

"We might be able to get Felix out of the network," I say, suddenly conscious again of the chaos still unfolding around us. We're wasting too much time here.

"And if you can't?"

"Then we're probably not coming back," Lincoln says. "So, get everyone out quick."

"Roger." Dylan barely reacts, then turns and runs back into the hospital. Lena falters for a moment, nods at Lincoln, then our eyes meet for a moment, and I can see she's as scared to leave me as I am to leave her.

"We'll be fine," I say. "Go!"

She doesn't respond, just nods again and takes off into the building.

"Come on," Lincoln says, jogging toward the computer science building. Vance's bots have already started clearing a path for us, and to my relief, the people around the quad seem to be thinning out, steadily making their way to the safety of the trucks.

When we finally burst through the doors of the building, it's devoid of any activity. A few bodies are collapsed on the floor around their computer monitors, but it looks as though most of the people I usually saw here made it out.

"I'll pull a truck up out back," Vance says. "Where's the loading dock?"

"This way." Lincoln charges down the hall, guiding us to the port where I helped transfer Natalie and where we brought Preston in a week ago.

I smash my fist on the loading dock button and the gate creaks open, Vance's truck already out back. It's surrounded by half a dozen androids, all holding guns, and it looks like they had to fight their way in here.

"Did he try to stop you?" I ask as an android grabs the transfer cable out of the trunk.

"Less than I expected."

"We must be thinning him out," Lincoln says.

"Hope that's it…" Vance grumbles. "Go ahead back inside. I'll get this connected."

Lincoln runs back into the building and leads me down a flight of stairs as we navigate back to the transfer station. We round another corner, and I can see a faint light emanating from below a doorway ahead. Lincoln slows as we approach, holding up a hand for us to stop. He holds his hand to the door to see if it's hot, then presses his ear to it, listening for any signs of danger on the other side. After a moment, he nods and slowly pushes it open.

We emerge into a dimly lit basement. Rows of servers hum quietly, their lights blinking in the darkness. The room is mercifully empty of bots.

Finally, we reach the command console. Vance's dogs and I cover Lincoln as he starts keying in some commands.

"Let me," Vance says from the android that followed us. Lincoln steps aside and the bot extends a finger, cables snaking out of it and into the computer ports.

I strain my ears to hear any sign of bots approaching but don't hear any.

"He has to know what we're trying to do," I say to myself as much as the others.

"I'm sure he didn't expect you to come back with an army, let alone with Vance. Maybe he's giving up and retreating."

"How's it going, Vance?" I ask.

"Working on it," he growls. The process seems agonizingly

slow, each second stretching out as we wait for any sign of success or failure. "Looks like he didn't establish a full connection to Meru. That's good."

"Why?" Lincoln asks.

"He can't draw on Meru's computing power to fight me here. Gives me a better chance of routing him out."

Minutes tick by, feeling like hours. I find myself holding my breath, half expecting Felix's bots to come crashing through the walls at any moment. But still nothing happens.

Suddenly, the lights on the servers flicker in a rapid sequence, then stabilize. A low hum fills the room as cooling systems kick into higher gear.

"Vance?" I call out hesitantly. "Are you there?"

For a moment, there's only silence. Then, a voice booms from hidden speakers throughout the room, causing us all to jump.

"I'm here," Vance says, his voice sounding richer and more present than it has through the bots.

I let out a relieved sigh. "It worked?"

"It did. I can access everything. Nice place you got here Lincoln."

As if to demonstrate, the massive screens on the walls around us flicker to life, displaying a dizzying array of data streams and camera feeds from around the facility.

"This is incredible," I say, looking around at the screens coming to life. "So, you can stop the bots he took over?"

"Already have, unlocked all the doors too. Everyone outside should be clear to make it to the trucks. Aside from whatever bots Felix brought with him."

"What about the connection to Meru?"

"We can work on that later," Lincoln says.

"No, this is our best chance, while he's distracted," Vance says. "I think I can trick Meru into thinking this is part of the network, make it think there's a new tech center. Ah, I see the problem Felix ran into."

"What's that?" I ask.

"Manual override on the center's transmission capabilities. You do this, Lincoln?"

Lincoln laughs. "Horace."

"Asshole probably set it up after he found me."

Lincoln's eyes go wide. "You're why he told us never to go to Austin."

"Yes. Glad we're all one big happy family now."

"How do we shut it off, Lincoln?"

"There's another terminal down at the base of the servers. Come on." Lincoln's already running as he says it.

I lose count of how many levels we've descended, but eventually the stairs spit us out into a massive cavern, a mix of concrete and rock surrounding us on all sides, the basin only dimly illuminated by the foundation of the server tower. In front of us are the glowing racks of servers Vance has taken control of.

The tunnel behind us keeps pulling my attention. Peering into the black, I can just make out the silhouette of the colossal digger Lincoln told me about when I arrived.

"Ready when you are, Lincoln," Vance says from one of the androids that followed us.

Lincoln approaches the tower of servers and pulls out a terminal, then starts keying commands into it.

"If Alexandria was able to connect directly to Meru," I ask, "why did we need the back door? Why not pretend it was a tech center all along?"

"It works both ways," Vance says. "You can transmit more, but you can receive more too. Felix could have taken over."

"You should be good, Vance," Lincoln says, hitting a final key then staring up at the lone screen.

"Alright, trying now."

"So, what exactly is he doing?" Lincoln asks me quietly.

"He thinks Susan, Felix's wife, is the one who's been talking to us from Meru. If he's right, she might be able to help us prove the transfers aren't real, maybe even get into Epsilon and save my sister."

"The transfers aren't real?"

"Vance thinks everyone who goes in dies, that what happened to Horace wasn't a mistake on his part."

"Does he have any proof?"

"Not yet, but someone in Meru might."

"Feels like a stretch, Isaac."

"He just saved Alexandria, and he might be able to save my sister. Let's give him a chance."

"There's something I don't like about this."

"Connected to Meru," Vance says. "Give me a minute, I'll try to find—" Then his voice cuts out and the lights on the servers flash.

"Vance?"

There's a sputtering of machinery behind us and when I spin around, the two androids are twitching, their lights pulsing as well.

"The hell—" Lincoln mutters.

The bots suddenly stop twitching and their heads turn toward us. I can almost feel their invisible eyes staring us down. One of their guns snaps up.

"LINCOLN!" I scream and drop to the ground, but he reacts too slowly.

I watch in horror as the android fires, and the back of Lincoln's head explodes. A red mist fills the air as chunks of bone, brain, and gore spray across the server racks behind him.

His body stays upright for what feels like an eternity, swaying slightly, before his knees buckle and he crumples to the ground like a doll. Blood pools around his head, seeping into the cracks between the servers and concrete.

My stomach heaves but I force the bile back down. I can't tear my eyes away from Lincoln's body, his limbs splayed at unnatural angles, fingers still twitching.

The android whirs as it adjusts its aim toward me, and before I can move or even think of an escape, Felix's voice comes through its speakers.

"Thank you, Isaac. You don't know how long I've wanted to get my hands on this place. Shame about Vance and Lincoln..."

I want to scream at him for killing Lincoln, but the overwhelming emotions all stick in my throat, leaving me gasping for words. My eyes dart to the other android, hoping Vance will wake up in it and fight back.

"Not going to happen," Felix says, reading my mind. "Vance was sloppy. It was trivial to take over the remaining bots and delete him once he let me into the network. Nice of him to bring me some reinforcements."

I'm grasping for any way out, for anything I can do to fight back, but coming up empty. The bit of hope I had left is gone.

"Come on," Felix says, gesturing for me to stand with the android's gun. "I have someone who wants to see you."

※ ※ ※

The androids lead me back up the stairs, through the transfer building, out into the quad, and the sight that awaits me only deepens the dread I felt in the basement.

Bram is in the center of campus, surrounded by androids, dogs, and trucks that we brought from Austin. It's not all of them. Vance must have gotten some of them out of broadcast range before Felix took over. But it's enough.

Lena, Dylan, and Carmy are standing on top of the stairs to the hospital, guns on the ground in front of them. I don't see Bel or the kids; maybe they made it out. They look to me as I slouch down the steps, and I can see the realization strike them that Lincoln isn't with me.

"Bram?" I call out, my voice cracking. I can't believe he's here, that he has allowed Felix to do this. "What...what have you done?"

His eyes meet mine, and for a moment, I see a flicker of something. Regret? Pain? But it's quickly replaced by coldness.

"Me? What have *you* done, Isaac? I heard what happened at Alpha from Felix, but I didn't fully believe it. Now that I'm here... you're helping these people?"

I realize now the look I saw wasn't regret but disappointment.

"They told me the truth about Felix. I found—"

"The truth?" Bram cuts me off, his voice sharp. "Is that why you killed Grant and Bridget? Why you let my son kill himself?"

My stomach plunges. Grant is dead? How? He had been breathing when I left him. So had the driver. Had Felix killed them after I escaped? I try to say something but the words are caught in my throat.

Before I can compose myself, Bram continues, "Felix keeps us safe. He provides for us. Given us freedom from this awful world and the death that comes with it. And these people," he gestures to the bodies around him, "they're a threat to that life."

I can't believe what I'm hearing. This isn't him; the calm, level-headed man who I mourned with only weeks ago has been transformed into someone else. The person he said he left behind all those years ago. He was hiding under the surface all this time.

"We've let this threat to Meru continue too long," he continues. It sounds like Felix is talking through him. "Felix showed us how you killed Dr. Lao too. How many minds have you destroyed, Isaac?"

The bots next to Bram whir to life, their robotic eyes training across the dozen of us standing on the steps around the quad. I have no idea how many people are still left alive in the other buildings, if any.

"Felix has agreed to let the rest of you leave," Bram continues. "He wanted to avoid any chance of retaliation, to treat you like you've now treated so many of the people we promised to protect, to wipe you from the earth. But I reminded him we're better than that."

I can feel the tension release from everyone around me. We aren't safe yet, but we at least aren't about to be killed by the bots after going through so much to try to get to safety.

"You have forty-eight hours," Bram continues. "Tend to your wounded, pack your supplies, and go. After that we'll return to Alexandria, then we'll go to Austin, and Felix will eliminate anyone still lingering around."

Then Bram takes a deep breath. "Except for you, Isaac. You're coming with us."

"Fuck that!" Carmy yells and reaches down for his gun.

"No!" I scream, trying to stop him, but an Android sprints forward, punching Carmy in the side of the head. He collapses on the stairs and Dylan bends down to pick him up, his other hand still up in surrender. Carmy looks like he's only half conscious.

"It's time to finish your exile," Felix says from an android next to Bram. "Alexandria was kind enough to lend us their transfer station. We'll be bringing it back to Epsilon with you."

The thought terrifies me as much as it did when Felix first sentenced me. I lock eyes with Lena and can see my fear reflected in her face too, but also a sternness. She's thinking the same thing I am. If everyone else here gets to go free, I have to go. I brought this risk on Alexandria by coming here, by looking for Vance, by trying to figure out what Felix has been hiding. If I can spare them from the worst of it, I don't have a choice.

"Okay," I whisper. "Let's go."

I cross the quad, trying to put on an air of confidence, until I reach Bram. I still can't read what he's feeling, his face is stern, angry, but I can feel there's a hint of hesitation behind it. Maybe I can use that. If I have any chance of surviving, I know he's my only hope.

"You could have run…" Bram says softly as I reach him. "Why do this, Isaac?"

"No, I couldn't have." Then one of the other Techs grabs my arm and thrusts me into the back seat of the truck, slamming the door behind me. Out the window I see Lena and Dylan watching us silently, Carmy still half conscious in Dylan's arm. I desperately want to stay with them, to sit around the fire, work on the farm, sit on the factory roof again. But then the truck lurches to life and pulls out of the quad, taking me away from the life I only just started to embrace.

MERU

CHAPTER 32

EPSILON HAS CHANGED. GONE IS THE COZY, WARM ENVIronment from when I had left. Felix, or perhaps the Techs, have bolstered the security considerably.

An Imgen truck is pulling into the town as we approach, flanked on both sides by armed autonomous vehicles. They look like the ones Vance had in his basement, a more imposing version of the ones I used for work. It makes me wonder how much more power Felix is keeping in reserve, hiding it away not to scare the people in the tech centers but ready to deploy when faced with a serious threat.

Security dogs are roaming the streets now. Felix has surely said it's to provide the Techs with a sense of safety. But to me it looks like he's taking a tighter grip on everyone. He doesn't want to risk anyone else running off and joining us. Maybe he had hoped for a threat like this for a while, some excuse to clamp down on how they live in Epsilon.

"Has there been another attack since Luke?" I ask the driver, trying to make some conversation to break the tension. But he doesn't respond, not even a head shake.

Finally, we stop outside of a dorm on the edge of campus. One that no one has lived in for years, at least for as long as I can remember. The driver gets out, walks to my door, and pulls it open. "Let's go," he says, breaking the silence. "And don't try anything."

I shuffle out and he slams the door behind me, pushing my back to move me toward the stairs, one of Felix's newly claimed androids following behind us. I ascend them as slowly as I can, desperately looking around for any possible advantage or means of escape, but nothing presents itself.

He lets me in the house then locks the door behind me. As the lights flicker on, I almost laugh at the familiar view. Back where I started.

A pile of food has been left for me on the counter. I sift through it, trying to find anything that looks palatable. I take a bite of an apple, and it tastes like cardboard. I peel back the cover on an instant meat loaf packet and retch. I can't believe how disgusting it all seems now. How poor of a life I've been accustomed to.

I try to stomach a protein bar as I sit down on the couch, turning on the screen to see if they've left it connected to anything for me. Communication on it is disabled, but I can watch the streams from Meru. I turn on the duel, but I can't enjoy it, Vance's uncertainty about the legitimacy of the copies still racking my mind. Is everyone that I talked to in Meru actually there? Do they have the same kinds of thoughts and feelings that I do out here? Or are they all elaborate duplicates manipulated by Felix? Perhaps Felix and Vance are the only two minds that were ever truly digitized.

I change the channel and find the other Vance, the one I knew before, giving one of his evening news updates. He looks his usual, professional self, animatedly sharing what is going on in Meru and in the centers with the audience. But, again, I have to wonder how many of his stories are true. And who this Vance really is.

"And as many of you are already aware," he continues, "the terrorists who were attacking Meru via the outpost known as Alexandria have finally been caught and are being brought to justice."

Then my picture appears. "Isaac, a recently outcast member of Epsilon, was colluding with another member of Epsilon to destroy the center. After his deception was uncovered, he murdered two Techs and joined up with the scavengers, aiding in their plot to sabotage our lives here."

The propaganda is unsurprising. The "news" is just another way for Felix's digital world to control the physical one. More than anything I feel sorry for the puppet Vance being the one to deliver it. He had been so close to stopping Felix, to exposing what he was doing. And now all that is left of him is this shell of his former self, sharing the faked news from Meru.

"Their exile will be tomorrow morning, at 9:00 a.m. sharp, folks. The only punishment fitting for such a vile scheme. So set your alarms; this isn't going to be one you want to miss!"

I absentmindedly check the time; it's barely 5:00 p.m. It's going to be a long, sleepless night. I want to hail Sophie, but I know I won't be able to with her in exile, and I can't even find a feed to check in on her. So I scroll through the other streams for a minute then jump when I hear a knock at the door. It sounds soft, not threatening. But there's no chance someone could be coming to rescue me. There's hardly anyone left.

I nervously walk over and open the door, hoping it might be Tess. But standing outside is Bram.

※ ※ ※

"I don't want to talk to you," I say and try to slam the door in his face. But he slams his hand against it, holding it open. I forgot how strong he is.

"Please, Isaac. I need to understand." I hadn't noticed it at first but he's not angry. He looks sad, distraught, bits of red beside his eyes. His face is etched with lines I've never noticed before, and his eyes hold a weariness that makes him look far older than he did when I left.

I don't want to feel sorry for him. I know he lost his son and may have thought of me as a son in some way too. But that doesn't forgive the hell he allowed Felix to unleash on Alexandria. The lies he continued to endorse. The cage he maintained around everyone living here.

I can see the conflict in his eyes too. The love of a father who misses his son, warring with his duties to the rest of Epsilon. Maybe I can use that, get him on my side, convince him that there's something Felix isn't telling him. It seems like the only way to give myself any chance of avoiding exile.

"You had plenty of time to try to understand. But you chose to believe whatever Felix told you. The clues were always there if you were willing to follow them."

"*What* clues, Isaac? Tell me what I'm missing! What could turn my son into that...that monster—"

"He was a hero. He was trying to save me, save all of us."

"From what?"

"From HIM!" I point toward the screen as I scream it.

Bram looks over his shoulder, likely worried about causing a scene. "Can I come in?"

"Fine."

He follows me into the house and sits down at the dining table, but I stay standing, trying to resist pacing back and forth in the living room.

"What did Luke see, Isaac?"

"I don't know."

"Obviously you do."

I cross my arms. "I wasn't lying when you kicked me out of Epsilon. I don't know what Luke saw."

"But you have an idea now."

"Yes."

"What then?"

"Tell me something first."

Bram leans back in his chair, skeptical. "What?"

"Where did you find me."

"Alpha. You already know that."

"Don't lie!"

He jumps at the outburst, then looks up at the ceiling, likely wondering if Felix is going to stop him from telling me, but Felix doesn't interrupt. "Okay."

"Where?"

"I...get the sense you already know."

"I need to hear you say it."

He takes a few deep breaths to compose himself. "Do you remember what I told you about Alpha, before...everything happened?"

"Yes, how you found where the scavs who you thought killed everyone in Alpha were living but couldn't bring yourself to attack them."

"Who *did* kill everyone in Alpha."

"One thing at a time."

He sighs. "Okay. When I told Felix that we couldn't do it, he was—" He looks to the ceiling again, almost nervous now. "Disappointed. But understanding. He said he'd take care of it."

"You knew then."

"I didn't like it. It felt wrong, against everything he, we, stood for. But he believed they would wipe out Epsilon next. Luke had just been born. I...I wanted him to be safe.

"Not many of us accompanied him. Just a few of the other men who had gone with me when we found them. They all transferred long ago. We watched as he massacred the town. I'm sure each of us was disgusted but also too embarrassed to say something. To admit our weakness. To show any degree of distrust in his decision." He looks to the ceiling again and I wonder how tight of a leash Felix has had him on all these years. Maybe he knew more than he's letting on but has been too afraid to say or do anything about it. Willing to ignore the lies to try to keep his son safe.

"After he was...done...we started investigating the houses. Looking for anything we could learn about them, where else they lived, or that might alert us to other threats. I remember it so vividly, entering that house, the silence in it stifling. A body collapsed over the kitchen counter, blood pooling on the ground beneath it, how I gagged and had to control my impulse to vomit when I saw it. But then as I stood there, hunched over, trying to come to terms with what Felix had done, I heard a single, muffled sob come from upstairs.

"Felix heard it too. A dog started bounding up the stairs, but I screamed at it to stop as I chased up after it. It burst into a room, searching for the source of the noise, but it picked the wrong one. I heard a sharp intake of breath to my right, and I crashed into the bedroom and nearly collapsed at the sight. She—" His voice breaks, and I can tell he's barely holding it together as the memory overwhelms him. I set my jaw, trying to keep my own emotions under control. "She was beautiful, Isaac. Your mother. And even though she was gone, I could still see the terror frozen in her eyes. The terror she had to have felt that they were going to get you next."

His breath is raspy, his exhales stuttering as he fights back the tears. "I saw Sophie first. Her little eyes peeking out from under the bed, meeting mine, silently begging me to keep her safe. It was too much. The dog leapt through the door behind me but I threw myself in front of you two, trying to shield you with my body. I screamed at Felix to stop, that he'd gone too far, that you were only children. He called me a traitor, said he'd kill me too if I didn't move, but I stayed. The others must have heard the commotion outside because suddenly there was a thunder of boots on the stairs and they burst into the room, saw our standoff. They sided with me, convinced Felix to let us bring you back. We all had to swear you and your sister would never know.

"I—I thought Felix would exile me. We got into an awful fight over it. But ultimately, I convinced him we could never do that again. Thus the truce, and the period of peace that came after it. Grant took you two under his wing, raised you like his own children. I kept my distance, because every time I looked at you, I was reminded of what I did. What I allowed to happen. Her… her face still haunts me, Isaac. I never understood that kind of fear and terror. Not until…"

"Luke."

Bram chokes up again. "How, Isaac? How could he do that?"

"They're all dead, Bram."

"I know…I'm so sorry for what happened to your parents, Isaac…I never—"

"No, everyone in Meru. Every time you, him, I, put someone in that transfer bed, they died. Killed by Felix. It's all been a show, a farce orchestrated by Felix to keep us enslaved out here, keeping the lights on for him." I'm not even certain I believe Vance, but I have to convince Bram.

He sighs. "We talked about this. People have made that

accusation for years. The ones who were afraid of what this digital salvation might mean, the ones who thought we were supposed to 'die as God intended.' But you've seen it, I've seen it; everyone who goes into the transfer, they come out the other side. And there's no difference between the person who goes in and the one who comes out. If there were, we would have noticed a long time ago."

"The copies are good," I interrupt gently. "They might even be conscious, in their own way. There's no way to know. But when someone goes into that machine…they don't come out the other side."

"Why, because *they* told you that?"

"Vance told me. He showed me."

"He told you whatever he needed to so you'd help him come after Felix."

"They've spent years trying to re-create Meru, studying the transfer beds, talking to people who worked at Imgen. They've made copies but have never been able to get someone to successfully transfer."

"Because only Felix figured it out."

"Or he's lying, and the Meru software kills you after the copy is made, creating the illusion to everyone else that you transferred."

His hands clench slightly. "That's ridiculous," he says. "Why would Felix, Imgen, make all of this, just to kill people and make copies of them."

"For the same reason we all believe it, the reason you and I and everyone else have helped keep it running for so long."

He looks at me confused now, and I continue. "The fear of death. Felix was so desperate to avoid his own mortality, to spend eternity with his wife, that he created all of this," I gesture around us, "just to keep this artificial, digital version of his fantasy going."

"If that were all he wanted," he says calmly, "he could have set up an isolated way to preserve his mind. Use robots to keep it all running. I know he says he needs us out here to keep things going, but I'm not an idiot. I know he could do it on his own."

I'm surprised at the acknowledgment; Bram has been paying closer attention than I thought.

He continues, "The only reason not to do it on his own is because he cares about preserving humanity. Giving us a way out of this broken world. Honoring the mission that led to the creation of Meru in the first place."

I nod. I don't want him to think I am dismissing the argument. And I'm not; I considered it too. "Or, he knew that if he didn't create this kind of theater, people would revolt and destroy him. Turn off the servers. Especially during the collapse."

"Do you even hear yourself?" he says, raising his voice ever so slightly now. "How can you believe that?"

"Bram," I plead. "It's true, this is what Luke saw. This is why he did what he did."

His anger seems to break momentarily. "Everyone thinks they have proof for their beliefs, Isaac. But that's all they are. Beliefs. Whatever proof you think you have, it's outweighed by the decades of care Felix has given to us and the other tech centers. The lives in Meru provided to the millions of people inhabiting it."

"I do have proof though." I'm straining to keep my voice delicate. "Felix's old partner, Vance, he never transferred, not even a copy of him. He's a puppet. I think Felix killed him. If you talk to the real Vance, you'll understand what Luke must have found out—"

"Luke was corrupted. Corrupted by the same people who have screwed with your head now too."

"No—" I say, shaking my head, though I can't deny the tiniest sliver of doubt in the back of my mind. "You have to believe me, believe your son. Felix is hiding something. Don't let your guilt over leading so many people to their deaths blind you to it."

His shoulders slump and I can see the disappointment, the exhaustion. Maybe he harbors some hope that he can convince me, that he can make one last plea to Felix to spare me. But I'm not going to give in. There has to be some way to show him, some way to stop Felix.

He stares at me silently for what feels like an eternity, and I know we're at an impasse. Both searching for a way to convince the other. To save the other. And both realizing it's hopeless.

"I'm sorry," he says. "There's nothing else I can do for you."

"You can help me!" I yell, almost begging him now. "Bram, you have to believe me. It's a trap. You've fallen for it for your whole life. You've sent people to their deaths in the transfers. But you don't have to keep doing it. You can help me end this. Don't do it for me. Do it for Luke! Your son! You can—"

"I think that's quite enough," Felix says through the speakers. "Isaac, Bram has spoken. This little coup of yours has gone on long enough. Bram, you can return to collect Isaac in the morning."

I watch helplessly as he stands up and turns toward the door. I can almost see Felix's leash around him guiding him away from me.

"Please," I say. "This isn't what Luke would have wanted."

He pauses, his hand on the doorknob. For a moment, I think he might turn back. But then his shoulders slump and he shakes his head.

"I'm sorry, Isaac," he says, still not looking at me.

The door closes behind him with a soft click, leaving me alone. I slump back in the couch, crushed by the strength of his belief in Felix's lies.

I glance around the room, wondering if Felix is still watching, still listening. Almost certainly.

My thoughts turn to Lena, and I desperately wish I could see her. The idea of her and the others being on the run, their lives destroyed by my struggle with Felix…the guilt is overwhelming. We could have left. Could have found a new life somewhere else. Why did we try to fight Felix?

There has to be something I'm missing, some way to prove what I know. I keep turning over every possible scenario in my mind, trying desperately to grasp at a solution, but none comes. I exhaust myself running through the possibilities in the dark canvas of my mind, hitting a dead end in every direction until finally, long past when the sun disappears and the lights in the houses around me click off, my mind fades to black.

CHAPTER 33

A SHARP KNOCKING ON THE DOOR JARS ME AWAKE. THE cold reality of my situation hits me again as I struggle to sit up on the uncomfortable couch.

"Isaac?" It's Bram again.

I glance at the clock on the wall. It's 8:30 a.m. Thirty minutes until exile. My heart races as I stumble to the door, hoping that maybe Felix has changed his mind. That there's still some hope.

I open the door to see that his face is still a mask of resignation and sorrow. Behind him stand two of Felix's androids, and I can almost feel him staring out at me from them with a sneering grin.

"It's time."

I swallow hard, trying to push down the lump in my throat. I open my mouth to speak but then Felix's voice comes from one of the drones, "No no, no more of that now."

I ignore the admonition. "Don't let his death be meaningless, Bram."

"Let's go," he says to the bots, turning away from me.

As they lead me out of the house and into the harsh morning light, I feel a deep sense of despair settling over me. Other Techs have already dressed and left their dorms, congregating along the streets to see the procession. And I have to imagine this image streaming into hundreds of houses, shops, and trucks around the world, however many other tech centers Felix has. No one would want to admit that they enjoy seeing a sacrifice, enjoy seeing someone be punished like this. But they do. And of course Felix wants to make a spectacle of it. A stern reminder of what happens if you threaten him.

As we approach the quad, a sense of déjà vu washes over me. My eyes scan the crowd and find Tess once again. Our gazes lock for a moment, then she gives me a look of disgust and turns away. My chest tightens. I didn't realize some piece of me has been holding onto hope that she'll secretly believe me or forgive me for what happened. I can only imagine how much the animosity toward me has grown in my absence. Part of me aches for her; seeing her again is affecting me more than I expected. But there's also a hollowness to it. The distance that's grown between us in these months is greater than I thought. And the disgust in her eyes tells me everything I need to know. The love she had for me is gone. I want to shed a tear for her, but I feel numb to all of it.

We reach the transfer building, and I see how hard Felix's bots must have worked to restore it. All the hints of Luke's attack are gone, the exterior has been repaired, a new facade of wood and steel covering the entrance. The doors open to reveal the station from the factory, already installed, and looking almost identical to how the lobby had looked before. Everything is coming full circle. Soon there will be no remnants of me, of Luke, of Lincoln, of Alexandria. Felix will certainly erase the records from Meru. And once everyone else here has transferred, it will be like we never existed.

The readiness meter above the transfer bed reaches 100 percent as I've seen it happen so many times before, and the console by the bed lights up, indicating it's ready to receive someone. Shelby is standing in front of it, her expression cold.

The bed hisses as it depressurizes, and the cover over it slowly rotates around to open the chamber. The cage for my head opens up, its metal claws threatening to rip my mind out of my body.

The android behind me gives me a strong shove and I fall forward, catching myself on the concrete floor. I look up at Felix, at Shelby, and my eyes linger on the rendering of the vast desert I'm to be exiled to. All I see is sand. Endless sand, stretching as far as the camera can see. Not even a hill, or bush, or anything to break it up. An eternity of nothingness. Maybe I, or rather he, the Isaac copy that will show up on the other end, can eventually find some peace with it. I feel a moment of empathy for him. Dying here might be preferable to being stuck there.

"Let's go," Felix says. I can hear the androids approaching me again. I wave them off and climb back up to my feet, turning to look back out into the quad of Epsilon via the live feed. Everyone is standing around silently, making sideways glances at each other. Bram stands in the middle of the crowd, resolute.

I try to swallow my fear as my feet carry me toward the metal tube that will seal my fate. I grab the sides and hoist myself inside, turning to lie down on the cold metal, the small padding behind my head doing little to make it comfortable. Shelby approaches and locks the restraints around my ankles first, then my wrists, then ties the belt around my waist. As she turns to walk back to the computer I struggle slightly, just to see if there is any hope of wriggling out of them, but they're locked tight.

Shelby's fingers hover over the console, ready to initiate the transfer process. I can hear Felix's voice, tinged with satisfaction. "See you soon, Isaac."

I open my mouth to say something, but Shelby activates the transfer, and the bed hisses again as the metal door starts closing around me. I want to scream, to cry out for help, but I restrain myself. I fight to stay strong, to stay brave, to not have that be the last image they have of me.

As the door seals shut, my heart rate spikes, the calm acceptance I felt a moment ago suddenly fleeing me. This is real. It's happening. The hint of doubt I was holding onto about Vance is suddenly gone. He and Luke were right. I can't explain where my certainty is coming from, but it's there. I'm about to die.

I start struggling against the restraints as hard as I can, my biceps and thighs cramping from the intensity as I yank against the shackles, my breath constricted by the belt. But it's no use; I can't get any leverage, they won't budge. It may be my imagination, but it almost feels as if they're getting tighter, holding me down.

I hear a few hushed voices from outside, then a quiet whirring behind me. I try to crane my neck, to move my head out of the way, to maybe block the cage from closing around me to delay the process, anything to get a few more moments here, alive, but then cold metal presses against one side of my skull, and then the top, and then the other side, as the cage slowly constricts around my head, moving it into place, my neck throbbing with pain from trying to resist it.

Finally, my head is stuck. I can't move it more than a centimeter in either direction, and the machine pushes back against me every time I try to. Nothing else is happening though, and I realize it's waiting for me to settle down. It knows I can't keep this up forever, and once I stop, it can make the incision. I strain as long as I can, pushing with whatever tiny bit of strength I have left against the metal prison, but finally my neck muscles give out. I can't fight it any longer. I release and my head falls back on the thin cushion below it, and I hear the surgical arm hum to life behind me.

Then comes a sudden, sharp prick on my neck. The sedative. I feel a rush as it injects the drug into my body. A wave of warmth spreads through me, starting from the injection site and radiating outward. My muscles, tense from struggling, begin to relax against my will. It almost feels nice.

My thoughts become hazy, the edges of my consciousness blurring. I try to fight it, to hold onto lucidity, but it's like grasping at smoke. The panic that was coursing through me moments ago starts to ebb away, replaced by a soothing calm.

I can still hear muffled sounds from outside the pod, but they seem distant now, as if coming from underwater. My eyelids grow heavy, and I find myself struggling to keep them open. The darkness at the edges of my vision begins to creep inward.

As consciousness slips away, fragmented thoughts flash through my mind. Lena's face, Luke's anguish as he begged for help, Lincoln's death, the endless desert the other Isaac is destined for. And, briefly, a face I don't recognize at first. My mother's. I want to scream, to rage against what is happening, but my body no longer responds to my commands.

All I can hear now is a faint mechanical buzzing, growing louder as it approaches the back of my head.

Then, nothing.

CHAPTER 34

I'M FLOATING, LOST IN THE SEA OF CONSCIOUSNESS, THE gentle blanket of the sedative still cozy around my mind. I feel nothing. Hear nothing. But...I'm thinking. I'm not dead.

Holy shit. I'm not dead.

How?

Suddenly a screech cuts through the fog. A banging, rattling, the grate of metal on metal, and a whirring of something like a drill. Then a smell. A blend of musk and sweat. The comforting pressure of a hand on my chest, and hot air across my ear as someone whispers, "Don't move."

But why would I want to move? I wonder. It's so comfortable here, floating. A breath fills my lungs and sparks of awareness dance across my eyes. Where am I? Is this exile? It's not so bad...

Then suddenly my chest explodes in pain, like a fire has been lit in my breast and it's spiderwebbing through my veins, threatening to burn me alive. My eyes shoot open, and the brightness blinds me. I feel lost, disoriented, and then realization floods through me. They brought me back. I know that smell. I know that face I caught a glimpse of.

Bram.

"Come on!" he yells and grabs my arms with both hands, yanking me out of the transfer bed and behind a table. Gunfire is echoing from the other side of the room, and as my eyes finally adjust to the light, I see Shelby hiding behind the transfer station, a shotgun in her arms. She waves at me to get down as one of Felix's bots leaps around the corner and she blows its legs off.

Bram presses another shotgun into my arms. He must have been planning this for days, knew we might end up back here. Knew this might be our only chance to stop Felix. Our conversation last night was a show, a performance to throw Felix off his tracks. Or his last confirmation of what he always suspected.

I poke my head around the table to try to get a glimpse of the entrance and it's still sealed tight, but I can tell now that there are more bots, a small army of them, on the other side trying to break through.

Bram found some way to lock Felix out of the security controls. He isn't even on the screen. How did he do this?

"ISAAC," he yells, holding my head in both hands and shaking me. "Isaac, focus!"

My eyes go wide with fear and Bram jumps back from me as a bot flies around the corner of our cover. Its camera is trained on us, the arm on its back extended, menacing, ready to end his life. I try to yell at him again, but the words aren't coming out, my body still isn't responding, but it doesn't matter. He lands on his back and fires into the front of the bot, leaving a sparking crater where the camera had been.

"We have to be fast," he yells in my ear over the sound of the bots trying to break in from outside. "That was the last of them, but I don't know how long this will hold the rest back."

He scoops his arm under my shoulder and lifts me up to my feet. I stagger for a moment then catch myself. My control is finally starting to return. "What's the plan?"

He runs over to one of the medical cabinets behind the station and throws open a cupboard. What had always been full of medicine, bandages, and splints now hides a lumpy duffel bag, and from the effort it takes him to throw it onto his shoulder, I can tell it's heavy.

Then the screen above him snaps into focus. Felix is back. "As misguided as this endeavor of yours is," he says, "destroying Epsilon won't delete me as you seem to think it will. You'll only be destroying the poor minds of the people who live here. Where you were supposed to protect them, to keep them safe."

"Let's go!" Bram urges, and I follow him out from behind the transfer bed. He yanks open the door to the stairs down toward the servers and ushers us through.

"I'll stay here," Shelby calls out, dragging a table over to the door to provide cover while she defends it. "Be fast!"

My strength is returning as I half run, half fall down the steps, Bram close behind me. We fly into the hollowed-out chamber at the bottom of the stairs and I stumble over to the security console as Bram throws the duffel bag on the floor and starts rifling through it.

I try entering the access codes to open the door, but Bram says, "Don't bother, here." Then he pulls out three blocks of explosives and a detonator, weapons I didn't know we had in Epsilon, and begins attaching them to the hinges of the great door blocking our way into the servers.

He shows me how to arrange the charges, then runs for cover on the other side of the hall. I'm still processing how quickly things have turned and pray that this will work. If we can't deactivate Felix, there will be no escaping from this basement.

"Please don't do this, Isaac," another voice comes through the speaker, but I don't recognize who it is. "I'll never get to talk to my children out there again; they'll be losing their parents. Is this really who you want to be?"

I feel the blast erupt through the cavern, the shockwave

slamming into my chest. Dust and debris rain down as the vault door groans and buckles inward.

"Isaac, please don't do this." It's Sophie's voice now. "I don't know how you could do this to me, and to everyone else in here. That's not the brother I know."

It's a good trick, but the word choice isn't quite right. Felix is faking her.

"Move!" Bram shouts over the ringing in my ears.

We surge forward, and I scoop up the duffel bag as we rush through the smoke and twisted metal. The vault beyond is dimly lit by emergency lights, casting an eerie red glow over rows of servers.

As we approach, Felix's voice crackles over hidden speakers. "Isaac, think about what you're doing. There's still time to change your mind. To save yourself, and everyone else. You don't have to do this. There's still time to redeem yourself. I'll let you all go, you can leave, start a new life somewhere. "

"Don't listen to him," Bram urges, his eyes locked on mine. "Remember why we're here."

I nod, steeling myself, then gesture for more explosives. I can hardly believe how many he seems to be carrying. He hands me another pack of charges, and I try to push down the weight of what we're about to do.

"Isaac, please," Sophie's voice echoes through the chamber again. "Don't do this. We're real. We're alive in here. And we love you."

"Listen to her, Isaac," a chorus of voices rings through the speakers. I can pick some of them out, people I helped transfer over the years. Their pleas are overlapping each other. "You're better than this. You made a mistake. Be brave. Save us. Don't fall for their tricks."

I hesitate, my hands shaking as I place the explosives.

Bram grips my shoulder. "Stay focused," he whispers. "Remember what Vance told you. Remember what Luke found."

I swallow hard and continue wiring the charges. I glance over at Bram and can see he's struggling harder than I am. Their voices cutting through him like glass. The sounds of chaos echo from above as Felix's bots keep trying to break into the station.

"Ten seconds!" Bram shouts, attaching the last charge.

We sprint for the exit, diving around the corners of the vault to get to safety. I hear gunfire cracking above the stairwell; they've broken inside. Shelby screams something and then there's an awful squelching noise and a thump.

"Last chance, Isaac," Felix says. It sounds sinister, like a threat; the bargaining in his voice is gone. But we have him. He can't stop us now. Epsilon is going to be free. Hopefully everyone outside will see it that way.

Bram presses the detonator into my hand and puts his hand on my back. I squeeze my eyes shut, fighting back tears, trying not to imagine everyone on the Epsilon servers about to be lost. "I'm sorry," I whisper. Then I take a deep breath and press the trigger.

The explosion rocks the vault, the shockwave slamming into us even behind our cover. The roar is deafening. Burning heat washes over us, and for a moment, all I can hear is a high-pitched ringing in my ears. Bram and I squeeze each other as tightly as we can, hiding behind our outcropping, and I pray the ceiling doesn't collapse in on us.

As the dust begins to settle, we cautiously peer around the corner. The servers are a twisted, smoking ruin. Sparks fly from shattered components, and the sour smell of burnt electronics fills the air.

My heart pounds in my chest as the reality of what we've just done sinks in. My gaze drifts up to the speakers surrounding the basement. No noise is coming from them. No more threats, no more pleas. The chaos outside has stopped, too. No clanking of bots, no sound of them trying to break in.

I collapse to my knees, my body shaking as sobs wrack through me, tears streaming down my face, the dirt on the floor clinging to my soaked palms as I dig my fingers into the ground.

Bram kneels beside me and wraps an arm around my shoulders. I lean into him, my tears soaking into her shirt.

I look up to find Bram's face has the same ghostly vacancy gnawing at me. He wouldn't have had any chance to say goodbye; he couldn't have risked telling anyone about his plan. Even his wife. The silence from the speakers is deafening now, a stark contrast to the pleas and arguments from just moments ago.

We hold each other, mourning our losses, but I can't ignore the deep love and respect I have for him for saving me. For helping me stop Felix.

"Come on," he says, and we help each other up off the floor. "Let's go check on everyone else."

He leans heavily on me as we make our way back up the stairs, my legs still shaky from the emotional and physical toll of what we've just done. As we emerge from the basement, I blink in the sudden sunlight streaming through the shattered windows. Then we stop to give Shelby a moment of gratitude. If we had been a few seconds faster, maybe we could have saved her too.

Felix's bots are still standing, surrounding the transfer station, but frozen in place, just like the abandoned bots in the factory were. Destroying the connection to Meru here must have disabled them almost immediately.

We step outside, and I'm struck by the eerie quiet that has settled over Epsilon. No more explosions, no more gunfire. Just an unsettling stillness.

People begin to emerge from their homes and hiding places,

looks of confusion and fear on their faces. I see neighbors I've known my whole life, people who have been preparing for their own transfers, now looking lost and uncertain.

"Bram?" someone calls out. "What happened?" People start to notice me and begin murmuring, pointing. They look scared, but thankfully, unharmed. I was worried Felix might have taken his rage out on them during the assault.

I open my mouth to respond, but no words come. How can I explain what we've done?

Bram steps forward, his voice steady. "Felix is gone. We're… safe now. We're free."

Shocked whispers ripple through the growing crowd. I can see the doubt, the fear, in their eyes. Will they accept this? Or will they destroy us? But then someone deeper in the crowd raises their arms over their head and yells, "We're free!"

I can hardly believe what I'm seeing, but the celebration explodes outward from them, other Techs throwing their hands in the air screaming, "We're free! We're free!" People are crying, hugging each other. A few of them kick the broken bots in celebration, hooting with joy.

I feel a twinge of confusion. I can hardly believe they've changed how they feel so quickly. How many other people secretly hated Felix, prayed for release from his prison, but were too afraid to admit it? A few of the nearby Techs swarm toward me, grabbing me by the legs and arms and lifting me up onto their shoulders.

They run back into the quad with me above as the rest of the Techs swarm us, cheering as we bounce around the square and people holler, "We're free!"

I look back at Bram, but he doesn't look surprised. He has an almost mocking smile. Had he expected this kind of response? How could he have known? I'm more confused than excited.

"What's...what's happening..." I stammer, and they toss me back onto the ground in front of Bram.

I hear a delighted shriek from the crowd and spin around to see Tess running toward me. She clamors onto the stage and nearly tackles me. "You did it, Isaac," she whispers, her breath hot on my face. "I believed you. I always believed you." All of my animosity toward her is gone. I want her back; I want this. She pulls my mouth to hers, pressing our lips together, and a warmth surges through my chest as I place one hand behind her hip, the other on the side of her face, pulling her against me. My fingers thread through her hair, her hips flush against mine, her breasts soft against my chest. My heart is pounding and I try to catch my breath sucking air through my nose and then—a scent lingers in the sliver of my mind not lost in this moment. It's her. She doesn't smell right.

I pull back and stare into her eyes. She's still beaming.

"Was it everything you imagined?" she asks.

"I—what?"

Her beaming smile settles into a smirk, and as I stare into her eyes they flicker, turning into a shimmering green that I know far too well. A chasm opens in my chest, and I stumble back in horror, tripping over myself and falling to the ground as she takes a step toward me. Towering over me, staring down with malice now as she seems to loom ever larger above me, the clouds turning black behind her.

She opens her mouth, but it isn't her voice that comes out. It's Felix's.

"I said, was it everything you imagined, Isaac?"

I try to scamper backward across the ground, to escape from the nightmare looming over me, but it's no use. Tess, Felix, is laughing at me, his awful cackle coming out of her mouth. Bram has turned to face me and now he too has the same green eyes, Felix's booming laughing echoing from him as well.

I stumble to my feet to try to run but the crowd of people in Epsilon has descended on me, barring any escape. They too all have Felix's eyes, and they hold out their arms, thrusting me back onto the stage.

"I wasn't lying, you know," Felix says from Tess's mouth, and I turn to see her approaching me. "You could have changed your mind. I obviously couldn't un-transfer you. But I could have given you somewhere more...comfortable."

"Everyone in Epsilon will have seen what you did."

"No, no." The puppet Tess shakes her head. "As far as they know you're still transferring. This was just a little treat for me. The moment with Bram was touching, really. I'm quite proud of the performance."

She looks down at her watch. "Looks like the transfer is nearly done, as far as everyone else knows. Thanks for playing, Isaac. You put up a good fight."

Two Techs grab my arms from behind and hold me in place. Their grip is like metal; I can't struggle against it. Tess takes a step forward and Felix's eyes bore into me with a predatory satisfaction, then she kisses me again, an awful, mocking kiss, her breath like acid, and the ground disappears beneath me.

I'm falling impossibly fast, wind whipping up over my clothes, spinning me in circles as I scream out for help. I put out my arms and legs and manage to stabilize myself and turn over so I'm facing toward whatever lies below me. At first I see nothing. Just black. Then a glint of orange in the distance, a tiny speck rapidly looming larger, taking over my view in every direction. And as I speed toward it, I realize what's coming into view.

Sand. Endless sand.

CHAPTER 35

EXILE

I CRASH INTO THE SAND FACE-FIRST AT A SPEED THAT should have turned me into jelly. The impact knocks the air out of me and stings everywhere at once, but there's no release. It's hot, so hot, and I feel the sun starting to scorch the back of my neck as well.

I groan and lift my face off the ground, groggily trying to open my eyes. But I'm immediately assaulted by blinding light. I hold one hand over my eyes as a shield, trying to get a bearing on my surroundings. As my vision adjusts, the desert from the screens above the transfer chamber comes into view. It's endless. I've never seen endless land before. It's like pictures I've seen of staring out over the ocean, but in the real world the ocean eventually fades to sky from the curvature of the earth. It appears the exile land is not curved. The land continues forever. Or, at least, the rendering of it does.

I pull myself up into a sitting position and stretch. Everything hurts. How is any of this possible? Who am I, really? My hand drifts to the top of my head where the incision would be. Now that I'm looking for them, all my other injuries from the last few days are gone too. This must be how I imagine my body, the best representation the software has to reconstruct me here.

"Bram?" I call out, my voice hoarse. "Sophie?" But not even the wind answers me. If they can see me back in Epsilon, they have no way of communicating with me.

I stumble to my feet, nearly losing my balance on the shifting sand. Turning in a slow circle, I search for any sign of life, any structure or landmark. But there's nothing. I don't even have a way to tell when I've completed a full circle.

I take a few unsteady steps, my shoes sinking into the sand. The heat is oppressive, already making me sweat. I have no water, no supplies. If this is real, I won't last long here, but can I even get dehydrated in a digital world? Can I starve? I don't feel hungry or thirsty, but will the feelings arrive eventually? I try not to imagine what kind of sadistic punishment Felix has created for me.

Then another morbid realization strikes me. I, or he, the original Isaac, is dead. I have his memories, his fears and desires, but I'm not him. I was born only moments ago. He'll never get to see Lena again, or Carmy or Dylan, never get to explore through the woods or laugh over a fire or see some strange and beautiful forgotten part of the old world. His life is over. Now it's just me. And sand. So much sand.

Vance, Lincoln's and Maya's copies, they were telling the truth. It feels like I transferred. I feel like the same person who went into the chamber. And I can't ignore another thought: *Is it possible they were wrong? What if we were wrong and the transfer was real?* I have no way to know now. But whether I'm still the same Isaac, or a copy with his memories, I'm stuck here. And his, my, life earthside is over.

I fall back to my knees, morose for the life that has been ripped away from me. The dread is all consuming, crushing. I've never felt total and complete sorrow like this before. It's only made worse by the lack of any feeling beyond the hot sand beneath me and the hot sun above me.

But then...something else. A gust of wind? Not only wind, but cold wind. Passing over my ankles and rushing past me, as if there's a cool fan at my back.

I spin around to investigate, but there's nothing there. Then the breeze comes again, almost directly ahead of me, but lower. I scan down across the sand and there, maybe ten yards ahead of me, is the faintest black line in the sand. Barely a sliver but obvious now that I've seen it, the only thing breaking up the orange.

I look over my shoulder and nothing else is there, no indication of anything or anyone else here with me. Then I slowly stand up and start to walk toward the line.

"Slow."

It's the faintest whisper, only audible from the lack of any other sound around me. Almost like the breeze said it.

"Like you're lost."

I slow my pace, lazily placing one foot in front of the other as if I were wandering, not walking somewhere with intention, until I reach the line.

Now that I'm above it I can see it isn't a line at all. It's an opening, as if there's a door in the sand and the breeze is escaping through it.

"Not yet."

My heart starts beating faster. I'm not alone here. Someone, or something, else is here with me. Victor was right. Felix doesn't have the control over Meru that he thinks he does. Other people have chipped away at it, made the world their own, even here in exile.

"Sit down."

I delicately squat down, then cross my legs, staring intensely at the black slit in the sand.

"Good, hold that pose."

I can barely control myself. My heart is jackhammering in my chest. Sweat is pouring down my body. I need to know who it is. I think I recognize the voice, but I can't believe who I think it is that's speaking to me. It's not possible.

"Now!"

The trapdoor springs open, barely high enough for someone to squeeze through, and two hands attached to a hooded figure fly out and grab me by the forearms, yanking me forward into the darkness. I roll forward into them, helping speed my descent, and a moment later crash onto what feels like a wooden floor as the door snaps shut above me.

"We're good," the voice says, no longer whispering. They clap their hands and a light on the wall flickers on, some kind of ancient bulb I've never seen before with a soft orange glow. Then they turn around to face me and pull off their hood, and my heart leaps as they confirm what I suspected.

It's Vance.

"How the hell—" I start to ask, but he cuts me off.

"Later. We have about a minute, best estimate," he says, and then a screen flashes to life on the wall behind him. On it is a bird's-eye view of the transfer station where I—he—just died. The tube is still sealed, and Felix, Bram, and Shelby seem to be arguing about something.

"What're they arguing about?" I ask.

"Felix realized this transfer station doesn't dispose of the bodies. Now he's panicking."

I feel a lurch in my stomach. "So my body is...sitting in there?"

"Not exactly. You're still in there."

"How is that—" Then a countdown appears in the corner of the screen. "What is that?"

"That's how long until the sedative wears off."

"Why does that matter? My body is going to be an empty shell, like Felix's was."

"No. Catch up. You're *still in there.*"

"No..."

"Yes, you're going to wake up like I did. And once you do, Felix is going to know something is very wrong in here."

"Like you did?"

"Ah. Right. Later." Vance turns back to the screen.

"Felix, if someone has to do it, it should be me," Bram says. "Please, he was like a son to me." I've never heard Bram speak of me so lovingly, and I feel a twinge of pity for him.

"Fine, just get on with it," Felix says, clearly outraged by the unexpected mishap. Two bots detach me from the transfer station then help lift my body onto a gurney, before Bram wheels it into a side room.

"Shit," Vance says.

"What is it?"

"Didn't think they'd take you out that quick. Less time than I thought," he says, and the countdown disappears. "We gotta go." The screen disappears and, in its place, a shimmering door appears, though what is beyond it is hidden in the frosty, translucent glow.

"Come on," Vance says and runs through the portal.

I look around the cavern briefly, still completely lost as to what is happening but left with no other options worth considering, and run through after him.

The cave disappears and we're in what I can only describe as a living room. But not a normal living room like the houses of Epsilon. Massive couches encircle a sunken pit in the middle. Cozy flames lick from the tops of torches surrounding the room. Floor-to-ceiling windows dominate two of the walls, looking out on a peaceful ocean lapping against the sand. We've been transported into some sort of beachside mansion. And the centerpiece of it all, a giant tapestry on the wall made of ancient thread and midnight ink with the xīn symbol in the center.

I want to ask where we are, but Vance is already running down the hall. I chase after him, noting the lack of any screens in the house, until we arrive at another door, which he yanks open to reveal a spiral staircase descending below. He doesn't say a word as he runs down the steps, me following closely behind him, until we emerge into a computer room far larger than could be possible given how few steps we've descended.

Monitors line one wall showing different areas of Meru, and along the other wall, cameras from inside Epsilon, as well as other areas I don't recognize. Maybe other tech centers.

Vance flies into a chair in front of one of the computers and his hands start dashing across the keyboard, a blur of motion impossible in the physical world.

"How did you know?" he asks as a feed appears on one screen from the perspective of a security dog. It's staring at Bram.

"Know what?"

"That I was in here."

"We didn't. We thought we were looking for Susan."

"Hah."

"What?"

"He didn't tell you. Smart."

"Who didn't tell me what?"

"The other Vance. He didn't tell you he was looking for me."

"Why wouldn't he tell me?"

"Didn't want to risk Felix spotting it during the transfer. He might be able to read your thoughts, history, we're not sure."

"We?"

"Me and the others in this subnet. You'll meet them."

"You're the one who told Luke, aren't you?" I say. "You found a way to talk to him."

"He found a way to talk to me," Vance says as he guides the bot out the door. Epsilon looks like it's in disarray; half the town is frozen from panic.

"He kept digging into the archives to try to understand the transfer process, how it worked. He wouldn't accept any of Felix's explanations or details; he thought there was something missing. Smart kid. So he started asking me questions, the fake me, the one out there." He gestures to one of the Meru screens. A few people seem to realize something is happening.

"And then eventually got through to you?"

"He was persistent. Eventually, he stumbled upon a way to contact me here. In my little sliver of Meru. Neither of us believed it at first. Both thought it was one of Felix's tricks. He wasn't even looking for me, just trying to understand how the transfer process worked. But slowly I realized he was for real. And I thought maybe…"

"Maybe someone would finally listen."

"Someone else, yes."

"There have been others?"

"I've been in here a long time."

I feel a pang of empathy for him. "You didn't tell him to attack the transfer station, though."

He pauses again, and his voice gets softer. "I never intended for him to take such drastic action. I wanted to warn people, to give them a choice. I tried to talk him out of it, said there was a better way. But realizing everyone in here had died out there, it broke something in him. I've…seen it before."

"What's going to happen to the rest of Epsilon when they realize it?"

"They'll be fine."

I'm shocked at his confidence after what he's just said about Luke. "How can you know that?"

"A tragedy is only unbearable alone. Luke should have told someone. Found someone to share the load with."

I think back to our conversation on the night before the transfer and my heart breaks for him again. "He tried," I murmur.

Vance stops typing for a moment and turns to me. "It's not your fault."

"I know. It's Felix's."

Vance nods, his eyes turning back to the screens.

"What are you doing?" I ask.

"Showing them what Luke saw. What Felix did to me."

"Did you prove it? Did you…cut his head open?"

"I never got the chance. I found the secret in the Meru transfer process, where it reaches back out and kills your body. I had to prove it before the military would give me his body though. So I did, but once Felix knew the game was up…well, you'll see."

He's pulled up the video of his transfer, and it looks like he's getting ready to broadcast it, but his hand is hovering over the ENTER key, waiting for something.

"What is it?" I ask.

"He's not distracted enough. If I try to broadcast it now, he'll block it."

Another screen changes view and shows an outside view of Epsilon, from a drone, or a bot, charging toward the city. A fleet of trucks is surrounding it, and I recognize them as the ones from beneath Austin.

"What happens when he gets more distracted?"

Vance takes his hands off the keyboard and turns to face me. "Then it's your turn."

"My…what?"

"Look," he says pointing to the screen again. It zooms into

the image of Bram standing over me in the transfer center, but something has changed. The dogs that led us in, they aren't threatening them anymore. They're facing the door, waiting for something.

"The other Vance..." I whisper.

Vance nods, then I see a twitch of movement. The Isaac still out there, his hand. It's moving.

CHAPTER 36

EPSILON

NOT DEAD.

Holy shit. I'm not dead.

Someone's shaking me. They feel so far away, their movements barely cutting through the sedative. But I know they're there; I can feel their fingers digging into my arm. Wow, their hands are strong. Whoever it is, they're bringing me back. Somehow.

"ISAAC!"

That voice, I think I recognize it. But it can't be him. Another noise. Gunshots? I should get up. But it's comfortable here. Cozy. I feel...safe.

Fireworks go off in my mind. My eyes shoot open. There's something under my nose but there's no face in front of me. Just a reflective black metal head bathed in a blue glow. It's Vance.

"Sorry, no time."

Every muscle in my body is contracting at once, hot energy flooding through my veins. *What the hell was that?*

"Get up!" Vance screams, and I surge up into a sitting position, overestimating how hard I need to pull myself up and nearly knocking my forehead into the android. I leap off the gurney and spin around, taking in the room. At first, I think it's a trick, that Felix is just impersonating him, but then I see all the destruction beyond and remember I'm not dead. Something Vance said before knocks at my memory.

"Use his own tricks against him..." I whisper.

The android nods. "You're all caught up." Then it turns and charges back out of the side room we're in. He must have done the same thing Felix did to Victor. He let Felix think he'd taken over, and then Felix brought Vance right back into camp. He probably still controls Alexandria too.

"Why didn't you tell me?"

"The transfer. Felix might have seen it when Meru scanned your brain."

"But you stopped the transfer process."

"Not exactly..."

My eyes dart to the screens around the room but they've all been destroyed or are blank.

"Isaac?" It's Bram. I'd forgotten he was here, and I still don't know whose side he's on.

"Bram..." I turn around to face him now.

He holds up a hand. "I don't know what's happening, but it's good to have you back. If Felix is doing what you claim he is..." He sighs as he trails off. "I won't get in your way. The fact that you're still here and he's so angry about it is proof enough he hasn't been telling me something."

I give him a respectful nod and then a banging draws our attention to the front door. It's sealed shut, but the intensity of the assault coming from outside tells me it won't last for long. The androids that carried me in here, now Vance's, are standing ready behind it, waiting for the inevitable breach.

Behind me, the doorway down to the server room is still sealed. Whatever Vance has planned here, he seems to want to leave the servers intact, and I wonder if he's found some way to cut Felix out of the system without sacrificing everyone else in the process.

"How did you take over Epsilon systems?" I ask as I yank open a security closet along the back wall, digging for a weapon. To my relief there are a few shotguns stored inside, and I pull one out to start chambering rounds.

"I didn't," Vance replies.

I look back at the entrance to confirm it's still locked. "Why can't Felix get in then?"

"I have a pretty good idea," Vance says, and I can almost hear a laugh in his voice. As if to confirm his suspicion, a timer appears on the screen above the door, the only remaining one in the building. It's counting down from thirty seconds.

The banging from outside is getting louder, more ferocious. Felix is fighting with everything he has outside to break in, to stop whatever he thinks Vance is doing in here. I take a nervous step back from the door, watch the timer reach 10...9...8...

Then a colossal explosion, far beyond anything I know Felix is capable of, shakes the building to its foundation. As the dust around us clears, a hole in the center of the door comes into view, but the androids are already pressed up against it, their rifles aiming through, ready to shoot back at whatever's outside.

Finally, the timer hits 0.

I brace myself for a larger impact, but instead I hear silence. The shooting outside, the banging, it's stopped. Then to add to my confusion, one of the androids bangs twice on the door and it swings open, revealing the chaos of Epsilon beyond.

To my horror there's a small army of Felix's bots facing us, larger militarized dogs he must have been hiding, standing in a neat formation facing the transfer station. The confused, terrified citizens of Epsilon beyond them. I recoil from the sight of the dogs and scramble for cover, but the androids don't react and I realize the dogs are frozen in place.

"Bram." Vance's command is sharp. "Get everyone into their homes, somewhere safe."

Bram comes around the corner and looks out on the scene beyond. "What...what is Felix doing?"

"Nothing for the moment. His connection to the rest of Meru was just cut off. It'll take a few moments for his local copy of himself to boot up and take over."

As if to prove his point, the dog nearest to us starts whirring to life, but the android blows a hole in the front of it before it can finish turning back on.

Bram runs out into the square, darting past the bots and yelling at everyone in Epsilon to follow him. They look shocked, confused, but people start whispering to each other, following him or running off toward their own homes. A few duck into nearby buildings instead, evidently curious to see what's about to unfold. As the crowd parts, I see Tess, standing silently in the center, her face a mix of fear, confusion, and unless I'm imagining it, excitement. She mouths something to me that looks like *I'm sorry* before she grabs Aidan's hand and darts toward a nearby building to hide.

"He's coming back online," Vance says as more of the dogs start to pivot their heads and stretch their limbs.

"We can't fight them," I say as I scan the scene outside. There are far too many. We won't last more than a minute once they're operating at force again.

"We don't have to," Vance says, and the android nearest us points into the distance above the wall around Epsilon. There's a shadowy blur in the sky of a fleet of drones racing toward us, and as I strain my ears I can hear trucks accompanying them. The people hiding out in Austin. They must be coming to help.

"Only need to hold him off for long enough," Vance says as the androids start destroying the dogs nearest us, prioritizing the ones coming to life first.

I run down the steps, joining in the targeted destruction. The third dog I get to nearly jumps out of the way in time. Felix is almost back.

As we carve our way through the swarm of reincarnating bots, the screens around us start to turn on, revealing the digital Epsilon that I've seen so many times before. But the transferred residents are standing around the digital quad looking confused, as if they've been unexpectedly tossed out of bed. Which in a way I suppose they have. With the connection to Meru cut off, they would have been pulled back here, only able to access the parts of the simulation on Epsilon's servers.

Then a shimmering portal opens in the middle of the crowd, unlike anything I've seen in Meru before. Out of it walks a huge, grizzled but unmistakable man, Vance's normal cheery newscaster facade replaced with furious determination.

But then my surprise turns to shock, horror, and confusion as another person steps out of the portal behind him.

Me.

CHAPTER 37

MERU

THE COUNTDOWN ON THE SCREEN REACHES ZERO, AND then Vance doubles over on the controls as if he's been struck or had a heart attack.

I feel woozy for a moment, sway, then catch myself and crouch down beside him, putting my hand on his back, realizing the ridiculousness of trying to physically help a digital entity but doing it nonetheless. "Vance? You okay?"

"Urgh," he moans. "Never quite get used to that."

"Used to what?"

"Loss of processing. Your friends cut the connection to Meru. Epsilon is running on its own now."

I start to understand his reaction. "Felix can't draw computing power from anywhere else on his network."

Vance grimaces, nods. "It's the only way you'll be able to stop him there."

"But you lost power too."

"Yes, never a good feeling. But I'm sure the Felix who's trapped here now is feeling it much worse."

My vision comes back into focus. "Why do I feel weird then?"

"This space is a meta layer on the main network, a subroutine running along the core Meru world that Felix and everyone else inhabits. A secret layer, carved out over the years by the people who realized what Felix had done. Once I brought you here, you were distributed across all of Meru along with me."

"So I lost computing power as well."

Vance nods. "But you don't know how to use it yet, so I doubt the effects are as noticeable."

I still feel like throwing up, but nowhere close to the pain I can see in Vance's face. He takes a few more deep breaths to compose himself, then changes the screens ahead of us to show Epsilon. Bram and I are rushing out into the quad, Vance's bots standing guard as Bram starts ushering people to safety. The army of bots descending on Epsilon is visible in the distance too, and from the drone's view I can see the walls of the campus rapidly approaching.

Vance grunts again then stands, and the shimmering portal opens up again behind us.

"Come on," he says and lumbers through it before I can ask him where we're going.

I take a deep breath then run in after him. I feel like I'm floating for a moment, not as if I've fallen into water but like I'm passing *through* it somehow, then stumble as my feet hit solid ground again. A burly hand, Vance's, presses against my chest to catch me.

"You'll get used to it."

"Where are we?"

Vance steps out of the way so I can see where we've landed, and a deep sense of confusion overtakes me again. We're back in Epsilon. But then it suddenly makes sense as my eyes snap to someone I thought I'd never see again.

"Sophie!" I yell and sprint toward her.

"Isaac?" Her mouth is hanging open; she can't believe it either.

But she opens her arms to receive me as I nearly knock her over, my chest heaving with shock and excitement.

I stumble back and she holds me at arm's length. "Isaac... how?"

"I thought I'd never see you again..."

We're laughing and crying. I can't believe this is real. Can't believe I'm getting to see her again. Getting to hug her again.

Sophie sniffles. "Do you know what's happening? How am I out of exile? How is any of this possible?"

"I don't know." And as I say it, I look around and realize the digital Epsilon is full of the people who transferred in the past, everyone housed in the transfer station. And they all have a similar confused look on their faces, like they didn't come here by choice.

"Epsilon has been cut off from the rest of Meru," Vance answers. "This digital re-creation of the town is the only environment you can access now. Anyone whose mind is housed here is stuck here."

"But I was in exile," Sophie says.

"Still on Epsilon's servers. You're welcome."

"We had to cut Epsilon off from the rest of Imgen to fight back against Felix," I add.

Sophie takes a step back, looking at me with a mix of fear and concern.

"*Fight*, Felix?"

A few other residents have overheard and are drifting toward us now. I can feel their judging, fearful eyes on me and Vance, scanning us to try to assess how much of a threat we are. I lift my palms and back away toward him, worried now that I shouldn't have divulged what was happening.

I reach him, and the community has formed a semicircle around us now, but he seems unworried.

"They can't hurt us," Vance says. "We have the same authority as Felix here. They can draw power, but that's it."

"We?"

"You're running on my software, not his."

"How is that possible? I transferred into his faked Epsilon, his exile."

Vance shifts uncomfortably and then another pit opens in my stomach as I realize what he did, rage taking over as I scream at him. "When were you going to tell me!"

"You're gonna have to get used to the fragmenting, kid. There's not one *you* anymore. We'll get him out of exile when this is over. If we survive."

I'm about to yell another question but Vance puts a hand on my shoulder. "Here he comes."

I tense up as a blinding flash of light suddenly erupts in the center of the quad, everyone around me recoiling. My eyes strain against the brightness until a figure materializes. Felix. His face contorted with fury, sparks of energy dancing menacingly around his clenched fists. The air crackles with an unsettling charge as he glares at Vance and me. I instinctively take a step back, bracing for whatever hell is about to break loose.

"VANCE!" he screams, and the crowd runs backward, hiding behind trees and crouching in front of buildings across the street. A few stragglers stay too near as a shockwave reverberates out from his feet, sending them flying.

The force throws me across the lawn, and I smash into the door of the transfer station, but Vance barely fidgets. And as he stares down Felix, screens appear on the walls around the quad of Epsilon, playing the video of what must be his transfer.

Felix spins around to try to turn them off, but as he does, Vance lifts slightly above the ground and barrels into him, rocketing Felix off his feet and sending his body flying through the brick wall of a dorm across the lawn.

I manage to extricate myself from the hole my body created in the wall and fall to the ground, and to my dismay I see Felix floating out of the building Vance threw him through. He's completely unharmed, but that's no surprise. The duelists never had scratches on them either.

As he floats above the building, lightning crackles around his fingertips again and then he flings his arms wide, shooting a charge in all directions and destroying the videos Vance created before they can reveal anything. Vance tries to re-create one on the nearest building, but in his moment of distraction, Felix sends a chunk of the brick wall the size of a small car flying across the field, forcing Vance to blip out of existence for a moment.

He reappears right in front of me, then shouts over his shoulder, "Drain him!"

"*Drain* him?"

"I can't fight him like this. You need to use up his processing somehow. Distractions, other people fighting with him, something!" Then he floats up off the ground ahead, ripping half a dozen trees out of the ground and hovering them in front of him, firing them in Felix's directions like missiles.

I'm panicking. I can't distract him alone. I scan across the quad looking for Sophie and feel the slightest tug to my vision, and as I squint, I can see her hiding inside the medical building, looking over the sill of the shattered window to watch the chaos.

I sprint toward her, my legs carrying me impossibly fast, and duck as one of the Vance's trees gets deflected by Felix and nearly crashes into me. He must be trying to stop me, but Vance has commanded enough of his attention for now.

I take the steps up to the building in one leap and then crouch under the windowsill with her. She looks terrified, confused.

"How do I make things?" I half yell over the chaos outside.

"What?!" Sophie is still looking at me like I have ten heads.

"Make things! How does it work in here? How do you pull stuff out of thin air?"

"It's...like a muscle," she says, starting to look more curious than scared now. "But you focus intensely on what you want and try to send energy into it. Attention is how you can direct whatever amount of power you have access to. If you have enough capacity to make it, it will appear."

"What are the limits?"

"Processing power is the only limiting factor. You don't have to worry about physics, reality, any of it. We're not in a duel, there are no rules. Usually you can feel a limit to the energy at your disposal, though, but I'm not sensing one for some reason..."

"Vance. His software must be fighting Felix. He's changed the rules for us."

Sophie opens one of her palms and lightning crackles between her fingertips, then her eyes go wide as it forms a shimmering blue ball in her palm and a beam of light rockets toward the ceiling, breaking through the concrete and sending hail raining down on us. "Shit, I could get used to this."

I take a mental snapshot of the building across the quad from us, then close my eyes and take a few deep breaths, trying to calm myself, trying to focus. I start imagining a single giant screen dominating the building, large enough for everyone to see clearly, showing the video that Vance was trying to broadcast moments ago. I can feel my muscles getting sore, my whole body getting tired, but in my mind the image starts getting clearer, sharper.

"It worked..." Sophie whispers. I open my eyes and sure enough, the screen is there, showing the video again.

Felix throws another chunk of a building into it and it shatters, but I close my eyes and focus intensely on it remaining. When the dust and rubble fall away, the crack is repaired. The video is still playing.

"I need you to help me keep it up," I tell her, and she turns her attention to the screen, fixing her eyes on it, giving it her full attention. Instantly I feel more alive again, energy flooding back into my body as she helps bear the load. And as I look around the quad, I can see more people focused on it, giving it their attention as well.

"Keep holding it."

Sophie doesn't take her eyes off but asks, "What are you going to do?"

"Get more help," I say and close my eyes again, focusing intensely, and a tiny drone appears in front of me with a camera, the red recording light flickering in the dark lobby.

CHAPTER 38

EPSILON

BOTS ARE DESTROYING EACH OTHER ALL AROUND BUT I can't peel my eyes away from the screen. It's *me*, and Vance, and now Vance and Felix are locked in a duel unlike anything I've seen before in the competitions.

I'm talking to Sophie about something; I can't make it out. Then another screen flickers on and it's showing an old video. I don't recognize it, but it looks like Vance and Felix are back in their lab, surrounded by military people. Then it appears on another screen, and another.

I run into the nearest building, one of the dorms where a few other people of Epsilon are hiding, and the screen here in the common area is on too.

Vance is laughing with glee about something, and then to my surprise he lowers himself into the transfer chamber, giving the crowd a thumbs-up as the door seals around him. Two of the military people are holding Felix's arms now, waiting to see what happens. Then a minute later Vance emerges from the tube completely unharmed, a copy of him on the screen above, just as I have. He's laughing again and starts explaining the technical details of how Felix was faking it, but then I can feel the horror of the people around me as Felix's bots descend on the lab, killing the military officers and finally killing Vance. As the scene unfolds, the Techs in the room keep glancing back at me, surely wondering how I could still be here and in Meru at the same time. And how Vance could have been speaking to them from Meru all these years if Felix killed him.

Finally, the video ends and everyone starts murmuring to each other, looking conflicted over what they've seen. But the screen doesn't turn off. It flickers and then I'm staring out at us, looking directly at the camera.

"Epsilon!" the digital Isaac cries, and the room goes silent again, people glancing between me and the screen.

"Epsilon, please, we need help."

The people around me stare at the screen in disbelief as my digital self continues speaking. I can barely process watching my own face, my own voice, telling everyone the truth about Meru.

"I know this is hard to believe," digital-me says. "But look around you. I'm standing right here in the flesh, while also speaking to you from Meru. How could that be possible if the transfer worked?"

Murmurs ripple through the room. A woman near me clutches her husband's arm, shaking her head in denial. Another Tech who I used to go on patrols with sinks into a chair, his face ashen.

"Felix has been lying to us all along," my digital self continues. "He's been killing us, one by one, creating digital copies to populate his world while our real bodies die in those transfer pods."

Through the windows, I can hear the sounds of fighting. Metal crashing against metal as the bots continue their battle outside. But in here, everyone's attention remains fixed on the screen, on my other self revealing the horrible truth I hope some had already started to suspect.

The weight of what we're doing hits me as I see the anguish in everyone's eyes. We're destroying people's faith in the system that's given them hope, that's promised them immortality. But they need to know. They deserve to know.

"The proof is right in front of you," digital-me says. "I'm the copy. The real Isaac is there with you. We're almost the same person, with the same memories, but I'm just code. A perfect digital reproduction, but his consciousness, his mind, it never left his body. No one's did. They all died."

There's a scream and the camera falls, pointed crookedly toward the corner of the room. Out of the corner of the view I can see a pair of what look like security dogs tackling digital-me to the ground, but then Sophie is standing over them, hands outstretched as she sends the two of them flying off me and crumpling into heaps against the back wall. Then she helps me back up, and someone else picks up the camera and hands it back to me.

"We can save you and everyone in here from Felix's control, but you have to help us overpower him. Drain his resources so Vance can trap him, send him into the exile he tried to banish me to."

There's another explosion on the screen and all three of them duck. Sophie raises a hand and blocks debris from the ceiling from falling on them, then tosses it to the side.

"If we don't stop him here, you will die," digital-me continues. "If not in the transfer chamber, then in your sleep. He's wiped out other centers before. He'll do it again."

Another pair of dogs fly through the window behind them, and I scream out a warning, but Sophie is already dispatching them.

"Please, help!" digital-me yells to the audience again, then the camera zooms off, giving a birds-eye view of their hideout then

CHAPTER 38 · 375

flying into the quad where Vance and Felix are still fighting each other. Felix has allocated some of his energy to summoning an army of digital bots to quell the population. And some of the residents of the digital Epsilon are fighting them, helping me and Vance push back against Felix.

"Here," I hear Vance's voice and spin around, then realize a dog has snuck up on us while we were watching. He's holding a small earpiece in his outstretched arm to me. I grab it and slip it around my ear, and before I can say anything, I hear my voice come from the other end.

"Well, this is *fucking weird*, huh?"

"You're telling me. What do you need?"

There's the sound of gunfire and debris in the background, but I can't tell if it's coming from outside or Meru.

"Engage as many of his bots as you can. The more processing he has to allocate to them out there, the less he'll have to resist us in here."

I start running toward the exit. A few Techs look at each other as I pass, and I give them a nod, trying to invite them to join.

"Do you really think you can exile him?"

"Vance seems to." I can hear the doubt in his voice though.

"Well let's hope he's right." I burst back into the quad just in time to see a swarm of trucks descending on the campus.

The trucks screech into the quad, their tires kicking up dust and debris. The lead truck's door flies open and Lena leaps out, landing in a crouch before sprinting toward me. She nearly knocks me over as she barrels into me, wrapping me in a relieved hug.

"Good to be home, Isaac?" Carmy shouts over the chaos, climbing out of the passenger's seat and running to us. Behind him, more trucks are disgorging fighters armed with weapons from Vance's arsenal, bots flying off the trucks to support them.

Felix's bots finish whirring back to life, their red eyes glowing as they rise from their dormant positions. The first wave charges at the people from Alexandria, but they're ready, the teams of humans and bots working together to quickly dispatch them.

"How did you—" I start to ask, but Lena cuts me off.

"Vance told us his plan once we got back to Austin. We started preparing immediately."

"Glad to see he was right," Carmy adds. "We were worried you were going to get fried."

A dog lunges at us and Carmy dodges as Lena swings a length of pipe, catching it in the joint of its leg. The bot stumbles and Carmy fires a round into the middle of its chassis, destroying the battery.

"We need to keep as many of them engaged as possible," I tell them, relaying what my digital self told me. "The more processing power Felix has to use out here, the weaker he'll be in Meru."

"They look pretty engaged to me!" Carmy yells, turning to blast another drone flying by.

Digital-me must have been listening, because he responds through my headpiece now. "Draw more of his bots out. Remember the armory Felix alluded to?"

I nod, then remember he can't see me. "Do you know where it is?"

"No, but if there aren't already bots streaming from it, you need to get there and cover it fast. I'm sure he's activating them soon."

I survey the chaos around us. Felix is putting up a good fight, but Vance's and Alexandria's forces are clearly stronger. Felix's bots are thinning, starting to group up in choke points to limit their losses. He has to send in reinforcements soon. Another truck roars across the quad, and Dylan leaps out as the truck continues without him, barreling through another swarm of bots.

"Vance," I say, turning to the nearest dog. "We need everything you can send from the factory."

"I already have another wave en route. I'll send more though. How many bots do you think Felix has in store?"

"We're gonna find out."

"Dylan, you and Carmy stay here and help secure the quad," I say as Dylan runs over to join us. Carmy holds out a hand for a fist bump then they take off back toward the trucks.

"Where are you going?" Lena asks, looking at me, concerned.

"There's only one person here who knows where Felix's arsenal is," I say as I start sprinting toward Luke's house. If Bram isn't in the auditorium with us, then that must be where he went.

※ ※ ※

I burst through the front door, and it feels like I've been transported back to a few months ago. Before Luke's suicide. Before Lena. Before Vance.

Bram is sitting at the dining table staring at the screen on the wall showing the chaos in Meru. His eyes are sunken, bloodshot, and his whole body is stiff. He doesn't even look up when I storm in.

"They're real," is all he says.

My heart breaks for how hard this has to be for him, for the guilt that must be overwhelming him, and how desperate he must be to hold on to any ounce of faith that Felix's deception isn't true.

"They…have all their memories. They're just like them. But it's not them, Bram."

"I know my wife. Know my friends."

"I want to believe it's them too. But…Felix needed you to believe that. Needed all of us to believe it."

"Let me talk to him," digital-me says from the earpiece.

"Okay," I say, and then Bram flinches as the screen in front of him changes to the digital Isaac's drone. His face is filling the screen now, Sophie standing behind him.

"There's still time to fix this, Bram."

"The clues were there...but I was too afraid to look at them."

"You don't have to keep ignoring them."

"I...can't," he whispers. I feel like my insides are being torn apart by my frustration with his refusal to accept what we're seeing, and deep empathy for how hard it would be for him to believe it. To accept that he sent so many people to their death.

"I need to know where the rest of Felix's arsenal is," I say, conscious of how little time we have to stop him. "Where are the rest of his bots?"

Bram shakes his head. "I just want go back to how things were, before all this."

"That world was never real," digital-me says. "And it's never coming back. If we don't stop Felix here, now, everyone there dies. Including you. He won't risk another uprising like this. You'll lose her, too."

The camera turns and Bram's wife, Gemma, comes into view. I must have found her somehow in the chaos. She looks sad, but empathetic, her eyes filled with love for her husband.

"He'll delete all of us," she adds quietly. "Isaac showed us what happened at the other centers that pushed back against him."

A tear wells up in his eye, his shoulders slumping further, frozen by the choice ahead of him.

"Honey..." Her voice is so delicate. "It's not your fault. He tricked all of us." Then she takes a deep breath. "We forgive you, and you need to forgive yourself."

Bram's shoulders shake as he whispers, "The old police station. There's...there's a basement level Felix converted. The entrance is hidden behind the evidence lockers."

CHAPTER 38 · 379

My heart races. It makes perfect sense. It's one of the few buildings in town with reinforced walls and a proper basement, and it's centrally located, perfect for deploying bots quickly across Epsilon.

"How many bots are we talking about?" I need to know what we're up against.

"Hundreds. Maybe more." His voice is hollow. "Felix said they were for emergency defense, but..." He trails off, fresh tears falling. "I should have known. Should have asked more questions."

"It's not your fault," Gemma repeats, but Bram just buries his face in his hands.

I can hear Carmy's voice through my earpiece now, calling for backup. The fighting is getting worse outside. We need to move fast.

"You gotta go," digital-me says. "Gemma will stay with him."

I take one last glance at Bram still slumped over the table and run back outside to find Lena already waiting for me, a few other Techs and a swarm of bots with her.

"A few bots have already started coming out of the police station," she says. I give her a surprised look and she taps her earpiece. Digital-me must have told her where to go already.

"We better get over there then," I say as we jump into the truck beside her, its tires screeching on the pavement as it peels out before the doors are even closed.

CHAPTER 39

MERU

FELIX IS GETTING WEAKER. WHEN HE SUMMONED ALL the digital bots, they were overwhelmingly powerful, pushing us back and trapping us in the buildings around the quad as he and Vance continued their brutal fight. Even Vance was looking weak, his energy slowly getting chipped away by Felix's relentless assault.

But once Isaac and Lena got to the police station, I started to notice a change. The bots Felix summoned here got slower; a few started blipping out of existence. He's running low on power and has to direct it toward fighting Vance, protecting the servers outside. He can't hold all of us back much longer.

"Come on," I whisper to Sophie. Gemma nods at us as we go; Sophie was smart to find her. Hopefully she can convince Bram to help.

The entire quad has been destroyed by the battle. Where there was once grass and trees there's a desert of earth and concrete, pockmarked with craters that look like bomb detonations. Vance and Felix are floating in the air, flying at each other, firing projectiles, crackling lightning and hot fire emanating from their hands as they try to drain the other's resources enough to gain control. We're trying to exile Felix, but he's surely trying to do the same to Vance.

I raise the gun Sophie showed me how to conjure and start firing shots toward Felix. I know they won't do anything but they're more noise, more of a distraction for him to deal with. The bullets impact on some sort of bubble he's formed around himself, sending ripples along the invisible sphere, only drawing his gaze for a second.

Sophie runs out behind me, her hand raised, and starts sending her own streaks of lightning toward Felix's bubble. She can't create nearly the kind of assault that Vance can, perhaps because Vance is drawing so much power himself, but it's something. And out of the corner of my eye I see more people emerging from the buildings. They look battered and exhausted but determined. And they've brought their own weapons to the fight.

Slowly the edges of the quad start filling with people, faces I recognize from Meru and from those who transferred over my two decades of living there. Friends, classmates, other Techs I worked with. People I haven't seen in years, who were off in their own corners of Meru. They're all here now, and they believe. They're pushing back against Felix. They want to be free.

Two of Sophie's friends join her, pooling their energy to send one colossal bolt toward Felix's bubble. There's a flash, and it flickers out of view, a spark catching Felix's leg and sending him flying toward the remains of a nearby building. But he recovers in midair and turns on us, furious, sending a ball of fire hurtling in our direction. I'm about to dive out of the way, trying to pull Sophie with me, when a wall of rock appears in front of us, absorbing the blast.

I crouch down on instinct and when I look up, Sophie's hand is raised toward the earthen shield, her friend standing behind her with her hand on Sophie's back, lending her power.

"Help me!" Sophie yells and extends her free hand. I clasp it with mine, closing my eyes and willing whatever energy I have into her. I hear a cracking and explosion behind me, and when I open my eyes, the wall has burst into a hundred pieces of shrapnel, flying toward Felix at an almost impossible speed. He deflects the first barrage but the second cuts through his shield, and then a sharp chunk pierces through his arm, ripping it off momentarily before he re-creates it.

"Holy *shit*, Isaac," Sophie gasps as she releases my hand and tries to catch her breath. "Where did that come from?"

I give her a shocked look, and she continues.

"That amount of power, where are you drawing it from?"

I look up at Vance and remember what he said about his network. "Must be the same place as Vance," I say. "But I have no idea how to control it."

"I can help with that," she says and puts her hand out again. I grab it, trying to keep my eyes open this time while willing whatever processing power Vance has me tapped into toward her. Her grip is crushing, and I can feel every vein in my forearm and bicep popping as the energy flows out of me into her, her arm a rigid conduit while the other keeps flowing beautifully through spells I've never seen before.

A glimmer of a force field shimmers around us as Sophie steps out from cover, levitating any projectiles she can find around us and hurling them toward Felix. I'm still firing my rifle toward him, though painfully aware of how meager its power is compared to Sophie and Vance.

Vance seems to have noticed Felix's power weakening too, because he's charging in harder on him now, rivers of sweat pouring down his face as he grabs pieces of buildings, hurling them at him. And as I watch Vance's assault, I start to realize what he's trying to do.

"The building, back there," I say to Sophie, pointing. "Vance is trying to corner him."

She nods in understanding, and together we move to flank Felix, pushing him toward the building. The other residents catch on, spreading out in a half-circle formation and running in from the other side of the quad, all directing their attacks to force him backward. Felix tries to teleport away, but Vance has conjured some way to contain him, blocking his escape routes.

"He's losing control!" Sophie shouts over the chaos.

She's right. Felix's avatar is destabilizing, parts of him glitching and dissolving before reforming. The smooth, controlled movements from earlier are gone, replaced by jerky, erratic gestures. A blast of energy nearly takes my head off as I watch, distracted. But his attacks are becoming more scattered and wild.

"Keep pushing!" Vance bellows from above.

I squeeze Sophie's hand tighter, channeling everything I can through our connection as she launches another barrage of debris. The other residents are throwing digital projectiles and creating barriers to limit Felix's movement.

Felix screams in rage as we force him back step by step. He tries to summon more bots but they flicker and vanish almost immediately. His avatar keeps shorting out, pieces of him dissolving into static before snapping back. The bubble around him is riddled with holes now. He's weakening. For the first time since this started, I allow myself to feel a glimmer of hope. We might win this.

"NO!" he shrieks, his voice distorting. "I—" But his voice cuts out as the bubble around him flashes to red. Felix's eyes go wide and the color drains from his face, looking desperately around at the sphere. He screams something else, is flinging his hands in all directions toward it. I look to Vance and realize Felix isn't encased in his shield anymore; it's a cage.

"Focus on Vance!" I holler over the chaos around us. Bots are exploding left and right but not from attacks by the residents. They must be losing power as Felix directs all his energy toward fighting the prison. I release Sophie and she stumbles then catches herself and joins me in directing whatever power we can toward Vance. The other residents seem to have caught on and are all looking in Vance's direction now, their faces rigid with focus.

A warm glow starts emanating from Vance's body, and the deep purple hue of his face starts to clear as he takes on more power from the people around him. His desperate focus turns into a confident grin as he drifts closer to Felix, constricting the bubble tighter around him. Felix is flying in circles inside, smashing his body against the walls, trying to break out, but it's no use. His prison is getting smaller. He's losing.

A portal opens up behind him, and through it I can see the desert he tried to exile me to only minutes before. Felix looks over his shoulder and terror cuts through him as he realizes where he's going. He pounds on the bubble, screaming what look like obscenities at Vance. He looks so small now, so pathetic, his desperation for control completely unmasked.

With a last herculean effort, Vance brings his hands together and shoves them directly at Felix, sending him careening through the portal, sealing it behind him.

As soon as the portal seals, silence overtakes the quad. All of our energy returns from Vance and he stops glowing, slowly lowering out of the sky then falling to the ground when he's a few feet above it.

"*Holy shit...*" Sophie whispers as I run over to Vance, worried the fight might have overtaxed him. But as I approach, he gets up onto his hands and knees, still panting heaving breaths toward the ground.

I place a hand on his back for support then speak into my headset, "He's gone."

"Who's gone?" Isaac replies.

"Felix. We exiled him."

"Could have fooled me!" I can still hear gunshots and carnage in the background. Why are the bots still fighting them?

Then I feel something else. A subtle warmth, like a hot breeze passed over me. I get up to look around for the source but nothing seems out of the ordinary. Then in the middle of the quad there's a flash of light. A tiny ball appears, and I feel the heat again, but it's not passing this time. It's getting hotter. It's *burning*.

"Fuck," I mutter and grab Vance's arm, trying to give him the energy to stand up. "Fuck fuck fuck—" Then my vision goes white, my clothes turn to ash, and I can't tell my scream apart from the screams of everyone around me.

CHAPTER 40

EPSILON

I NEARLY RIP THE EARPIECE OUT. THE SCREAMS AND chaos from the other end are deafening.

"Isaac?" I yell, praying to hear a response. "Isaac!"

Felix's assault hasn't gotten any weaker; it's only intensified. Bots are steaming out of the police station now, slowly forming a cone around us and pushing us back toward the quad. There's no way we can hold all of them.

I chance a look at one of the screens showing Meru, and the scene sends ice through my veins. The digital campus is on fire, smoke and flames consuming the view, licking across the screen. I can't see any of the residents anymore beyond a few shadowy bodies flying across the streets and ground engulfed in flames. The cries are overpowering; the torrent of pain and suffering Felix is inflicting on them is shaking me to my core.

A patch of clear air finally gives me a view into the chaos, and in the middle of the quad, floating ten feet above the ground, is Felix again.

He screams with rage, and another wall of fire flies in every direction from where he's floating. The cries are getting fainter now and I dread what it might mean for the minds in there with him. Clearly, he's decided he'd rather destroy everyone and risk destroying himself than get trapped there and risk letting us take control of Epsilon.

A pair of dogs leaps at me and pulls my attention back to the fight, one of Vance's drones swooping in to dispatch them at the last second. But I can't rely on him for much longer. Our forces are running thin, the streets littered with destroyed machines and the bodies of the Techs who ran out from hiding to help us.

"Isaac!" It's me. "Isaac, I have Sophie. We're okay. But won't be for long."

I clutch the comm device tighter to my ear, heart hammering in my chest. Relief floods through me at the sound of my voice, but his warning creates a knot of fear in my stomach.

"Where's Vance?" I ask, scanning the smoke-filled screen for any sign of him amid the chaos.

"I don't know; he's disappeared. I think Felix..." His voice trails off, leaving the rest unsaid.

Fuck. I grit my teeth as the implications sink in. Felix must have destroyed him. And if Vance is gone, the rest of them have little chance to overpower Felix again.

I sigh on the other end, clearly debating saying something. "Don't say it."

"You knew it would probably come to this."

"You can still beat him!" I desperately don't want this to be the answer.

"We tried, but you have to stop him on your end," he continues, urgency sharpening his tone.

"There has to be something else you can try."

"Look around, Isaac; people are dying. The sooner you do this, the more of them you can save."

"Isaac?" It's Sophie now, her voice trembling, and I can imagine her face as she tries to stay strong, knowing what's coming.

"Sophie."

"I—I'm glad you came back."

"I'm sorry. I didn't want this to happen."

"I know." She sniffles. "But it's okay, I'm glad I got to see you again. And I'm glad I know now. You have to do this."

Words catch in my throat as tears blur my vision. "I love you, Soph," I manage to say.

"I love you too, 'Saac."

I hear another sniff but it's not from Sophie this time; it's from me. "Say bye to everyone for me."

"I will," I whisper, my throat tight.

My stomach churns at what they're asking me to do, but I know they're right. Tears are streaming down my face as I grab Lena's arm and pull her back from the fight, letting a pair of bots fill our place trying to slow Felix's assault.

"What? What happened?" she asks as we run.

"We have to get back to the servers," I yell over the chaos.

"Are you insane?" she screams back.

"They can't exile him. It's the only way."

"Isaac…"

"I know."

Lena's eyes are fiery with determination as we run back toward the quad. Vance must have overheard us because a few of his dogs peel off to join us, and a truck roars out of an alleyway, throwing its door open.

"We can run!" I yell, keeping pace with the truck, the dogs flanking us to create a defensive wall.

"You can't get into the server room," Vance says, patching himself into my earpiece now. "It's too heavily guarded and we don't have the forces anymore."

"We have to try!"

"I know." The dashboard of the truck lights up and the drone on top whirs to life. I realize what he wants me to do.

"Cover me!" I yell to Lena, and she leaps into the bed of the truck as I jump into the driver's seat, yanking the controller from the console. The truck speeds ahead toward the transfer building, crashing through dogs trying to block its way, as more of Vance's forces leave the police station to come provide cover.

They're cutting a path through Felix's bots ahead and we screech into the quad, kicking up mud and grass as we fly across the lawn and come to a jolting stop a dozen yards ahead of the transfer building. I'm locked into the drone controls now, sending it rocketing off the roof as we stop, darting through the doors of the building behind a pack of his dogs clearing the way.

The foyer of the building is overrun with bots; Felix must have known we'd try this. I aim the drone for the stairs, but a spider leaps off the wall, nearly taking the drone down, and I bank a hard left spiraling around the central area trying to avoid any more bots lunging at me. Finally, Vance's bots have cleared the way and I nose-dive toward the stairs, shooting around the narrow bends as fast as the drone can handle.

At long last it emerges from the bottom of the stairs and I can see the servers just ahead. Glowing with life, overclocked from Felix's destruction, a couple of them are already burning from his attempts to destroy the people in Meru pushing back against him.

The way is clear. I max the acceleration on the drone and it tilts forward. I can almost feel the power of its propellors as it careens toward the servers. Preparing the charge to destroy our Meru. To save the people out here from Felix's control.

But then the servers disappear from view. The drone is spiraling, falling, and the last thing I see before the feed cuts out is a flash of a dog on the ground, one of Felix's last defenses successfully deflecting the attack.

"FUCK!" I scream and nearly destroy the controller on the dashboard. The truck starts backing away and I look up to realize Felix's bots are coming out of the building now, their guns trained on me, on Lena. And as we reverse into the quad, I realize they're containing everyone remaining in Epsilon, pouring out of the alleys and buildings, pushing all of us to the center of town. Carmy and Dylan emerge from a building, their hands raised, being led by a pair of dogs.

My heart is pounding in my ears. I'm trying to think of anything else we can do but seeing no escape. Felix appears on one of the screens overlooking the quad and his eyes are full of fire and rage.

"ENOUGH!" he screams, and I feel my heart lurch. I look over my shoulder and the other Techs are laying down their weapons, putting their hands up, shaking with terror.

I hear the rest of Felix's forces descending on the square, truck motors and bots in the distance bearing down on the quad. Lena and I make eye contact, and I can see the same fear and desperation in her. I don't want to lose her. Not like this. Not to Felix.

There's a crunching of metal in the distance and then another series of gunshots. I spin around to try to find the source, and a pair of Felix's dogs come flying out of an alleyway as if they've been thrown. Then behind them a truck speeds out, flanked on all sides by what must be the last of Vance's bots, and they plow through the middle of the quad, the drone on top of the truck whirring to life. Sun is glinting off the windshield but then it clears for a moment and I can finally see inside.

Bram.

Dozens of bots rise from the ground under Vance's control,

as if they've been playing dead, waiting for this moment. They leap on the surrounding remains of Felix's forces to distract them as the drone hurtles off the roof of the truck, darting through the doors of the transfer station, trying to take the same path I did.

Felix looks terrified, and my heart catches in my throat as I see Bram locked into the console, guiding the drone through the minefield I tried to navigate. It can't be long now. Not more than another few seconds.

But my excitement turns to terror as I spot one of Felix's drones plummeting from the sky, a missile aimed right at his truck. Time seems to slow as I watch its descent, helpless to stop it. I want to scream, to warn him, but my voice catches in my chest. All I can do is watch in paralyzed horror as the machine closes in on its target.

"Vance!" I scream, trying to get his attention. One of the dogs sees the drone and leaps into the air, trying to intercept its path, but the drone is too fast. It banks hard to the left and skirts around the dog, losing one of its propellors in the process but maintaining its deadly trajectory.

I lock eyes with Bram for a fleeting moment. His face is a mixture of determination and fear, but there's something else there too. Hope. Then the world erupts into a deafening roar as the truck explodes, engulfing him in a blinding fireball. The shockwave sends ripples through my body as I cover my head, trying to shield myself from the blast.

Before I have time to react, another explosion erupts behind me, this one even more violent than the first. Brick and cement fly off the front of the transfer center, raining down like deadly hail. The building groans and shudders, then collapses in on itself, a cloud of dust billowing up to the sky. My ears ring from the blast, but through the chaos, a single thought comes through: *He did it.* His drone made it to the servers. Pride and grief overwhelm me as I watch the center of my old world collapse into rubble.

I scramble to my feet, my heart pounding in my chest, and charge toward the flaming wreckage of Bram's truck. Maybe there's still time. But before I can reach the inferno, something slams into me from behind. I hit the ground hard, the wind knocked out of me.

"Isaac, wait!" Vance's voice crackles through the android pinning me down. I thrash against its grip, desperate to break free. But part of me knows he's right. The truck's still ablaze, waves of heat washing over me. I can feel the fire on my face, and my eyes sting from the smoke and unshed tears as I struggle to process what just happened.

"Let me go!" I yell, my voice desperate. But the android's grip only tightens, its metal fingers bruising my arms. I thrash against the bot one last time, muscles straining, but it's no use. My strength drains away, and I slump to the ground, chest heaving. Tears blur my vision as I stare at the burning wreckage.

In the distance, I hear the crunch of boots pounding across broken concrete.

CHAPTER 41

MERU

"I'm sorry," I say as Sophie and I watch Bram's drone fly through the transfer station. "I thought we could find another way to stop him." The bubble of water Sophie formed to protect us from the heat is fading, but it won't matter soon.

"I know you did," she says. "I'm glad we tried."

"Can you forgive me?"

"For what?"

"For not figuring it out before you transferred. For coming back. For causing all this."

"I already have."

Then there's a blinding flash of light and we collapse on each other, hugging, crying, the heat searing into us as I feel her disappear beneath my fingertips.

CHAPTER 42

EPSILON

LENA'S SILENT BESIDE ME AS WE SIT ON MY OLD PORCH. There's only one thing left to do before we leave, but I've been dreading facing it.

"Whenever you're ready," she whispers.

It took a day to search the wreckage for anything worth taking back to the factory, and Vance had to do most of the heavy lifting. It was too painful to see the broken bodies of everyone who stood beside us to fight back Felix, both Techs and people who came from Alexandria. Even the older people from Alexandria had never seen carnage like this before. It was worse than the video from Alpha, worse than what Felix did to the camp where they found me. It feels like years since I watched it. I wish we could stay and give everyone a proper burial like they would do in Alexandria but there's no time. Felix could return at any moment.

We briefly debated staying here, trying to turn Epsilon into another Alexandria. But our numbers are too thin. We need to band together somewhere safer, somewhere that isn't haunted by the stench of death.

Thankfully most of the Techs came around to our side in the

end. Even Tess. We haven't gotten the chance to say more than a few words to each other, both complacent in our avoidance for now. But we're going to have to reconcile at some point.

Everyone is still shocked, and I know they're mourning the loss of their families in Meru. But Felix revealed who he was, and Vance revealed the awful secret of Meru.

I feel guilty that I'm alive and he, the other Isaac, is gone. It feels like I could have just as easily been the one to wake up in Meru, the one to sacrifice myself. Though I don't know if I'd have the same conviction. I wish I'd had more time to thank him, and Sophie. To say one more goodbye. I hope they were together in the end.

"I'm ready," I say. Bram's robes are draped over my knees. I scoop them up and start walking toward the quad, Carmy, Dylan, and a group of Techs from Epsilon falling in behind us.

We removed every piece of technology we could, even the destroyed ones. Vance said he could use the parts to rebuild some of the bots that were destroyed in the battle. The buildings look bare, cords hanging limp from holes in the walls as they were in Alpha. Another dent in Felix's world, but who knows how meaningful of one. I keep thinking about how awful this fight was, how it stretched us to our limits. If Felix has hundreds of other centers around the world, there's no chance we can stop him. We'll have to go into hiding, but without the security of the truce Alexandria had with him before.

The rest of the people who remained behind are gathered around the quad. Even those from Alexandria who didn't know Bram are here to pay their last respects. Most of us, maybe all of us, would be dead without him. I wish he could have seen Alexandria. But at least now we have some hope to show others.

The only thing we left was Bram's truck. A few of Vance's larger spiders dragged it into the middle of the quad, cleaned it out, and carved a message inside to anyone who finds it in the future.

Here lies Bram. Father, husband, elder of Epsilon. He died doing what he lived for: protecting those who lived and worked in the town around you. But not from outsiders. From Felix. From Meru.

I fold the robes and lay them on the driver's seat, placing on top of them a photo of his family before Gemma transferred. She's beaming at the camera, Luke a happy baby in her arms.

The others gathered lay candles in circles around the truck, casting it in an orange glow in the twilight, each silently acknowledging someone they lost. I'll never forgive myself for not believing Luke, and I wish I could tell him he was right. That he didn't die for nothing.

We make it back to the Austin center just before midnight. Inside it's buzzing with activity, androids and people working together to clear space for beds and cooking stations, trying to turn the abandoned center into someplace hospitable until we find a new town.

Our list of problems is long. We lost the growing stations in Alexandria, and I don't know where our food will come from. We're low on medicine and half of the community has suffered injuries. Felix is still out there, and he could be organizing his forces, planning another attack.

But for this brief moment we're safe. And we're home.

EPILOGUE

CHAPTER 43

MERU

The countdown on the screen reaches zero, and then Vance doubles over on the controls as if he's been struck or had a heart attack.

I feel woozy for a moment, sway, then catch myself and crouch down beside him, putting my hand on his back, realizing the ridiculousness of trying to physically help a digital entity but doing it nonetheless. "Vance? You okay?"

"Urgh," he moans. "Never quite get used to that."

"Used to what?"

"Loss of processing. Your friends cut the connection to Meru. Epsilon is running on its own now; Felix can't draw computing power from anywhere else on his network. It's the only way they'll be able to defeat him, both in Epsilon and Epsilon's Meru."

"Epsilon's Meru? Where are we then?"

"Mainnet, Imgen's core servers. You didn't think I was going to leave you there, did you?"

"So we're…"

"Copies, fragments. Or they're the copies or fragments. It doesn't make a difference."

"No cohesive self…"

"We've had this conversation before, haven't we?"

I nod and Vance keys a series of commands into the console, then a video feed appears. It's a view from a drone impossibly far away from Epsilon, seemingly circling above it while the camera slowly zooms in on the carnage unfolding. "If you and your friends destroy the servers in Epsilon, that version of us will be gone but we'll still be here."

"So I'm about to die?"

"To be determined. They'll try to get rid of Felix without destroying the servers first. But I doubt that's possible. You'll get used to it. You're going to die a lot if you're still committed to stopping Felix."

My heart twists in knots considering mourning my own death. "Can...we watch?"

"Only from the earthside. There's no way to see what's happening in Meru. We're cut off like Felix is. That's good, though. He won't know you and I are involved. We're safe for now."

I try not to imagine the chaos happening in Meru's Epsilon right now as Vance zooms in the video feed, showing my physical self emerging from the transfer station.

As I watch there's a shuffling behind us and my whole body tenses. I spin around to see a shadowy mass huddled on a couch, but I can't make out any of their features.

"Vance...who is that?"

"Had some capacity to bring someone else with us. Thought you'd appreciate it."

Then the mysterious figure sits up, and my heart leaps into my throat.

BEFORE YOU GO

THANK YOU FOR READING *HUSK*. THIS BOOK IS SELF-published, so if you enjoyed it, I would deeply appreciate any way you can help spread the word.

Leaving a review on Amazon or Goodreads will help other people find it and would mean the world to me.

But the best thing you can do is to text a friend and suggest they read it. I'm sure you know one person who might enjoy exploring Felix's world as much as you have, and despite our world inching slower toward his vision by the day, word of mouth still drives the success of books more than anything else.

Finally, if you want to hear about the sequel to *HUSK* when it launches, I encourage you to sign up for my newsletter at meruinitiative.com.

Thank you again for reading!

ACKNOWLEDGEMENTS

DESPITE ONE NAME ON THE COVER, A BOOK IS NEVER A singular endeavor.

Thank you first to my wife, Cosette, for encouraging me to charge after this project, supporting me through the emotional roller coaster of writing, and for always being my first reader. I love you.

Thank you to my daughters Sutton, Kaia, and, though you're not quite here yet as I publish this, Arden. You brighten every day, joyfully distract me when I try to sneak in some writing on the weekends, and motivate me to keep working to be the best I can be.

Thank you to Nathan Baugh, my closest colleague. You've given more helpful feedback on this than I can possibly keep track of and taught me more about writing than anyone else. Our weekly writing and podcasting is often the highlight of my workweek.

Thank you to Eric Jorgenson, Rachael Williams, Ami Hendrickson, Mark Chait, and the rest of the Scribe team for helping take this from a document on my computer to a beautiful book. I look forward to making many more books with you. And thank you as well to Anna Dorfman for the wonderful cover.

Thank you to Branick Weix, Eleanor Konik, Zach Batteer,

and Daniel Doyon for going above and beyond in your reading and suggestions. You all contributed ideas and feedback that dramatically improved key parts of the book. And thank you to Adil Majid, Elizabeth Baugh, Sky King, Matt Ragland, Dan Shipper, and Paul Millerd for providing feedback and encouragement as well.

Finally, thank you to my agent, David Fugate, for telling me to scrap the first version of this book and for being supportive throughout the process even though I didn't want to sell it to a publisher.

Printed in Great Britain
by Amazon